THE PALE BLADE

EMPIRE OF FLAME & FANG

ALEC HUTSON

Mom, I love you and I miss you

The Reading Mother

I had a Mother who read to me
Sagas of pirates who scoured the sea,
Cutlasses clenched in their yellow teeth,
"Blackbirds" stowed in the hold beneath.

I had a Mother who read me lays
Of ancient and gallant and golden days;
Stories of Marmion and Ivanhoe,
Which every boy has a right to know.

I had a Mother who read me the things
That wholesome life to the boy heart brings —
Stories that stir with an upward touch,
Oh, that each mother of boys were such!

You may have tangible wealth untold;
Caskets of jewels and coffers of gold.
Richer than I you can never be —
I had a Mother who read to me.

by Strickland Gillilan (1869-1954)

1

Insects rose from the depths of the tall grass as Bren waded through the field in search of the wayward goat. She grimaced, swiping at the swarm with her free hand, for a moment afraid that she had blundered into a nest of those ornery purple-and-black-banded wasps. It would not be the first time. Last summer, she'd spent the Night of the Three Sisters trapped miserably at home while the rest of the village danced and celebrated, her face a swollen mess. Thankfully, these bugs were fat and fuzzy and bumbling, and they dispersed without putting up a fight. Still, her patience for this chase was wearing thin.

"Where are you?" she murmured, searching for her quarry. The little goat's mottled black and white coat should have been easy to spot, but the dark green grass in this corner of the meadow grew thick enough that the kid seemed to have been swallowed whole. Bren spared a glance over her shoulder at the rest of her herd. They were still plodding along the path that wound down the hill, a routine so ingrained that Bren sometimes wondered if they even truly needed a shepherd at all. The old queen that ruled the herd seemed to know exactly the time to return to the farm, late in the afternoon when the shadows began to creep across the meadow and the pale outline of the Silver Mother appeared in the sky.

There. The nubs of two little horns poking up from within a patch of red clover. Liquid black eyes lifted to meet her own, brimming with what Bren suspected was feigned innocence. The kid's jaw worked frantically as he hurried to chew the clover as quickly as possible, clearly aware that his little adventure had come to an end.

"Naughty beast," Bren grumbled, smacking the small goat's rump with the flat side of her sword's wooden blade. The kid gave a surprised bleat and began to bound back towards the rest of the herd, and with a sigh, Bren followed. Every year there seemed to be one willful fellow who refused to stick by his mother, consuming her attention when she'd rather be doing other things. Like practicing her forms. Bren slashed at a bowed puffball rising from the grass, scattering its spores to the wind. Her arm ached, a testament to the effort she had been putting in when she wasn't running after the goats, but she still felt like she hadn't made nearly enough progress with the sword her uncle had given her. Though he likely wouldn't be visiting this summer anyway – Bren had heard that there was fighting to the east, over the mountains. As an officer in the Bright Company, her uncle Merik likely would have marched to meet the raiders from across the sea.

She did a quick count as she rejoined the herd, making sure none of the other goats had wandered off. When she finished, she found the queen had stopped and was staring back at her, as if in annoyance at being doubted.

"Well, fine, let's go," Bren called out, and with a braying snort the old goat turned away and resumed her slow meander down the path.

The sun continued its descent as Bren trailed the herd, gilding the peaks of the distant Snowspears and making the lake at the bottom of the hill flash like a sheet of beaten gold. She whistled tunelessly to herself, working on strengthening her wrist by cutting patterns in the air with the practice sword. When she finally arrived at the Bright Company – and she would, no matter what her mother said – she'd be very familiar with the weight of their blades. That was important,

Merik had told her. Most times a soldier missed a parry, it was because of exhaustion, not the skill of their opponent. She'd make sure to impress them with her stamina from the first day.

Bren was jolted from her daydream when she caught a flash of movement high above. She squinted into the fading day, trying to make out what had drawn her eye. A bird was soaring on the wind, and it must be huge because it was more than just a smudge in the sky, yet still far enough away that she couldn't make out any details. It looked to be big even for the blackwings that sometimes swooped down from the mountains to carry away young goats. She tightened her grip on the hilt of her sword, wishing she'd brought her crook today. The extra reach would have come in handy if one of those great raptors tried to make a meal of her charges.

Bren frowned as the distant bird glinted briefly in the sunlight, as if it were bearing away something metallic in its beak. How strange. What could that—

"Oh!" she cried, stumbling over a goat that had found its way between her legs. It bleated something that sounded rude and then scampered ahead, and by the time Bren looked up again the bird was nothing but a dwindling speck in the molten sky. She watched until it vanished, considering whether she should tell her father. If she did, then he'd probably keep the herds in the lower meadows for a few days at least, and Bren preferred being up here, removed from prying eyes. After all, if her mother looked out the window and saw her practicing her forms, she'd make an almighty fuss and maybe even forbid Bren from bringing her sword along in the future when she tended to the goats.

And Bren needed the practice. She was going to be a warrior, just like her uncle. He'd once been a shepherd in these same fields, and now he commanded men and women in the Bright Company, the most famous mercenary troop along the Flowering Coast. Merik had demonstrated that in the Company it didn't matter where you came from, only what you accomplished.

The path they followed jagged around a lichen-scarred boulder, and then the pace of the herd quickened as the thatched roof of their barn appeared up ahead. She would keep quiet about the blackwing, Bren decided . . . but maybe tomorrow she'd lug both her crook and her sword to the high meadows.

To Bren's surprise, the barn doors had been left open, and as the goats streamed inside they started jostling for the best sleeping spots. She followed, whacking the leg of a buck that had paused to gnaw on a rotten carrot lying in the dirt. As it scurried into the barn's dimness, she began to pull the doors closed, but then stopped, her eyes widening.

An unfamiliar horse was tied to one of the hitching posts in the barn. For a moment, Bren thought he must belong to Merik because this was most definitely a warhorse, but he seemed too fine a steed, even for her uncle. He looked like the mount of a prince or general, a sculptor's vision of the perfect horse. His coat was an unblemished white, and though he stood in the shadows his long mane appeared to be the color of spun silver. Frog, the old nag that hauled their vegetables to market, looked almost embarrassed to be forced to stand beside such a noble beast, his head hanging low.

Bren cautiously approached the mysterious horse, but he seemed unfazed by both her presence and the milling goats that now filled the barn. Great blue eyes watched her calmly, and Bren had to restrain herself from reaching out to stroke his glorious coat. Uncle Merik had told her once how the destriers of knights and other cavalry were trained to bite, and she truly didn't want to startle him and lose a finger. Instead, she made a circuit of the horse, careful to keep out of kicking range. He had been ridden hard recently, as sweat still lathered his muscled flanks where they were not covered by a blue caparison trimmed with silver. Despite her fear of alarming the horse, she couldn't resist reaching out to brush her fingers over this beautiful fabric. Different phases of the moon were stitched onto the caparison, and Bren's mouth went dry when she realized what these symbols suggested.

But surely that was impossible.

Slowly, she backed out of the barn and latched the doors, her heart hammering. A warhorse bearing the symbols of the Silver

Mother. Her gaze went to the farmhouse. Who was inside her home right now? And *why*?

Squawking chickens flung themselves out of her way as she hurried across the yard. She ran her fingers through her tangled hair, trying to pull out the snarls, and when she reached the farmhouse door she paused and took a deep breath before slipping inside.

Bren had been hoping to enter without drawing too much attention to herself, but that immediately proved impossible. An armored man surged from the chair where he'd been sitting beside the fire, his hand on the hilt of his sword.

"No!" Bren's mother cried, dropping the spoon with which she'd been stirring a bubbling cookpot and throwing herself before this warrior. "Please, m'lord, it's just my daughter."

The man blinked in surprise, but he did not let go of his blade. "She is one of them," he said, an almost musical lilt to his voice. His skin was a shade darker than the olive of most who lived in the Seven Valleys, which meant he was probably from the southern coast, or maybe the Umber Isles.

"She's not," Bren's mother said, speaking so quickly now she was almost babbling. "She's our daughter. I found her many years ago in the woods. She was just a babe, no more than a few weeks old."

The door to the larder banged open, and her father tumbled into the main room. Links of sausages were looped about one arm, and in the other he clutched Bren's brother Helat to his chest. Terror twisted the small boy's face when he saw the warrior looming over his mother, and with a shuddering wail he began to cry.

The stranger's hand moved from his sword's hilt as he returned to his chair. "She certainly looks ready to fight," he muttered, almost sheepishly.

To her great surprise, Bren realized she'd raised her practice sword into one of the defensive forms. "I'm sorry," she said, letting it slip from her hand to clatter on the floor, feeling foolish. What good would wood do against steel anyway . . . though that might not even be what the warrior's sword was forged from. If the legends were true, a shard of captured moonlight filled his filigreed scabbard, called down by the priestesses of the Silver Mother.

For, beyond all belief, a paladin was in their home.

"Apologies, Ser Dahlen," Bren's father said, handing her squalling brother to her mother and then kicking the wooden sword into the corner. "She has foolish dreams of joining the Bright Company."

A shadow passed over the paladin's face as he leaned back in his chair. "I'm afraid that may not be possible anymore," he said hollowly. "The Company was broken on the field of Manoch Tir, scattered to the winds, along with the rest of the armies under our queen's banner."

Bren gasped. The Bright Company had been defeated? What had happened to Uncle Merik?

Her father paled at the paladin's words. "Grim tidings," he whispered, as he put his hand on the edge of the table to steady himself. "My brother is in the Company."

"He may yet live," Ser Dahlen said, though his tone was not reassuring. "Many of us escaped when we knew the day was lost. Nothing would have been gained by a final charge into that field of fire." He closed his eyes, and for the first time Bren saw his weariness. Lines scored his young face, and from the dark circles it looked like he hadn't slept in many days. She could imagine what his finely wrought armor must have looked like gleaming in the morning sun, but now it was dented and crusted with mud and filth, the image once embossed into his cuirass obliterated by a heavy blow that had partially staved in the metal.

Bren's mother went to her and gathered her into an embrace. She smelled of sweet cedar woodsmoke and lavender, the familiarity steadying Bren's racing heart.

"I was worried about you," her mother said, then she pulled back and looked her up and down. Her mother was a thin woman, hair mostly gone to gray these last few years, but Bren knew the strength in her. She could spend all day in the fields, then set the house in order and have a hearty meal on the table by the time Bren and her father returned in the evening. Her mother's hand drifted up to brush aside a lock of dark hair that had fallen across Bren's eyes.

"You're a woman now, and it will be a dangerous time to be out alone. Ser Dahlen"—and here she inclined her head towards the warrior, who was watching them with his lips pursed—"said that there will be bands of broken men slipping over the mountains. A great battle was lost in the east. So from tomorrow, you must stay inside."

"I can protect myself," Bren insisted, her gaze going to the sword in the corner. "I'm not afraid."

"Your . . . mother is right," said the paladin. The pause was noticeable, as if he had not yet come to grips with the idea that Bren was truly her mother's daughter. "Those who survived Manoch Tir will be desperate, and whatever oaths they once swore were sundered with the defeat of their lords. Many will consider themselves brigands now, not soldiers."

"Is Queen Alyssa truly dead?" Bren whispered. Her legs felt so weak she wanted to sit, but she hesitated at the idea of crossing to the empty chairs near the paladin.

"She was on the field," the paladin replied with a grimace. "One soldier told me he saw her fall. But another claimed her Wardens brought her to safety after the Velaschin shattered our middle. I do not know who among the great names still live. The ones that draw breath are being hunted."

A coldness filled Bren's gut. The farmers and shepherds who lived in the Seven Valleys rarely spared a thought for the crown that claimed dominion over these lands. They had been part of the kingdom of Felaesia for a century, but the kings and queens in distant Chalice had ruled with a light touch, whatever edicts they passed from the Petaled Throne rarely affecting the lives of the peasants here. Would these new overlords be cruel? How would the fall of Felaesia change the Seven Valleys?

"Who are these invaders?" Bren asked. She'd heard of the Velaschin before, but only as a distant trading people. They were famous for their goods crafted from obsidian, somehow treated to make as strong as steel and even sharper. Goodman Pelas had bought a Velaschin hand-ax and shown it to her, and at the time she'd been awed by its lightness and how well it chopped.

The paladin did not answer her for a moment, and since his eyes were still closed, she thought his exhaustion might have overwhelmed him. Then he sneered, shaking his head. "The Velaschin are liars. They spoke of friendship while secretly making ready for war—"

A series of thumps came from outside the farmhouse, the ground trembling. The paladin's eyes flew open. "They are here," he said heavily, rising from his chair. A bleakness was in his voice, but no fear or anger. Bren scrambled out of his way as he strode past her. The paladin hesitated, his hand hovering over the handle, and then after drawing a deep breath he pushed open the door and stepped outside. His large body blocked most of the view, but Bren saw a flash of color beyond him before the door closed again, along with the movement of something impossibly huge.

No one inside the farmhouse dared to speak. Even little Helat had stopped sobbing, shoving his thumb into his mouth and laying his head against his father's chest. Bren and her parents looked at each other with wide eyes, waiting for some indication of what was happening. She was expecting to hear screams or shouting, the clash of metal, but there was only silence.

"Brenna!" her mother hissed in panic as she started to creep towards the window, but Bren ignored her. Very slowly, she cracked open the wooden shutters, just enough so she had a view of the yard . . . and of who had pursued the paladin to their doorstep.

The edge of the shutter nearly slipped from her trembling fingers.

"Oh," she whispered numbly.

Three warriors faced the paladin in a rough semicircle, their gauntleted hands resting on the hilts of swords driven point-first into the earth. The blades were black, glistening in the last red rays of the day. Their armor was dark as well and vastly different from what the paladin across from them wore: while the silvery sections of his plate flowed together into a unified whole, their armor almost seemed at war with itself, all brutal angles and barbed ornamentations. Their faces were hidden inside spiked helms fashioned to resemble the heads of roaring monsters, but that was not what terrified Bren.

Behind each of these warriors was a dragon.

Her mind struggled to accept what she was seeing. Bren had heard stories, of course, about dragons with swords for teeth and scales of iron, but they had not been seen in these lands for many lifetimes – it was said that if they still existed, they did so at the fringes of the world, far beyond the realms of men. Hidden deep in barren wastes or curled around the peaks of distant mountains.

And yet . . . and yet . . .

Here they were.

They crouched with long tails tucked under their massive bodies, wings folded upon spined backs, and slitted yellow eyes trained on the paladin. Two of the dragons had scales of deep forest green, while the last and largest seemed molded from the same gleaming darkness as the swords of its masters. Claws that looked capable of rending a man into pieces carved furrows in the ground, and leather straps were wound around their chests. These looked like some sort of harnesses, so that the warriors would have a way to mount the beasts. But what kind of men could tame dragons?

Bren's insides felt like water. These monsters were too huge, too terrible. They should not exist, let alone fly. She realized that the flash of metallic color she'd seen in the sky earlier must have been one of these dragons. Or perhaps others were out there, searching for this paladin.

To his great honor, Ser Dahlen did not try to flee or beg for mercy. Deep beneath Bren's terror a breathless pride stirred to see the chosen of the Silver Mother meeting certain death without flinching.

"What's going on out there?" her father whispered from across the room. He was cowering beside the table, clutching Bren's mother and brother tightly.

"Dragons," she replied, surprised by the calmness in her voice. "And men."

"Dragons?" her father repeated incredulously.

She couldn't blame him.

"Who are they?" he pressed. "What do they want?"

Bren opened her mouth to tell him that of course she had no idea, but the words died when she noticed movement from the warrior who stood in front of the black-scaled dragon. Keeping one hand on the pommel of his strange sword, the stranger reached up and undid the straps of his helm, then pulled it off.

Bren's heart skipped. His skin was milk white, his cheekbones high and sharp, and hair like a raven's wing fell nearly to his shoulders. His mouth was set in a thin line.

Bren had never seen a more dangerous-looking man.

Or one that looked so much like her.

While she'd been staring at the stranger, the other two dragon riders had also removed their helms. One was a man well into his twilight years, and though he still stood tall and straight-backed, his hair and drooping mustache had gone to silver. The other was a woman, and from her appearance, she could have been Bren's older sister. Her lip was curled in disdain as she watched the paladin.

Slowly, the warrior in front of the black dragon raised his sword, pointing the slightly curved tip at the paladin. He said something, but Bren was too far away to hear the words clearly. She could guess what it was, though, as the Silver Mother's champion drew his own sword smoothly. Light flared as his blade cleared its scabbard, then dwindled to a shimmering opalescence that slid along the tapering length. Bren's fingers tightened on the shutter. It truly was moonlight sharpened into a sword, the goddess's will made real.

As the paladin settled into a guard position, Bren wished she could see his face. His movements were precise and assured, and she wanted to believe he was showing no fear. This was a hero from the stories, and in the stories, the hero always triumphed. Bren allowed a small trickle of hope to worm its way into her heart.

Something unspoken passed between the two warriors, and then they came together in a rending clash. Glistening darkness struck pearly metal, and a discordant chime shivered the air. A flurry of blows commenced, almost too fast to follow, and then they separated again and started to circle each other warily.

The other riders watched without expression, unmoving.

Another grating shriek as the swords crossed, then the dark warrior lunged, sending the paladin stumbling backwards. Ser Dahlen caught himself quickly though, and a moment later he was on the attack, driving his foe towards the great black dragon watching the fight with heavy-lidded interest. Bren gasped with every ringing parry, her pulse rising as the tempo of the duel grew ever faster. This swordfighting was different from anything she had imagined. Her uncle had taught her the forms used in the Bright Company, patterns learned to protect the soldiers beside you even as they protected you. But this . . . there was no pattern here, at least that she could see. Yet it was as graceful as a dance.

And then it was over before Bren even realized what had happened. The black blade flickered out, and the paladin was late with his parry, the cut opening up his thigh. He stumbled, his leg collapsing beneath him, and the dragon rider fluidly stepped within the paladin's guard to plunge the dark sword into his chest, parting his battered cuirass like it was made of cloth. Bren moaned in dismay. The paladin swayed, staring down at the length of obsidian emerging from him. Then the rider ripped his sword free, and the paladin collapsed, his radiant blade slipping from slack fingers.

No. This wasn't how the stories were supposed to end.

For a long moment, the warrior stood looking down at the body of the paladin. Then he raised his gaze, and to Bren it seemed like he saw her peeking through the cracked-open shutters. Slowly, he lifted his free hand and then made an almost dismissive gesture in the direction of the farmhouse. Behind him, the two green-scaled dragons shifted, their great jaws opening. Deep in their gaping mouths, beyond rows and rows of monstrous teeth, red flowers of flame suddenly bloomed.

"Run!" Bren screamed, turning back to her family just as the world was obliterated by blinding light.

2

Pale light filtered through skeletal branches, blazing on bone-white bark. Bren's feet sank into thick, cool moss. Serpentine roots rippled the earth, reaching for her.

She skipped away, searching the lees of the trees for the sky-blue flower her mother wanted. It grew for only a brief time in the early days of spring, emerging after the snow had finally receded, and when crushed and mixed with other herbs, it was the most effective remedy to relieve her father's knee pain. They had come into these woods every year since she could walk, gathering up enough of the fleeting blossoms to last until the next winter. Bren always loved the hunt. When they got home, she'd show her father what she'd collected, and he would sweep her into a hug and spin her around and tell her mother she should make honey cakes. Which her mother then would do, singing the songs in the old language. Bren never understood the words, but they still always stirred something inside her.

There. A blue blossom, almost hidden in the shadow of a fallen tree. Bren crouched to pluck the flower, ignoring the finger-length beetles scurrying into the rotten wood. She wasn't afraid; she'd suffer any kind of scary insects to help her father. Just to demonstrate her bravery, Bren flicked one of the beetles that had dared to linger. It landed upside down, its tiny legs flailing, and she watched it struggle until it finally managed to flip itself over and flee. Then she picked the flower, placing it into her pouch as she stood again.

And she saw she wasn't alone.

Three other children were close by, staring down at something. They appeared to be from the village, though she hadn't seen them before. There were two girls who looked about her age, maybe eight years old, and a boy a few years younger. All had dusky skin and deep black hair, like most of the Seven Valley folk.

"Hello," Bren said, coming up beside them. One of the girls glanced at her, then went back to poking the body of a rabbit with a stick. The other girl grunted her own greeting, squinting at Bren like she was confused about what she saw.

"Where's your mama?" Bren asked, wrinkling her nose as she caught a whiff of the dead animal.

The girl with the stick waved her other hand vaguely in the direction Bren had come from. "Over there. Looking for bluesnaps."

"Mine too," Bren told her, lifting the pouch that dangled on a cord around her neck. "And I'm helping. How about you?"

The girl shook her head. "Can't. Have to watch my brother." She jabbed her stick at the small boy, who had decided to investigate a cluster of white-capped mushrooms. "Don't eat those," his sister said, whacking his hand as he reached for them. Then she turned away, ignoring him as he began to cry.

"Are you a ghost?" asked the other girl suddenly.

"What?"

The girl tilted her head to one side, giving her a look not very different from the way she had been recently examining the dead rabbit. "A ghost. You're so white. Kellus saw a ghost once, and he said it had skin like new snow."

"I'm not a ghost."

The girl frowned like she didn't believe her. "Well, what about them?" she asked, pointing behind Bren.

She turned. Three figures – two men and a woman – stood motionless among the trees. Somehow in the time Bren had been talking to the children, the day had abruptly changed: the forest floor was now blanketed by

a strange mist, and the sunlight trickling down had vanished, replaced by a
sourceless glow. The strangers were clad in intricate dark armor that made
Bren think of the beetles, and their pale faces stared out from the open jaws
of terrifying monsters. Tendrils of mist curled around their legs like great
blind worms.

"I don't know them," Bren told the girl, but that was a lie. She'd seen
them before. But where? The knowledge hovered at the edge of her memory,
taunting her.

"You do," the girl said confidently.

Bren took an involuntary step backwards as the three strangers raised
their arms, hands open like they were beckoning her to approach. The mist
had thickened, clotting the woods and reducing all but the closest trees to
vague shadows.

"Mama," Bren murmured, her panic rising. "Mama, where are you?"
She whirled in a circle as the mist closed around her. The children had
vanished, along with the silent, watching figures. She couldn't see anything,
and from that slithering whiteness, clammy fingers reached out to brush
her skin . . .

BREN AWOKE TO DARKNESS, clawing for breath. Something heavy
pressed against her chest, pinning her legs and one of her arms. The
pain was excruciating, rolling over her in pulsing waves; she moaned,
then coughed as what tasted like ash slipped into her mouth. This
sent an even sharper agony stabbing through her, and tears prickled
her eyes. Her thoughts were fractured, and she struggled to understand what had happened. Where was she?

She sensed something hanging above her, but she couldn't tell
what. Everything was silent except for her hoarse gasping. The air
was stale but carried a burning smell. Was she underground? Had
she been buried alive? Her fear rose, and she fought to beat it back.
Swallowing hard, she focused on slowing her breathing, and gradually she brought herself under control.

As her panic subsided, her memories returned. The paladin in his
tarnished armor standing across from the terrifying strangers. Two

dragons, their jaws hinged wide, crimson light swelling in their throats. Her mother and father hunkered against the far wall, shielding her brother with their bodies.

"Mama," she croaked, fear flooding her again, but this time it was not for herself. "Papa!" *Helat.*

There had been searing light and then darkness. She tried to parse out what exactly had happened. Spears of flame had erupted from the dragons, enveloping the farmhouse, but Bren couldn't remember her flesh burning. She ached, but it was the pain of falling from a great height, like when she'd slipped and tumbled down the side of a rocky hill. Half the day had passed while she'd lain at the bottom with a badly twisted ankle until one of the goats had led her father to her. Bren wanted nothing more than to have him come now and dig her out of wherever she was – most likely the ruin of their house – but she knew that would not happen. She had to do it on her own.

Grunting with effort, she pulled her trapped arm free, and though her shoulder ached, nothing seemed broken. Then she reached up, trying to feel what was above. Her fingers brushed something dry and prickly. It felt like straw and crumbled under her touch, sifting down to sting her eyes. This was the thatch that had covered their roof. Some of it must have survived the dragon's flames and then fallen onto her when the walls collapsed. But if the house had burned, why hadn't she? Hope stirred in her – if she had survived, maybe her family also still lived. Maybe they were up there right now, looking for her.

"Mama!" she cried again, louder than before.

Bren strained, and the debris pinning her lower body moved. She shifted her hands and pushed hard at what was on top of her – it felt like charred wood – and pieces of it broke away under her fingers. Hissing in triumph, Bren squirmed free, then lifted herself so she could tear at the thatch. It came away in clumps as she clawed frantically, and she sobbed in relief when her hand finally pushed through the straw.

Cold licked her fingers. Bren brought her face up to the hole she had made and breathed the fresh air. It was also dark on the other side, but not as seamless as where she'd been trapped. Stars like tiny diamonds glimmered on a great dark cloth. Was this the same night? Or had she been buried and unconscious for more than a day? She considered calling out again. Her parents or other rescuers might hear her, but so would those frightening warriors if they were still nearby. She should be cautious.

More dry thatch rained down on Bren as she widened the gap she'd made, until it was large enough that she could reach and pull herself up. Bren flopped half out of the hole, gasping, her cheek pressed against the straw. When her head stopped spinning, she dragged her legs from the wreckage and then rolled onto her back, absolutely exhausted, staring up at the night sky as she searched for any reservoir of strength that hadn't yet been fully drained. Above her, the Silver Mother was almost full, the scars from where the demon Maliskaith had clawed Her etched clearly upon Her surface. Her three daughters dangled like a jeweled necklace beneath Her face – Arela, a gleaming yellow circle; Nasai, a crescent of green; and the dark gap in the stars where Kez hung. Gold, jade, and iron.

Bren struggled into a sitting position, then forced herself to stand. She shivered as the wind strengthened, suddenly realizing she was almost naked – only a few ragged scraps clung to her, more charcoal than cloth. The flames had consumed the house and her clothes, but not her flesh. Had the Mother protected her? What about her family? She had to find her family. She fought through her dizziness and looked around desperately.

The Silver Mother was bright tonight, her spectral touch gilding what remained of the farmhouse. Most of the walls had collapsed with the roof, but the brick fireplace still stood – she remembered her mother and father huddling there, Helat clasped between them.

Bren didn't want to go look, but she had to. Steeling herself, she carefully picked her way through the ruin, her apprehension rising. There would be nothing, she assured herself, because if she had been spared, then they had as well . . . perhaps they had gone to seek help, not realizing Bren was trapped under the rubble.

Something glinted atop a dark mound, and Bren stepped closer to investigate. It was a silver disc infused by the moonlight, a representation of the Mother just as She was hanging above Bren right now. She frowned. Her mother had worn an amulet like this — in fact, she had rarely ever taken it off. Why would she have left it behind?

The mound. It wasn't ash or charred wood but a tangle of something knotted together, almost like the roots of a tree. It wasn't that, though. Her dread strengthened as her eyes followed the line of a limb where it curled around what might have been a bowed head . . .

"No," she whispered, falling to her knees. A hollow opened inside Bren, and she tilted her head back, staring up at where the Silver Mother was now blurred by the tears wetting her cheeks.

BREN CAME to herself huddled amidst the debris and clutching her mother's amulet to her chest. She had no memory of taking it up. A gray dawn had seeped into the sky, though the night's chill lingered. Her throat felt raw, and her eyes ached from crying.

Mama. Papa. Helat.

Gone. *Dead.*

Slowly, she pushed herself to her hands and knees and then to her feet. She felt stiff and sore, but it didn't seem like anything was broken. In the ghostly morning light, she could now clearly see that her tunic and trousers had been reduced to charred scraps. Bren shivered, wrapping her thin arms around herself . . . before she did anything else, she needed new clothes. Everything in the house was ruined or buried under debris, but there was a small chance that her mother hadn't brought in the washing before the paladin had appeared on the doorstep. Bren stumbled around the edge of the one wall that remained standing, then gave a little sob of relief when she saw clothes draped over the lowest branch of the tree where her mother hung the laundry. She quickly peeled off the tattered remnants and dressed herself in the shirt and pants she'd worn two days ago. Her shoes were also falling apart, toes peeking out where a flap of doeskin had been torn away, but they would have to last for now. She was still cold, so she wrapped herself in a hooded cloak of green-dyed wool that had belonged to her father; it was far too large, but it made her feel safer because she could pull up the cowl and vanish into its depths. The faint smell of her father's pipe smoke clung to the wool, bringing with it a pang of sadness.

She couldn't put off what she needed to do any longer. One of the blankets her mother had woven last winter was also hanging there; it wasn't large, but the dragon flames had left little enough behind. Bren turned back to the farmhouse, holding the blanket so tightly her fingers hurt.

BREN'S ARMS trembled as she placed the last stone atop the cairn. She swayed, feeling lightheaded, and then dropped to her knees in the dirt. The gray morning had slowly lightened as she labored, and now the sun was high overhead in a wash of cloudless blue. The beauty of the day sickened Bren. When she'd first started digging and gathering the rocks, the sky had been the color of a funeral shroud, and that had felt right and fitting. Now the warmth on her shoulders and the gentle breeze in her hair made her want to scream at how unjust and monstrous this all was. She should be with the herd in the high meadow while her father turned the earth in the western fields and her mother worked her loom beside the hearth, Helat playing at her feet. Not this. Not this.

Her mother's amulet was in her hand, and she squeezed the silver disc until she felt its edge cut her palm. She vaguely sensed the pain, but it was far away, overwhelmed by the numbness that had filled her since she'd set to work burying her family. Blood welled, and using her thumb, she smeared it across the amulet's blank face. Bren didn't know what she was doing, but it felt right.

"Silver Mother," she said softly, "please help me."

She rubbed the amulet, imagining her blood seeping into the metal. The sight of it summoned memories of the solstice festival –

every autumn when the Mother was full, swollen with the next month's sun, the Seven Valleys would gather to cut the necks of goats to feed the goddess while She was in the throes of birthing. The blood would give Her strength, a small contribution to help Her keep the Everdark away for another little while. One night, as the rain lashed the roof and the wind rattled the shutters, Bren's father had told her that in olden times it had been children who were chosen to feed the goddess. A great sacrifice, but there was power in such blood. The nights had grown longer and darker since the lives of goats had replaced those of children.

Bren brought the amulet to her lips, breathing in the coppery scent of her own blood. *Hear me, goddess.*

"They killed Mama," she murmured hoarsely. "They killed Papa. My brother. Their souls are with You now, so You know this. I'm alone. I want You to let my family know that I won't forget. Or forgive." She paused, gathering herself. "Give me the strength, Mother, to bring vengeance to the ones that did this."

Bren kissed the metal, tasting her own blood on her lips. Then she slipped the amulet around her neck without wiping it clean. The silver did not feel cold against her bare skin, and that must have been the blood's fading warmth.

Bren rose to her feet, for the first time in a long while feeling something other than numb disbelief. She fingered the edges of this new emotion as it grew, letting it swell to fill her breast.

Anger.

Bren knew the oath she'd just sworn to the goddess was a foolish fantasy. She was just a girl of sixteen summers. Her enemies had swords and armor and *dragons*. Bren breathed in deep, then let it out slowly. But it also meant she had time. Time to grow and learn and train. Those three warriors had been young once. Weak. They had become strong, and so would she. Bren turned and gazed out over the ruin of her house, then at the pile of stones marking the resting place of the three people who had once filled her heart.

THE BARN WAS STILL UPRIGHT, but it looked like a great carcass that had been ripped open. On the side where once the set of double doors had stood there was a massive splintered hole, and as Bren approached, she dreaded what she might find within. She was expecting a gristly scene – like when a weasel had gotten inside their chicken coop last summer – but the sunlight pouring through the rent in the wall instead illuminated nothing except scattered hay, long gouges in the floorboards, and a few dark splotches of blood. The dragons had fed on her goats, she had no doubt, but they must have swallowed each of the poor animals whole. Remembering the size of the monsters, Bren was not surprised.

The horses were too large to have suffered a similar fate, but they had also vanished. From the broken ropes beside the hitching posts, it looked like they had panicked and thrashed themselves free, probably when they'd first caught the scent of dragons. Bren hoped they had escaped and were even now cropping the grass in a distant meadow. Frog had been a good and loyal horse, and she had feared finding him torn apart.

Bren set to scavenging what useful things she could find. A satchel her father had used for his trips to market was hanging on a peg, and she took it down, then filled it with some of the less-rotten carrots kept in a bin near the back, treats used to tempt Frog to help pull the plow. There were some torches, lengths of wood dipped in tree-pitch that they'd used at night to scare away wolves. And to her great good luck, she found a rusted knife among the tools on her father's workbench. It wasn't much, but it made her feel safer.

Would this be enough to get her to Leris? Bren had a vague idea of the distance to the City of Roses, as it had once taken her father four days to travel there and back when he'd gone to visit his brother. But that had been by horse, and even though Frog was slow and plodding, he surely was much faster than Bren would be on foot. She looked down at her ravaged shoes, wondering if her feet could possibly survive such a journey. After chewing her lip for a moment in consideration, Bren cut strips from a burlap sack and wrapped them around the remnants of her shoes. She would get new footwear when she got to Leris. Her uncle might not be in the city if the Company had indeed fought in that battle the paladin had spoken about, but Bren could stay with his wife until he returned.

If he returned.

Bren shoved those thoughts aside and stood, studying her cloth-wrapped feet critically. She hoped that would help, even though it made her look like a beggar. And maybe that would be for the best, as other travelers on the road wouldn't think she had anything of value to steal. Shouldering her carrot-laden satchel, she turned to leave the barn.

And stumbled back a step. The paladin's horse was silhouetted by the daylight pouring into the barn. He watched her with the same calmness as before, and Bren couldn't help but wonder how he had gotten so close without her hearing.

"Hello, boy," she murmured soothingly, slowly approaching the horse. "Where did you go? Did you take old Frog with you? Why are you back here?" She bent down and rummaged in her satchel, drawing forth a carrot. "Is this what you want? Are you hungry?"

The stallion's tail flicked in reply. His brilliant blue caparison was streaked with mud and had accumulated a fair number of burrs and thorned brambles. It looked to Bren like he had run into the forest after bolting from the barn.

"Here," she said, bringing the carrot to the horse's mouth.

He sniffed and then nibbled delicately.

"Go ahead," she urged, laying her hand on the side of his head. Watching her with eyes that showed no fear, he took a larger bite and soon the carrot was gone. "Very good," Bren whispered, reaching up to rub his ear in the same way Frog had liked. The stallion made a *whuffing* sound, and she hurriedly pulled her hand back, but then he leaned in closer to press his head against her.

"All right, so you do like that," Bren said. She realized that she was smiling, and guilt stabbed at her that she could feel anything except sorrow right now.

Suddenly the horse swung his head away from her, as if he'd heard something, and stared towards the ruin of the farmhouse.

"What is it?"

The horse whickered in reply, then turned and trotted from the barn. Bren quickly shouldered her satchel, hurrying to follow.

He came to a stop in the yard outside her home. The dirt had been churned by many boots and bore the indentations where the dragons had rested their huge bodies. The evidence of the size of the monsters made Bren shiver, and there was a somewhat sour smell lingering in the air that made her think of charcoal and sweat. She wondered what was compelling the horse to brave the dragon's spoor, especially here where it was strongest.

His hoof kicked at a clump of trampled grass, and then the horse lowered his head, almost bringing his muzzle to the ground.

"Something there?" Bren asked, circling the area the horse was interested in. It looked like the rest of the yard, torn up from what had happened.

She stiffened. Her gaze flicked from the charred remnants of the farmhouse's entrance and then back to where the horse was prodding the earth with his hoof. Yes, this would have been the spot. She remembered a length of glistening blackness sliding into the paladin's chest, his legs buckling as he collapsed.

Right there.

"Oh," Bren murmured, stepping closer and laying her hand on the horse's caparisoned flank. "I'm sorry. He's gone."

The horse stopped kicking the dirt and raised his head to look at her. It was foolish, but Bren imagined she saw a question in his blue eyes.

"I don't know what they did with him. Maybe they honored him with a warrior's pyre." *Maybe they fed him to their dragons*, she thought, though she did not give voice to such a horrid possibility. "He's dead; I saw what happened." Her last words were barely whispered, more for her than the horse. "We've both lost everything."

And maybe that meant they were supposed to be together. Bren's hand drifted to the amulet under her shirt, still crusted with her blood. Was this the Silver Mother's doing? Had She heard Bren's oath?

It would certainly make getting to Leris easier. Then she could return the stallion to the paladins and explain what had happened here. Still, if someone saw her riding on the road with the symbols of the Silver Mother so prominently displayed, they'd assume she was a horse thief. Bren stepped closer to the destrier and unbuckled the straps of his saddle, then took hold of the heavy cloth draped over his back. She worried the horse might shy away or nip at her, but he simply continued to watch her placidly.

"You'll feel more comfortable not having to carry this around," Bren murmured, then with some effort pulled the caparison hard enough that it slid from the horse to puddle on the grass.

Bren sucked in her breath, awed by the beauty now fully revealed. Even at rest he was impressive, and she could only imagine the force and speed with which he could gallop across a battlefield. His coat was pure white, absolutely unblemished, although there were the scars of old wounds along his flank. They almost looked like the claws of an animal, Bren thought, though such a beast would have had to be massive.

"Well, if I'm going to ride you, I need to give you a name," she said to the stallion. Her finger gently traced one of the old wounds on his side. It reminded Bren somewhat of the scratches the demon Maliskaith had given the Silver Mother, which were visible on clear nights.

"Moon," Bren decided, and as soon as she said that it felt right. The color of the horse's coat, the scars, the fact that he had been the mount of a paladin . . . it was fitting.

She rubbed the horse's side. "Your name is Moon now."

The horse whinnied and tossed his head, stamping his hooves like he was ready to depart.

Which was not a bad idea. Bren squinted up at the sky, trying to figure out how long it would be before the sun began to sink. Her family's cairn had taken her until midday to build, but she thought there was still quite a bit of light left. She supposed she could spend the afternoon scavenging in the ruin of the house, then sleep in the barn and depart on the morrow. But this would mostly just be a delay, and she barely had enough food to last until they reached Leris.

"I agree, let's go," Bren murmured to the horse. She hefted the saddle that had come off with the caparison and returned it to Moon's back. Better to start her journey now while the memory of what had happened still burned bright.

"To the City of Roses, Moon," she said, swinging herself up into the saddle.

3

A rose had been carved into the rock placed beside the road, along with the number fifty-seven. Bren sat up straighter in the saddle, shielding her eyes from the sun. They were perched on a small rise, and the black stone of the ancient imperial road they traveled was easy enough to follow, a dark thread wending between dun hills until it finally vanished into the hazy distance. The last marking stone had displayed the number sixty, so at least they were going in the right direction. Still a long way from Leris, though. Bren supposed they could travel a few more leagues at least before they would have to stop for the evening. She applied gentle pressure with her legs, and Moon resumed his easy trot.

The City of Roses. Bren had begged her father for years to allow her to visit Uncle Merik, but he had always demurred, promising that next season would be a better time. She knew he didn't like the city, as each time he'd returned he complained for days about the filth and squalor. Her uncle, though, had given her a different vision of Leris when he'd come to the farm. Stone houses with facades veined by white roses towering over streets filled with men and women hailing from all along the Flowering Coast and even more distant lands. When he'd regaled them with his stories, she had almost been able to smell the strange spices and hear the clamor of Leris's famed golden bells.

Bren had always been inclined to believe her uncle over her father. After all, if the city was such a terrible place, why did so many people choose to live there?

But this was not how she'd imagined her first visit to the City of Roses. She'd daydreamed about kissing her mother and father farewell, giving Helat a bone-crushing hug, then embarking on a journey that would end with her enlisting at the office the Bright Company kept in Leris. Instead, she had left with her heart under a cairn, and there might not even be a Company to join anymore if what the paladin had said was true. She shook her head, trying to clear it of these black thoughts. If she allowed herself to dwell overlong on what had happened, she wasn't sure she'd have the strength to continue.

To distract herself, Bren concentrated on the clip-clopping of Moon's hooves over the road of perfectly fitted black stones. The way was beyond ancient, from the days of Old Gith and its Empire of the Dawn. That distant city was now a demon-haunted ruin, but the roads it had built still bound together cities and kingdoms far beyond just the Flowering Coast. Gith had been the center of a vast web, and the strands remained even though the spider was long since dead. Those other places she knew only from stories told by firelight on festival days: Akesh, a land of bone-pierced tribesmen guarding haunted barrows; Zenovia, where the children in ancient, decaying cities were schooled in poison before they learned to read; the Crimson Dominion, with its dragonfly knights and thorned towers; and the black-sand deserts of Than Kamis, scoured by flensing winds and wandered by madmen who had gazed upon the faces of the gods. Mostly lies, Bren was sure, but there had been many long afternoons spent under a tree in the meadow, yearning to see for herself what lay beyond the Seven Valleys as the goats milled around her.

Then again, not long ago Bren would have thought dragons to be creatures of myth. Now she had seen their scything claws and gleaming scales. She had seen their fire. Bren swallowed at the memory of those terrible jaws opening wide and the roiling flames within, birthed from nothing.

Flames that had not harmed her. The farmhouse had been razed, its wooden frame reduced to charcoal. Her family burned almost past recognition. But the fire that had washed over her had not singed a hair on her head.

Why? It had to be the Silver Mother. The goddess had reached down and enfolded Bren in Her hands, granting protection from the dragon's wrath. Bren knew there was nothing special about her – she was just a shepherd girl from the Seven Valleys. But then again, the Sage of Pearls who had cast the demons from the shores of the Flowering Coast had once been but a fisherman. Perhaps the Silver Mother was weaving a great destiny for her. The thought was both exciting and terrifying.

A purple twilight crept into the sky, darkening the forest. They had descended into a valley, and now the hills rose in shadowed swells around her. The jagged remnant of a tower was picked out against the sky, and she wondered if this might be a Gith ruin, for the old empire had left traces of itself scattered all over these lands. Every few years, the Seven Valleys would be chattering about some treasure looted from an old tomb or temple. Despite this, most folks refused to go near anything that was suspected of having been built by the Gith. Danger and dark curses clung to the vestiges of the old empire.

Bren's stomach grumbled, and she rooted in her satchel for a carrot. A poor meal, but it would keep her from starving until she arrived at her uncle's house. She took a bite, and Moon's ears perked up at the sound, his head turning slightly so he could see her out of the corner of his eye.

"You want some, too?" Bren mumbled through a mouthful of carrot. "Maybe it's time to stop for the night." She had been hoping a good rest spot would materialize on the road, perhaps a willow tree with spreading branches that would keep her dry if it rained, alongside a stream clean enough to drink from, but it seemed no such spot was likely to appear. And if they did not stop, they would soon be blundering around in the dark. Sighing, Bren brought Moon to a halt and slid from his back, then led him off the road and into the woods.

She was afraid he might stumble in the underbrush or turn his hoof on a rock, but he was as surefooted as he was good-natured, and when they reached a small clearing far enough away that she could no longer see the road Bren looped Moon's reins around a stump and began setting up camp. She gathered fallen branches and leaned them against the trunk of a tree, making a crude shelter from the wind. There was more than enough wood left over for a fire, but Bren did not know how to start one without flint or steel. It would be cold, she knew, but it couldn't be any worse than how she'd spent the previous night.

Moon had been admirably patient, and she rewarded him with a half-dozen carrots from her satchel. As he crunched on his dinner, Bren stroked his flank and rubbed his ears, praising him for the good job he'd done today. Then she removed his bridle and saddle, piling them near where she thought she'd sleep.

Night had fully fallen by now, and the forest's tangle of branches and briars had been swallowed by the dark. Bren could just glimpse a slice of the Silver Mother through the thick canopy, but very little of Her light was trickling down. She shivered, wishing she'd found a blanket in the barn and chiding herself for not bringing along Moon's caparison. At this moment, the risk of attracting unwanted attention was far outweighed by the thought of curling up beneath that thick, weighted cloth. Or she could have simply reversed the caparison, hiding the holy symbols. Bren sighed, wishing this idea had occurred to her earlier.

The breeze slithering between the trees and rustling the branches suddenly died. In the silence that followed, Bren felt a rising panic. Alone at night in a strange woods, the darkness so deep she couldn't even see her hand in front of her face . . . what could be prowling out there, stalking ever closer? The Gith ruins weren't too far away, and that ancient people had consorted with demons. Her heart quickened, and she silently implored Moon to whicker or stamp his hooves so at least she would know she wasn't alone.

Wait. She cocked her head, listening. Faintly she heard raised voices, and thankfully it sounded like men, not demons or monsters. A grating laugh drifted through the forest, and relief swelled in Bren. Just the knowledge that there were other people out there comforted her . . . though for all she knew, they could be robbers or worse.

Then again, they might be merchants or a family of farmers traveling to Leris. Bren clasped her knees to her chest, chewing on her lip. The thought of sitting around a fire, maybe begging for a taste of meat or bread while enjoying the company of others . . . that held a powerfully strong appeal.

Bren made her decision. She would approach quietly through the woods, and if these travelers seemed friendly, she would show herself. And if they did not, she would creep back here and hunker down in her little shelter and pray to the Silver Mother for sleep to come quickly. There was a danger, of course, of getting lost in the darkness, so she couldn't go too far. Fifty steps in the direction she thought the voices were coming from, and if she hadn't found them by then, she would turn right around and retrace her way.

"I'll be back," she whispered at the great black shadow where Moon was tied up, and taking a deep breath for courage she started moving through the woods as quietly as possible. That was difficult, and she winced with every crackle and snap she made, but the continued murmur of voices told her the attention of these strangers was fixed somewhere other than the forest.

Soon the glow of a fire appeared ahead, flickering between the trees. Bren continued her careful approach, ready to retreat at the slightest hint of danger. The voices were all men, she realized, which was not a promising sign. If she'd heard the laughter of children, she suspected she would have wept in relief.

Finally she found a gap through the dense underbrush where she could see who was sharing the forest with her. Four men lounged around a fire in a mossy clearing. They were all wearing tabards emblazoned with the same flower, but from this distance, Bren couldn't tell what it was. Maybe an orchid, which would have meant these were men of Velessi, or perhaps that was the hyacinth of Chalice. Not a rose, she thought, although the uniforms were so dirty and disheveled that it was hard to tell for sure. Soldiers, then, and not brigands. Bren was still uneasy. She remembered the paladin's warning about broken men fleeing a disastrous battle, no longer bound by their oaths. How could she tell if they were broken? She had to admit these soldiers certainly did not look whole. Their clothes were ragged, and in the reflected light of the fire, Bren could see thin, hollow-cheeked faces. A few of them were smiling, though, as they held out skewers threaded with meat to the flames, and one of the men said something that resulted in more raucous laughter.

When that finally died, the red-haired one that had spoken stood, and Bren tensed, afraid he would come closer to where she crouched. She held her breath as he moved towards the edge of the clearing, but luckily he was far enough away that if she hunkered down and stayed silent, he would almost certainly not see her.

And then she noticed the boy.

He was sitting with his back against a gnarled trunk. His hands and legs were bound, and a strip of cloth had been tied around his head, filling his mouth. A lock of his long black hair covered one of his eyes, while the other watched the soldier approach with surprising calmness. His boots and tunic looked to be of fine make, though like the soldiers' clothes, they had seen better days.

Who was this? A criminal captured by these men? A runaway being returned to his family? He didn't look any older than she was, Bren thought.

The soldier squatted down and reached around to untie the gag in the boy's mouth. He worked his jaw like he was trying to dispel some lingering soreness, then flashed such a disarmingly cheery smile that Bren blinked in surprise.

"Thank you," he said earnestly.

The red-haired soldier snorted, but the boy's smile didn't waver.

"Do you think you could loosen these straps as well, good sir? I'm afraid they also aren't very comfortable."

This seemed to entertain the men around the fire greatly, and they dissolved into laughter again. The soldier looming over the boy shook his head, his gap-toothed grin wide, and then held out his skewer of meat.

"I was just tellin' the boys, I think ye might be even more tender than this here coney. Reckon maybe we should carve off a little piece o' ye and see how it fries up."

The boy's gaze slid from the soldier to the dripping meat. "I must confess that I have no idea. While I have a sense of my own softness, that meat you're brandishing is a mystery. It looks juicy enough, though. Perhaps if I were allowed just a nibble, I could furnish you with my honest opinion."

The soldier's response to this was an expression of absolute incredulousness, like he couldn't believe what he'd just heard. "Still trying to steal our food, lad?"

The boy's expression became pained. "As I told you, there's been a misunderstanding. I was merely checking to see if you'd caught enough rabbits that you might be willing to trade one away."

The soldier raised his face to the night sky, then pointed through the smoky haze to where the Silver Mother hung over the clearing, huge and swollen. "Yer a fortunate lad that we caught ye when Her face was already shining down. It's bad luck to stretch a man's neck while the goddess is watching, otherwise we'd already have ye dangling from a tree."

The boy laughed, but to Bren it sounded forced. "Surely that's a bit of an overreaction. Even the rabbit would agree that such a punishment is not justified."

"Army discipline would be a dozen lashes," the soldier said, lowering his eyes to the boy again. "But we ain't in the army anymore." He crouched down, holding taut the cloth they'd used as a gag. "When the Mother leaves the sky, ye hang."

"Unfortunate, but if that's the case, you must agree that I deserve a last meal, and as it turns out, you *do* have rabbits to—"

The soldier shoved the cloth back into the boy's mouth. Then he rose, chuckling and shaking his head as he returned to his grinning comrades. Behind him, the boy continued to try to speak through the gag, but all that came out was incomprehensible gibberish.

Bren set aside any thought of approaching these men. They may still be wearing the uniforms of soldiers, but it was clear that was not what they considered themselves anymore. Once a warrior lost his lord or his city, what did he fight for? Himself? That sounded more like an outlaw.

She had a strong desire to creep back through the forest to her horse, then, while the Mother was high, return to the road and ride until Moon tired. But what about the boy? He may have been a thief – his claim to be otherwise hadn't been very convincing – but did he deserve to die for trying to steal from these once-soldiers? What if he was starving . . . or maybe his younger sister was even now watching the woods, waiting for him to return and trying to ignore the ache in her belly?

Bren settled down, trying to make herself more comfortable. She could save this boy. The soldiers had already said they wouldn't kill him until the morning. Eventually they'd sleep, and then she could sneak closer and cut his bonds. By the time the soldiers realized he was gone, they'd be galloping down the road. Surely these men wouldn't bother hunting for a boy who had attempted to steal a rabbit.

Bren tried to ignore her own grumbling stomach as the once-soldiers finished their dinner. One of them produced a long-necked bottle, and they passed that around, singing songs and telling ribald jokes that made Bren's ears burn. After they'd licked all the grease from their fingers and the empty bottle had been smashed to a chorus of groans, most of the men stretched out beside the dwindling flames. A pox-scarred soldier with the biggest ears Bren had ever seen remained on watch while the others tried to sleep, taking out a chunk of half-whittled wood and a dagger. He quickly became absorbed in his work, his face a mask of concentration.

As the night deepened, the forest came alive with the thrumming of insects and the mournful cry of a lonely songbird. The fire subsided until it was little more than glowing embers. Bren watched the head of the soldier on guard slowly lower several times, then jerk back up as he fought to stay awake. Finally, his chin settled onto his chest and stayed there, the wooden dog or wolf he'd been carving slipping from his fingers.

It was time. Bren began to move as quietly as possible, staying recessed in the shadows as she skirted the edge of the clearing. Her heart was hammering so loudly that it seemed like it should wake the soldiers, and she froze for a moment as one of the men grumbled something in his sleep. When he quieted again, she let out her breath and continued until she found herself behind the tree the boy was slumped against. She crept around the trunk, his unruly mop of black hair gradually coming into view.

"Don't be frightened," she whispered, and to her relief, she saw the boy's head twitch slightly towards her. She'd been worried she would have to wake him up. "I'm going to free you. I have a horse nearby, and he's big enough to carry both of us. Do you understand?"

The boy jerked a quick nod. He turned his head so he could see her out of the corner of his eye.

And winked at her.

Now nervous that she was about to cut loose a madman, Bren edged further around the trunk and knelt down beside the boy. His wrist-bindings were made of tough leather, and it took a few terrifying moments for her rusty old knife to cut through. As soon as they fell away, he reached up and ripped the gag out. Bren prayed fervently to the Mother that he'd keep his fool mouth shut until she finished freeing him. The strap around his legs was thicker and proved even harder to cut. She sawed away frantically, the leather barely parting, and then his hand covered hers as he added his strength. The knife sliced through the bindings, sending Bren falling forward, and her free hand thumped the ground as she just caught herself from sprawling face-first in the grass.

She looked up and met the gaze of the pox-scarred soldier. For a moment he simply goggled at them, his mouth opening and closing like he was a caught fish, and then he surged to his feet screaming something unintelligible.

"Let us be off," said the boy calmly, and then his hand closed around her arm and pulled her stumbling into the forest.

Brambles and branches clawed at Bren, snagging her clothes and leaving burning lines across her cheek. She couldn't see anything, and the fear of running into a tree or tumbling down a ravine made her stomach clench, but shouts rose up behind them, along with what sounded like an enraged bear crashing through the woods in pursuit. She didn't know where they were going, but it was definitely in the wrong direction.

"This isn't the way to my horse," Bren gasped. She nearly fell as her ankle turned on a rock, but the strong grip on her arm kept her upright.

"Excellent," came the reply. The boy sounded barely winded and not the least bit worried.

"What?"

"Well, they're right behind us, yes? We don't want to lead them back to our means of escape." He stopped talking for a moment as they struggled up a steep incline, leaves slithering under their feet. "Once we lose them in the woods, we'll circle back to your faithful steed."

"In the dark?"

"You must know where you camped relative to the road. We find the road, then your horse."

Bren winced. Her sloppily repaired shoes were on the verge of fully coming apart, and she felt every sharp stone under her feet. "What if those men find my horse first?" she asked between gasps of pain.

The boy paused, clearly unsure which way to go. To their left, the ground seemed to rise further, while on the right, it sloped downwards. A loud bellowing not very far behind them made Bren jump, and the boy muttered something that sounded like a curse and pulled her upwards.

"If they find your horse, I shall get you another one."

"This is a very nice horse."

"I promise the replacement will be better."

Bren couldn't help but snort. "Are you a better horse thief than you are a rabbit thief?"

He seemed at a loss for words after that, and Bren thought she might have wounded his pride.

They were scrambling up the side of a rocky hill now, and the trees had thinned enough that she could occasionally glimpse the Mother or one of Her daughters. When they paused to catch their breath, Bren glanced behind and saw a faint glow bobbing through the forest. It seemed the soldiers weren't foolish enough to career around in the dark. Voices carried up to them, and Bren recognized the man who had threatened the boy earlier.

"This will do," the boy said with no small satisfaction.

Bren dragged her gaze from the lights moving among the trees. "What will do?"

"This," he replied, tugging her towards a pile of tumbled dark shapes. Huge rocks, Bren realized, as the boy wriggled between two of them, the way so narrow his chest scraped against stone. He'd finally let go of her to do this, and Bren hesitated before following.

"What if we're trapped in there?" she asked, also wary of what might be lairing inside this cleft in the hill.

"We won't be," the boy replied, his disembodied voice floating from the darkness. "It gets wider quickly."

Tamping down her fear, Bren turned herself sideways and slipped into the crack. She could feel the pressure on her front and back, along with the weight of the stone hanging above her, and for a terrifying moment this summoned the memory of being buried in the ruin of her house. She imagined becoming wedged here, unable to move, slowly dying of thirst as the desperate boy further inside the cave pulled vainly on her arm . . .

Bren shuddered with relief as she emerged into a larger space. For a few heartbeats she stayed doubled over with her hands on her knees, her panic slowly draining away.

"They're not fitting through that," the boy gloated. Bren jumped at his voice; she hadn't realized he was standing right beside her. The darkness in this cave was absolutely impenetrable.

"How long do we have to hide?" Bren hissed back, her skin

crawling as she considered what else could be crouched in here with them.

There was the sound of movement and the rasp of cloth on stone, and Bren assumed he must have found something to sit on. "Until the morning. I suspect they'll tire of this chase soon, but if they don't, they'll certainly have given up by dawn. Then we'll slip out and find your horse and be off."

"As simple as that."

"Indeed."

Bren couldn't think of what to say to this. She sighed, feeling around beneath herself until her fingers brushed rock, and then she sat heavily with her head in her hands. How had she ended up in a cave with a stranger? Would Moon still be there when she finally returned to her little camp? She was an utter fool.

The boy seemed to abhor silence, and Bren wasn't surprised when he broke it. "What's your name?"

"Brenna, daughter of Gelin."

"Well met, Brenna. I am Tal of the Shadows."

In the darkness he couldn't see her frown. There weren't many orphans in the Seven Valleys, but Bren had heard that those children who did not know their fathers chose a name when they came of age that they thought best suited them. She now knew this Tal was an orphan and that trying to steal a rabbit was most likely entirely in character for him.

"Call me Bren."

"Bren, then. Thank you for what you did back there. Unnecessary, but appreciated."

"Unnecessary?"

"In truth, I was waiting for those fools to fall asleep before I made my escape."

"Oh, really."

"Indeed. I have a razor sewn into my inner sleeve. Quite handy, I recommend everyone carry one."

"*Hm.* Do you have anything else useful hidden in your shirt?"

Tal chuckled, sounding far too satisfied with himself. "Now that you ask ..."

Bren stifled a surprised cry as pale light swelled in the darkness. It traveled over the inside of the cave, illuminating a jumble of rocks and a ceiling that was higher than she expected. The ghostly radiance emanated from something the boy held in his hand, but it did not flicker or dance like a flame.

"What is that?" she breathed, leaning in closer to see what he held.

"My pebble," he told her smugly. It was actually larger than a pebble, but not by very much, perhaps the size of a fingernail. The light spilling from it masked its form, but Bren thought it was shaped like a sphere.

"Where did you get that?"

"I seduced a beautiful sorceress," he told her breezily, "and she gave me a token of her love."

"Did you steal it?"

"I did not," Tal said with a sniff. "As I said, it was a gift."

"*Hm.*"

The light abruptly vanished, darkness flooding once more into the cave. A pulsing island of white lingered in Bren's vision.

"We don't want to draw anyone's attention," he explained, returning the object to wherever it had been secreted with a rustle of cloth.

Bren had much preferred the cave when she could see, but he was right. If those men realized where they were hiding, they'd be trapped in here. Sighing, she settled down to wait.

THE NIGHT CRAWLED along with excruciating slowness. Several times, Bren went over to the crack and peered through it, hoping to see a lightening in the small slice of sky that was visible, but she was always disappointed. The boy had finally fallen silent, and when he mumbled something incomprehensible, she realized he was asleep.

Bren wondered how he had possibly gotten comfortable enough to nod off – the rocks she was sitting on seemed to be all pointy edges, not to mention that once she had felt something long and many-legged scurry over her hand.

She leaned her head back against the stone, then sat forward abruptly when she imagined a corpse-white centipede undulating into her hair. That made her skin prickle, and she considered standing on top of a rock to avoid almost all contact with what might be scuttling around in the cave. Maybe if she—

Bren stiffened, listening hard. She could have sworn she'd heard something. Perhaps it had just been her imagination . . . No, there it was again, but so faint. As if to taunt her, Tal chose this moment to begin snoring. Scowling, Bren considered pinching his nose closed but instead reached out into the darkness and tapped him lightly.

"*Uh?*" he murmured, coming awake. "Is it morning?"

"No," she hissed. "Be quiet."

"Are they here?" he whispered, his voice finally containing a hint of fear.

"No. But listen."

He complied, and Bren also focused during the silence that followed. Had it been real? It must have been . . . or had she fallen asleep for a moment and dreamed it?

Then it came once more, fluttering on moth wings.

A faint whispering.

"Can you hear it?" she asked.

"There's nothing," Tal assured her. "I have superb hearing, I promise you. I can tell dice are hollow even when thrown in a crowded tavern."

"I hear a voice."

"My voice?"

"Be quiet."

Bren strained. The whispering did not grow any louder, but the more she concentrated, the clearer it became. It sounded like . . . She swallowed, a chill washing through her.

It sounded like someone she knew.

"I think it's my mother," she whispered.

"Aha," Tal said after clearing his throat. "Perhaps she's worried about you and has come looking."

"She's dead."

"Well, let's hope it's not her, then."

Bren rose from where she was sitting and carefully picked her way over the treacherous rocks to the back of the cave where the whispering was loudest.

"You know," Tal said, "the soldiers must have given up by now. I think it would be an excellent time to leave this place."

Bren ran her hand along the wall until her fingers found a gap in the rock. Trying to ignore the sour feeling in her stomach, she brought her ear to this crack and listened.

Her mother's voice carried to her clearly, whispering in the old tongue. But she wasn't singing, as she always had been before when she spoke that language. It almost sounded like she was pleading.

Pleading for help.

Bren's fingers tightened on the edges of the crack, and to her surprise, she felt the wall shift. It wasn't one solid slab, she realized, but rather a pile of not-very-stable stones. She pulled, and the gap widened, fragments of rock bouncing to the floor.

"What are you doing?" Tal asked nervously, hovering at her shoulder.

"I'm going to try to find my mother."

"That is *not* a good idea," Tal hissed in her ear. "You just said she was dead."

"I'm not going to leave her again," Bren growled, straining with all her strength. The rock she was pulling suddenly slipped, and she had to jump backwards as a small avalanche began.

The darkness in front of her had not changed, but now cold fingers of air brushed her skin, making her shiver. She had opened a passage to somewhere.

"What have you done?" asked Tal in a strangled voice.

"I need light. Give me your pebble," Bren commanded.

"Ha! No."

"I risked my life to save yours."

"And I'll return the favor by not letting you go in there."

"I'm going. I have to." She reached out and found his arm in the dark. "Please," she asked, her voice softening.

Tal was quiet for a moment. "Aren't you scared?"

Bren frowned. She should be scared. She should be *terrified*. And yet she wasn't.

"Yesterday I watched my family die, and I had to crawl out of the ruin of our house and bury them. Trapped under that wood and ash, the weight pressing down on me so hard I could barely breathe . . . That's what I fear. Not my mother, even if she's a ghost. Maybe she has something she needs to tell me."

"Oh, by all the sundered sages," the boy muttered, and then the spectral radiance swelled, filling the cave again. In front of them was a jagged opening half the height of a man, and from the light spilling through this hole, Bren could see a passage curving away into the darkness.

"Our ledger will most definitely be balanced after this," Tal grumbled, stepping closer so that the light slid further down the tunnel.

Bren knelt to peer into the black. "You can also hear those whispers, can't you?"

Tal gave a sharp shake of his head. "If I heard any whispers, I'd right now be running down the hillside begging for those soldiers to tie me up again. I'm assuming you're a madwoman, and when you go in there, you'll eventually come to a dead-end and have to turn around."

Bren held out her open palm. "Let's find out. I assume you don't want to go first."

Tal muttered something unintelligible, but he tipped the thing he called a pebble into her hand.

"Thank you." She had been expecting it to be warm, but it felt just like a cool, smooth stone, polished for an age at the bottom of a river.

Bren crouched, and before she could truly consider what she was doing, she went down on her hands and knees and entered the tunnel. She held the pebble loosely, the light leaking from between her fingers. Ahead, her mother's whispering voice beckoned her on.

"I'm coming, Mama," Bren murmured, crawling forward. Behind her she heard scraping as Tal joined her in the tunnel.

After about a score of paces, the ceiling no longer brushed her head, and soon she found she could stand. Packed earth had replaced rock on either side of her, and she had no doubt that tools had shaped this passage. Her hands brushed the walls, dirt sifting down.

"You know what this must be, yes?" Tal asked, looking around with wide eyes as he slowly came to his feet.

She shook her head, her fingertip tracing a whorled design cut into the wall.

"Old Gith," Tal said softly. "These hills are full of their ruins and tombs."

He put his hand on her shoulder, stopping her. "The stories say they danced with demons, Bren. I know you've heard the same. Think what really could be calling to you."

Bren shrugged his hand away. "If it's a demon, I'll wring its neck for pretending to be my mother."

She continued but soon stopped again as the pale light revealed two blocky pillars flanking an entrance into a larger space. One of these pillars was bare of any ornamentation, but the other was covered in countless spiraling lines of squirming runes.

"Last chance to turn around," Tal said hopefully, but in response she strode forward into the black.

And came face to face with the dead.

Bren stumbled back a step. The narrow chamber was empty save for a large, rough-hewn stone chair set against the far wall.

Sitting on that ancient throne was a corpse.

Given the age of this barrow, Bren thought there should be only a pile of crumbling bones, but the corpse's papery skin was still stretched taut over its withered body. Its skull was tilted backwards, jaw open as it stared with empty eye sockets at the low ceiling. Whatever clothes it had once worn had rotted away, and Bren couldn't be certain if it had been a man or woman.

Skeletal fingers were curled around the verdigris-stained bronze hilt of a sword, its blade lying across the corpse's lap. Bren swallowed, her mouth suddenly dry. Light from the pebble slid over the length of the strange pale blade, which looked as sharp as if it had recently been polished and whetted.

"Mother, save us," Tal said hoarsely, joining her in the chamber.

Bren's hand went to the amulet under her shirt. It was as cold as ice against her skin, and she shivered.

"What are the whispers saying?" Tal asked, rubbing his arms as if he could also feel a chill.

"They've stopped," Bren replied, crossing the room to stand before the looming stone throne.

"Perhaps we should go," said Tal, his words spilling out in a tumbling rush. "Certainly this poor thing would prefer not to have its rest disturbed – wait, what are you doing?"

Keeping her gaze fixed on the dead warlord's sunken face, Bren reached out slowly to grip the sword's hilt, her fingers brushing bone.

"I don't think you should touch that—"

The blade scraped across ancient skin as Bren pulled it free. She had been half expecting the corpse's finger bones to tighten around the hilt and yank it back from her, but it gave up the sword without a struggle. Bren let out a shuddering breath.

Its weight surprised her, as it was lighter than the wooden practice sword her uncle had given her. The unadorned bronze grip felt comfortable in her hand despite the scarring from the patina, and light rippled along the odd metal. She jumped as a sound came from the corpse, but it was just the arm shifting after losing the sword, bone cracking against stone.

"Are you taking that?" asked Tal in disbelief.

"Yes."

The boy made a disapproving noise. "Plenty of other swords in the world. Most can be acquired without upsetting ghosts or demons."

Bren slid the sword into the loop on her belt she'd made to hold her wooden practice blade. She should find a scabbard soon, but this would do for now. She'd just have to be careful not to cut herself with the naked metal hanging at her side.

"That is the problem," she told Tal, rubbing her thumb on the pommel. Bits of green flaked away, revealing the dark metal beneath. "So many swords in the world, and I don't have one." She inclined her head towards the corpse. "He doesn't need this anymore."

"He?" Tal repeated with a frown. "That was a woman."

The sword of a warrior queen. Perhaps she had been meant to find it, Bren thought. Perhaps this was the will of the Silver Mother.

But if that was true, why was the goddess's amulet so cold? She swallowed, stepping back from the throne. It almost felt like something was watching her from the depths of the corpse's empty eye sockets.

"Let's go."

4

Wan morning light was trickling down through the trees when they finally made it back to where Bren had set up camp the night before. She had been afraid that Moon would be missing, either stolen by the soldiers or having freed himself with the same trick he had used to get loose in the barn, but when she pushed through the underbrush they found the horse still in the clearing. He stared at Bren like he was severely disappointed in her, then tossed his head.

"I'm sorry," Bren said, feeling guilty. She went over to where she'd hidden her satchel among the roots of a tree, hoping to make it back into his good graces with the offering of a few carrots, but the bag was empty. For a moment, she thought some wild animal had snuck from the forest to pilfer their food, but then she noticed the hoofprints in the soft earth. Bren blinked, comparing the length of the rope – which was still around the stump – to where she'd left the satchel. She didn't see how Moon could have reached the bag. Was it possible that the horse had freed himself to devour all the carrots, then somehow looped it over the stump again just so he could claim innocence later?

She turned back towards Tal to ask him if he'd ever heard of a horse that could do such a thing and found him staring wide-eyed at Moon.

"What's the matter?" she asked, and her words woke him from his stupor.

"Sages, you were right. That is a magnificent horse."

"Thank you."

"He looks like a king's mount."

Bren bit the inside of her cheek. It was probably best if he did not know the truth about Moon.

"Your family raised him?"

"Yes," Bren said, hoping her face wasn't turning red. She'd always had a problem with flushing when she lied. It had been very hard to fool her mother . . . Bren pushed that thought away. She couldn't think about her.

Tal approached Moon slowly, holding up his hands as if he were trying to show the horse he wasn't armed.

"You don't know much about horses, do you?" Bren asked.

"I'm city born. Lived my whole life in the City of Roses."

"Oh," Bren said. "I'm going to Leris."

"I guessed that," Tal replied, having come close enough to Moon that he could lay his hand on the horse's flank. "There's little else around here. But I don't think visiting the city is a very wise decision right now."

Bren turned her satchel inside out, hoping a carrot had escaped the horse's notice. Her stomach was twisting itself into a knot. "Why?"

He looked at her like she was simple. "Because you're a Velaschin. Lots of folks are scared and angry right now at your people." He hesitated, then hurriedly continued when he saw her frown. "Not that I'm one of them."

"I'm not Velaschin," she said.

"But . . ." His hand slipped from Moon as he gestured vaguely towards her. "Your skin. Your hair."

Bren slung the satchel over her shoulder. "I've lived my whole life in the Seven Valleys," she told him, anger edging her words. "Do you know why I'm out here, riding on my own to Leris? Because Velaschin murdered my family."

He swallowed. "I'm sorry."

"A paladin took shelter at our farm. He was fleeing some great battle, and the Velaschin hunted him to our doorstep. They killed him, then burned my house to the ground with everyone I loved inside. They left me for dead."

"A paladin . . ." Tal looked down at the ground, his face troubled. "I thought if anyone could defeat the Velaschin, it would be the Silver Mother's chosen."

"They had dragons."

Tal's head jerked up. "You've seen them."

There was something in his voice. "Have you?"

He nodded. "I was there with the army over the mountains. Never thought I'd go, but a month past, a royal messenger arrived in Leris recruiting for Her Majesty's army. He said Felaesia would soon be at war, that the ungrateful barbarians from across the sea whom the queen had allowed to trade with the kingdom and settle in the port of Yestra were now preparing to invade. He spoke of glory and the riches that could be looted from the enemy, and many of us pledged ourselves. He said we were *irregulars*." Tal's mouth twisted bitterly. "Irregulars. We didn't have the slightest notion what those were, but for the great lords commanding in the field, it meant we were the chaff that could be discarded first so that their knights and sworn swords were kept safe. I slipped away after most of my company were cut down in some nameless swamp." His eyes looked past her, reliving the memory. "I buried myself in the mud and pretended to be dead and watched the dragons circle in the sky like carrion birds. The Velaschin who weren't riding those monsters marched right over me. I think I've been trodden on by half their damn army. After they passed, I crawled out of the muck and decided I preferred my life in Leris."

"Your clothes seemed to have survived the ordeal."

He glanced down at his finely tailored tunic. "Ah. My current garments were liberated from someone who wasn't in such dire straits."

"Just as you tried to liberate a coney from those soldiers?"

Tal shrugged. "Much the same. I have always held fast to the belief that those with more should share with those who have less."

"Even if they don't want to?"

"*Especially* if they don't want to. That means they deserve to lose it."

"*Hm.*"

Tal cleared his throat. "Well. We're both headed to Leris. Perhaps we could travel together?"

Her uncle Merik had told her of the guttersnipes who inhabited the City of Roses, children born and raised on the streets. He'd spoken of them with contempt, and she remembered him warning her father to give them a wide berth when he visited the city, as they were known to prey on visitors. Tal was clearly one of them. He'd as much as admitted to being a thief. And yet . . . she found that she trusted him. He'd pulled her through the forest when he could have left her behind for the soldiers, and then he had followed her into a Gith barrow even though he'd feared what might be calling to her.

"Can you ride a horse?" she asked.

The boy glanced at Moon uncertainly. "It's just sitting, yes?"

"There's a bit more to it than that. You'll likely get a little sore if you haven't ridden before."

"Pain doesn't bother me," he said with the confidence Bren had started to expect, and she had to restrain herself from rolling her eyes.

"Then we can ride together. Moon should be able to easily carry both of us."

"Moon," Tal said, running his hand through the horse's silvery mane. "A fitting name." He turned to her, smiling broadly. "Very well, I accept your offer. We shall be companions."

Bren nodded, then took up the reins and began to lead the horse through the forest to the road. Tal kept pace with her, showing his agility by leaping lightly from fallen log to rock, never touching the ground.

"And what are your plans for when you reach Leris, Brenna?"

"Bren. And I have family there. My uncle is an officer in the Bright Company, and he lives in the city with his wife."

"Ah, the Company," Tal said. "They can be a stuck-up bunch. Most of them also come from the streets or farms, but they think they're better than the rest of us."

Bren silently agreed with that. Uncle Merik had indeed expressed disdain for those who refused to hoist themselves from whatever poor situation they had been born into. In truth, he probably would have respected Tal's decision to join the queen's army. Not his subsequent desertion, though.

"Then you know where you're going?" the boy asked.

Bren helped Moon skirt a thorned bush, pulling aside the grasping branches. "It's my first time in the city. I've never been to my uncle's house. I believe he lives somewhere called the Garden."

Tal teetered on a pointy rock before finding his balance. "That would make sense if he's an officer in the Company. Nice area, the Garden. Most of the well-to-do merchants and tradespeople live there. It's large, though. Takes up nearly a quarter of the city."

"I'll ask around in the shops or visit the Bright Company's offices."

"A good plan, but even so, I would be happy to help you. Some might not be willing to talk with a Velaschin girl, and I know Leris as well as anyone."

"Even the Garden?" She glanced at him, and when he caught her look, he winked.

"I've actually spent quite a lot of time in that district."

"Liberating things?"

"Sometimes," he replied, grinning slyly.

"Showing up at the city gates with you isn't going to get me thrown into prison, is it?"

He snorted. "Highly unlikely, though I suppose it depends who's on guard duty when we arrive."

Bren shook her head and sighed. "Well, let me know, please, if it is the wrong person so I can pretend I don't know you."

Tal grabbed at his chest like he'd taken an invisible sword thrust. "Unsettling lack of loyalty, I must say, after all we've been through."

They emerged from the forest and found themselves on the old imperial road, Moon's hooves ringing again on the black stone. The horse pranced for a moment as if pleased to be out of the woods with its rocks and roots. Bren couldn't help but compare the crudely carved stone barrow they'd discovered with this masterfully constructed road, still in excellent condition after an age of heavy use. The Gith may have built both, but she'd have wagered anything that the tomb was far older, from a much earlier time. Or perhaps she was wrong, and that barrow had been dug by an even more ancient, vanished people.

Bren swung herself up onto Moon, careful that the sword hanging naked at her hip did not accidentally harm the horse. Then she scooted forward until she was pressed against the front of the saddle and slapped the leather behind her.

"Sit here. It's best I'm in front if you've never ridden before."

It took Tal a few failed attempts to climb up, but finally he settled himself on the saddle. He was still unsteady, and when Moon shifted slightly, he gave a little yelp and grabbed hold of Bren's waist.

"Apologies!" he cried in horror, quickly letting go.

"It's all right," Bren replied, glad he couldn't see her blush. "I used to ride double with my father to the village sometimes. I have the reins, so there's not much else for you to hold on to. I won't consider it untoward if you need to put your hands on me. Just watch out for the sword. And don't kick his flank by accident unless you want to be thrown."

"You're sure the horse can bear both of us?" Tal said, sounding like he wanted an excuse to return to the ground.

"He's carried things much heavier than you and me," Bren said, digging her heels into Moon's side.

"Sages save us!" Tal cried as the horse surged forward, his arms tightening around Bren.

Bren realized she was smiling. Certainly that was in large part because of the fear she could hear in his voice . . . but there was something else as well.

It felt good not to be alone.

TAL LASTED ALMOST until midday before he begged Bren to bring Moon to a stop so he could dismount. When she did, he hopped down gingerly, tottering away from the horse with an awkward, wide-legged gait. Bren remembered the first time she'd ever ridden a horse and how sore she'd felt, and that had been the much smaller Frog at a slow plod in the pleasantly soft lower pastures. Bouncing up and down at a good pace with his legs stretched across the wide back of Moon had put lie to the claim that pain would not bother him.

"Perhaps I'll walk a ways," he said loudly, rubbing the inside of his thighs. "Stretch my legs a bit."

"I suppose we don't have to hurry," Bren replied amiably, nudging Moon into a slow trot. "Though I am starving."

"We'll come across an inn sooner or later," Tal assured her.

"I have no money."

Tal pulled out a pouch and gave it a shake, and Bren heard the jingle of coins. "I would be happy to share."

"*Hm.* If you had money, why did you not simply buy one of the rabbits the soldiers had caught?"

The pouch disappeared again. "If I'd shown my coin to those bastards, they would have taken it away, and I'd have ended up just where you found me anyway. They were not honest men. And believe me, I know the type."

Bren believed him.

They continued in silence for a while. The dark forest gradually thinned, then vanished altogether, becoming a rolling meadow spattered with crimson blossoms that stretched away on both sides of the road. Bren startled as Tal suddenly plunged into the tall grass, but he soon returned with a few of the bright red flowers, their long stems braided into a crown. He handed it up to Bren, and this time she couldn't hide her blush.

"For you, my lady," he said dramatically, flourishing a bow.

She leaned forward to place the crown between Moon's ears. "It will look better on him." For a moment it perched there, but then with a whicker of annoyance the horse tossed his head, sending it flying.

Tal stared at the ruin of the crown for a moment. "You are different from what I was expecting."

"What do you mean?"

"I thought peasant girls would be more . . . traditional."

"Traditional?"

"Dresses and babies and such. Gossiping by the well about who can't properly pluck a chicken. Pleased to be crowned with flowers by a handsome boy. Fewer swords."

Bren snorted. "I was going to join the Bright Company. My uncle gave me my first sword to practice with." It had been wooden, but she kept that to herself. Thinking of her uncle brought with it memories of her family, and her mood suddenly darkened. "But now . . . I have other dreams."

"And what are those?"

Her hands tightened on the reins. "Revenge."

He blinked up at her, evidently surprised by her change in tone. "For your family?" When she nodded, Tal frowned and ran his fingers through his dark hair. "But you said the ones who burned your farm rode dragons."

"Yes."

"Are you planning on killing the dragons too?"

Bren shrugged. "Aren't dragons just dumb animals? I wouldn't swear vengeance on an enemy's horse."

"Well, that's something, I suppose. I don't think anyone in the army has figured out how to kill those big scaly monsters." Tal turned away, blowing out his cheeks. "It's rank madness, but best of luck to you. The Sages know Felaesia needs a champion right now."

The doubt she heard in his voice annoyed her. "Thank you," Bren told him, kicking Moon into a canter. She glimpsed Tal's surprised face as she thundered past, then she reined up further down the road to wait for him.

When he finally caught up to her, panting, she gestured for him to get up in the saddle again. "Tired of walking yet? I want to hurry – I'm hungry, and I have dragon lords to kill."

TWILIGHT WAS DARKENING the sky when they finally reached an inn. It was a rambling, two-story structure of timber and stone situated at a crossroads, and it looked to be doing excellent business, the fenced stable yard filled with horses and wagons. Bren wondered if there would be any beds available for the night.

"Your cloak," Tal whispered in her ear, and Bren pulled up her cowl. She didn't like hiding, especially since she had been raised under the Mother's gaze in the Seven Valleys, but it was probably for the best if she didn't flaunt her pale skin. Who knew what other atrocities the Velaschin had committed in this land? Hers couldn't have been the only farm they'd burned.

A boy with a withered leg limped towards them as they approached, leaning on a length of wood. He whistled in admiration, wide eyes fixed on Moon.

"*Eh*, travelers," he called out. "Welcome to *The Grinning Gallows*."

Bren slid from Moon's back, and then Tal thumped down beside her. "Thank you. Are you a stable hand?"

The boy spat out something he'd been chewing on. "Aye. It's a copper venmark for the stall, and I'll make sure this handsome fellow is well fed."

"*The Grinning Gallows*?" Tal said, fishing a coin from his pouch. "Odd name."

The boy gestured vaguely behind him, still staring at Moon, and after a moment Bren realized that he was pointing at where a gibbet had been erected in the shadow of the inn.

"Used to be they thought crossroads were the best place to hang folk 'cause angry ghosts wouldn't know which way to go to catch the ones who strung 'em up." He spat again, wiping his mouth with the back of his hand.

Tal flipped the boy the coin, which he deftly plucked out of the air. "Always this busy?" he asked, gesturing at the wagons scattered about.

"Nah," the boy replied, biting down on the coin. "Everyone's scared, fleein' for Leris's high walls. The queen lost her head on the battlefield, and now there's an army of baby-eatin' barbarians roamin' around."

Tal cast her a sidelong glance. Bren receded deeper into her father's oversized cloak, keeping her hands hidden.

The boy didn't seem to notice, his eyes only for Moon as he stepped closer to take up the reins.

"No amount of pampering is too much," Tal said with a smile, then grabbed Bren by the arm and began guiding her towards the inn's entrance.

"Perhaps we shouldn't stay here," Bren whispered uneasily. "I don't want to cause a problem."

"Don't worry," Tal replied as he pushed open the door. "We'll find a dark corner to eat our supper in and then retire to our rooms for the night. I'm so hungry I'll soon be gnawing on saddle leather if we keep riding."

The common room of the inn was crowded, patrons sitting cheek-to-jowl on benches running beside two long trestle tables. They looked like the folk she had grown up with, good Seven Valley stock, farmers and tradespeople dressed in roughspun clothes, and there were as many women and children as men. Entire families seeking solace in Leris before the invaders arrived. Or perhaps bands of roving soldiers-turned-brigands had driven these refugees from their homes.

It felt strange hiding herself from her own people. Tal led her to a bench and with a friendly smile cleared some space. Bren slipped onto the wooden plank, trying to keep her head lowered so that others wouldn't be able to see her face in the depths of her hood, but she couldn't help but stare at the food scattered about the table. The man beside her noisily slurped a brown stew with chunks of meat and vegetables from a hollowed-out trencher of bread, and across from him a woman with bruises under her eyes and stringy black hair was ripping apart a roasted capon. It had been several days since she'd eaten anything except raw carrots, and her belly began to ache while watching them devour their food.

Tal beckoned for a harried-looking older woman to approach, then pointed at the bread bowl near Bren.

"Two of these, Auntie. And a pitcher of ale."

The woman gave a curt nod to show she'd heard, then turned towards someone else demanding her attention.

Tal stared at the swirling chaos of the common room for a long moment, his eyebrows raised. "Leris must be in an uproar," he muttered with a shake of his head. "I wonder where everyone will sleep."

"Do you think the Velaschin will really cross over the mountains in force?"

The boy shrugged. "Who knows? I assume so. They are invaders, after all, and our army is scattered."

Bren's hand drifted to the hilt of the sword hidden under her cloak. Her enemy would come to her, it seemed, but what could she do? She needed years of training and an army of her own.

Silver Mother, help me, she thought, her fingers stroking the bronze pommel.

I will.

Cold surprise washed through Bren, and she nearly toppled from the bench. Tal flashed out his hand, just catching her before she tumbled backwards.

"Whoa! Careful there," he exclaimed, concern in his face.

She swallowed, trying to decide if that whisper in her head had been real. Surely not. The goddess never responded to prayers directly unless one was a sage or a prophet. It must have been her imagination. After the ordeal of the last few days . . . any strange voices in her head were understandable, she supposed.

"Here you go, my lovelies."

Bren's attention returned to the table as the serving woman set two circular loaves of bread down, each filled with steaming helpings of stew, along with a clay pitcher and a pair of worn wooden cups.

Maybe her hunger was making her mind play tricks on her. Tal had already decided she was fine, ignoring the spoons the serving woman had tossed onto the table and lifting his bread bowl to directly gulp the stew. When he finally lowered the bread, he looked almost drunk, chin glistening and eyes glazed.

"Sages, that's good," he moaned and then reached to fill their cups from the pitcher.

Despite her lingering apprehension about the strange voice, Bren couldn't resist anymore. She ripped off a chunk of the crusty bread, dunked it in the stew, and then shoved it into her mouth with all the decorum of her goats swarming their feed.

Mother, that *was* good.

She realized Tal was holding out a cup for her. After she took it, he lifted his own in a toast.

"A pleasure to meet you, Brenna, daughter of Gelin. May you never need to save my life again."

They touched cups, and Bren drank deeply. She didn't often drink ale – her father had only ever allowed her a few sips on festival days – and her head was already swimming when she set the empty cup down.

No meal had ever tasted as good as—

Stew splattered Bren as Tal's face was smashed into his bread bowl. A moment later, fingers closed tightly around her shoulder, and then she was flung from the bench. Her head struck the wooden floor hard, and she could only lie there in shock, blinking up at the dark shapes looming over her.

"Good to see you again, lad."

Bren knew what she would see even before her blurred vision finally returned.

The red-haired soldier who had taunted Tal in the clearing now stood behind him, his hand tangled in the boy's long hair. She recognized the three grinning soldiers clustered around, including the pox-scarred one who had been keeping watch. Droplets of stew flew from Tal's face as he thrashed, trying to break loose from the grip, but the soldier only laughed and cuffed the boy hard. Tal's head struck the table, and to her horror he immediately went limp and started to slide from the bench. Two of the soldiers stepped forward and caught him before he fell, each grabbing him under an arm.

"Tal," she slurred, struggling to stand. Just as she found her feet, someone kicked her legs out from under her, and she went sprawling again.

More rough laughter came from the soldiers, followed by a stab of pain as a boot slammed into her ribs. She curled up holding her side, tasting blood in her mouth.

Through the haze that had descended, she saw Tal was being dragged away. His head was hanging down, and though his long hair was obscuring his face, she assumed he was unconscious. Bren reached out a trembling hand as the soldiers threw open the door and hauled Tal outside.

Silence filled the common room for a long moment, and then voices swelled as the shocked patrons began discussing what had just happened. A plump, balding man crouched beside her, his face scrunched up in concern.

"Are you all right, lass?" he asked, putting a hand on her.

Gritting her teeth, Bren struggled to her feet. She realized her cowl had slipped when gasps erupted around her.

Velaschin she heard someone cry. *Milkie.*

The man who had knelt beside her rose and took a stumbling step back, drawing the circle of the Silver Mother in the air.

Ignoring the stares and exclamations, Bren limped across the common room holding her side and pushed open the door. She swayed on the threshold, blinking in the fading light and trying to understand what she was seeing. Tal's splayed legs were dragging in the dirt as the soldiers carried him across the yard. What were they doing? Where were they taking him?

Then she noticed that one of the soldiers had a length of rope over his shoulder, and she hissed in dismay, steadying herself with a hand on the door frame.

They were taking him to the gallows.

"Stop!" Bren cried, staggering after them.

Most of the soldiers ignored her, but one of them turned back. It was the pox-scarred whittler who had seen her cut Tal's bonds, and his mouth fell open when he saw her.

"Bloody 'ell," he said loudly. "It's a bloody milkie, just like I said. See, I ain't crazy. Besh, Nok, come look at this."

"Aye," growled another of the soldiers as they wrestled the boy onto the gallows' platform, the heels of Tal's boots thumping on the stairs. "Must be a spy. Once this one's danglin', we'll deal with her."

"Put him down!" Bren yelled, her fingers closing on the bronze hilt of her sword. She slid the blade free from the loop on her belt, stumbling slightly. It felt awkward in her grip, very different from the wooden sword she usually practiced with.

Harsh laughter erupted from the men up on the platform. When it finally subsided, one of them called down to the pox-scarred soldier.

"Careful there, Jessap. She looks mighty dangerous."

The others shook their heads, still grinning as they looped one end of the rope around Tal's neck and tossed the other over the gibbet's beam.

Bren started towards them, her sword raised, but the soldier they'd named Jessap placed himself between her and the stairs.

"Someone'll pay good coin for a milkie spy that can still talk," the pox-scarred man said, drawing his own sword. "So don't make me stick you."

Bren's heart thudded in her chest as she settled into one of the forms Merik had taught her.

The soldier's brows lifted in amusement. "Had some trainin', lass? Do the milkies fight same as us?"

Up on the gallows, the soldiers had hoisted Tal into the air. He'd come awake, and his fingers were scrabbling at the rope around his neck as his legs kicked wildly.

Cold fear filled Bren. She had to get past this man and cut down Tal quickly.

She lunged forward, swinging her sword. Metal clanged as the soldier caught the blow easily, his mouth twisting into a smirk. She tried another quick attack, but it was also turned aside. Snarling in frustration, she thrust at his belly, but he danced out of the way, laughing.

"You got some quickness, lass, but I'd wager you never swung in anger. Fighting ain't just the forms." He rushed closer, and she raised her sword to block him, but at the last moment he changed the angle of the blow, and his hilt struck the side of her head hard.

Bren tasted dirt. She was lying on the ground, but she couldn't remember falling. Pain throbbed behind her eyes, spots of light flaring.

She had to get up. Her fingers scrabbled in the patchy grass, trying to find her sword, and she expected at any moment to feel something sharp sliding into her back.

"Stay down, lass," Bren heard over the ringing in her head.

She raised her face from the ground to see the soldier turn away. Beyond him on the platform Tal spasmed, his face purple.

Her hand closed around the bronze hilt. Stand up. She had to stand, even though she knew it was hopeless. These were trained soldiers, and she was just a poor shepherdess who had foolishly dreamed of being a warrior. The pressure in her head seemed to be building, as if the blow she'd taken had broken something inside her skull.

Let me in.

Words, echoing.

"What?" Bren mumbled, wondering if she had lost her mind.

I will help you. Let me in.

There was something hovering at the edge of her comprehension. "How?" she whispered.

Reach for me.

There was a sensation of something swelling inside her until she felt like her head would split asunder. It was vast, too huge to be confined in her, but still it could not push into her deepest recesses. There was a barrier within her keeping it from going too deep.

More grating laughter. Bren focused on Tal, now barely twitching.

"Yes," she hissed and unclenched the fist that had been closed tightly about her mind.

It began as a trickle. Strange, foreign thoughts she couldn't understand worming inside her, and then that dribble strengthened, something buckled, and she was drowning in a sudden torrent, gasping for breath as she sank below the surface.

Bren climbed to her feet holding her sword. The metal that had felt so wrong in her grip a moment ago now seemed an extension of her arm. She started walking towards the gallows, the tip of the sword dragging in the dirt.

"She's not learned her lesson yet, Jessap," cried one of the men, and the soldier who had struck her turned. He clattered down the steps scowling, his sword raised.

"Lass, I've had enough o' yer—"

Her blade slid into his stomach. The soldier gawped, staring down at the length of pale metal and blinking like he couldn't understand what had just happened.

Bren wasn't exactly sure, either. She had lunged forward with a quickness she had never shown before, the thrust executed perfectly.

The soldier collapsed when she pulled the sword free. Blood streaked the blade, and she felt her gorge rise.

She'd mortally wounded a man.

And it had been so easy.

Cries of alarm erupted atop the gallows. Bren forced her gaze from the bloody blade just as Tal tumbled down to lie in a heap on the platform, the soldiers who had been pulling on the rope now reaching for their own swords.

Bren stepped back calmly as they rushed down the stairs. One of the men crouched beside the pox-scarred soldier, desperately trying to staunch the gushing blood with his hands. The other two stalked towards her, their faces twisted in rage.

Bren knew she should feel fear. These men wanted to kill her.

There would be no mercy granted, no quarter given. But it was as if ice had hardened inside her, for she felt no fear.

A sword lashed out, and she stepped to the side, letting it slide past. Another blow was aimed at her neck, and she turned this with her blade. The force sent a shiver up her arm, but it was on the very edge of her senses. Her sword flickered, cutting a pattern she'd never learned, and the soldier bellowed as he struggled to ward away her blade. She felt the slight resistance of metal meeting flesh. He reeled away, and her sword entered his throat. Continuing the same motion, her blade caught the other soldier's thrust and knocked it aside. He screamed and swung again, and she ducked beneath that blow, then drove her sword between his ribs as she straightened. His shocked eyes stared into hers, and she ripped the sword free.

The last soldier was still beside his dying comrade, disbelief writ clear in his face. Then he screamed, lurching to his feet as he started to draw his sword, only to pause in confusion as pale metal plunged into his chest. He toppled, dead before he struck the ground.

Bren felt like she was waking from a dream. Four soldiers sprawled at her feet, and none of them had come close to touching her with their swords. Men who had been trained to kill. Men who were stronger and faster. The memory of what she had just done seemed unreal, as if she had been watching someone else.

The pressure in her head receded, and as it pulled away, emotions rushed in. Fear. Revulsion. Bren shakily slipped the sword back into its loop at her belt; her hand was trembling so much that it took her several attempts. The pox-scarred soldier with the belly wound was mewling now, his face drained of color. He stared at her with empty eyes, and she couldn't help herself from wanting to do her best to stop his life from leaking away.

"Brenna."

She tore her gaze from the soldier. Tal was on his knees, the rope that had nearly ended his life limp in his hands. Livid markings burned red around his neck, and he was looking at her in confusion and fear.

Bren rushed up the rickety stairs. "Tal! Are you all right?" she asked, crouching beside him on the gallows' platform.

"Yes," he rasped, rubbing at his throat with trembling fingers. "What . . . what did you do?"

Bren glanced at the four soldiers lying in the grass. Three were motionless, and the last was squirming weakly. Then her gaze went to the inn's entrance, where a crowd of patrons had gathered to watch. They were silent, but Bren saw their horror. Shame at what she had done flooded Bren, but she did her best to ignore it.

Hooking her hands under Tal's arms, she hauled him to his feet. His legs wobbled, but after a moment he steadied himself.

"Come on, we have to go now."

5

——————

Moon raced along the Gith road, hooves clashing on black stone. They had been riding long enough that the sun had slipped below the horizon, and stars had emerged to attend the Silver Mother and Her daughters. Yet the great stallion showed little fatigue. Maybe his head was bobbing a bit more than when they'd burst from the inn's yard, his breath coming slightly faster. Bren wondered how long he could keep up this pace – it certainly seemed like he could continue on through the night if necessary.

She knew that riding in the dark was a terrible idea. The Silver Mother was bright and full, but the dark stone of the Gith road drank the moonlight, and all it would take would be one unseen rock to lame Moon. And Tal was in no condition to walk. He slumped in the saddle in front of her, his head hanging down. The only indication that he wasn't already asleep was when his hand drifted up to touch his neck.

They reached the ruins of a town, white stone gleaming like bone under the gaze of the Silver Mother. Most of the buildings had been reduced to their foundations, although the broken remnants of a few pillars stabbed the sky. Bren couldn't see much in the way of shelter, but she thought they could hide from the road behind one of the crumbling walls. She slid from Moon, keeping a hand on Tal so he wouldn't topple without her sitting behind him, and led the horse off the road.

"Where are we?" Tal mumbled, raising his head.

"Just a ruin," Bren replied, helping Moon navigate the large blocks of stone rising from the grass. These evidently had once been plinths, as several pairs of eroded feet were set atop them, though the statues they had supported had long since vanished.

They arrived at a pool of water, and from the stone steps descending into the silvery surface Bren thought this might be an amphitheater that had flooded. She'd seen similar white-stone ruins before when exploring the Seven Valleys – the Gith or some other ancient people had left these half-buried skeletons scattered about, sundered arches curving skyward like broken ribs.

Bren helped Tal dismount as Moon bent his head to the pool and began to drink. The boy staggered when he stood beside her, and she wondered if the blows to the head the soldiers had given him were more serious than she had thought. He sat heavily on a chunk of stone next to the pool, staring emptily out over the still water.

"What happened back there, Bren?" he finally asked, his voice hoarse.

She swallowed, unsure what to say. Moon had turned his dripping muzzle towards her, as if he were also waiting for an answer.

"I don't know."

"You killed four men. Soldiers. Where did you learn how to wield a sword like that?"

"I . . . I never did."

"I saw you."

"That wasn't me. I mean, it was. But there was something else guiding my hand."

He regarded her solemnly for a long moment. "Then nothing like that has ever happened before?"

She shook her head sharply. Should she tell him about the voice? Or would he think she was mad?

Tal's gaze settled on the hilt at her side. "The sword."

Bren closed her fingers around the bronze grip to try to show she wasn't scared. She half-expected to feel that pressure swelling again, the sense of a foreign presence invading her mind . . . but nothing happened. Slowly, she drew the sword from the loop at her side. Moonlight played along its length, and in that moment the strange metal almost looked like ceramic, as there was no gleam to its flat whiteness. Something occurred to her, raising gooseflesh on her arms. She hadn't wiped the blade clean after the battle, but now she couldn't see a speck of dried blood on the sword.

"Toss it in the water," pleaded Tal, fear in his voice.

He was right, of course. She had heard it speak. Seen what it could do.

Bren raised her arm, bringing the sword back to throw it . . . but then hesitated. She remembered her mother and brother knotted together in death, seared by dragon fire. The paladin staring at the black blade in his chest as his own radiant sword slipped from his fingers. The dragon lords in their barbed armor and monstrous helms.

"No," Bren said thickly, sliding the sword back through the loop.

"You must," Tal said, his tone desperate. "This is dark sorcery. Gith magic."

"I need it," Bren told him, her thumb tracing the design cut into the center of the hilt. Most of the verdigris had flaked away by now, as if the sword was slowly being reborn.

"For revenge?"

"Yes."

He ran his hand through his hair. "I know something of sorcery, Bren." He licked his lips, hesitating a heartbeat before continuing. "My mother was in the House of Jade." Ghostly light swelled in his hand as he pulled the pebble from his pocket. "That's where I got this. A present she gave me the last time I saw her . . . before she disappeared. I didn't know what happened to her until years later, and I hunted down another servant of Nasai who had known her in the House. She was lost trying to recreate an old Gith ritual. Power always comes with a cost, Bren. Your life, your soul, or your freedom." He held her gaze, and she could see how much he wanted to convince her.

"My life, my soul, or my freedom," Bren repeated slowly, shaking her head. "If I was offered that bargain right now in exchange for vengeance, I would take it." She knew she spoke true, even though she wished she did not. "They destroyed my life. And to them, it was nothing. They killed my baby brother!" she cried, wiping angrily at her eyes. "I need help." Her hand tightened around her sword's hilt, half hoping and half dreading that whatever presence dwelled inside would make itself known again. "Help like what happened back there at the inn."

Tal hung his head. He looked exhausted. Which he had every right to be, given what had happened.

"Are you all right?" she asked.

He nodded and raised his head to give her a wan smile. "It's been a hard few days. I think a night's sleep would do us both wonders."

"I agree," Bren said, her gaze sweeping the ruins. There were some patches of grass between the shattered buildings that looked comfortable enough, so long as it didn't rain. Should they set a watch? Tal was in no condition to stay awake, and from her own bone-deep weariness, she suspected she wouldn't last much longer. But she had to be strong. She had to try.

"I'll take the first watch," she said.

Birdsong woke her. Bren raised her head, blinking groggily. She was sitting splay-legged in a patch of grass, her back against a piece of crumbled wall. Pale mist the same color as the morning sky coiled upon the surface of the pond.

"Oh, hells," she muttered, reaching up to massage her stiff neck. She'd fallen asleep before she could wake Tal and have him take over for her. Anyone could have snuck up on them during the night and cut their throats or made off with her horse.

Moon.

Bren twisted around in panic but then subsided in relief when she locked gazes with the stallion. Was that disappointment she saw again in his eyes? Bren was willing to bet Ser Dahlen had never dozed off when he was entrusted with the first watch.

"I'm not the paladin," she called out to Moon. He *whuffed* something in reply that might have been '*I know*' and lowered his head to start cropping the grass.

"Talking to the animals?"

Tal emerged from the ruins and found a seat on a chunk of stone beside the pond. His voice was still scratchy but not nearly as hoarse as it had been the night before.

"You sound better," Bren said, standing and stretching.

His hand drifted to his neck. "Still aches. But I think my beautiful voice will return soon, so please don't worry."

"Oh, I was excited that we might actually be able to enjoy some companionable silence on the road to Leris."

Tal crooked a grin, then skipped a stone across the water. Ripples disturbed the stillness, reaching for the edges of the pond. "And leave you to your brooding? Perish the thought."

Bren realized she was smiling. It surprised her how much of a relief it was to hear Tal's sorry excuse for wit again. She had worried during their frantic escape from the inn that his near hanging would weigh on his spirit, but he seemed to be recovering well. Had she been affected by what had happened? Seeing him up there, his legs kicking as his face purpled . . . The memory made her feel ill. And then she'd also killed four men. That had an edge of unreality to it, as if it had been someone else holding the sword. Which might be true. She swallowed, glancing at the hilt at her side. Was there a demon inside waiting to possess her again?

As she had told Tal, she found she didn't care very much. She needed all the help she could get.

Four men. One moment they were laughing, and the next they had been sprawled on the ground with their lives leaking away. Each had family, most likely. Someone who cared for them. A wife, a mother. A child. Bren shook her head, trying to clear it of these thoughts. Those soldiers had been wicked men. They had looked into Tal's face as he gasped for breath and grinned. They would have killed her even if they'd realized she wasn't a spy, just a shepherd girl from the next valley over.

She let her hand rest on the bronze pommel, which was cool and slick from the morning mist. "Thank you," she murmured, quiet enough that Tal wouldn't hear. Speaking to swords was even worse than speaking to animals.

THE SUN HAD BARELY CRESTED when Bren glimpsed the high white towers of Leris rising over the treetops, red banners snapping in the wind. She knew they had been drawing closer, as the press of people on the road had thickened, but still she was surprised they had made such excellent time. The city was closer to her family's farm than she'd realized – Frog's plodding had lengthened her father's journeys back and forth, while Moon was proving to be indefatigable. He'd kept up a good pace ever since they'd left the ruins, and he showed no sign of flagging.

"Where will they all stay?" Bren asked as they passed a chain of wagons carrying what looked like an entire village. Grubby, red-cheeked children pointed at Moon and tugged on the dresses of older women slumped in the back of carts. The exhaustion was writ clear in the faces of these peasants; it looked to Bren like they had been forced to abandon their homes at a moment's notice and had not had a chance to rest for days.

"I don't know," he replied. One of the little girls giggled, and Bren twisted around to find Tal making monster faces at her.

"The city looks big enough," Bren admitted. In truth, she was awed by the size of the walls, far larger than she'd ever imagined.

"Much of the city is taken up by the Garden – like where your well-to-do uncle lives – and the Brocade, where the truly rich merchants and nobles keep sprawling manses. The Duke of Thorns has a fortress there worthy of a great king. And if you think any of *these* folk"—he made a sweeping gesture that encompassed their ragged fellow travelers—"are going to be allowed to sleep within the walls of those districts, you're very mistaken. No, if they're allowed inside, they'll be herded into the Tangle with all the other lowborn."

Bren hunched deeper into her cloak as they neared the gates, remembering the outraged cries of 'milkie' back at the inn. She wished she had gloves to hide her pale hands and almost asked Tal if he would take the reins from her. There was little worry, though, of them being denied entrance – guards wearing white tabards emblazoned with the rose of Leris appeared to have given up trying to control the flow of people entering the city and were now just waving everyone through.

"Finally, a bit of luck," Tal whispered in her ear as they passed into the shadow of the soaring gate. She nodded, rendered speechless by the stone arching high above their heads.

The stream of travelers emptied into a vast cobbled plaza hemmed with timber and stone buildings and intersected by several broad avenues. Bren did her best to navigate Moon through the swirling chaos of overloaded wagons, bleating animals and confused newcomers trying to figure out where they should go. Here, the city guard was being more aggressive, funneling those seeking refuge either to the buildings along the edge of the plaza – which Bren assumed were inns – or towards the roads that appeared to lead to a poorer area of the city. The Tangle, Bren guessed from what Tal had said earlier. The other exits around the square were guarded by halberd-wielding guardsmen, and as Bren watched, a man in rough homespun was turned back when he tried to leave by one of those ways.

"That's the route to the Garden," Tal said, raising his voice to be heard above the din and gesturing towards where the man had just been rebuffed.

"Should we try to talk our way past those guards? My uncle's house is in the Garden."

"No," replied Tal decisively, shaking his head. "They might want to take a close look at us, and when they see you're Velaschin, someone will grumble that you should be locked up in the Maw."

"But I've lived my whole life just a few days' ride from here."

"The city is on edge. I've never seen it like this, even during the Wilting Riots. I would guess the watch right now is not taking any chances." He rightly assumed that she was about to start arguing and continued quickly. "But don't worry. There are alleys and side streets we can use to slip into the Garden. And you said you wanted to visit the Bright Company's office to find out where your uncle lived, yes? It's in the Tangle."

"Truly?" That surprised her – Uncle Merik had told her the Company was the most famous mercenary troop on the Flowering Coast, retained by all barons and dukes to settle disputes.

"The offices are used for recruiting, and the kind of folk who join mercenary companies are not usually welcome in the more . . . prosperous areas of Leris."

"Then that's where we should go first," Bren agreed, turning Moon towards the only large thoroughfare empty of guardsmen wearing white surcoats emblazoned with bright red roses, though it was still jammed with the other recent arrivals.

The flood of travelers slackened to a trickle as Bren and Tal rode down the street, many drifting away to investigate the cheap inns and flophouses where pretty girls or husky men lured them by calling out about the fabulous amenities that could be found inside their establishments. Most of the houses in this area were smaller and shabbier than the plaza where they'd entered the city, but their walls were still veined with roses, blossoms of red and white and yellow. And everywhere reminded Bren of her village's market day, but many times larger – carts piled high with vegetables lined the roads, along with stalls selling all manner of trinkets and tools and clothes. Faded wooden signs hung above the doorways of shops, advertising what was sold within. Horseshoes for a farrier. A pair of goblets for a bronzesmith. A curved razor for a barber . . . or a bloodletter, she supposed, depending on the need.

Tal tapped her on the shoulder and pointed at a shop with a sign carved into the shape of a boot. "Let's stop there first," he told her. "Easiest way to judge someone is by what they have on their feet, and I doubt we'd even get inside the Company's offices with you looking like a beggar."

Bren glanced down at the ragged remnants of her shoes, only a few steps away from falling completely to pieces. "I don't have any money."

"Don't worry. I owe you my life," Tal replied with a smile. "But if you feel guilty, maybe your uncle could pay me back later."

They slid from Moon and tied the horse to a post outside the shop. Bren noticed eyes lingering on him, but she was fairly sure that anyone foolish enough to try to make off with the stallion would end up with a hoof to the stomach.

A bell chimed as they pushed open the door. Bren breathed deep of the heady smell of tanned leather, marveling at the array of goods on display. It wasn't just shoes in the shop – belts and jerkins and travel bags were arrayed on shelves or hung from pegs. A wizened little man with a bald pate fringed with tufts of white hair bustled out from a backroom, wiping his hands on a stained apron.

"Welcome," he said warmly. "What are you young folk looking for?" His friendly expression faltered when Bren pulled back her cowl, but to her relief, he recovered quickly. Apparently, some folk at least did not hate everyone who looked like they might be Velaschin. To her surprise, this knowledge made a lump form in her throat, and she swallowed it back.

"Boots," Tal said, gesturing at the toes poked through the ends of Bren's shoes.

The old man made a *tsking* sound, shaking his head. He looked visibly pained by the state of her footwear.

"Indeed," he agreed, guiding them towards a long table covered with a dizzying variety of shoes. He hefted a beautifully-tooled red boot that looked soft enough to be used as a pillow, its heel high and graceful.

"A fine choice if you have the coin," he said, then arched an eyebrow at them. "You do have coin, yes?" Tal's money pouch materi-

alized in his hand, and he gave it a shake. At the sound of metal clink-
ing, the shopkeep's smile broadened. "Excellent! Would you like to
try them on, my dear?"

To Bren, the boot he'd selected looked like something a lady
would wear while strolling through her garden. She couldn't imagine
trying to swing a sword while tottering about on those heels.

"I think this is a better choice," she said, picking up a traveler's
boot of gnarled black leather.

"Certainly functional," the old man said with a sigh as he
returned the fashionable – and no doubt expensive – lady's boot to
the table. "*If* you plan on marching somewhere."

"I do," Bren replied, unwrapping the strips of cloth she'd used to
keep her shoes together and slipping her feet into the boots. The
callouses and blisters she'd accumulated over the last few days
protested, but she could immediately sense the quality and durability
of the boots, and she even set her feet into one of the forms to test
how easy it would be to move through the footwork her uncle had
taught her.

The shopkeeper watched all this with a wry smile. "A fighter, are
you? Then those are the boots for you. And is that a sword I see?"

Bren realized she had drawn back her cloak to give herself more
freedom of movement, revealing the bare blade hanging at her side.
She hurriedly concealed the sword, but the old man crooked his
finger for her to show it to him again.

"Let me have a look, my dear. I was a soldier myself in another
life, and I'm not sure I've ever seen a weapon like that before."

Bren glanced at Tal, who shrugged.

"Come, come. I happen to believe all young ladies should carry
swords, especially in these troubling times."

With some reluctance, Bren drew forth the sword. The old man
whistled, pulling on his scraggly whiskers.

"An interesting piece," he mused, reaching out to touch the white
metal. "Antique, I would say. Is this a family heirloom, or did you
unearth it somewhere?"

"It's—"

"It belonged to her grandfather," Tal interrupted. "He was a bit of a collector."

"I see," murmured the old man, still entranced by the blade.

Bren shot Tal a questioning glance, but he shook his head curtly.

"Well," the old man finally said, wandering over to a shelf cluttered with various leather goods, "perhaps I can interest you in a scabbard? Dangerous keeping it bare like that, and it won't be good for the metal."

Bren doubted that, since the sword had apparently remained untarnished in a barrow for a very long time, but she kept quiet as Tal clearly didn't want the shopkeeper to know where they'd found the blade.

The old man returned with a few sword scabbards of varying lengths. Some were plain and unadorned, while others were lacquered or had designs incised into the leather. He hummed to himself as he held up several beside her sword and then set all but one back on the shelf.

"Your blade is short but not as narrow as how the bravos like their swords. An odd shape, to be honest. But this might be suitable."

He handed her the scabbard he'd selected. It was dyed a deep forest green and tooled with intricate knotwork that almost resembled the design set into the hilt. After a moment's hesitation, Bren slid her sword into the sheath and was surprised at how perfectly it fit.

"I'll throw in a sword belt as well," the shopkeeper said, sounding satisfied with how well he'd sized up the blade. "And then you'll truly look the part of a young swordswoman."

As he wandered away to rummage through a basket filled with belts, Bren sidled over to Tal. "Can you afford this?" she whispered.

He patted her on the arm reassuringly. "Do you remember what I told you? A man who has more than others should share his wealth, or he deserves to have it taken away."

"Well, thank you," she said, feeling another swell of emotion. She hurriedly looked away, not wanting to let him see her face.

The old man brought a fine-looking belt to her and watched with some pride as she undid the charred length of twine she'd been using. There was even a small buckle of reddish metal to secure it, something like she had seen her uncle Merik wearing. She wondered if he had bought his belt at this very shop.

Tal whistled as she secured her new scabbard. "You're ready for war."

Bren turned this way and that, making sure the way the sword hung did not impede her movements. She had to admit she liked looking at her new scabbard and belt and boots. Days ago, she'd been dreaming in the meadows of adventure while she watched her flock – now she had a magic sword at her side and a maybe-magic horse to ride and boots to take her from one end of the Flowering Coast to the other. It all seemed so unreal. Was this truly the goddess's doing? It must be.

Bren set these thoughts aside and realized that Tal had already finished bargaining with the shopkeeper. More coins than she had ever seen at one time changed hands, but the boy did not seem upset about spending so much money. That more than anything else made her feel a trickle of unease. Was he being generous so she'd let her guard down? Would he betray her later, perhaps steal away Moon or her sword? Bren forced herself to ignore these niggling doubts. If the boy's behavior towards her was all part of an elaborate ruse, then he must be a swindler of tremendous skill. She refused to entertain the possibility, not least because she deeply did not want it to be true.

"The Mother's blessing be with you both," the shopkeeper said as she followed Tal back outside.

A crowd of ragged urchins had gathered around Moon, and as she watched, one of the children darted forward and slapped the horse's flank, then scrambled back shrieking as his compatriots laughed uproariously. Moon responded with admirable stoicism, watching the boy for a moment with his calm blue eyes before turning to Bren. It was probably her imagination, but she could almost sense him imploring her to end this nonsense.

"Enough! Get away!" she cried, wading into the throng of children like she was trying to convince her goats to leave the meadow.

The children fled, some of them bumping into her as they rushed past. Bren staggered, but none of the urchins even slowed as they continued their squealing stampede . . . at least until Tal's hand flashed out and caught a little freckled girl by the arm. She squirmed, trying to break free, but he tightened his grip and dragged her up higher until her toes were barely touching the cobbles.

"It's all right," Bren told him, but Tal didn't look at her, instead staring at the smudge-cheeked little girl with narrowed eyes.

The urchin wasn't thrashing anymore, having gone limp as she grinned up at Tal.

"Give it back," he growled, and in response the girl fluttered her eyelashes innocently. The other children had regrouped across the street and were jeering and pointing at their captured friend.

"I don't have nothing."

"Last chance," Tal said, a warning in his voice, "before I turn you upside down and start shaking."

The girl giggled, and with a flickering movement almost too fast to follow, a knife appeared in her hand.

"Watch out!" Bren cried, but the girl only held it up for Tal to take. Bren frowned when she realized the knife looked familiar. Rusted blade, cloth-wrapped handle . . .

Tal snatched it away and then handed the knife back to Bren. "Lucky I'm here, and you don't have anything else more valuable."

Bren returned the knife to her pocket, alarmed at how easily the urchin had lifted it from her.

"So you're back," the girl said, still smirking up at Tal. Despite her youth, she had the smug confidence of someone much older.

"Just arrived today, little mouse," Tal told her, still not letting go.

"Seen the Ratman?"

"Not yet."

The girl's free hand darted up to wipe her nose. "He'll be wanting to see you, *Tal of the Shadows*." The way the little girl said his name was almost mocking. "Best you don't keep him waiting too long."

Tal scowled. "Well, run back to the Burrow and tell him that I'm coming soon," he said, then released her. The girl flashed him a final impudent sneer before sticking out her tongue and darting away.

Bren watched her vanish into the gang of her whooping friends, and then the lot of them scattered into alleys and alcoves like insects fleeing the light.

"Who is the Ratman?" Bren asked.

Tal stared at where the one he'd grabbed had disappeared, a faraway look in his eyes. "An old . . . friend," he muttered, then shook himself. "Not your concern. Come on, the Bright Company offices are ahead."

BREN COULD UNDERSTAND why this section of Leris was called the Tangle. Streets twisted and turned, knotting together like the branches of an overgrown bramble. Bren was grateful that she had Tal as a guide, as she was sure she'd have ended up going in circles even if she'd asked for directions. Most of the buildings were pressed tightly together, several stories tall and built of ancient wood, and some were even listing like they'd had too much to drink. An uncontrolled fire would cause terrible destruction here. She remembered the ruins of her own house and shuddered as she imagined the dark shadow of a dragon soaring over these houses, drenching the city in fire.

They passed a large stone building with intricate frieze work and a white-domed roof. A steady stream of people were passing in and out of its pillared entrance, many with arms in slings or bandages wrapped around their heads. All manner of folks – young and old, men and women and children – their only commonality being that they all looked to have some ailment.

"What is that place?" she asked. They were both walking beside Moon now – Bren reveling in the feel of her new boots and Tal hobbling along, still clearly suffering from his days in the saddle.

"The Tangle's House of Gold," the boy told her. "The biggest in the city, no doubt, but far from the fanciest. In the Brocade, the House's dome is covered with gold leaf that flashes like a second sun during the day."

She should have known just from the sight of so many sick and injured. Arela, the golden daughter of the Silver Mother and Her eldest child, was the goddess of healing and new life. Her acolytes dedicated themselves to alleviating suffering, and it was said that her most favored priestesses could heal by touch alone.

"Do all the daughters have temples in Leris?"

Tal looked away, his face darkening. For a moment, Bren was confused, and then she remembered that he'd told her his mother had served in the House of Jade.

"Yes. The Iron Daughter's House is across from the barracks. She also has shrines scattered about – you'll see one when we reach the Bright Company offices."

That made sense. Kez was the patron of soldiers and war, and the blacksmith in her village had kept a statue of the goddess in his forge that he'd cold-hammered himself from a hunk of black iron. The brutal angles and blade-sharp limbs had scared Bren as a child, but now she realized it was truly the best representation of the goddess of war. She'd seen the horror and ruin war brought firsthand.

"The Houses of Jade are always hidden," Tal said, a sharp edge to his words. "Nasai's servants prefer the shadows, for sorcery withers in the light of day."

Bren weighed for a moment whether she should ask about his past dealings with that secretive House before her curiosity finally got the better of her. "You said you tracked down someone from the House of Jade."

Tal nodded tightly. "There are clues if you know where to look. I searched for nearly two years, and in truth, I never found the actual House, only an establishment some of the sorcerers frequented. After I confronted one about my mother . . . well, I never saw any of them again there. And I went back every night for months."

Bren swallowed, impressed with Tal's courage. Nasai was the most dangerous and mysterious of the Silver Mother's daughters, and it was she who had first taught sorcery to men so they would have some way to stand against the demon-magic of Old Gith. And while sorcerers may have liberated the lands from that yoke long ago, it was well known that some delved too deeply into the forbidden.

"And here we are," Tal said, seizing the opportunity to change the topic. The street had emptied into a small plaza dominated by a statue of a portly man with a crown, his shoulders thrown back and his hands on his hips. It might have been a regal pose if his entire upper body had not been painted white with bird guano. Behind this defiled fellow was a squat building with arrow slits for windows and a door that looked like it had been designed to keep out a horde of invaders.

"*Hmm*," Tal murmured.

"What is it?"

"Something isn't right. There were always Bright Company men on guard at the door in their silly crimson and silver armor when I came here before."

Frowning, he started across the plaza, and Bren followed. When he reached the door, he rapped loudly, though it looked so thick she wondered if anyone could possibly hear them knocking.

"Hello?" Tal shouted. He went over to one of the arrow-slit windows and put his mouth to the narrow gap. "Is anyone there?"

"Ain't nobody there."

Bren jumped back as a pile of rags lurched from the alley beside the offices. A man, she realized, covered in lesions and smelling like a stable. Tal didn't seem alarmed by the beggar's sudden appearance, turning to face him with arms folded.

"Where are they?" he asked.

The old man scratched at his pockmarked face and shrugged. "Dunno. But they left in a hurry few days back. Tryin' to keep ahead of the dragon lords, maybe. Rumor has it an army is marchin' this way to pluck the City o' Roses."

Bren's heart fell. How would she find where Uncle Merik lived now? The city was so huge, so confusing. She could wander for weeks knocking on doors and never find his house.

Tal must have seen her expression. "Don't worry," he promised. "We'll find your family."

The ragged beggar cleared his throat and spat out something unsettlingly green. "Lookin' for someone?"

"None of your business," Tal snapped.

The beggar grinned, showing more gum than teeth. "There's a fellow who keeps his ears to the cobbles. Might be he knows where yer friend can be found. But you know that already."

"What do you mean?" Bren asked, but the old man's milky eyes were fixed on Tal instead of her.

"I'm talkin' about the Ratman. Time for you to go say hello again, boy."

6

_____

After the beggar had croaked a laugh and shuffled back into the shadows, Tal took Moon's reins and led them down a crooked street, traveling deeper into the Tangle. His face could have been carved from stone. Dark shapes flitted at the mouths of alleys or uncoiled where they had huddled in alcoves and on stoops, but he ignored them. Bren felt their gazes skitter hungrily over her, and she made a show of letting her hand rest on the hilt of her sword. This area of the city may have still been considered part of the Tangle, but it was different from the vibrant, bustling streets they had seen so far. Here, most of the buildings looked abandoned, and the sun-bleached streets were empty of anyone except a few mangy dogs and clumps of moldering night soil.

"Where are we?" Bren whispered, stepping over the corpse of a rat the size of a cat.

"This is where all the lost and forgotten of Leris end up," Tal replied, the confidence in his stride helping Bren to overcome her misgivings. "It was my home after I ran away from Saint Natok's."

Bren eyed the shadows, sensing the attention of whatever was hidden in their depths. She jumped as a child ran shrieking with laughter across the street from one alley mouth to another, and Bren couldn't be sure, but she thought the urchin might have been one of the gang that had previously accosted them.

"So they know who you are?"

Tal snorted. "Oh, they know."

They continued on while the shadows lengthened until Tal stopped outside the collapsing portico of what once had been an impressive manse. The roof had caved in on the second floor, and Bren peered past the pillars flanking a gaping entrance, its door long since vanished. Inside, she glimpsed a dusty, rubble-strewn floor stabbed by spears of light and a wide staircase ascending into a heap of debris.

"This place?" Bren asked skeptically.

Tal nodded, then raised Moon's reins. "Where are the greeters?" he said loudly, but not to Bren, his voice echoing.

"Here, Shadows," a voice behind them drawled, and Bren turned to find a lanky boy sauntering from across the street.

"Whispers," Tal said, no warmth in his voice. "The Ratman has you on door-duty? I thought you'd be running things by now with me gone."

The boy sneered a smile, pushing back his mop of chestnut curls. "Special favor to the big man. Wanted to see your return, how you looked. Any scars on that pretty face? Or did you hide in the back, let the others do the fighting?"

Tal's jaw hardened. "I did the Tangle proud, put all the lessons I learned here to good use. That's why I'm still breathing."

The boy made a show of looking around. "An' where are Quiet and Knives? They still breathing, too? Or did ya leave them behind? That's a lesson you taught a few o' us."

Something trembled in Tal's cheek, and the smile he was forcing faded away. "Careful, Kint of the Whispers, or you and me will go round."

The boy held up his hands in mock surrender. "Just needling you, Shadows. No offense intended. Now you should get inside – the Ratman don't appreciate waiting, you know that."

Tal nodded tightly, tossing the reins to the boy.

"What are you doing?" Bren asked in surprise.

"He'll take care of Moon until we come back," Tal told her, starting on the crumbling steps leading up to the manse's portico.

Bren hurried to come alongside him, her boots scuffing on the stone. "We can trust him?"

"Whispers? In most things, no. But to watch your horse until we finish our audience with his boss? Then yes."

As they entered the foyer, Bren glanced apprehensively at the rotting ceiling. Her attention was jerked back down when their arrival disturbed something small and furred, sending it scrambling into a chink in the wall.

"Was that the Ratman?" she asked, trying to lighten Tal's mood.

"Ha-ha," he replied sarcastically, leading her through a listing doorway and into an even larger and emptier room. Whatever furniture had once filled the manse had long since been looted or destroyed. There were mounds of stone, though, crumbled bits of masonry that looked to have fallen from the ceiling or walls, and Tal headed towards one particularly large pile topped by the severed head of a statue, its features gouged away by some sharp implement.

Bren wrinkled her nose at the musty smell. "What are we looking for?"

Behind the rubble, someone had laid a half-rotted chunk of wood that might once have been the elaborately carved front of an armoire, and Tal dragged it aside to reveal a set of stone stairs leading down. The steps didn't disappear into complete darkness, as a ghostly radiance was welling up from below; it didn't flicker or dance like the light cast by a flame, which disturbed Bren, but Tal didn't hesitate before he started descending.

Bren followed, trying to ignore her growing unease and glad she had a sword at her side. Voices were rising from the depths, mostly high-pitched and childlike, and after about twenty steep steps, they passed into a large chamber, the stairs pressed high up against the wall and then plunging precipitously to the floor far below. Bren felt dizzy when she glanced down, but once she did, she found it difficult to look away. The space was vast and sprawling, its recesses lost to darkness. The light was spilling from an area near the base of the stairs, where a dozen statues carved of some pearly material had been placed around a collection of antique-looking furniture. The radiance seemed to be seeping from this strange stone, but Bren felt no heat or warmth rising up as they descended. Flitting around these statues and crawling over the tables and chairs were children, their laughter echoing in the high-ceilinged hall. In the middle of the ring of statues was a divan of gilded metal and plush purple cushions, and reclining on this was the fattest man Bren had ever seen. He stirred when he noticed Bren and Tal, beckoning them to approach.

"What is this place?" Bren asked, unnerved by this bizarre scene.

"The Ratman's Burrow," Tal replied as he reached the bottom. Without hesitating, he slipped between two of the statues as he made his way towards the divan and its huge occupant.

"But what was it before?" Her fingers brushed the nacreous stone of a dancing man with the head of a stag and found it cool and smooth to the touch. All the statues were monstrous, unnatural combinations of beasts and men. Some had the bodies of animals with beautiful, expressionless human heads, while for others it was reversed, the eyes of snakes or fish or wolves watching the children scurrying about at their feet from atop beautifully sculpted human bodies.

"Part of the undercity," Tal murmured out of the corner of his mouth as they neared the Ratman. "Leris was built on Gith ruins."

"So these are Gith," Bren breathed, mesmerized by the inhuman faces staring down at her.

"Gods, demons, who knows. Or maybe this is what the Gith really looked like. The Ratman found them in the depths and dragged them here to illuminate his Burrow. Glowstone, we call it."

"Tal!" the fat man bellowed, struggling to sit up among his mounded cushions. "Welcome back, little mouse! How does it feel to be a war hero?"

Beside the divan was standing a girl older than the other children, her hands clasped in front of her. She had long, straight black hair and a face so thin she looked almost skeletal. Her thin lips twisted into a smirk at the Ratman's greeting.

"Does one still get to be a war hero when their side loses so terribly?" she murmured softly.

The Ratman's pudgy face crinkled. "I don't know. Good question, little mouse! What do you say, Tal?"

"I'm no hero," the boy replied, folding his arms across his chest. "But I fought for Leris, which is more than anyone else here can say."

"For the Queen and the Petaled Throne!" cried the Ratman dramatically, thrusting his fist into the air. The urchins – most of whom had paused their games to watch Tal and Bren – shrieked in laughter.

"You look comfortable standing in my spot, Bones," Tal said, his attention shifting to the painfully thin girl.

She bristled, her eyes narrowing. "My spot now, Shadows. With you and Quiet and Knives all going off to find glory, someone had to step up."

"And she's done a fine job," the Ratman rumbled. "The mice have never danced to a better flutist." Plump fingers fluttered to his mouth, as if he had just noticed something shocking. "My little mouse, did someone try to *hang* you?"

Tal's hand drifted to the mottled red markings around his neck. "A misunderstanding," he muttered.

"Would that misunderstanding have anything to do with the *Velaschin* you've brought into my home?" he continued, then gave an oddly high-pitched giggle.

The girl standing beside the Ratman's divan gaped, squinting at Bren. "Sages, you're right," she said as surprised gasps rippled through the watching urchins.

Bren felt two dozen pairs of eyes peering into the depths of her cowl. She gritted her teeth, made uncomfortable by the sudden attention.

"Come, girl, let us see you," urged the Ratman. "You might be the only one of your people left in the city. The empire's trading houses emptied not long before the queen's army began to muster, may the

Silver Mother shelter her soul." His beady black eyes flicked to Tal as he said this.

Grimacing, Bren pulled back her hood. The muttering swelled so loud that Bren had to yell to be heard. "I'm not Velaschin! Well, perhaps my parents were. But I never knew them, and I was raised in the Seven Valleys. The Velaschin burned my farm. I pray to the Silver Mother and her daughters, same as you all, and I've sworn an oath to take revenge."

The Ratman clapped his hands together, his eyes bright with excitement. "And so you've come to the City of Roses to start your quest. So stirring."

"The very beginning," Tal interjected. "Bren first needs to find her family. Her uncle and aunt live in Leris. He is an officer in the Bright Company, and their house is in the Garden."

"Ah," the Ratman said, nodding knowingly. "That is why you went to their office in the Tangle instead of coming straight to the Burrow. My heart was heavy because I thought you were avoiding me!"

"I'm not coming back to work for you. What I said before still stands. But that doesn't mean we can't help each other."

The Ratman's face had fallen at Tal's words. "But why would I help? You were so cruel before you went off with my sneakiest little mice."

"I have money," Tal said over the chorus of angry murmurings that had grown in the wake of the Ratman's question. "I know what it costs to find out where someone lives in the city. I'll give you a silver venmark to send the mice scurrying and another silver when they return with the address."

The fat man swooned, putting his hand to his head as his eyes fluttered closed. "Oh, how have we come to this? Negotiating like businessmen when once our bond ran thicker than blood?" He snapped his fingers, then winced at the sound. "My dear, I need a compress, if you would be so kind."

A damp towel materialized in the girl's hand, and she gently laid it on the Ratman's brow. Immediately, the lines on his face smoothed out, as if whatever had momentarily afflicted him had just as quickly vanished.

"Tal, my boy, I shall do what you ask. But you must come to see me again – there is much we still have to discuss."

Bren sensed some of the tension seeping from Tal. "We will wait at *The Coronet* for one of the mice to bring us the information." He paused, then swallowed. "And thank you."

"My uncle is Merik Kaelingsun," Bren said, finally daring to speak. "His wife is named Heralia. She's a gardener, I think."

The Ratman waved at them languidly, settling deeper into his divan. "Very well, they will be found. Go, my once-mouse and his new friend, and let it never be said that I am not a forgiving and generous soul!"

BREN SAT on the edge of the bed with the ancient sword across her knees. She ran her finger along the length of the pale blade until she reached the blocky bronze cross guard. Then, taking a deep breath, she closed her hand around the grip and waited for something to slither into her mind.

"Do you feel it?" Tal asked.

Bren frowned at her distorted reflection in the strange metal. "No," she said, lifting her eyes to where the boy had folded himself into the windowsill, his back pressed against the frame. He turned away from her, gazing out over the city. *The Coronet* was a rambling old inn that had clearly once been something else, six tall, thin towers ringing its central structure like the points on a crown. The old woman who had been so pleased to see Tal had put them in the highest room in one of those turrets, and the view over the rolling sea of rooftops as twilight fell was spectacular. Only a few other buildings soared as high as *The Coronet*, mostly in the distant district that Tal had informed her was the Brocade. And everything in Leris was dwarfed by the Briar, the hulking abode of the Duke of Thorns. Bren wondered if the sharp crenellations fringing that fortress's high curtain wall were meant to evoke a thick rose bramble.

"Maybe that voice was your imagination," Tal said, drawing his knees up to his chest.

"I would love to believe it was only me back at the inn since that would mean I'm some sort of swordfighting savant." She thrust the sword back into its scabbard and tossed it on the bed. "But it's not true. Maybe it was the sword . . . or maybe it was the Silver Mother or the Iron Daughter reaching down to help. It certainly wasn't me."

Tal let out a long sigh, turning back to the window. "Old Gith things are trouble."

Bren snorted. "Says the boy who used to live in an underground lair built by the Gith."

"That's exactly how I know to be careful. There are things down there that do not sleep. Every year, a few of the Ratman's mice vanish after they decide to go exploring."

Bren crawled up higher on the bed and leaned against the rickety headboard. The mattress was as lumpy as days-old porridge, and she'd already glimpsed several many-legged critters scurrying into its depths. The nest of blankets Tal had made on the floor for himself looked far more inviting, but she didn't want to make him feel like his chivalrous act of giving her the bed wasn't appreciated.

"What was it like?" she asked, watching him watch the city. "Being one of the Ratman's mice, I mean."

Tal was quiet for a long time. When he finally spoke, his voice sounded distant. "Warm."

"Warm?"

"Safe. Protected. Before I joined his gang, I was scrounging a living on the streets. I'd run away from the orphanage and had nothing and no one. The Burrow was a place to live, the mice a family. The Ratman . . ." Tal paused again, and Bren could see his throat moving as he swallowed. "He was like a father."

"But you left."

Tal nodded. "I had to."

"Why?"

He tapped a tuneless melody on the window's dirty glass. "When I was younger, I didn't understand why the older mice always left when they reached a certain age. It seemed to me like a betrayal since the Ratman had given them so much. But slowly I came to understand. The Ratman doesn't care about us. He acts like he does, says sweet things, but in the end, we are just tools. He abandoned a friend of mine to the blackness of the Maw, and her only crime was getting caught stealing something the Ratman wanted. He could have returned what was stolen, at least used it to bargain for Essa's freedom, but it was more important to get on the right side of some powerful patron." He ran his hand through his thick black hair. Tal wasn't handsome in the way that had made the other girls in the village swoon, but there was a certain charm to the way he looked, with his mess of dark curls and long thin face.

"So we decided to leave," he continued finally. "Quiet and Knives and me. Grel and Peshka, their mothers had named them, though we had abandoned our birth names when we became mice. We'd been friends for years, back to when we were the smallest mice in the Burrow together. It was Quiet's idea to join the army. Get out of Leris, leave the Ratman far behind, be part of an even bigger and stronger gang. And we'd have each other."

He was crying, Bren realized. She didn't hear it in his voice, but tears had wet his cheeks.

"They died in that swamp. The arrows were falling like rain, and the bastards hadn't even given us helmets or real armor. I was pressing my hands to the hole in Quiet's belly, and he was still trying to talk to me. After he stopped breathing, he didn't look at peace – he was scared, even in death."

"I'm sorry," Bren whispered.

Tal wiped at his face. "You can't keep looking back at the past, or you'll get smacked in the head by the future you don't see coming. One of the oldest mice told me that my first night in the Burrow."

"You can still hold them in your hearts," Bren said softly.

Tal nodded jerkily. "I do. I miss them, but they're gone." He cast a

shy glance towards her, and she thought she knew what he was thinking. At least he wasn't alone anymore.

Bren's fingers tangled in the threadbare blanket. A warmth was
growing inside her, emotion rising up into her throat. She blinked,
surprised to feel the prickle of her own tears.

"I—"

"Blood and fire!" Tal cried, tumbling from his perch on the sill. He
scrambled to his feet, brandishing a curved dagger at the window.

Bren's hand scrabbled for the scabbard among the sheets. What
was it?

Then she gasped. A familiar grinning face was staring at them
through the yellowed glass, almost invisible with night having fallen
over the city.

Muttering angrily to himself, Tal sheathed his dagger and
unlatched the window. The girl hovering outside shifted so the
window could swing wide, then she slipped inside and dropped to
the floor. She examined her hands as she straightened, rubbing at the
red abrasions covering her palms.

"You again," Tal said, folding his arms across his chest.

"Me again," replied the freckled girl, grinning impishly.

He inclined his head towards the door. "Any reason you didn't
take the stairs, little mouse?"

The girl snorted, then swallowed whatever she had just
dislodged. "Me and Gram Rhelga don't get along so well. Didn't want
to risk gettin' smacked with a ladle if I came in through the front
door."

"That wouldn't have anything to do with your sticky fingers,
would it?" he asked.

"Maybe," she replied, her grin widening.

Bren remembered how this girl had lifted her knife from her
without her knowing. If she owned a business, she certainly wouldn't
let this one inside.

"I also just needed the practice," the girl continued, flexing her
fingers. "Couldn't let an opportunity to climb *The Coronet* slip past.
Took me a while to find you, though." She snickered, running her

fingers through her sweat-damp curls. "Surprised you didn't hear the screams from below. Scared the britches off a few poor folk when they saw me pass by their window."

Tal sighed, rolling his eyes. "Well, I assume you didn't make this climb for the fun of it. Did the Ratman find out what we want to know?"

"Aye," the girl said, wiping at her nose and then jerking her thumb in Bren's direction. "This one's uncle lives just off the Street of Swords, near where it crosses the Street of Silver. House with blue shutters and a knocker shaped like a rooster."

Tal nodded. "That makes sense. I know a lot of the Bright Company brass in Leris live on the Street of Swords. It's how it got its name, though a few smithies have also set up shop there now."

The girl unfolded a grubby hand, and, careful not to touch her skin, Tal deposited a silver coin in her palm. It vanished into one of her many pockets, and then she leaped up onto the windowsill. Before she disappeared into the night, she twisted around, locking gazes with Tal.

"Oh. Almost forgot – Ratman wanted me to tell you that he don't want to hear you pulling any jobs. You want back into the life, you gots to go have a sit down with him first, work out some kind of arrangement. Understand?"

The corner of Tal's mouth lifted, but there wasn't any humor in that half-smile. "Tell him he doesn't have to worry. I won't step on any tails."

The girl's eyes narrowed, as if she was turning over what he'd just said for any hidden messages. Then with a wink she threw herself over the ledge and was gone.

Tal crossed the room and closed the window, making sure it was latched securely before turning back to Bren.

"That was easy," she said, feeling a swell of relief to know where her uncle lived.

Tal chewed his lip as he considered something, then shrugged. "It's too easy, though. I'm surprised the Ratman didn't make me dance a bit more for that information."

"Should we go now or wait till the morrow?"

Tal cast a glance at the window. It was a cloudy night, the city almost completely lost to darkness. "It's up to you, though it will take us a while to cross the city, and the watch patrols are more numerous and less gentle after the sun goes down. We'll leave Moon here in the stables. I know the girl who takes care of the horses, and she owes me a favor."

"The morning, then," Bren said, hugging a pillow to her chest. The giddy excitement she was feeling might make sleep difficult, but she was also exhausted. "We'll leave at first light."

7

The house was easy enough to find, one of a row of two-story cottages that looked almost identical save for the color of their shutters. This district of Leris had little of the Tangle's chaotic bustle, with tidy shopfronts frequented by well-dressed women and a noticeable lack of nightsoil in the streets or dead rats in the gutters. The few unaccompanied children she'd seen were plump, bonnets framing scrubbed apple-red cheeks. None of them had the ragged look of the Ratman's feral charges. Bren noticed that Tal looked more nervous and out of place here than he had in the deepest, darkest part of the Tangle. He hung back as she approached the blackwood door with its heavy iron knocker shaped like a rooster.

"Come on," she said, beckoning him closer. "My aunt doesn't bite."

"I've had someone yell for the watch to chase me away too many times in the Garden," Tal said, but he still came up beside her as she took hold of the rooster's comb and rapped it hard against the wood. From inside, she heard the faint sound of a woman's voice yelling that she was coming.

"Bren," he said, and she glanced over at him. Tal licked his lips, his eyes darting to the street and then back to her. He looked very uncomfortable. "I'm going to leave you to your reunion. I have things I have to do, people I need to see, and I don't want to intrude on your family matters."

"What's wrong?"

He blew out his cheeks, raising his gaze to the sky. "I just don't feel like I should be here for this. You need some time alone with your aunt to talk about what happened."

Bren frowned. "Then are you leaving me? For good?"

"No, no," Tal replied quickly. "I'll come see you again soon. But you're not the only one with reasons to come to Leris. I brought you here safely, and now I have to attend to my own obligations."

"All right," Bren said. Her fingers slipped from the knocker, and she briefly took Tal's hand, giving it a squeeze. "Thank you."

Surprise crinkled his face, though he mastered it quickly. He winked at her as he pulled away, then he skipped down the steps and started walking quickly back the way they'd come.

Bren watched him for a moment, flustered by the welter of emotions she was feeling, and then her attention was drawn back to the door. Someone was fumbling with a deadbolt on the other side. She swallowed nervously, trying to put Tal out of her mind and focus on the here and now.

The door opened slightly, a slice of a familiar face appearing in the crack. "Yes? Who is it?"

Bren pulled back her cowl, eliciting a gasp from the other side of the door.

"Oh, by the Mother, Brenna!"

More scraping as a chain was hastily removed, and then the door was flung wide. A stout woman lunged forward and gathered Bren into a crushing embrace. She was pulled inside and heard the door slam beside her, but she saw none of this as her head was still buried in her aunt's ample bosom.

"Saints and sages, my girl," Heralia exclaimed, finally releasing Bren and letting her stumble back a step. "What are you doing here?"

"I . . ." Bren began, but then her words failed her. She swallowed hard, feeling a knot she'd kept tight inside her for days start to unravel. With this came a swell of sadness that made her chest ache. Her aunt watched her with concern as she struggled to speak. Finally, Bren fought through her rising emotions. "Auntie, Mama is dead. They're all dead."

The walls she'd built to protect herself ever since she'd buried her family crumbled away. She swayed, hot tears spilling down her cheeks. Before she could fall, her aunt was there, dragging her back into her arms.

"Child," she murmured, stroking Bren's hair. Still holding her tight, Heralia walked with her further into the house and then sank down onto a settee. Bren let herself feel everything she'd been fighting to keep at bay, and she wasn't sure how long she sobbed, but when she finally pulled away, her aunt's blouse was soaked with her tears.

Heralia cupped Bren's face with her hands. Her fingers smelled of flowers – she was one of the gardeners who helped take care of the countless roses in Leris. "What happened? Can you speak of it?"

Bren swallowed, trying to find her voice. "Warriors came to our home. Dragon-riders. They were chasing a paladin of the Silver Mother who had stopped at our farm for shelter. After they killed him, they . . . they . . ."

She trailed away, unable to continue.

"The Velaschin?" Heralia asked softly, and Bren nodded.

"I'm so sorry," her aunt murmured, brushing at the tears wetting Bren's face. "Your mama and papa were good people. The very best. And I never met your brother, but I heard all sorts of stories from Merik after he returned from his visit last summer."

Bren sniffled, finally bringing herself under control. She glanced around the small house, hoping that she would see some sign that her uncle was here. It was a cluttered home – nearly every bit of space was filled by a ceramic pot containing a flower or plant. Roses, of course, red and yellow and white, but also pale blue lilies, ebon-blooms black as pitch, and ethereal moonblossoms that would only unfold when the Silver Mother appeared in the night sky. But there was no crimson officer's cloak hanging from the pegs on the wall, no mud-spattered marching boots by the door.

Heralia noticed her looking around. "He's not here," she said quietly.

Bren's heart fell, and her aunt must have seen that in her face. "Doesn't mean he's gone," she said quickly. "Rumors is that the Company is gathering itself further to the west after the debacle at Manoch Tir. Merik would have gone with them. Or he might have been captured. He's an officer – the milkies would want to ransom him back." She paused, realizing what she had just said. "Oh. I'm so sorry, Brenna."

"It's fine," she said, but she had to stop herself from pulling her cowl back up. "I'm not Velaschin. I may share their skin, but I'm from the Seven Valleys."

Heralia patted her arm. "You are, dear, I know that." She was quiet for a moment, her lips pursed. "How did you get to Leris?"

Bren wiped away the last traces of her tears. "The paladin's horse survived the Velaschin. I rode him here and left him stabled at an inn called *The Coronet*."

Heralia frowned in disapproval. "I've heard of it. It's those tall towers rising out of the Tangle, yes? Not really the place for a young lady on her own."

"I wasn't by myself," Bren said. "I met a boy on the road, someone who was from Leris and had volunteered to fight the Velaschin, but was returning after the battles. He helped me find you." Bren didn't mention their foray into the unsavory undersoil of the City of Roses. She was certain her stolid, respectable aunt would be aghast to hear about the Ratman and his burrow teeming with ragged little mice.

"And where is this friend of yours now?"

"He brought me here this morning and then left to go settle his own affairs. But he said he'd come to see me later."

Heralia laid her hand on Bren's leg and gave it a comforting squeeze. "Good. I want to thank the lad for bringing you here safely. Trust is a dangerous thing to give out, Brenna, and it may have worked out this time, but you should be more careful. This war has stirred up all sorts of trouble, and there will be wicked people trying to take advantage of the chaos."

Bren nodded. The emotions that had flooded her a moment ago were finally receding, and in their absence was a bone-deep weariness. She wanted to sink down into this settee and let her exhaustion carry her away.

Her aunt rose, clapping her hands together like she was a baker dusting away flour. "Well, let's get you settled. We have a spare room for when my sister or your father . . ." She hesitated for a moment, then continued. "When your father used to come visit. And it looks like you haven't eaten anything in days. I have some meat pies I baked this morning cooling on the back window. Should be about ready to eat. And then you can sleep for as long as you like. Silver Mother knows you deserve it."

THE NEXT FEW days passed in a blur. She slept on a decadently soft feather bed, waking when golden light trickled through a window that looked out over a fruit-tree-filled courtyard shared by several families. Songbirds nested in those branches, and she'd lie there listening to their sweet sounds as her racing heart slowed and the sweat cooled on her skin. Nightmares continued to torment her, but at least they dissipated quickly now. Eventually, cooking smells would lure her from the bed, and she'd drag herself to the table and find a plate heaped with eggs, fried meat, and flaky bread. Aunt Heralia was an excellent cook, and she seemed to enjoy having someone to feed. After breakfast, Bren would accompany her aunt when she went out to care for the countless flower beds and trellises in the Garden. They'd meet other women while they pruned and weeded, friends of a similar age to Heralia, and there was much gossip and laughter, the darkness of the times forgotten for a short while. Which may have been why they did this work – Bren wasn't even sure if they were even paid to keep the city beautiful or if this gardening was purely a social occasion. She returned to her aunt's home every evening sweaty and smelling of flowers, with dirt under her fingernails and a sense of having accomplished something that day.

The third night after Bren's arrival, they were just sitting down to enjoy a dinner of buttered leeks and barley porridge, a light rain pattering upon the roof tiles, when a knock came. They shared a glance, and Bren could see in Heralia's face a flicker of something like hope before her aunt swallowed and pushed away from the table.

"Who is it?" she called, her hand hovering over the door's chain.

"Heralia?" came the muffled response. "It's Gevin Lux. Open the door; I don't have much time."

Her aunt gasped, fumbling with the deadlock and chain. A cloaked figure pushed his way into the house as Heralia stumbled back a step, her hand fluttering to her chest.

"Gevin! What are you doing here? Where's Merik?"

"In a moment, goodwoman," the man said, pushing back his cowl and looking around the small room. He had a lean face covered in stubble, and a livid scar that still glistened wetly curved down one side of his face. His cloak and boots seemed more mud than leather, and a sword that looked like the twin of the one Bren's uncle had let her hold last summer was belted at his waist. "I've been riding for three days straight, and I'd kill for a dram of the good Stoneswallow whiskey I know your husband keeps on hand." His eyes alighted on Bren at the dinner table, and he frowned. "Who's this?" She saw his fingers twitch like he wanted to draw his sword.

"My niece," Heralia said, bustling over to a cabinet and pulling out a bottle half-full of liquid amber. "The daughter of Merik's brother. She was an orphan; she's not one of them."

"He mentioned her before," Gevin said slowly, his hand moving from his sword hilt as he came over to the dining area and collapsed into a chair. Even with the table between them, she could smell him, sweat and horse and something sour. He ignored her attention, tilting back his head and closing his eyes, his face slackening in exhaustion.

For a moment, Bren thought he was going to fall asleep right there, but then her aunt returned and slammed the bottle on the table in front of him, and his eyes flew open again.

"Gevin," she said, her voice like iron, "*where is my husband?*"

"Sages, woman," he said with a sigh. "You scared me half to death." The Bright Company man rubbed at his face, then pulled the cork from the bottle and poured a healthy amount into a cup. Gevin threw back the drink in one motion, then grimaced. "Thank you," he said, and he sounded like he meant it. "I needed that."

Bren's aunt had put her hands on her hips and looked to be on the verge of demanding information yet again, but Gevin held up his hand to forestall her.

"All right, Hera. All right. I just needed a moment to compose myself. I stopped here to tell you about Merik when I was explicitly instructed not to attend to any personal matters, so a little gratitude would be appreciated."

Heralia crossed her arms, looking less than understanding, but still she stayed quiet.

Gevin refilled his glass and took another sip. "He's alive, Hera. Or at least he was when I left camp."

Her aunt swayed, and Bren leaped up to steady her.

"Oh, thank the Mother," Heralia murmured, raising a shaking hand to cover her mouth.

"What happened?" Bren asked as her aunt let out a few shuddering sobs. "Where is he?"

"What happened?" Gevin repeated bitterly. "The kingdom fell, that's what. And after Queen Alyssa did what most had long considered impossible – she brought together the armies of all the dukes and duchesses and hired every one of the great mercenary bands: the Bright Company, the Last Men, the Azure Swords. She even convinced a renegade prince from the Crimson Dominion to throw in his lot with Felaesia. It was the greatest force gathered since her great-grandfather united the Flowering Coast." He shook his head, grimacing. "I wasn't privy to the strategies laid out in the high tent, but my understanding was that we hoped our archers and the ballistas we'd dragged into the field would bring down their dragons. None of those monsters fell, at least that I saw. No arrow can fly that high, and the bolts of our siege weapons were simply too inaccurate and easy to dodge. We could not strike them, but they had no such trouble. Fire, searing blood, lightning, even a darkness that ate away at flesh like acid . . . How could we stand before what the beasts were vomiting on us from above? So we broke."

"But you know my Merik is still alive?" Heralia asked, and Bren thought she looked like she could use a drink of the whiskey as well. "You saw him?"

Gevin nodded, then drained his glass again. "Aye. He was commanding the Third, and I was his adjunct. It was chaos there for a while, but he led what was left of our men from the field and into the foothills of the mountains, where it was easier to take cover from those lizards. After a few days of hiding, we got word that what was left of the Company was reforming to the west."

"So the fight goes on?" Bren asked, leaning forward with her elbows on the table. "The war isn't finished?"

Gevin stared into his empty glass as if the answer could be found in the dregs. "I don't know if the war is truly over, but the Company's part in it is done. At least for now. Commander Khelus plans on taking the Company into the Dominion if the archons will have us. He's a proud man, the commander, and a true son of the Flowering Coast. He won't bend the knee to invaders."

"Then what are you doing here?" Fear had crept back into Heralia's voice, and Bren could understand her concerns. What would happen to her if the Bright Company stayed in the Crimson Dominion? Would she leave her home to go be with her husband? Or wait for him to return?

"The fools who fled the office here left some documents of great import behind. Contracts, promissory notes, blackmail, those sorts of things. I was tasked with gathering them up and then returning." He splashed another finger of whiskey into his cup. "But don't fear, Hera. Your husband wouldn't have let me come back here without bringing a message for you. He said to be patient and be safe. The Duke of Thorns is a coward and will not try to resist the Velaschin, so the city won't be sacked. When he can return, he will."

"Why does he not come back now?" Heralia asked, her fingers white against the wooden tabletop.

Gevin sighed. "Because the commander is stubborn, and Merik is loyal. But the Company will not stay in the Dominion forever. Either we will march out to face the Velaschin again – unlikely, so long as they have their dragons – or the commander's resolve will be worn down by the men who want to return. Too many are like Merik, with families on the Flowering Coast."

"So just wait," Heralia said sourly.

Gevin reached over and covered one of her hands with his own. "I'm sorry, Hera. But your husband lives, and he loves you, and Silver Mother willing, you'll be together again soon." He slowly stood, moving like he'd already stiffened up. "And I have to be off. The outriders of the dragon lords will be closing in on Leris, and I don't want them to stumble across me when I leave the city."

"Take me with you," Bren said abruptly, also rising from her chair. "Uncle Merik was teaching me how to fight. I was going to join the Bright Company as soon as I was old enough."

Gevin regarded her with raised eyebrows. "I'm sorry, lass. The Company is no place for you right now. And I need to move fast. You'll just make me slower."

"I have a horse," Bren continued, meeting the Bright Company man's gaze with what she hoped looked like steely resolve. "A fast horse. And a sword. Please, my family was killed by the Velaschin, and I swore to the Silver Mother that I'd get revenge."

Gevin smiled sadly. "Your uncle would murder *me* if I dragged you across the realm to where we've holed up. You're much safer here. The city will prostrate itself to the dragon lords, and I expect life will go on almost as normal. The Velaschin are brutal on the battlefield, but they have not yet sacked a single city. They're planning on ruling these lands, not razing them."

"How are you so sure?" Heralia asked, glancing at the door like she expected the Velaschin to burst in at any moment.

Gevin snorted and shook his head. "Does it look like the city is preparing for a siege? A conquering army is days away, and there's no sign of any resistance. I suspect the duke has already informed the dragon lords that the city will open the gates to them, and in exchange, there will be no sack or purging of those with noble blood."

"I beg you—" Bren began, but the soldier cut her off brusquely.

"Stay safe. That's what Merik wants most." He drew up his cowl as he moved for the door, then paused and turned back when his hand touched the handle. "May the Mother watch over you both," he said, and then he was gone, the hiss of rain swelling briefly as he vanished into the night.

BREN EMERGED from her bedroom the following morning to find Heralia humming to herself as she bustled about preparing for their day of gardening by filling a basket with her tools and a few cloth-wrapped lunches of bread and cheese. She seemed lighter on her feet, smiling at Bren brightly.

"Morning, my dear. It's a beautiful day to keep the City of Roses blooming!"

Bren grumbled something unintelligible and sat heavily in a chair, staring blearily at the hard-boiled eggs and leftover porridge her aunt had laid out.

She'd lain awake for much of the night, unable to quiet her thoughts. The news that her uncle was alive had brought a tremendous sense of relief, but she was also deeply disappointed that Gevin wouldn't take her when he returned to the Bright Company. And learning that the Velaschin were only days away from Leris was unsettling. Gevin had seemed confident that some accord had been reached and that the dragon lords would not sack the city, but Bren still felt nervous. She'd seen firsthand how little these invaders valued the lives of the common folk.

Bren ate as quickly as she could, but when she looked up from slurping the last of her porridge, she still found her aunt hovering near the door, obviously impatient to start the day. Bren considered telling Heralia that she'd prefer to stay home and rest, but she had to admit that some fresh air and sunshine would probably do her more good than moping around here.

The city was busier than Bren had expected, given the early hour, but perhaps the glorious weather was pulling people outside. Her uncle's house was situated near the intersection of several busy streets – Silver and Swords – and usually the silversmiths and weapon mongers received their business later in the day. After all, few people went shopping for a sword just after rolling out of bed. There must have been a fresh batch of fish brought in from one of the nearby lakes, as several older women were carrying poles laden with the recent catch. Sometimes the smells from the nearby Street of Scales wafted into her uncle's neighborhood, though this morning the breeze was blowing in the opposite direction and was decidedly more floral.

"We'll start down by the House of Gold," Heralia said, clattering down the steps and into the street. "I noticed the wall across from the temple was getting a little ragged."

Bren was about to follow her, but then she paused, squinting into the distance where their little avenue emptied into the larger Street of Silver. Something was happening, some commotion. She heard faint, panicked cries, and people were running towards them like they were being chased, but Bren couldn't see anything.

"What's going on?" she asked. Heralia had stopped her humming and was shading her eyes to try to figure out what had caused the disturbance.

"I don't know, dear. A thief, perhaps? Those urchins from the Tangle are getting more brazen every year."

Bren frowned as she watched the fleeing folk dash into alleyways or pound on doors to beg to be let inside. "I don't think – Mother save us!"

Bren stumbled, nearly collapsing as a frozen dread filled her chest, stealing her breath away.

Dragon.

It came soaring over the rooftops, black as night and nearly as vast.

Somewhere far away her aunt was screaming – no, Heralia was right beside her, but there was a roaring in Bren's ears drowning everything else out. The dragon had a long serpentine neck fringed with spines, its dark wings were infused with the light shining through from above, and a barbed tail coiled and snapped like a banner in the wind.

The monster passed over them, its shadow plunging everything into darkness for a moment, then it banked on whatever currents coursed through the sky and winged its way towards the Brocade.

Bren stared after it, numbed. She had seen a dragon that looked just like that before . . . It had crouched behind the man who had passed the death sentence on her family.

She returned to herself, realizing Heralia was desperately trying to drag her back inside.

"Brenna!" her aunt gasped. "Come on!"

For a moment, she let herself be pulled towards the door. Then she shook herself free of her aunt. Heralia gaped, her face slack with surprise and fear.

"Go inside," Bren said quickly. "Pack some food and clothes in case we need to flee. I'll be back soon."

"Where are you going?" her aunt cried. Heralia lunged, trying to seize her again, but Bren was already off and running in the direction the dragon had gone.

Chaos followed in the monster's wake. Most people scattered, rushing for shelter, though a few stayed rooted to the spot with ashen faces and eyes glazed with fear. Only she was trying to follow it, weaving among the terrified Lerisians as she sprinted in pursuit. The streets in the Garden were straighter and more orderly than in the Tangle, but still she had to dash down alleyways and side streets to keep going in the general direction it had flown. She paused and glanced behind her after a few twists and turns and was relieved to see that her aunt had given up the chase. Then she was off again, following the dragon.

More formidable manses were rising up around her – this must be where the stolid burghers of the Garden gave way to the wealthy nobles of the Brocade. There were men here in the rose-and-white livery of the city watch, and on another day they would have seized Bren, but now they didn't even look at her, terrified faces turned to the sky.

She passed beyond the great houses of the rich and arrived at the outskirts of a vast garden. The entrance was a gilded gate wrought of some glimmering metal set in a high wall entirely smothered with roses. Beyond this barrier, the crenellations of the Briar clawed at the sun-washed blue, and atop the peaked turret of the tallest tower, the dragon of living darkness had perched to survey the city, shadows leaking from its mouth to stain the sky.

8

Heralia was furious when Bren finally returned. She didn't yell, but her anger was evident in the way she stalked around the house pruning her flowers in a decidedly violent manner. Bren tried to apologize, but eventually she retreated into her room to lie on her bed and consider what she had witnessed. The dragon had resembled the mount of the warrior who had killed the paladin, but it was also true that Bren knew little about these creatures. Perhaps there were many that looked the same. What she did know was that when the dragon had alighted on the Briar, there had been no effort to dislodge it. No alarm had been sounded, no arrows had arced from defenders on the walls. The monster had not been conquering the city . . . the city was already conquered. Gevin had been right – rather than resist, the Duke of Thorns had bent the knee to the invaders. At first this angered Bren, but the more she considered the situation, the more she sympathized with the duke. If the enemy had boasted only infantry and cavalry, the high walls of Leris could keep them camped outside for months. But dragons . . . what could anyone do against dragons? Bren imagined the beasts soaring over the city far beyond arrow range and breathing flames into the close-packed wooden buildings of the Tangle. It would be a disaster. A massacre.

Bren stayed in her room for a while, polishing the odd metal of her sword with a rag. It seemed to make little difference in the flat luster of the blade, but Bren secretly hoped the spirit inside would appreciate the effort. She assumed her aunt would ignore her for at least a few days as punishment for what she'd done, so she was surprised when a knock came at her door and she heard Heralia say that dinner was on the table. Sheathing the sword and returning it to its hiding place under her bed, Bren left her room to find her aunt sitting at the table, having prepared a simple meal of dark rye bread and porridge. The cold fury Bren had seen earlier in her face had been replaced by what looked to be bone-deep exhaustion, the emptiness in her eyes suggesting to Bren that her aunt was already drained of emotion.

It was a feeling she knew all too well.

Bren slid into her chair, watching her aunt warily. "I'm sorry," she said, and Heralia's gaze moved from the steaming bowl in front of her to Bren.

She sighed. "Accepted, Brenna."

"That dragon . . ." Bren began as her aunt broke off a chunk of the bread and dipped it in the porridge. "It looked the same as one of the monsters that burned my house."

Heralia chewed slowly, watching her. "And if it was?"

"Then that means its master might be here as well."

Her aunt frowned. "Even if he is, there's nothing you can do about it. You're just a shepherdess from the Seven Valleys. "

"Uncle Merik was once a shepherd."

"Where is your uncle now? Far away, hiding from these dragons. And he has swords under his command, the finest warriors in all Felaesia." Her aunt reached out and laid her fingers gently on the back of Bren's hand. "Dear heart, in times like this us common folk have to hunker down and try to stay safe. There's nothing you or I can do. If we try to resist the men with swords, they will not hesitate to cut us down."

Bren pulled her hand away from her aunt's touch, but still she nodded, pretending agreement. She wondered if Heralia would say the same if Gavin Lux had told her Uncle Merik had died from Velaschin blades, and she began to tear her piece of bread into smaller chunks, her appetite soured. Heralia appeared satisfied by Bren's behavior, as she gave a slight smile before returning her attention to the food.

What about the oath Bren had sworn to the Silver Mother? Her life ever since that day had seemed guided by a higher power – she had a horse now and a sword, and the Velaschin were here, in this city. Surely she could not—

Bren noticed that her aunt had cocked her ear to one side as if listening.

"What is it?" she asked, but Heralia only furrowed her brow.

Then Bren heard it as well, a faint rumbling. It was like when something had startled her flock and sent them fleeing across the meadows in terror, a hundred hooves pounding the ground.

Slowly, she rose and went to the door, her aunt a step behind her.

"It sounds like the Bright Company on parade," Heralia whispered.

Ignoring her aunt's command to stop, Bren opened the door a crack and looked outside.

Twilight had bruised the sky, and the spectral outlines of the Mother and her daughters were visible over the city, accompanied by a dusting of the brightest stars. Lamplighters had already finished their rounds, flames flickering in the lanterns lining the street. It could have been any night since Bren had come to the Garden . . . except this evening, an army marched through the city.

Her fingers tightened on the door frame as she gazed once more upon the soldiers of the Velaschin Empire.

They marched in tight formation, filling the Street of Swords. Black-metal pikes rested on shoulders, wickedly barbed, and their banded mail had the same sharp angles as the armor of the warriors Bren had seen before, though lacking in the more elaborate flourishes. A shudder passed through her at the sight of those helms and the solemn pale faces staring out from within monstrous iron jaws.

The largest man Bren had ever seen rode at their front on a black stallion. He wore no helm, and his hairless, grub-white head was crisscrossed by ancient scars. Bren flinched as his gaze passed over her, and she thought she saw his mouth twitch in amusement. A huge greatsword was strapped across his back, big enough to cut a horse in half with a single blow. Above this host rose a banner: the outline of a dragon's head, etched black against a field of white.

Bren realized her aunt had a hold of her arm, and after one last long look at the Velaschin soldiers, she allowed herself to be drawn away from the door. Her heart was pounding in time to the steps she still felt reverberating up through the floor. They were truly here, inside the walls. The defenders of Leris – if they could be called that – had simply given up their city.

"Come, dear," her aunt said, trying to lead her back to the table. "Finish your dinner and forget about what's going on out there. Worrying won't change anything."

Bren shook her head, pulling away. "I'm not hungry," she said before quickly crossing the room and entering her bedchamber. She shut the door and leaned against it, closing her eyes as the terrifying memory of that scarred giant rose up again in her mind's eye. She suddenly remembered something her Uncle Merik had told her long ago when she'd asked him if he'd ever been scared in battle.

"Fear is good," she murmured as she went to her bed, hearing his voice in her head as she dragged out her sword. "Fear is caution. But it cannot stop you from doing what needs to be done. You must master your fear, or it will master you." She sat on the bed, the sheath across her knees. Then she pulled the sword free and held it up, studying her distorted reflection in the strange blade. "Fear is good," she repeated, and she thought she felt the hilt twitch in her grip.

THE NEXT MORNING, Bren was roused early by a loud banging, as if someone were trying to break down their front door. She groped towards wakefulness, then hurriedly dressed and left her room clutching her sheathed sword. Heralia emerged out of her own chamber at the same moment, and from her bewildered expression, she was also alarmed by the thought of someone announcing themselves in such a manner.

"Who is it?" Heralia called to whoever was outside, wrapping her shawl tighter around herself as she edged towards the door.

"It's Melichai d'Garivoux, goodwoman! For the love of all that's sacred and pure, open this door immediately!" It was a man's voice, surprisingly high-pitched and emotional. The speaker sounded like he was on the verge of panicking . . . or perhaps breaking down in tears.

"Melichai," Heralia muttered. Bren let go of her sword's hilt when she saw the fear drain from her aunt's face.

The knocking suddenly grew even louder and more frenzied until Bren could actually see the wood shivering. "Please! We've no time to waste!"

Sighing, Heralia crossed the room and flung open the door. A man stumbled inside, dressed in billowy clothes so garishly bright they could have been motley. An oversized hat that might have begun its life as an embroidered cushion slipped from his head, revealing a shock of white-gold hair. He must have had some Dominion blood in his ancestry; his skin wasn't as dark as most on the Flowering Coast, though he was nowhere near as pale as Bren.

With a small cry of distress, he scooped his hat from the floor and dusted it off, then settled it on his head again. Behind him, two hulking soldiers in the livery of Leris hovered in the doorway.

"Goodwoman!" the man cried, flourishing an elaborate bow. When he straightened, he turned towards Bren, but before he could offer her a similar greeting his eyes widened, and his mouth fell open.

"Fire and ashes, Heralia, what in the name of the three daughters is a *Velaschin* doing in your house?"

"She is the daughter of my husband's brother," her aunt said primly, going over to a shelf and pulling out a blue glass bottle. "A drink, Melichai? I know it's early, but I remember this is your favorite."

The man wrenched his gaze from Bren to the bottle, his longing very obvious. "No, no, goodwoman," he said quickly, shaking his head. "As much as I would enjoy a tipple right now, I must perform my duty today with utmost alacrity." His eyes drifted back to Bren. "Your husband's brother, did you say? But I have met your husband – fine fellow, good Seven Valley man. Old farming family, I believe."

"I am a foundling," Bren said, suddenly realizing how rude it was to be brandishing a sword. She hurriedly laid it down on a side table, but the man didn't seem to notice her embarrassment.

"Interesting," Melichai said, tapping his chin. "And perhaps fortuitous. But before we pursue that, let me first tell you why I've come."

"Yes, please," Heralia said with a sigh, folding her arms across her chest. "I don't think I've ever seen you out before midday."

"It is dreadfully early, isn't it?" the man answered, his expression pained. "The sun is far too bright right now for any reasonable person to be outside." He pulled out a silken handkerchief and daubed at his face like he'd labored through the desert to reach their house. After tucking it back away, he straightened his shoulders and turned his attention fully to her aunt.

"I need a gardener," he said dramatically, then waved his hand quickly like he'd made a mistake. "No, no – let me amend that. I need the best gardener in Leris. Today. Right now."

Heralia blinked, looking like she could use a swig from the bottle she'd just put back on the shelf. "*Now*?"

"Indeed," Melichai continued. "For we have an emergency. As you certainly know, Duke Tassehone has opened the gates to the milk –" He paused, his gaze flicking to Bren. "Uh, to the Velaschin. Very unfortunate, but what is to be done? Sage's mercy, they have *dragons*." He cleared his throat, his attention returning to Heralia. "Well, there is to be a ceremony today at the Briar where the duke will formally bend the knee and pledge his allegiance to their emperor. But of course such a momentous moment shouldn't be lacking in pomp and grandeur. The duke wishes to show the dragon lords why we are the City of Roses, the most beautiful of all the blossoms on the Flowering Coast. A mural must be prepared at the ceremony site, a wall of colored roses depicting one of their fearsome monsters in all its terrible glory." Melichai hesitated again, licking his lips. "I think, perhaps, he hopes to flatter them. And a demonstration of why damaging our fair city would be an affront to whatever gods they follow."

"You want me to make a rose mural?" Heralia asked, sounding incredulous. "Why not have Ferin or one of the other royal gardeners do it?"

Melichai sighed. "Unfortunately, old Ferin's heart gave out yesterday when a dragon swooped just over his head on the way to finding a perch atop the Briar. Very tragic. And none of his apprentices have nearly the same experience and skill as you. He told me many times about how much he wanted you to join him in the Brocade, as he felt your talents were being wasted out here."

"The Garden is my home."

"And such a beautiful home it is," Melichai said warmly, looking around in admiration. "Certainly you will be able to fill it with all sorts of expensive trifles once you complete the masterwork I have envisioned . . . because I promise you a purse with a hundred gold venmarks for the work you will do today."

Bren's jaw dropped at the amount. If her father had sold his farm and all his animals, he wouldn't have gotten nearly that much, and she doubted her Uncle Merik earned the same in a year on an officer's pay. The duke must indeed be desperate.

Heralia's face had also gone slack with surprise, but she controlled herself quickly. "I shall do my duty to Leris," she told him solemnly.

"Wonderful!" Melichai cried, clapping his hands together. "Then gather what tools you need and join me at the Briar as soon as possible. I'm having the apprentice gardeners cut a thousand roses right now, so you'll have plenty of flowers to work with." He spun on his heels, the two slouching guardsmen snapping to attention. Something must have occurred to him, as after a few steps towards the door, he turned again.

"Oh – and your niece should come as well."

"Why?" Heralia and Bren replied together.

Melichai's long fingers fluttered in the air. "These Velaschin . . . they're a bit of a mystery, I'm afraid. There were a few of them living here quite peacefully, but after news arrived that we were at war with their people they abandoned the city. They weren't mistreated, I assure you," he added hastily with another glance at Bren. "Simply nervous, I believe, that they might be blamed for the actions of their kin." He flipped back a glittering tassel that had fallen across his face. "The duke was just expressing to me yesterday evening that he wished some had remained so they could be trotted out when he swears our city's fealty to these new masters. You know, a reminder that we have welcomed their people in the past."

"She's not from across the sea," Heralia said, a note of worry in her voice.

"But they will not know that," Melichai replied, flashing a winning smile. "Just look happy and well cared for, yes? Dress nicely and be pretty." He snapped his fingers. "In fact, I'll send over my tailor as soon as I return to the Briar. He'll get you sorted while your dear aunt makes my mural, and then you can join us for the ceremony."

"I don't know . . ." Heralia murmured, her fingers kneading her shawl nervously.

"I do," Bren said quickly, glancing at the sheathed sword she had set down earlier. "I'd be honored to attend."

～

AFTER MELICHAI HAD SWEPT from their home in a flurry of silk and lace, Heralia collapsed into a chair looking stricken.

"Who was that?" Bren asked.

Her aunt had begun to massage her temple vigorously, as if trying to forestall a headache. "The First Gardener of Leris," she said, sounding emptied of emotion. "Although he knows about as much about gardening as you do. It's quite an exalted and lucrative sinecure in the City of Roses. He's responsible for keeping all the districts blooming, but in truth, nearly the entirety of his efforts are concentrated on the Brocade and the Briar. Still, if the Duke of Thorns ever descended into the Garden or the Tangle and was disappointed by what he saw, Melichai would lose his position and maybe even his head. So he sometimes comes by to visit me or some of the other gardeners to make sure our jobs are getting done."

"Is he a noble?"

Heralia shrugged. "I don't know. Perhaps? He affects their mannerisms, but it's clear he's also got Dominion blood. I suppose he could be someone's bastard, but I'm not privy to the gossip about those who dwell in the Brocade. He might simply be a clever grasper who has wormed his way into the duke's inner circle."

Bren ran her finger along the length of her sheathed sword, tracing the intricate knots decorating the leather. "And you're going to help him?"

Heralia sighed, pinching the bridge of her nose. "Of course. A hundred venmarks is a fortune. And if I refused his request, I'm sure he'd find some way to punish me."

"Then I suppose I'll see you at the Briar."

Heralia's gaze snapped to Bren. "You can't truly be thinking about going up there."

"It didn't sound like I had much choice in the matter. The First Gardener said he'd be sending his tailor over shortly."

Heralia rolled her eyes. "I could smell the whiskey on his breath from across the room. There's a good chance that he'll have completely forgotten about you by the time he crosses back into the Brocade." Her aunt rose abruptly. "But if he came down into the Garden, likely others are expecting me at the Briar. I need to dress and go quickly. The Duke of Thorns does not value much – even the oaths he once swore to the Petaled Throne, apparently – but he is passionate about his flowers. Gardeners have disappeared into the Maw for disappointing him."

Bren picked at the heel of last night's bread as her aunt rushed about, gathering everything she thought she would need. Then, after giving Bren a quick hug and a kiss on the brow, she dashed from the house, muttering to herself about the madness of the world these days.

The hunger Bren usually felt when she woke had been crowded out by the butterflies fluttering in her stomach, and after a few more nibbles she went over to one of the shelves and began perusing its contents. Eventually, she pulled down a thick book that had caught her eye, running her fingers over the strangely coarse binding. It felt almost like bark instead of leather, as if someone had carefully skinned a tree after turning its leaves into pages. Though perhaps such things were common. Her parents had not owned any books – or even known how to read – but Bren's mother had sent her a few times a month to deliver eggs and things she had knitted to their elderly neighbor, who had lived by himself in a hut on top of one of the hills. She'd looked forward to these visits, as he was always excited to see her, and sometimes he'd let her carefully leaf through his collection of beautifully illustrated manuscripts. He'd taught her to read, patiently guiding her to sound out stories about brave paladins and wicked sorcerers and crafty demons. When he'd died, Bren had felt like a door to another world she'd just started to explore had been closed.

The spine crackled as she opened the great tome. Inside, she found intricately detailed drawings of various flowers, some of which Bren recognized. A flowing script filled the rest of each page, detailing the properties of each flower and how it might be used in medicine and cooking and other, more esoteric applications, like the warding away of fell spirits. She tried reading some of these descriptions out loud, stumbling over the longer words after so many years without practice. When her voice got tired, she read silently, awed by how much wisdom had been collected on these pages. Her mother would have given much for the knowledge she held in her hands. That thought made Bren's chest ache, and she closed the book for a while, lost in bittersweet memories.

She was still far away in misty dells herb-gathering with her mother when a knock came at the door. It wasn't the impatient pounding of the First Gardener, and if she had been in her room, she doubted she would have heard it at all. Shifting the heavy book from her lap, Bren went to the door and opened it. She'd been expecting the tailor Melichai had dispatched to be dressed in the same ostentatious finery as the nobleman, but the small, slight man standing in the entrance wore only a simple gray shift. He had an unremarkable face, and his hair had been shaved into a tonsure. Behind him loomed a giant carrying a chest that looked large enough for Bren to fold herself up inside with room to spare.

She blinked in confusion. This certainly did not look like the man responsible for Melichai's outfits.

"Well met, my dear," the man said in a soft voice. "May I come in?"

Bren tamped down her surprise, moving aside to let him enter. He gave her a slight smile, then motioned for the huge man to put down his burden in the middle of the room. Bren eyed the chest as the giant retreated to one corner, his expression blank.

"Are you the tailor?"

The man offered a crisp bow. "I am. My name is Selasin, and I have been instructed to dress you appropriately for the ceremony that is to be held at the Briar later today."

Bren tensed as the tailor swept closer to her while pulling something from the front pocket of his shapeless robe. She relaxed when she realized it was just a long piece of string.

"Arms up," he commanded her, and after she complied, he quickly took her measurements, laying the string alongside her limbs and wrapping it around her waist. His movements were efficient and practiced, and when he finished, he glided over to the chest and flipped it open.

"Now, unfortunately, we have no time for me to make you something new," he murmured, perusing the contents before him with a hand on his chin. "We'll have to do what alterations we need here and now."

He reached deep into the chest and, after a moment of rummaging around, pulled out a glistening length of emerald-green silk. When he unfolded it, a long, narrow-waisted dress was revealed, its neckline and cuffs fringed by white lace. Bren had to admit it looked beautiful. It was also something she had no desire to wear.

"This would work," Selasin mused, coming closer to her while holding up the dress. "Green is popular this season, and you'll draw more than a few envious eyes. An excellent contrast with your striking complexion."

Bren tried to keep the disappointment from her face, glancing to where her sheathed sword still lay on the side table. She couldn't wear a sword with any dress.

"Lovely," she told the tailor, forcing a smile. "But Velaschin women never wear dresses. At least not, uh, at important moments like this." Bren desperately hoped that this lie hadn't brought a blush to her face.

Selasin's brow crinkled in surprise. "Truly? I've never heard of such a thing." He tapped a finger against his cheek. "I'm sure I saw the wife of that Velaschin merchant Azar wearing a sumptuous gown during the last Wintertide festival."

"Well, at a seasonal festival that would make sense," Bren said, her mind racing. "But this is to be a formal ceremony where the duke swears allegiance to the emperor. Have you seen the women the Velaschin have in their army? Even riding their dragons? Putting one of us in a dress would be insulting to them."

"I see," Selasin intoned, not sounding at all convinced as he returned the green dress to the chest. "Then what would be appropriate?"

"Tunic and trousers."

"Tunic and trousers," Selasin repeated slowly, clearly unimpressed.

"There's very little difference between men and women among the Velaschin," Bren continued, surprising herself with how easily the fiction was now rolling off her tongue. "Truly, I would love to don one of your dresses for the evening, but most important is not insulting our new lords."

"*Hmm,*" Selasin murmured, digging down to the bottom of the chest. "We are lucky I'm always so well-prepared." He dragged from the depths a rumpled shirt of fine blue weave, twining flowers embroidered on its breast. "This was to be the riding shirt for Lord Haling's daughter, but she was thrown from her horse and broke her leg before I could deliver it. Functional and fashionable, those were the instructions given to me."

"Perfect," Bren said, trying not to look too pleased.

"And these black damask pants will pair nicely. If you bring that" —he nodded towards her sheathed blade, apparently having noticed her earlier glance—"you'll look like quite the dashing young bravo. Just please don't stab anyone." A snort erupted from the huge servant standing in the corner. Bren joined in the mirth, summoning forth a laugh that she hoped sounded like she also found the very idea ridiculous.

9

They perched on the mighty fortress like buzzards in a dead tree, staring down at the city spread below as if it were a carcass ready to be stripped bare. Bren counted six, talons curled around battlements as tails lashed the air, sunlight sliding across scales. The smallest was russet-colored and lacked the two front limbs of the others, making it look like a monstrous cross between a rooster and a dragon. This impression was reinforced by the way it stalked back and forth upon the high curtain walls, occasionally pausing to unleash a terrible shriek. Several other dragons resembled the green beasts that had burned her farmhouse, but she couldn't be sure if they were indeed the same monsters. These drakes snapped and nipped at each other, wisps of smoke leaking from their jaws. Their antics apparently did not impress the dragon sprawled on top of the keep as it watched its brethren with disinterest. If its dangling tail had not been flicking back and forth, Bren might have convinced herself this one was a statue, as it had a pebbled hide that more resembled stone than scales. But it was the last dragon that Bren kept her gaze fixed on as she approached the gates. Larger than the rest, it was a shadow hunched atop the tallest tower of the fortress. Bren was certain she knew this dragon.

And that meant the man she'd sworn to kill was here.

As she approached the gate, the guards flanking the raised portcullis eyed her suspiciously. Bren supposed she couldn't blame them. She was a girl dressed like a noble with a sword at her side, and her skin marked her as one of those who had so effortlessly conquered their proud city. How surprised they would be if they knew she was from a farm a few days' ride outside the city and that the weight of the pale metal she carried was in truth quite unfamiliar to her.

The guards did not challenge her as she passed into the shadow of the gate. Her heart was beating fast, but what fear she felt was more for the dragons looming above. It was hard to be worried about soldiers when predators with claws longer than swords were nearby. She could imagine the numb hopelessness Tal and his fellow soldiers must have felt watching the Velaschin dragons soaring overhead. She truly couldn't blame the duke for the surrender she was about to witness.

There was something else as well. Strange emotions were infringing upon her mind, things she could not understand. It was both like and unlike when the spirit in the sword had manifested – that had been just as alien, but different. These . . . reverberations were pressing from outside, vague emotions rather than the fully formed language of the voice from the inn. And while the sword-ghost had been a single will, now she sensed several, and they were not fixed solely on her. Could everyone feel what she did now? Bren swallowed, wrenching her eyes from the dragons. She had to focus on what she had come here to do.

The ceremony was taking place in the fortress's bailey. Two distinct crowds milled on the other side of the gate, and one was much larger and dressed in colorful finery similar to what Melichai had been wearing. The women wore long gowns of shimmering fabric, their hair pleated into elaborate weaves with gold flashing at their necks and fingers. The men all had blood-red roses pinned to the breasts of their doublets, and Bren was relieved to see that swords hung at their sides, though the hilts were so encrusted with jewels that she doubted they had been forged to be swung in anger. These nobles of Leris shifted nervously, their conversation barely rising above a whisper as they cast glances at the dragons roosting on the Briar's crenellations.

The other group was Velaschin. Barely more than a dozen men and women, all hard-eyed and dressed for war. A few wore the more baroque and intricate armor of the dragon riders that had hunted the paladin, and the rest looked drawn from the army Bren had witnessed marching through the streets. The huge man with the scarred head was there, looking bored by the proceedings. Her chest tightened when she also saw the older dragon lord with the drooping silver mustache. Outside her farmhouse he had appeared grim, but now he was staring up with an appreciative half-smile at the massive flower mural that had been built on the outer wall of the keep.

This must have been what her aunt had been summoned to do. It was quite impressive, she had to admit. Red and white roses were set into a metal frame bolted onto the side of the stone wall, carefully arranged to conjure up a massive crimson dragon with wings outspread against a field of white. The colors of Leris, but the rose had been replaced with the symbol of the Velaschins. A clever way to demonstrate the city's new allegiance, Bren thought, and a worthy backdrop for the ceremony.

Her aunt and the other gardeners who had so hastily constructed this impressive display were nowhere to be seen. No doubt they had been ushered away before the guests had arrived. The First Gardener was here, though, mingling with the great and powerful of Leris. He saw her as well and arched an eyebrow at her. Melichai looked like he was about to disengage himself from the plump, silk-bedecked woman clinging to his arm, but before he could do that, a great chime shivered the air.

All eyes turned to the keep's arched entrance. With slow, measured steps an impressively rotund man emerged into the daylight; his belly strained against a uniform that resembled what the officers in the city wore, but it was of some finer red fabric and this – combined with his shape and rather florid face – made him resemble a giant, waddling strawberry. On his brow rested a diadem of twisted green metal spotted with jeweled flowers, and from the low bows and curtsies his arrival elicited from among the Lerisians, Bren had to assume this was the famous Duke of Thorns. She noticed the Velaschin did not even dip their heads in respect.

"Fine men and women of Leris," the duke proclaimed loudly, spreading his arms wide as if to encompass all those gathered, "we are here for a *momentous* occasion, the wedding of our great city to the glory of the Velaschin Empire." His voice did not tremble, but Bren could see the duke's face glistened, and he cast a quick, nervous glance upwards to where the dragons perched. The monsters had stopped their playing and were now peering down intently at what was happening in the bailey. Bren frowned, wondering just how intelligent they truly were. She'd thought them dumb beasts, but the way they were watching the duke suggested they understood this moment's significance. Also, those . . . emanations she was feeling seemed surprisingly complex. If these emotions were truly radiating from the dragons, then they were indeed no simple animals.

Before she could consider this further, an uneasy murmuring rippled through the nobles of Leris. The black dragon that had been atop the tallest tower moved, then suddenly launched itself into the air. The duke appeared ready to flee back inside the keep, but after a brief struggle that Bren saw play out in his face, he controlled himself. The dragon soared around the tower, then folded its wings against its sides and plummeted towards the courtyard below. Gasps turned to shrieks, but before the nobles could stampede for the gate, the dragon arrested its fall, its wings unfurling. Wind and dust swept over them all as the dragon hovered over the flagstones, wings churning the air.

Bren was rooted to the stone, overwhelmed by the power of its presence. She felt fear, yes, but also awe at its terrible beauty. The dragon seemed molded from darkness – its scales did not flash or glitter like its brethren above, instead greedily devouring the daylight. It looked like a slice of the night given life. The pressure she'd felt in her head returned, far stronger than before.

"You must master your fear," Bren whispered to herself. "Or it will master you."

Easier said than done . . . Whoever had coined that phrase had certainly never been standing before a dragon. The nobles of Leris were now stumbling away from the monster, and the resolve of a few broke completely as they began running for the gates in panic. But Bren did not cower or step back. Ignoring the thudding of her heart and the voice in her head that was screaming at her to flee, she set her shoulders and raised her chin defiantly.

The dragon settled on the ground, regarding the crowd with slitted yellow eyes. Its belly brushed against the stone as it hunkered lower, and at that moment, the alien emotions Bren sensed seemed to crystallize. She felt its disdain, a smug dismissal of the fleeing men and women, laced through with boredom. And there was something else, an affectionate warmth directed towards the one on its back . . . In surprise, Bren's gaze went to the figure half-hidden by a fringe of neck spines. She hadn't realized someone was mounted on the dragon. As she watched, the rider threw down a knotted rope, then swung himself out of the saddle with surprising grace and quickly descended. When he stood on the ground, he laid a gauntleted hand on the glistening black scales, and the emotion Bren had felt a moment ago radiating from the dragon strengthened. Then the rider turned, facing the ashen-faced Duke of Thorns.

It was him.

Bren's legs wobbled, and the world seemed to tilt. The fear that had been battering against her broke through the barriers she had erected, and for a moment she was again hiding behind the shutters of her house.

"My lord," the dragon rider said loudly, striding towards the duke. "Let us get on with it."

His accent was strange, almost archaic, and it took Bren a moment to understand what he had said.

Being addressed roused the duke from his stupor. He blinked watery eyes at the tall warrior, then nodded shakily.

"Yes, yes," he murmured. "The wedding."

The dragon rider's face could have been carved from marble. "Wedding?"

The duke gulped; it looked like he was trying to swallow his fear and failing. "The wedding between Leris and your empire."

A humorless smile cracked the dragon rider's face. "This is no wedding, my lord. Your city is merely another concubine for the emperor's harem."

The huge, scarred general barked a laugh at this, and the sound jarred Bren from her paralysis. She drew in a deep, shuddering breath, suddenly realizing just how close she was standing to the man who had killed her family. Her fingers twitched, brushing the pommel at her side.

Let me in.

The voice swelled in her mind. Accompanying it was a vision etched so fine Bren could have believed it was a memory if she didn't know better. She saw herself stepping forward from the crowd and quickly crossing the distance to where the duke knelt before the Velaschin warrior. Cries of alarm erupted, but she was too fast, her sword flickering from its sheath as she lunged. The man turned, his eyes widening in surprise just as the pale metal took him in the neck. Flesh and bone parted, and then his head was toppling from his shoulders as the dragon bellowed.

She came to herself. Her hand was gripping the hilt so tightly her fingers ached. Her body trembled, straining to rip the sword free and make true what she had just witnessed.

Let me in.

Her heart flailed. The images in her head had been a promise. Death, for the one she had sworn to kill. Vengeance.

The duke was kneeling in front of the dragon lord, but whatever oath he was intoning was lost to the roaring in her ears. Cold sweat prickled her skin.

Now! She had to give herself over to the voice *now* before the chance was lost.

The vision rose again, showing what might come after. She saw herself twisting and spinning through a storm of blades, blood arcing as her sword plunged into white Velaschin flesh. A shadow loomed above her, and then claws were tearing through her back, flensing her to the bone. She fell forward, surrounded by dead Velaschin, the dragon lords that still lived lunging forward to stab her with their black-bladed swords.

Bren returned to herself with a gasp. The image of her mutilated corpse lying on the stone lingered in her mind, slowly fading.

A glorious death.

That voice again, echoing from elsewhere.

Death. She would die, but she would have her revenge. Hadn't she told Tal she would make that trade? Why was she hesitating? *Why?*

The dragon lord turned from the still-kneeling duke. He held the twisted green diadem with its glittering jewels in his hands. He did not place it on his own brow but held it up as a roar rose from the gathered Velaschin. The Lerisians looked less pleased, the women in their frothy dresses clutching at the arms of stone-faced men.

"A glorious day for the empire, isn't it?"

It took Bren a moment to realize that someone was speaking to her. The Velaschin were still cheering, thrusting their closed fists into the air as the dragon lord brandished the crown to the crowd.

She turned to find the older Velaschin warrior with the silver mustache standing at her shoulder. He smiled at her when he saw he had her attention, the lines around his storm-grey eyes crinkling.

Bren felt disoriented by the friendliness she saw in his face . . . and the realization that he had used the same word as the strange voice in her head. *A glorious death, a glorious day.*

"I said this is a glorious day for the empire," he repeated, raising his voice as the cries from the Velaschin crested. He had the same odd accent as the other dragon rider, but even more pronounced.

"I suppose so," Bren replied, her mouth suddenly dry. She glanced at the warrior who had received the duke's oath of fealty – he was moving among his fellows now, accepting their praise. Bren's hand trembled, still clutching her sword's hilt.

"Are you a trader?" the old dragon rider asked. "You're not with the army. Did you stay behind in the city when the others left?"

"No," Bren replied. "I'm not a trader."

The Velaschin's face creased in puzzlement. "Not with the army, not a merchant, dressed in such finery with a sword at your side, your words flavored like the people of this land . . . I have to admit, I'm intrigued. You look like a blademaiden from the old stories!" He said this jovially, but a stab of shame went through Bren at his words. She didn't know what a blademaiden was, but she was sure they wouldn't be standing frozen as the man they'd sworn to kill celebrated victory only a few steps away.

"I was a foundling," Bren heard herself saying. "I was raised near Leris."

Surprise deepened in the old warrior's craggy face. "A foundling? You have never been to Velasch?"

She gave a tight shake of her head. The voice inside her had gone silent, as if accepting that she had made her decision. She just wasn't ready to die today, the Silver Mother curse her cowardice.

"To never see the Wraiths rising through the mists, the gray shores of Gesian, the tombs of Yiss . . ." He blew out his breath, making his mustache tremble.

Around them, the Velaschin had begun to mingle with the larger crowd of Lerisians. The nobles still looked nervous and a bit numbed by all that had happened, but the Velaschin had clearly been instructed to try to put them at ease. Servants carrying trays with fluted silver cups had appeared, offering drinks to nobles and dragon lords alike. Evidently, they were meant to be celebrating this new union.

"I am Agiz ben-Ahzan, sworn to the Flamehold and the Second Wing," the old warrior said, clapping his fist to his chest before bowing shallowly. He paused, watching her expectantly, and it took Bren a moment to realize he was waiting for her to introduce herself.

"My name is Brenna. I was the daughter of Gelin Kaelingsun."

"Was?"

"He . . . died."

The dragon rider touched two fingers to his brow. "Condolences. I know the pain of losing the ones you love."

Bren could only stare at the old warrior, her thoughts scattered. She was being comforted by the man whose dragon had burned her father alive.

He seemed to sense her distress as he hurriedly continued. "Not that it brings back those you have lost, but you should be gladdened at what we have witnessed here today." He swept out his hand, indicating the milling crowd of Velaschin and Lerisians. "We might have taken this city with fire and blood if the Duke of Thorns had been a less reasonable man or Vanoc ben-Karth not so merciful. Thousands would have perished."

Bren nodded at the dragon rider who had received the duke's surrender. "Is that Vanoc ben-Karth?"

"Aye," the old man said, and Bren could hear the pride. "He is the best of us. The hero that will unite these lands."

"A hero, is he?"

The old man glanced at her sharply, surprised by her tone. "He is. Three cities have already fallen to the First Army and the Second Wing, and none were sacked. Under another command – such as General Haethan Varyxes – the streets would have run red." He gestured at the huge, scarred warrior who had withdrawn from the crowd and was leaning against the rose mural with a silver cup in each hand. He didn't seem to care that he'd obliterated much of one of the dragon's legs, the crushed blossoms strewn about his boots.

"I must be away, Brenna," the old man told her, his friendly smile returning. "Vanoc wants us to ingratiate ourselves with these popinjays, convince them that our rule does not threaten their stations." As he started to leave, he hesitated, turning back to her. "May I ask how old you are?"

The question caught Bren off-guard, and she answered without thinking. "Sixteen."

The old warrior stroked his mustache thoughtfully. "You know, I have been watching you since you arrived. You can feel them, can't you? The dragons."

Bren wanted to deny this, but she found herself nodding slightly.

Agiz's smile returned. "I thought so. You're one of the Blood, then. How interesting."

"The Blood?" Bren whispered, her throat suddenly dry.

He shook his head as if amazed by her ignorance. "Of course, you wouldn't know. It means an ancestor of yours belonged to one of the four great houses of Velasch. I wonder how you came to these shores! But that does not matter, I suppose." The old warrior's gaze went to one of the green monsters perched far above. "Those born of the Blood can bond with the dragons if they are lucky and strong enough to claim a hatchling. Now, there are hundreds of others with the same potential, but still it is a great opportunity. You should not squander it."

"What—"

Agiz snapped his fingers, interrupting Bren.

"Aha! I just remembered. There will be a Winnowing next month in Yestra on the eve of the summer solstice. An egg was laid by Vera's storm not long after she fell. Terribly sad, for she would have been overjoyed to see Mist a mother."

"A . . . Winnowing?"

"Yes, it's the ceremony when all those with the Blood compete for the favor of the hatchling. In Velasch, there would be hundreds vying to bond with the new dragon, but here in these lands, I doubt there are forty Blooded of the proper age. Not terrible odds, I have to say. You should attend – the Sisters cannot turn you away. Every child of Velasch who is descended from the first four and has seen at least fifteen summers must be allowed to compete in the Winnowing."

Bren found she couldn't drag her eyes from the creature looming over them. Her, a dragon rider? Madness.

"I must leave you, Bren. But think about what I've said. And if you do decide to take your chance, remember my name: Agiz ben-Azhan. It will open any door in the empire."

With a final smile, the old warrior left her, moving towards where Vanoc ben-Karth was now holding court surrounded by a few other

Velaschin and what looked to be the most important Lerisian nobility, including the Duke of Thorns.

Bren was not alone for long, though, as almost immediately the First Gardener materialized at her side. He was holding one of the silver cups, and from the flush in his cheeks, it wasn't his first.

"Don't you look dashing," he said, spilling some of his drink as he gestured at her. "And you seem to have charmed that dragon rider. Tell me, was that Agiz ben-Azhan?"

She nodded slightly, still trying to accept what she'd just been told.

Melichai whistled. "A legend of his people. The Old Drake, they call him. At his age, most would have been put out to pasture, yet here he is. What did you two talk about?"

Bren shook her head, feeling foolish to even give voice to what the dragon rider had told her. "He said I should attend something called the Winnowing. That I might end up with my own dragon."

Melichai goggled at her, then burst out laughing. "You, a dragon rider? Lucky he didn't see you dressed like a peasant." He reached up to pinch her cheek, and she had to restrain herself from slapping his hand away. "Still, you served your purpose. Now he knows we do not mistreat milkies."

Bren felt an intense wave of dislike for the First Gardener, but he seemed oblivious. An elegantly coiffed Lerisian lady touched his arm, and he turned away, instantly forgetting Bren as he disappeared into the swirling crowd.

Her fingers brushed the pommel at her side, but the sword remained quiet. Grimacing, Bren whirled and began striding back towards the gate, her stomach churning with self-loathing and no small amount of confusion.

10

A gray lethargy settled over Bren during the days that followed. She ate, she slept, she accompanied her aunt out into the Garden to prune the flowers and help with the shopping. Life in Leris seemed to have changed little with the Velaschin occupation. Guardsmen in rose livery patrolled the streets, matrons frequented the market, and old men still lounged outside in the evenings on stools playing calat. There were some small differences that Bren noticed through the haze in which she was drifting. Children had all but vanished. Where before the little ones had been allowed to play and scamper about so long as they were within sight of their homes, now they were locked away inside. And Bren noticed nervous glances directed skyward and towards the distant, looming fortress where the dragons still perched like terrifying gargoyles.

She found it difficult to make idle talk, even when her aunt tried to draw her out. A hollowness had been growing inside her ever since the ceremony at the Briar. She felt numb, emptied of all emotions except one.

Guilt.

She had stood a dozen paces away from the man who had murdered her family. The spirit in the sword had shown Bren what could be. Her blade separating his head from his shoulders. Then an avalanche of steel and scales falling on her, sending her to join her family. And when she stood before them in the shadow of the Silver Mother, she could look them in the eyes and say they had been avenged. A shepherdess slaying a dragon lord.

Yet she had hesitated, letting the moment slide past. Bren had no illusions about ever having such a chance again. It had only been an unlikely confluence of events – or perhaps the goddess's guidance, and this thought made her shame burn hotter – that had put her within sword reach of the dragon rider.

She had learned she was a coward. Bren had dreamed about being a hero since she was small, but in the end she had proven herself unworthy. Just a foolish, selfish girl.

"I'm going to buy some bread for tomorrow."

Bren roused herself from the mire of her thoughts. She was standing in the middle of a busy street, but she'd barely taken notice of what was going on around her. Heralia was looking at her expectantly, poised at the threshold of a bakery. The rich smell of baking bread slipped from the open door, and for the first time in days Bren felt her appetite stirring.

Her aunt appeared to notice this. "Would you like something? A fruit tart, perhaps?"

Bren shook her head, for some reason feeling guilty. "No, I'm fine."

Heralia stared at her a moment longer, her lips pursed, and then vanished inside the bakery. The disappointment Bren had seen in her aunt's face made her feel even worse, and she almost followed her into the shop. But after a few steps, the bleakness rose up in her again, and she turned to stare blankly at a tired old nag as it clopped down the street hauling a cart half-filled with vegetables.

"Bren!"

She blinked, looking around to see who had spoken.

"Over here!"

The voice had come from the darkness of a narrow alley beside the bakery, a space barely wide enough to squeeze into.

Bren approached cautiously, peering into its depths. "Hello?"

A familiar face emerged from the shadows.

"Tal!" Bren cried, just stopping herself from rushing over to embrace the boy.

He smiled, though she thought it looked a little forced. Even in the dim light, she could see the dark circles under his eyes.

"How's life in the Garden?" he asked, staying in the alley. She assumed he must be wary of the watch, so she left the street to join him, casting a quick glance to make sure her aunt was still inside the bakery.

"It's . . . good," she said slowly.

He must have seen something in her face. "Bren, what's wrong?"

Something cracked inside her. Her face crumbled as she fought and failed to keep the tears at bay.

"Bren!" Tal said with fresh worry. "Did something happen?"

"Yes. No." Bren slumped against the wall of the bakery. She angrily wiped at her face, disgusted with her weakness. "I was there at the Briar when the duke surrendered the city. With my sword. I could have *killed* the man who murdered my family. But I couldn't bring myself to do it. I knew I would die, and I was too scared, too much of a coward . . ."

She swayed, feeling light-headed, and then Tal was there. His arm went around her shoulder to help steady her.

"I didn't know your family," he began, and she could tell he was choosing his words carefully, "but I am absolutely certain they would not want you to die for them."

Bren blinked into his tunic, dampening it with her tears. She thought of her mother, singing as she cooked. Her father dandling Helat on his knee. Tal was right, she knew – they would not want her to avenge them if it meant her death. That terrible, constricting knot inside her loosened slightly.

She pulled away from him, feeling like she could breathe freely again for the first time in days. "I think . . . I think you're right. Thank you."

Tal crooked a smile. "It's nothing. I owe you, Brenna, daughter of

Gelin." He paused, then glanced at her sidelong. "And actually . . . there's something else as well."

"What?" Bren asked, wiping the wetness from her face.

"Someone wants to meet you."

"Me?" Who even knew her, save for the First Gardener, his tailor, and an old dragon rider?

"Aye. The Ratman was the one who reached out to me, but it's not him who's interested in you. He's just the middleman setting this up."

Bren frowned. "You have no idea who it is?"

Something flashed in his face and was gone. "No. But whoever it is wants this meeting to be secret. The location is somewhere far from the eyes of the Velaschin."

"And why would I want to go?"

Tal ran his hand through his thick hair. He looked nervous, she thought. "The word is that whoever will be waiting for you is offering something he or she knows you desire."

"But I don't want anything." *Except revenge. And to go on living, apparently.*

The boy shrugged. "The Ratman wouldn't have come to me unless he was certain this person was someone worth meeting."

Bren chewed her lip, considering what Tal had said. Could this stranger truly offer her what she wanted? What did she have to lose by meeting with them?

"Brenna!" Her aunt's voice came, loudly calling for her. "Where did you get to, girl?"

Bren glanced at the alley mouth, wondering what her aunt would think if she saw her skulking about in the shadows.

"I have to go," she told Tal.

"Will you come?"

Bren nodded. "So long as you think it's safe."

Another flicker of something in his expression, quickly controlled. "Good. Meet me here tonight after your aunt goes to bed. And we'll be back before morning, I promise."

"Brenna, where are you?" The panic creeping into her aunt's voice made Bren feel guilty.

"Coming!" Bren shouted. As she began moving towards the street, his hand suddenly grabbed her wrist.

"Oh, and Bren," he said quietly, as if he was afraid someone was listening. "Bring your sword."

THE NIGHT WAS DARK, the Mother and her daughters hazy smudges behind a thick blanket of clouds. Despite this, Bren found it easy enough to find her way back to the alley. The lamplighters in the Garden kept the streets well-illuminated, and warm light spilled from many of the windows and doors. In the Tangle, half the buildings had been dark, with shadows scurrying at the fringes of what little could be seen, but the Garden was a much more welcoming place.

Which made Bren wonder why Tal had told her to come armed.

"Hello?" she whispered as she approached the darkened mouth of the alley. "Are you there?"

The darkness shivered as Tal stepped out into the street. His clothes blended with the night, and he moved silently.

"I can see why you chose your name," she murmured as she came up beside him. "You look like a shadow."

After glancing up and down the street, he beckoned for her to follow him. "Come here, out of the light," he said quietly. "If any of the watch see us skulking about, they'll either chase us away or drag us to the Maw for questioning."

Bren hurried to join him, and together they plunged into the darkness. "What is this all about?" she asked, then gasped in surprise as something small with sharp claws scrambled over her foot. "And where is this meeting?"

"Someplace safe," he replied, his fingers tangling with hers as he drew her deeper into the black. "You have to trust me." He paused for a moment. "You do trust me, don't you?"

"I do," Bren said without hesitation. Was that foolish? Tal was a thief and an orphan. But the thought that he would betray her seemed almost impossible to contemplate. They'd been through so much together. Tal didn't reply to her, but she felt his hand tighten in hers.

The vague map that Bren had constructed in her head of the Garden was rendered useless almost immediately. Tal stuck to the alleys and side streets, only dashing across the main thoroughfares when he needed to reach the shadowed entrance to another one of the small passages that veined the district. Bren tried to orient herself by finding the Briar, but though she caught brief glimpses of its bulk, the twists and turns of the path they followed quickly confused her again. She noticed with some unease that Tal paused several times, his head tilted as if listening for something. Pursuit, she assumed . . . but why would anyone be following them?

Finally, they arrived at a massive, crumbling gate. In the guttering light of the lonely lantern, Bren saw that the stonework of the pillars was carved with faces. Some stared serenely, lips pressed together, while the mouths of others shrieked, eyes wide and wild. Beyond the cracked-open barrier stretched a dark expanse – there were no streets or buildings, though she could see a vague tangle of shapes picked out against the night.

"Leris's lichyard," Tal whispered, letting go of her hand as he slipped through the gate.

Bren hesitated, staring at the graves closest to the entrance, which were illuminated by the hanging lantern's light.

"Why are we going in there?"

"Far away from prying eyes," Tal whispered, motioning for her to join him. "Come on. We're already late."

"Late for *what*?" Bren grumbled, tempted to grab Tal and shake him until some answers spilled out.

"Our meeting. It's not far now."

Bren gritted her teeth, but she followed Tal as he moved deeper into the lichyard. The clouds had thinned, and the hazy outline of the Silver Mother gilded the monuments and gravestones with a spectral light. Statues of men and women looking heroic or pious loomed from the darkness, and Bren couldn't help but imagine their trespassing was watched with disapproval.

At last they came to an ancient, tumbled tomb set into the side of a hill. Tal picked his way through the shattered entrance, the ghostly radiance of his pebble swelling to play upon scattered chunks of stone. Earth had burst through the far wall and spilled across the floor. Bren could see shards of white gleaming in the dirt – bones, she suspected at first, but when she moved closer she saw they were actually pale roots, glistening like entrails.

Tal went to a corner of the tomb and crouched, his fingers tracing the outline of something embedded in the floor. A handle, Bren realized, and now that she was looking, she could see a hatch. Grunting with the effort, Tal pulled the trapdoor open to reveal a chute leading down into darkness.

"The undercity again?" Bren asked dubiously as the boy swung himself over the edge and began to descend quickly using the metal rungs bolted onto the side.

Tal paused; only his head remained above the floor, and the darkness had rushed into the tomb to replace the pebble's light. His face was still lit from below, making him seem like a wraith rising from its grave.

"It's the safest place in the city," Tal told her. "No guards or dragons down here. Only mice."

His head vanished, and Bren had to hurry to follow so she wouldn't be left behind in the tomb.

Her sheathed sword bumped against the narrow walls as she descended hand over hand; some of the rungs shifted slightly, but most were firmly fixed into the earth. Bren wondered what had compelled the builders of this tomb to include an entrance to the catacombs below Leris. Or perhaps that had been its purpose all along, hidden in plain sight.

They entered a soaring chamber up near its vaulted ceiling, and she tried to avoid glancing down at the floor far below her. If one of the rungs pulled loose now, she'd likely shatter every bone in her body. Forcing herself to stare straight ahead, she tried to ignore the drop, not daring to look down until her boots touched the ground.

Tal's light crawled over the room, though it dissipated before illuminating the far reaches. What could be seen was impressive. Faded frescoes covered the walls, images of animal-headed giants cavorting madly with men and women wearing flowing robes. In the scene closest to Bren, the Gith were dancing around a stag-headed creature playing upon shepherd's pipes, but as her eyes traveled along the wall she saw other, more macabre moments: a demon dangling a babe by his foot over its gaping crocodile jaws as a human woman – presumably the child's mother – clutched at its leg. The vast chamber was empty save for these decorations, though a circular pit had been cut in the center of the floor. Tal was already on the lip of this abyss, peering over the edge, and he beckoned her to approach.

"Listen," he said and then tossed a chunk of rock into its depths.

Bren waited, then frowned. "I don't hear anything."

"Exactly," Tal said, crouching down so that his pebble's light slid further down the smooth sides of the well.

"How deep does it go?" Bren asked, unnerved by the strangeness of this place.

Tal shrugged. "Who knows? We used to enter the undercity here, Quiet and Knives and me, exploring to look for treasures, and though we dared each other to climb down, no one ever did. Some things are better left alone."

Bren dragged her gaze from the blackness welling up from below, suppressing a shudder. "I don't like it here."

"We call it the Dread," Tal said, standing and moving away from the hole. "That sense of . . . wrongness."

"I feel like we're being watched," Bren said, her gaze lingering on one of the Gith demons. Black eyes stared at her from a falcon's head, seemingly tracking her as she followed Tal towards one of the chamber's high arched exits.

"Don't worry," the boy said as he led them into a broad corridor, holding his pebble high. Webs clotted the ceiling, spiders the size of her fist hanging among the ghostly threads like bloated fruit. "There are dangers here, but the parts we frequent have had many visitors."

"I thought you said when we were in the Ratman's Burrow that mice occasionally go missing in the undercity?"

"Well . . . that's because they were foolish and strayed from what was known."

"Do you know that for certain, or do you only hope?"

Tal didn't answer her, and Bren chose not to press him further. He did appear to be very well versed in the layout of the undercity, hardly hesitating as he led them down twisting passages and across great echoing chambers. His pebble was not the only light in this labyrinth – high up on the walls, glowing shards were set into the stone, spilling out the same spectral radiance as the statues in the Ratman's lair. Glowstone, she remembered Tal had called it.

They came to an entrance flanked by stone wolves with the heads of snarling men. Despite their ferocity, Tal visibly relaxed at the sight of them, some tension he'd secretly been holding seeping away. He was not as confident as he had appeared, Bren realized with a trickle of fear.

The vast space beyond the wolf-thing guardians blazed not only with the light of glowstone but also a dozen torches held by those waiting for them. They were mostly rough-looking men, clad in battered leather armor with swords at their sides, but Bren also recognized a few of the older mice she'd met during her foray into the Burrow – the boy who had been guarding the door, Whispers, with his mop of curls, and the thin girl Tal had called Bones who had been at the Ratman's side. Of the fat thief, there was no sign.

This chamber was different from any they had yet seen. In its center was a featureless block of some black substance, almost like an anvil or an altar, a ring of stone about knee high encircling it. That circle was then enclosed by another about a half-dozen paces away and then another and another, all the same height, although the distance between them gradually widened. The last nearly brushed the walls, and they had to clamber over it to approach where the others were clustered near the chamber's middle.

"Took your time," called out Whispers, his voice echoing in the great space. It must be fear making Bren giddy because having someone nicknamed whispers speaking so loud almost made her let loose with a panicked little laugh.

"Not like you had anything better to do tonight," Tal replied in the swaggering manner he affected when around his old compatriots. He paused, making a show of looking around. "Where's the Ratman?"

"Surely you didn't think he'd drag himself here?" Whispers said with a snort.

"His gout is getting worse," the wraith-like girl Bones added. "He rarely leaves the Burrow these days."

Tal paused and held up his hand for Bren to do the same. "He was supposed to make the introductions," he said, a note of warning in his voice. "Without him here, how do we know it's safe?"

"Ain't nobody knows about this place except us," Whispers said with a shake of his head. "This is the mice's kingdom, you know that."

"Not entirely true."

Cries of alarm rose up, and steel scraped as the Ratman's men whirled towards this new voice. Bren's hand went to her sword hilt, her heart thudding when she saw that a cowled man now loomed behind the black stone at the chamber's heart. She could have sworn he hadn't been there a moment ago. Next to him was a boy about the same age as Bren, his silver hair shimmering in the torchlight. He leaned against the dark altar with his arms folded and the ghost of a smile on his sharp-featured face.

The shrouded figure ran a spidery finger along the top of the black stone. "This place is known to us. Long ago, it was sacred to the Gith, then later it was repurposed as a temple to the Mother in those early days of her church when Her worship was still forbidden."

"Who are you?" Whispers called out, drawing himself up and puffing out his chest.

The silver-haired boy's smile broadened, and Bren realized it had always been mocking. The man beside him pulled back his cowl, revealing a sunken, hairless head covered in squirming blue markings. And this was not his most unsettling feature, for his eyes were pupilless pools of deepest black. "Do not fear. I am the one who summoned you here."

"Sorcerer," Bren whispered. No wonder Tal had told her so little.

She would have balked if she'd known she was meeting a servant from the House of Jade.

Those sworn to the goddess Nasai were shrouded in mystery. Their help had been vital in casting the demons from the Flowering Coast, but their own willingness to court the darkness was well known. Sorcerers were just as often the villains in the stories as they were the heroes.

The boy's gaze settled on Bren, his smug smile vanishing. "Do you see it?" he asked warningly, his hand going to the hilt at his side. "She looks like the Huntress."

Despite the boy's alarm, the sorcerer's calm expression did not waver. He held up his blue-tattooed hand to keep his companion from drawing his sword.

"She is far too young. And such a resemblance will only be for the best, I believe."

Bren swallowed back her unease and stepped forward. "Who are you?" she asked, repeating Whispers' unanswered question.

The sorcerer slipped his hands into his loose sleeves and attempted what must have been intended as a comforting smile, but it looked ghastly in his cadaverous, blue-painted face. "Greetings Brenna, daughter of Gelin. I am Tharos, and this is Desian. As you have certainly guessed, we are residents in the House of Jade and the servants of holy Nasai." He turned his head, sweeping all those gathered with his gaze. "Great thanks to the Ratman for organizing this meeting."

"Was there a reason you wanted so much muscle here tonight?" asked Whispers, the bravado in his voice sounding forced.

"That does not concern you—" replied the silver-haired boy sharply, but the sorcerer cut him off with a raised hand.

"We are pursued," Tharos said. "The Velaschin do not worship the Mother, and they fear the power of Her second daughter. These dragon lords have assassins trained to hunt sorcerers, and many of my brothers and sisters have already fallen to their knives. The one we call the Huntress very nearly caught us recently, and if the Mother is merciful, then she still believes us dead. But we cannot take that chance."

"What do you want with me?" Brenna asked, surprised by how steady her own voice sounded.

The sorcerer studied her for a long moment with his fathomless eyes. "Very little fear. That is good. And it is not what *I* want, but what I can give you." He paused, letting the weight gather behind his next pronouncement. "Vengeance."

Bren's heart leaped in her chest; she certainly felt afraid, despite what the sorcerer had claimed. But what was he really offering her? Her hands were clenched so tight that her fingernails bit into her palms. "I stood a dozen paces away from the man who killed my parents," she found herself saying. "I could have stepped forward and stabbed him through the heart, but I did not."

The sorcerer's bloodless lips twitched upwards. "So brave and honest. Perhaps we have found a replacement for our paladin."

"Perhaps she fears what we will ask," said the boy at his side.

"I think not," Tharos said, gliding closer to loom over her. Bren sensed Tal stumbling back a step, but she refused to be intimidated by this apparition, lifting her chin to meet his empty gaze.

"You see, Desian? There is steel in her. Tell me, child, was it fear of death that stilled your hand at the Briar . . . or perhaps the fear that a single death would not be worth your own?"

Bren blinked. Could he be right? Did she want to strike a greater blow against the people who had murdered her family?

The skeletal grin widened. "Yes. One death for four is not a fair trade." He reached up, running his finger along her jawline. She did not flinch, though his touch was freezing cold. "Brenna, I am offering you the chance to inflict a great vengeance on our enemies."

"How?" she whispered hoarsely.

Tharos looked away from her, towards the crowd of cutthroats. He turned to the girl Bones, somehow having realized that she was the true leader here.

"Send your people elsewhere. The matters I have to discuss here are not for your ears."

Bones nodded, looking shaken, and then with a few barked commands ordered the men she had brought to take up positions guarding the entrances to the chamber. The sorcerer frowned at Tal when he realized the boy was not going with them.

"And you as well, little thief."

"No," Bren said firmly, reaching out to take Tal's arm. "I trust him."

The sorcerer narrowed his eyes. "Would you trust him with the fate of the kingdom, girl?"

"Yes," Bren replied, refusing to be intimidated.

He held her gaze as if searching for something, then shrugged like Tal's presence truly was of no great importance. "Very well. Perhaps the thief can be of some use."

"My name is Tal," he interjected. "And you're not the first sorcerer I've dealt with."

Hollow eyes slid to the boy beside her. "Oh, I know who you are, bastard. Your birth ruined one of the most promising adepts in the House of Jade. She was never the same after."

A shiver passed through Tal, nearly wrenching his arm from her grip. "You knew my mother?"

"Of course I did, boy," the sorcerer replied, an edge of frustration to his words. "But your sordid story is irrelevant at this moment. Brenna is the one who carries the Mother's hope."

The Mother's hope? "Why me?"

"Surely you can guess, child." His black eyes bored into her, making her skin crawl.

"Because . . . because I look like them. The Velaschin."

His thin lip curled. "Almost. Because you *are* Velaschin. And not just one of their common people . . . I believe you carry the blood of the great houses, the blood that can tame dragons. Tell me, your parents in the Seven Valleys treated you well, yes?"

"Yes," Bren whispered.

"Like their own flesh? Even though your true parents came from across the sea?"

She nodded, her throat tight.

"And they are dead by Velaschin hands."

"By dragon fire," she said softly. "They burned our house after slaying a paladin who had taken refuge with us."

"And how did you survive?"

Bren held up her arm, showing her pale, unblemished skin. "By the Mother's grace. I felt the flames washing over me, consuming my clothes, but when I awoke in the ashes of my house I was untouched."

"It was indeed the Mother's blessing," the sorcerer agreed. "We know this to be true, for what happened was shown to Nasai's servants in a vision. The Mother has a task for you."

"But what can I do? I am nothing. A girl. A shepherdess."

The sorcerer stepped backwards, the tips of his fingers spreading across the surface of the black altar. "Tell me, Brenna, why our kingdom has fallen. Why were our armies routed at Manoch Tir, why did that cowardly duke throw open the gates of this city?"

"Dragons," she murmured.

"Indeed," he said gravely. "Nothing can stand before the Velaschin's monsters. The sorcery of the Jade House, the moonblades of our paladins, the skill of our archers . . . The dragons are as unstoppable as the rising tide." Blue sparks drifted from where the sorcerer's fingers brushed the black altar, as if summoned by his rising passion. "And we are but a steppingstone. After all the cities of the Flowering Coast have bent the knee, they will turn their attentions inward, towards the Dominion and other lands, until they straddle the entire continent. They will not stop until Old Gith is whole once more . . . except this time, the tyranny will be brought on dragon wings, not with demon magic."

Bren jumped as azure light flared from his fingertips, but the sorcerer did not seem to notice this had happened. He was staring so intently at her that she felt like she was on the verge of being swallowed by the absences that were his eyes.

"We need dragons of our own," he said.

Bren blinked. "But . . . how . . ."

"The Winnowing," the sorcerer continued, speaking over her

confusion. "A test to determine which of the Velaschin youth are worthy of becoming a dragon lord. We know you were already told of this by the old rider Agiz ben-Ahzan that day at the Briar."

"How do you know about what we spoke?" she asked, feeling like she was floating outside herself.

The sorcerer fluttered his fingers as if such a question was irrelevant. "The Jade House has many servants, and not all are sorcerers. If something of great import happens, we have eyes and ears in attendance. The *how* is not important . . . What matters is that we know what the old dragon rider told you, of his invitation for you to attend the Winnowing that will be held in Yestra."

"But I am no true Velaschin. Surely that means I would fail this test."

The sorcerer smirked. "Perhaps that would be true if you were to make the attempt as you are now. But I believe we can put our finger on those scales."

"Quite literally," the silver-haired boy interjected, then chuckled at his own wit.

A coldness was stealing into Bren. What was the sorcerer saying? That he could help her claim a dragon?

"There are two parts to this Winnowing," the sorcerer continued, the tone of his voice becoming more academic. "In the first, the Velaschin children on the cusp of becoming adults are brought before a dragon's egg. If the beast inside stirs, this means the child has the potential to bond with it. We know the old rider believed you to be Blooded, but there are far more born with this potential than there are dragon eggs."

Bren tried to ask a question, but the sorcerer raised a finger to silence her.

"So a second test is needed to determine who is truly worthy. What this is exactly we do not know. It is a closely guarded secret, and it may change with each new Winnowing." He turned his finger until it was pointing at her chest. "Brenna, you must pass these tests. You must claim a dragon, train in their empire across the seas . . . and then you must steal for us our own clutch of eggs."

Bren felt like she was drowning as the full weight of the sorcerer's words washed over her.

"But . . ." Tal interrupted, his face showing his concern. "How do you know the dragon will recognize her? Perhaps the old rider was wrong? She might not even pass this first test."

"We would leave little to chance," the sorcerer replied. Something green and glistening was in his hand now, though she hadn't seen him reach into his robes. He held up this object, and she saw it was a thin, flat disc of jade, smaller than her palm. Streaks of darker color swirled within, reminding her of the summer sky during a storm. "We have infused this disc with the same sorcery that burns in the heart of dragons. We believe that any hatchling in its shell will instinctively respond to one that bears this artifact."

Bren stared at the disc warily. "So I would . . . carry this?" The madness of this all was making her dizzy. Her, a dragon rider? And then a thief stealing away eggs? She should turn around and leave now. How could *she* be responsible for the sorcerer's insane plan succeeding?

"We do not know if jewelry is allowed to be worn during the first test of the Winnowing," the sorcerer said, holding out the disc. "Give me your arm."

She hesitated, unsure what he intended.

"Now, girl!" he hissed, and against her better judgment, Bren held out her hand.

The sorcerer did not place the object in her palm – instead, he reached further up her arm and pressed the disc against her skin. It felt as cool and smooth as a river stone.

"Bren . . ." Tal murmured.

"It's all right," she told him. "It doesn't hurt."

Bren gasped as the sorcerer's other hand suddenly closed around her wrist. Instinctually she tried to pull away, but his grip was like iron.

"What are you—"

Bren screamed as burning pain flared where the jade disc touched her skin. Flames raced through her veins, darkness pressed at the edges of her vision, and she collapsed to her knees. Her bile rose, and she spilled the contents of her stomach on the stone in front of her, spattering the hem of Tharos's robe. The sorcerer ignored this, holding her arm as the strange words he spoke shivered the air. She sensed motion near her, and with tremendous effort, she focused enough to see Tal struggling frantically with the silver-haired boy.

"Bren!" he screamed, but her name was like the murmur of thunder in the very great distance.

The sorcerer let go of her wrist and she fell forward, her cheek striking the cold stone. Blood mingled with the taste of vomit in her mouth. Moving her arms and legs weakly, she tried to push herself to her knees, but it was like all her strength had drained away. There was nothing inside her except for the fire consuming her muscles and bones and blood, leaving behind a hollowness filled with ash.

More screams. It didn't sound like Tal, but who else could it be? She recognized the faint shriek of metal. Had Tal wrested a sword from somewhere? It sounded like he was fighting his way through an army to get to her.

She had to help him.

Gathering every shred of her will she could muster, Bren lifted herself from the floor with trembling arms. Grunting with the effort, she shoved herself into a sitting position, her aching arm dangling limp in her lap. Her head lolled, and she squinted to try to determine where this clamor was coming from.

She didn't understand what she was seeing. The largest of the chamber's entrances was filled with men, a knot of churning chaos. Torchlight glinted on silvery steel and was swallowed by curved black blades.

Velaschin.

Bren tried to stand, but her legs were like reeds, and she collapsed again. Her arm was still burning where the sorcerer had pressed the jade disc to her flesh, and a less painful but still uncomfortable warmth was spreading through the rest of her.

One of the Ratman's men screamed, clawing at his throat as a filament of glistening darkness wound around his neck. In her half-conscious stupor, she followed this squirming tendril to a handle held by a Velaschin warrior. Bren gasped – it was the third dragon rider from that terrible night. With a flick of her wrist, the Velaschin uncoiled the whip from around the man's throat, and as he fell to his knees gasping for breath she slashed with the black-bladed sword she held in her other hand, severing his head from his body. She was grinning fiercely, her pale face spattered with blood. Around her, the slaughter was almost complete, only a handful of the Ratman's thugs still standing.

"The Huntress!" the silver-haired boy hissed, and Bren could hear his fear. "She's found us!"

"Run," the sorcerer said hollowly. "I will stall them. Take the girl to Yestra before the Winnowing. Prepare her well."

The boy looked stricken. "And leave you?"

"You must," the sorcerer barked, the blue markings on his face starting to writhe.

Strange words spilled from his mouth, making the air tremble. To Bren, it seemed like a stone had been dropped onto the surface of the world, sending out ripples. The dragon rider had also noticed the sorcerer's chanting, and as the last of the Ratman's men fell she screamed a command and pointed with her obsidian sword towards where they stood, the whip she held in her other hand twisting like a living serpent.

Every torch was instantly extinguished, darkness rushing into the ancient temple. Cries of surprise rose up, and Bren nearly joined them before she realized that panicking would only lead the Velaschin right to her.

She almost screamed anyway when a hand closed around her wrist.

"We must go," the silver-haired boy growled in her ear. He pulled her roughly to her feet, and this time her unsteady legs didn't collapse beneath her.

"Tal," she slurred, a thickness in her throat.

"I'm here," she heard him say from close by. A spectral radiance swelled, and the light from his pebble pushed back the dark. She saw him standing a few paces away, etched in gray, and then the silver-haired boy holding on to her snarled one of those strange, echoing words and the light abruptly vanished.

"Fool!" the sorcerer cried as he began to drag Bren through the black. "You'll get us all killed!"

More shouts were rising up behind them – the Velaschin had certainly seen that brief flash.

While she was being pulled forward, Bren reached back desperately in the direction of where she'd last seen Tal, and she gasped in relief when her fingers closed around cloth, maybe the hem of his sleeve. A heartbeat later, his hand found her arm, and she hissed in pain as he touched the spot where the sorcerer had pressed the jade disc.

Across the chamber, a flower of green flame bloomed and then wilted, sending a wave of hot air washing over them. Bren stumbled and nearly fell, and it was only the boy's strong grip on her that kept her from sprawling face-first on the stone.

More blasts erupted from behind them, dust and small stones sifting down from above. The triumphant cries from the Velaschin several moments ago had turned to screams of pain and fear.

"Careful, there are stairs here," the silver-haired boy said, somehow calm despite the chaos.

Even with his warning she would have tumbled down the steps, but the sorcerer had been expecting this and braced himself to catch her.

"Oh!" she cried, her face slamming into the boy's chest just as Tal collided with her back, and they all teetered dangerously at the top of the steps.

The boy steadied himself, letting out what sounded like a rather colorful curse in a language Bren did not know, and then he started descending the stairs.

"Quickly," he whispered, and with great care Bren followed, testing to make sure there actually was another step every time before she committed fully. The thought of what might happen if the stairs suddenly ended in a great drop made her queasy.

When they finally reached the bottom, Bren could have kissed the stone beneath her feet.

"We need light," the sorcerer commanded. There were still screams and rumbling coming from above, but the sounds were muted.

"A please would be appreciated," Tal muttered, but a moment later his pebble's ghostly radiance appeared.

They stood at the base of a broad set of stairs leading up into darkness in a chamber much smaller than the temple they had just fled. Sconces lined the walls, their tarnished metal fashioned into heads that looked vaguely man-like despite their elongated features. The silver-haired boy glanced back the way they had come, as if hoping to see the sorcerer hurrying down the stairs, then frowned and started towards the lone arched passage.

"Come on!" he snapped. "They'll be following our trail soon!"

11

They fled through the echoing halls of the undercity, taking corridors seemingly at random. When they came to a massive domed chamber, its ceiling veined by a tracery of golden threads, the silver-haired boy hesitated only a moment in front of the three darkened exits before choosing the only one without jagged runes carved above the lintel. They descended spiraling stairs and crossed a gallery where hooded glowstone statues glowered from niches set in the walls. The passages bent unnaturally, twisting in upon themselves like a maze designed by a madman, and more than once they found themselves where Bren was sure they had been before.

The weakness in her legs gradually faded and was replaced by a stitch in her side. At first, it was like the tip of a knife pressed against her skin, but before long the entire blade was plunged deep. When they finally stopped, Bren doubled over, gasping.

"Do you hear anything?" the sorcerer asked.

Bren tried to ignore the stabbing pain and straightened, tilting her head as she listened for any pursuit. They now stood in a circular chamber, curving walls meeting at a point high above where a monstrous face carved of glowstone sneered down at them. Glimmering points that might have been constellations were incised into those walls, and in the center of the room was a cistern of dark water. Benches were arrayed around this pool, and Bren let Tal take her by the arm and lead her over to one. She collapsed heavily on the slab of cold stone, her body trembling.

"Don't get too comfortable," the silver-haired boy said. "We'll have to go soon."

Tal slipped onto the bench beside her. "We lost them, sorcerer. There's no way they're following us through that labyrinth."

The boy shook his head. "That was the Huntress, bastard. She's tracked down a dozen powerful sorcerers, and somehow she can see through all our guile. We thought we'd fooled her with an illusion showing our deaths, but she has some power we do not understand."

Bren felt Tal stiffen beside her when the apprentice called him a bastard again, and she glanced over to see him glaring at the boy in distaste.

"It's sorcery she's tracking?" Tal spat back. "Then we should go our separate ways. You're the only sorcerer here."

The boy ignored his tone. "I would if I was certain she'd follow me. But the girl has just experienced a powerful incantation. For all I know, the Huntress would be more likely to stay on her scent."

"I'm not 'the girl'," Bren said sharply. "And he's not 'the bastard'. I'm Bren, and he's Tal."

The silver-haired boy arched an eyebrow. "Well, you *are* a girl, and he *is* a bastard, but very well. And if we're now on familiar terms . . . I am Desian, an initiate in the House of Jade."

"A sorcerer's git," Tal muttered.

Desian chuckled at the venom in his voice. "Didn't you hear? Bren wants no more name-calling."

"I don't care," snarled Tal, rising from the bench. "You're a snake, just like the other sorcerers. If I'd known it was your master who the Ratman arranged that meeting with, I never would have brought Bren here."

The boy with the silver eyes shook his head and sighed. "Did you forget what just happened? Tharos pulled the attention of the

Huntress onto himself to give us time to escape. He *sacrificed* himself."
The sorcerer's jaw was clenched, and the smug amusement he'd shown a moment ago had vanished. "This isn't just about our lives or who rules this city or that kingdom. The Velaschin will destroy the Houses of Gold and Iron and Jade. They will cast down the Silver Mother Herself."

"They can't do that," Bren said quietly.

The boy whirled at her. "Truly? Do you remember what Tharos said? That place was once a temple dedicated to the Mother. Her followers gathered down there in the dark to worship her, because to do so in the city above would mean their deaths. These lands were once ruled by men who still revered the demon princes of Old Gith, even though that city had fallen long ago. It took much blood and struggle before the Sage of Pearls cast the last of the demons from the Flowering Coast. The Velaschin would tear the Silver Mother from the sky and return her to the depths we stand in now."

Tal did not respond to this outburst, though he was staring daggers at the boy. Could the Velaschin truly wage war against the goddess herself? The Silver Mother was woven into the very fabric of these lands, held fast in the hearts of its people. Surely these invaders would fail if they tried to destroy belief itself.

Or was this mad plan to steal the eggs of dragons the last dice throw of a desperate goddess? Bren's gaze went to the spot on her arm where the sorcerer had pressed the jade circle. Something that might have been taken for a birthmark darkened her skin, and when she brushed this new blemish, she felt a hardness beneath. She glanced up and found Desian watching her with pursed lips.

"Yes," he said with a knowing nod. "You may need that artifact to ensure the hatchling's interest. Tharos has hidden it in your arm so that it will not be taken away before the Winnowing begins. We understand little of the test's true nature, but we do know that those attempting to entice a dragon are not allowed to bring anything with them into the trials."

Bren traced the outline of the disc embedded in her flesh. It still ached, but the searing pain she'd felt earlier was but a memory. Still, the thought of having something *sorcerous* lodged in her body like a splinter was deeply unsettling.

"What is the plan, then?" Tal asked, folding his arms across his chest.

"Much of the plan was just recently torn to shreds and scattered to the wind," Desian replied mockingly, running a hand through his silver hair. "Tharos was planning on taking her under his wing, training Bren so that she would have the best chance of passing the Velaschin's tests. Now . . ." He swallowed, and for a moment, Bren saw the uncertainty he was trying to keep hidden. "Now that task falls to me . . . unless Tharos still lives."

Bren shifted, trying to get more comfortable on the cold stone of the bench. "But you don't think he does."

Desian stared at Bren bleakly. "I do not. I've seen the handiwork of the Huntress. She is a ruthless killer."

"I've seen her before," Bren said softly.

"What?" Tal exclaimed.

"She was there when the dragons burned my farmhouse . . . burned my family."

Tal put a comforting hand on her shoulder as Desian folded his arms across his chest, looking troubled. "How long ago was this?"

"A fortnight, perhaps? Why?"

Desian frowned. "It's nothing. But did she see you?"

Bren thought back to that moment when she'd been peering through the thin crack of the shutters at the three dragon riders standing over the paladin's corpse. "No. I'm sure of it."

"That's good," Desian said, sounding relieved. "If she did and then recognized you at the Winnowing, the game would be up."

"Will she be—" Bren began, but then she gasped, lifting her hand from where it had rested on the bench. The stone had suddenly become painfully cold, like touching ice.

"What is it?" Tal asked.

Bren rose from the bench. The cold had seeped through her leggings, numbing her backside. "I don't know," she said. "This stone suddenly feels frozen."

"Look!" Tal cried, pointing at the pool of black water that filled the center of the chamber. Something had disturbed it, sending tiny ripples traveling across its surface. But there was nothing except the hazy reflection of the glowstone face fixed to the ceiling, floating like a drowned man in the pool's depths. Confusion grew in her when she realized that this image was slowly growing larger. Bren glanced upwards, but the face on the ceiling hadn't changed its position. Which meant . . .

"Something's in the water!" Bren said, scrambling away from the pool.

"Don't let it touch you!" Desian yelled, dashing for the chamber's exit.

Bren followed, Tal beside her, and she saw pure terror in the boy's face when he glanced over his shoulder.

"Sage's mercy," he moaned, then put his head down and ran harder, pulling Bren into the passage where Desian had vanished.

Bren also risked a glance behind her before they left the chamber, and what she saw chilled her to the bone. The ghostly glow had brightened, but now it was coming from the pool, the waters churning like a vast school of fish was feeding just below the surface. Something was emerging from the froth, and to Bren it looked like the demonic face carved into the ceiling, though it was perched atop sloping, spined shoulders, and in the center of its chest was another huge mouth filled with fangs. That lipless maw was stretched wide, and crazed laughter chased Bren as she turned and ran.

They caught up with Desian quickly because he had slowed, clearly unwilling to career blindly through these passageways. Then together they ran until their legs gave out in a small chamber filled with nothing except dust and cobwebs.

"What was it?" Tal asked between panting breaths. "What did you see?"

Bren shook her head, unable to answer through her own labored breathing, and motioned for them frantically to continue their flight.

No one needed convincing.

BREN WASN'T sure how long they ran, but it felt like forever before Desian finally halted, collapsing against a wall in a room mercifully free of monstrous statues or fathomless pits. The sorcerer pressed his face against the crumbling stone, breathing hard. Tal was doubled over, his hands on his knees as he sucked in lungfuls of air. Bren's legs were trembling again, and the stitch in her side had returned, but she seemed to be holding up better than her two companions.

"What was that thing?" Tal asked again, this time directing the question at Desian.

The silver-haired boy scowled, with some effort pushing himself from the wall. "Why should I know?"

"You're a sorcerer – you make deals with creatures like that."

Desian snorted. "You know nothing, *Tal*." The emphasis on the name sounded the same as when he'd called Tal a bastard.

"It was a demon back there, wasn't it?" Tal pressed.

Desian shrugged. "Was it? I don't know; I've never met one. The House of Jade forbids any attempts at contacting powers from places beyond this world, which are what you so ignorantly refer to as demons. Your mother is a cautionary tale for the rest of us."

"Do you think it's following?" Bren interjected quickly before Tal could unleash the anger clouding his face.

Desian slumped, running his hand through his sweat-damp hair. "I don't know. I don't think so. If it *is* an entity from the beyond – and there's no certainty in that – then it's likely bound to that pool of water. Otherwise, it would have fled back to its home long ago. That's something most don't realize about the things you think of as demons – they usually don't *want* to be here."

"Well, I don't want to be here, either," Bren murmured, looking around the chamber. "Tal, do you know where in the undercity we are?"

His brief, humorless laugh was all the answer she needed. "*Ha.* We are far, far off the beaten paths. The mice never venture this far, or if they do, they don't return to tell about it. We are in the deep undercity, and whatever we find down here likely hasn't been disturbed since the Gith roamed these halls."

Bren shivered, staring at the blackness beyond the reach of Tal's pebble. What could their presence stir awake after so many ages?

"If there's any sunlight shining on this situation," Bren finally said, trying to find something good in what had happened, "it's that the Velaschin aren't going to find us. I imagine they'll let the horrors down here do the work for them."

"Yes," Desian muttered, staring at her flatly. "Wonderful."

"We're not dead yet," Tal said, and Bren was pleased to see that the despair she'd glimpsed in his face had been replaced with resolve. "In the Burrow, we had rules about what to do if we took a wrong turn and got lost in the undercity. Take every passage that slopes upwards. Don't touch anything, no matter how valuable it looks. If you feel a wind or hear something that sounds like it might be air flowing, follow it. And whatever you do, *don't* follow any lights that aren't yours."

"That sounds reason . . ." Bren began, but the rest of what she was about to say died in her throat. She squinted, peering more intently at the darkness beyond the pebble's glow.

"Do you see something?" Desian asked, his hand going to the silver hilt of his sword.

"I . . . don't know," Bren murmured. For a moment, it almost looked like the darkness had rippled. Was the boundary of the light shrinking? "Is the pebble fading, Tal?"

"It's never happened before," the boy said with a note of worry. "But it does seem like—"

A tendril of blackness slipped into the light, groping blindly towards them.

"Desian . . ." Bren said, backing away from the glistening black limb.

"Run!" the boy cried, but before he'd taken more than a few steps towards a passage he gave a strangled cry and skidded to a halt. The darkness in front of him was writhing like a nest of shadowy snakes.

"This way!" Bren cried, bolting for the arched doorway that led back the way they'd come, but a black tide rose, cutting off their escape.

"What do we do?" Tal cried. The circle of radiance thrown by his pebble was rapidly dwindling before the roiling darkness. More tendrils were entering the light, questing towards them. Bren dared hope that they were as insubstantial as shadows, but then she heard a wet thwacking as one slapped against the stone. And from somewhere was the sound of a vast bulk being dragged across the floor . . .

Steel scraped as Desian drew his sword. He mumbled something under his breath, and emerald flames flared, coiling around the blade. Tal fumbled a dagger from somewhere, baring it at the encroaching darkness. Bren gripped her hilt and was surprised to find it warm. She unsheathed her sword just as a dozen shadowy arms reached for her.

Let me in.

That familiar pressure came again, swelling in her mind. Immediately, Bren gave herself over to the presence, begging for its help.

"Come in!" she screamed, and out of the corner of her eye she saw Desian's head snap towards her in alarm. "For the love of the Mother, take me!"

"No!" Desian cried, apparently thinking she was speaking to the abomination. Indeed, the living blackness may have thought the same, as shadowy tendrils lunged at her as if they were all commanded by the same will.

And she found her body was no longer her own.

Bren watched in mute astonishment as her sword leaped to meet the first of the grasping arms. The pale metal sliced through it like it was flesh, and a chunk of wriggling black tumbled to the floor. The tendrils seemed to pause, a ripple passing through the darkness pressed against the faltering light, and then they thrust forward again with renewed vigor. A shriek echoed in the undercity unlike anything she had heard before.

Bren twisted, the sword dancing in her hand. Shadowy arms reached for her, but she was too quick, slipping between their attempts to seize her, the blade a flashing scythe. One tendril did wrap around her ankle, and a jolt of coldness traveled up her leg, but she severed it, what pain there was seeming far away.

Screams came again, but human this time. The presence controlling her spared a glance to her left, and Bren glimpsed the silver-haired boy vanish as tendrils dragged him thrashing into the darkness beyond the light. His cries abruptly ended, and the emerald flames crawling along his blade guttered and went out as soon as his sword entered the black.

"Bren!"

The ghost inhabiting Bren ignored Tal's anguished plea for help, focused on slicing apart the arms grasping for her, but with some effort Bren wrenched her head to where the cry had come from. The presence fought her, intent on keeping her from being overwhelmed.

Still, she managed to turn her head enough to see Tal being swallowed by a wave of blackness. His terrified eyes locked with hers, and before he was fully submerged, he threw the ball of ghostly light that was keeping them from being plunged into absolute darkness.

The presence inside her must have realized the importance of Tal's pebble, as her free hand flashed out to catch the light even as she spun into a slash to cut another tendril in twain. The sword thrummed in her grip, seemingly aware of the dozens of grasping arms, shearing through them before they could reach Bren. The light leaking from between her clenched fingers now barely illuminated more than a few paces, but still the blackness could not seize her.

It *wasn't* truly her, though – Bren had given herself over fully to the spirit in the sword. She could only watch numbly as the pale blade reaped the shadows, the black limbs writhing around her feet briefly before dissolving into nothing.

But she knew it was only a matter of time. For every tendril she cut, two more took its place. And losing them seemed not to hurt the thing at all – if anything, the living darkness looming outside her tiny circle of light appeared to be growing larger, as if more of the creature was oozing into the chamber.

Tal and Desian must be dead by now. Their screams had stopped, and the only sounds she heard were her own heavy breathing and the scrape of shadow limbs on stone. Tears wet her cheeks, and her mouth opened, but instead of a sob she heard herself *laugh*. No, not her – it was the ghost.

Searing cold encircled her sword arm. She did not let go of the hilt, but her blade could no longer flicker as the tendrils wrapped her other limbs. Bren wanted to scream, but the blackness rushed over her face, forcing its way into her mouth, clawing down her throat. She choked and spluttered as a thick numbness filled her chest, drowning her . . .

Suddenly, Bren could breathe again. She felt the darkness slither back up from her insides, wrenching her mouth open as it fled her body, and she collapsed. After a moment of gathering her strength and wondering dazedly why she wasn't dead, she pushed herself to her hands and knees with trembling arms. Bren coughed, spattering the stone in front of her face with blood. Spots danced in her vision, and she came dangerously close to passing out.

The spirit was gone. Blinking, Bren found the verdigris-stained hilt lying not far from her. It must have been torn away as the darkness washed over her, and perhaps that was what had cast out the spirit. Her body was clammy, but still she trembled with the exultation of battle, her heart pounding wildly.

Tal.

Groaning, Bren forced herself to stand. She swayed, just managing to find her balance. The rippling black that had filled the chamber had vanished, the light from Tal's pebble once more pushing back the natural dark. Bren scooped the glowing sphere from where it had fallen, searching the edges of what it illuminated.

She heard a hacking cough, and Bren rushed towards the sound, then gave a cry of relief as the light revealed Tal sitting on the floor with a dazed look on his face. He stared at her blankly for a moment before recognition sparked in his eyes.

"Bren," he murmured and then yelped in surprise when she threw herself at him, wrapping him in an embrace.

Looking over his shoulder, she could see Desian a little way off, his arms and legs weakly moving on the stone as he tried to rise.

"I thought you were dead," she said, squeezing him harder.

"Better loosen up a bit," he rasped, "unless you want to be the one that kills me."

Bren couldn't hold back a relieved smile as she released the boy. "What happened?" she asked.

"I don't know. The darkness was holding me; I couldn't move, and there was a coldness spreading. I felt myself drifting away like I was falling asleep. Then I came back to myself sprawled on the floor and feeling like I'd been eaten and eventually coughed back up."

"It was the same for me," Bren said. "I thought—"

"Shhhh," Tal hissed, and she feared he had heard the scrape of that vast bulk returning. She concentrated on the silence, immediately realizing what had drawn his attention.

It didn't sound like the living darkness, thank the merciful Mother. But still a shiver passed through her, as she could only imagine what other horrors roamed these cursed halls.

It was a repeating crack, like wood striking stone. The sound was definitely getting louder, approaching from one of the corridors choked with blackness.

Desian had heard it as well – he'd climbed to his feet by using the wall for support, and now he was leaning against the stone with his head tilted, listening intently. His expression was bleak, as if he had given up all hope of ever escaping this abyss.

Bren quickly went to where her sword lay on the stone. She swallowed, remembering the feeling when she had surrendered herself to the presence inside the blade. This time in her panic she had allowed it to take too much – she'd been like a passenger in her own body, reduced to watching helplessly. But without the sword she would have been overwhelmed immediately by the crawling black. Bren glanced at the shadowy corridor, uncertain what she should do. If the creature hadn't forced her to drop the sword, would it ever have relinquished its grasp on her body? Did she dare wield it again . . . but if she left the haunted blade here, how would they ever survive the undercity?

Bren made her choice. She scooped the sword from the floor,

expecting to be flooded again by the presence, then exhaled in shuddering relief when nothing happened. Steeling herself, she turned to where this new sound was coming from.

A hunchbacked shape draped in heavy robes shuffled from the darkness. It leaned on a cane of twisted wood, and as it clumped closer Bren realized that this was the source of the sound. There was something else as well, a softer clicking that she could only hear now that this stranger had entered the chamber.

Desian was the first to find his voice. "Who are you?" he asked, stooping to grasp the hilt of his own sword.

The robed creature paused as if surprised to be addressed, then swung its head towards the sorcerer.

Bren hissed, her hand tightening on the sword's hilt when she saw what was emerging from the depths of the cowl. It reminded her of something she'd seen years ago when a chirurgeon had come to the Seven Valleys to investigate a suspected case of the blackbelly plague. The doctor had worn a mask with a long, curving beak like a buzzard, and her father had explained to her that this was done so herbs could be packed inside to protect him from the disease.

This time, Bren did not think this was a mask. That softer clicking came again, and her eyes were drawn to the stranger's feet . . . which were splay-toed and clawed like a great bird. She was just about to lunge forward, thrusting her sword, when it suddenly spoke in a halting, reedy voice.

"A fledgling, but with power. Foolish. Do not try your tricks on me, slaver."

Desian drew himself up. "I am of the Jade House, an initiate of the deeper mysteries. You are an abomination of Old Gith, and I reject you, creature, and whatever offers you would make."

The beak opened, emitting a strange croaking. Bren thought the creature might be coughing, but then she realized this was laughter.

"Bargain with you, fledgling? Already you are in this one's debt, yes? Ka-ntelik fled, for the Crawling Doom remembers Res."

"You saved us?" Bren asked, finally lowering her sword.

The hunchbacked creature swiveled to her, recessed eyes briefly gleaming gold in the pebble's light. As the weight of its attention settled on her, the hilt in her hand twitched.

A shudder went through the thing, and Bren heard something like the rustle of feathers. "Ashika. So you survived, in a sense." It dipped its head in a shallow bow. "The Exiles stride the city above – can you feel it? Or were they cast out after your age had already passed? It grows so difficult to remember . . ."

Bren blinked, unsure how to respond. This creature almost sounded like it recognized her. Knew her.

"Come, blademaiden," it continued, the lumps on its back shivering. "Surely your memories are still as sharp as your edge. You could ever hold a grudge, this one knows." The creature moved closer, its cowled head craning forward as it examined her.

"I remember you, trickster."

Bren glanced around in alarm, searching for the source of this voice. She met Desian and Tal's wide eyes – both of them were staring at her.

The voice . . . the voice had come from her. It had been deeper, laced with old anger. Bren reached up to touch her face, as if to make sure her body was still her own.

The creature croaked again. "Much have you missed. Your people were lost, and Belach led Gith to ruin. But what a glorious ruin it was! Such fine feasting in the long decay."

"Belach," the voice spoke through Bren's mouth. Hate swelled in her breast, hot and fierce.

"Aye, blademaiden," the bird-thing said, bobbing its head. "Your deepest fears came to pass; the door was flung open so wide that it could not be easily shut again." The creature spread its arms, indicating the chamber in which they stood. Bren saw its hands were clawed just like its feet. "But much greatness was accomplished. Mighty works were fashioned, such as this labyrinth. The first of the great mazes to be built in this folding."

Bren's head moved of its own accord, her gaze traveling over the ancient chamber. "It is but an emptiness, prowled by ghosts and shadows."

"What are you saying, Bren?" Tal asked. His fingers tugged on her sleeve, pulling at her, but she could not move her head to face him.

With great effort she managed to force out her own words. "I don't know," she gasped, the tendons in her jaw refusing to cooperate.

"It's the sword," he said, and then she felt his fingers prying at her grip on the hilt. The presence inside her ripped her arm away, and the desire to strike him down swelled bright and hot. Pale metal gleamed as the sword twisted in her grip, sweeping towards Tal's throat.

"No!" Bren cried, and the blade halted, trembling, so close to killing him that a line of red had appeared on his neck. The presence inside her strained, but with a tremendous surge, Bren wrested back control of herself. Her arm dropped, though she still couldn't let go of the hilt.

"No," she repeated in shuddering relief.

Tal stumbled away, his hand clapped to his neck to staunch the bleeding, his face ashen.

The cowled figure made a strange crooning sound, tilting its head as if intrigued by what had just happened.

"This child is strong, Ashika. Worthy of you, perhaps?"

Bren was breathing hard, emotions churning within her that were not her own. She felt rage, hot and billowing. But that was not all . . . beneath this anger there were other, deeper currents. Shame, to have come so close to striking a killing blow for this offense. She was too proud. It had always been her greatest weakness, this pride. And . . . fear. Memories of darkness and silence, the endless echoing ages with nothing but her papery skin pressed against us . . .

Bren cried out, falling to her knees.

I . . . am sorry.

The sword moved in her grip, a wash of cold traveling up her arm.

The boy does not deserve death.

"Who are you?" Bren whispered.

Ashika, blademaiden of the People. Long have I waited. Long have I been lost in dreams.

"The People?"

Gith, we later called ourselves. Or perhaps we were named thus by the men of the Black Mountain only after the war. I cannot remember.

Bren felt her sense of self strengthening, the presence inside her unwinding from around her mind. She suddenly realized she had the advantage, and with all her will she thrust the presence away, forcing it from her head.

The silence was sudden and deafening. Bren dropped the sword; it clattered on the stone like it was nothing more than ancient metal.

The hunched stranger cocked its head, the motion reminding Bren of a bird studying something of interest. "Ashika bested by a fledgling. How interesting."

"Please," Bren rasped, feeling lightheaded. "Help us escape this place." She stumbled and would have fallen, but suddenly Tal was there, holding her up.

The stranger made a clicking sound, then reached inside its voluminous robes and withdrew something red and round. Bren struggled to focus on what it held, and it took her a moment to realize that inside that cage of clawed gray fingers was a ball of crimson twine. The creature released the ball, letting it fall to the floor, and as soon as it touched the stone, it began to roll, leaving a thread in its wake. In moments, it had vanished into one of the corridors.

"Follow, fledglings."

"How do we know we can trust you?" Desian asked, still brandishing his sword, though no emerald flames crawled along the blade now.

The stranger shrugged. "This one offers help but cares not if you refuse. Though be warned – worse than old Ka-ntelik dwell down here, in the deep places. Many things scurried into the cracks of the world after the Gith fell." The thing made a grunting sound, and this must have been meant as a farewell, for it turned away and began hobbling towards another passage, different from the one where the thread had unspooled.

"What do we do?" Tal asked as the stranger was swallowed by the shadows, the sound of its clumping passage growing fainter.

"I suppose we have to follow the thread," Bren replied.

"You called it Trickster," Desian said, coming up beside them. "Do you know what that thing was?"

Bren shook her head, which made her feel dizzy. The act of expelling the presence in her head had cost her more than she'd thought. "That wasn't me. It was the sword speaking."

"The sword?" Desian breathed in surprise, his narrowed eyes going to the pale blade that Bren had returned to the scabbard at her side.

"There's something inside it," Bren murmured, struggling to talk through the dryness in her throat. "Something terrible." With some effort, she managed a few faltering steps in the direction the ball of twine had disappeared. "Let's go. I want to get out of here.

12

"Well, that was quite the adventure," Tal said. He lifted his flagon of ale from the table but then apparently decided against offering a toast and set it back down. Bren could see that his hand was trembling, despite the lightness of his tone.

Desian did not even glance in Tal's direction, his face troubled and his glass of shimmering goldenwine untouched. From the tightness of his jaw and the haunted look in his silver eyes, the sorcerer might have been reliving the nightmare of the undercity.

Bren's chair creaked as she twisted half-around to check the tavern's entrance for about the twentieth time, her attention drawn by the sound of the door opening. But the new arrival in this charming little rat-hole was a bent-backed, sallow-faced man who seemed completely focused on only one thing as he stumped over to the bar. The tension that had briefly flooded her drained away. Every time Bren turned, she half-expected to see a raven-haired woman with a whip of writhing shadow framed in the doorway, a squad of dark-armored Velaschin at her back. She'd had to restrain herself several times from resting her hand on the hilt of the pale sword – the last thing she wanted now was to hear that voice in her head. It had been a struggle not to leave the sword in the undercity, but it had now saved her more than once. She knew she needed it, though she found that thought disturbing. She had to trust the Silver Mother had sent the sword to her.

"No one is going to find us here," Tal said quietly, noticing where she was looking. "If the Velaschin or the city watch marched this deep into the Tangle, folks would be running into *The Serpent's Legs* warning everyone to clear out. Half the miscreants in here right now are probably wanted by the authorities."

Bren suspected Tal spoke the truth – the other patrons in this forsaken grotto of a tavern looked like the kind of men and women her mother had warned her about: hard-eyed and dangerous, the hilts of weapons prominently displayed. Most hunched over their drinks alone in dark corners, though some were engaged in furtive whisperings. At one table a game of knaves was unfolding in silence, the only sounds the snap and rustle of cards being dealt and the clink of coins being tossed.

Desian's lips curled. "You're a fool if you think the Huntress is going to announce herself so brazenly. She's canny. We won't know she's here until her shadow darkens this table." He shook his head, tracing a knot in the wood with his finger. "The ambush in the undercity only happened the way it did because the Ratman's thugs necessitated overwhelming force. She's usually more subtle. Half of the masters in Leris's Jade House died before they even knew they were being hunted."

"If she followed us deeper into the undercity, then she's likely dead," Bren said, trying to convince herself. As they would have been if not for that creature. Even still, it had taken them half a day of following the crimson thread before they'd found themselves in the basement of an abandoned building in a dark corner of the Tangle. Bren had never been so happy to see the sun, and the first breath she'd taken when they'd stumbled out onto the street had been the sweetest in her life.

"I would have said that's impossible," Desian replied, "but now that I've experienced what's down there . . ." A far-away look came over his face, and he shuddered. "Maybe she's dead. We can hope."

"Are the masters truly all gone?" Tal asked him.

Desian woke from his daydream. "I saw only a single corpse, but Tharos claimed he was the last. That would mean seven sorcerers steeped in the power and mysteries of the jade moon were murdered in the span of a few days."

"This Huntress must not be a mere warrior," Bren murmured, remembering the first time she had seen the Velaschin dragon rider, the hate in her eyes as she'd glared at the poor, doomed paladin.

"She is not," Desian agreed, finally lifting his glass and studying its contents. The goldenwine eddied and roiled, far thicker than any other wine Bren had seen before. She remembered seeing glasses of this stuff at the ceremony where the duke had bent the knee to the Velaschin. It certainly looked like a drink for nobles. When Desian had placed his order, the grubby serving girl had looked at him like he'd suddenly grown a second head, yet still they'd procured a dusty bottle from somewhere.

The sorcerer's apprentice sipped his drink, rolling it around in his mouth before swallowing. "The Velaschin have their own magic, far different from what was taught to us by Nasai. While our sorcery can bend the physical world to our will, the power of the dragon riders is focused on the mind. Memory-magic, illusions, even the ability to enter the thoughts of others. Tharos and I discovered one of the Jade House masters after the Huntress had finished with him, and before he died, he could only gibber apologies about the secrets he had given up. She had flensed his mind like it was a rabbit she'd caught in a snare, peeling away layers to expose what had been hidden within."

Tal's fingers drummed the lip of his mug. "So she knows your secrets."

"Not my secrets," Desian said sharply. "The secrets of Nasai. Though I hope the Huntress does not understand all that was revealed to her."

"Is that how she knew about the meeting in the undercity?" Bren asked, and the sorcerer shrugged.

"Tharos's plan was borne of desperation. Only he remained of Leris's House of Jade. There was a traitor, I suspect . . . Perhaps the Ratman hoped to curry favor by delivering the last sorcerers to the Velaschin."

Bren frowned. "Those were his men killed down there," she pointed out, but the rest of what she was about to say died in her throat when she saw Tal's face. He looked troubled as he studied his drink.

"Desian could be right," he said slowly. "Much as it shames me. The thugs were not the Ratman's typical muscle. Hired swords . . . expendable. I don't want to believe it . . . but I also can't remember seeing Bones or Whisper after the Velaschin flooded the chamber. Bones is smart enough to flee at the first sign of real trouble, but if I know Whispers, he would have been sorely tempted to stand and fight. Since he didn't . . . it makes me think he was told not to."

"Does the thief have no loyalty to his city?" Bren asked, and Tal responded to this with a look of exasperation.

"He is the Ratman," Desian muttered. "His namesake is not the most honorable of animals."

"To be fair," Tal added, "the Duke of Thorns *has* sworn fealty to the Velaschin emperor. In truth, if the sorcerers of the Jade House were working against Leris's new overlords, the Ratman would be doing his duty as a good citizen of the city."

Desian snorted. "The duke may be feckless, but there are deeper bonds that knit together the Flowering Coast. We all owe the Mother our lives – She has protected us since She blessed the Sage of Pearls and helped him banish the last of Gith's demons from these lands. To let these infidels cast Her down would be a monstrous betrayal."

Bren remembered kneeling beside her parents in front of the little altar they'd kept to honor the Mother, and her hand drifted to the silver amulet beneath her tunic. The oath she'd sworn was still etched sword-sharp in her mind. *Give me the strength, Mother, to bring vengeance to the ones that did this.* And the Mother had been at her side ever since that terrible night. She'd given her a horse to carry her to the City of Roses. A sword that could cut demon flesh. And perhaps most importantly, others to share her burden.

Her gaze went to Tal, and she found him already watching her. The Mother must have brought them together . . . and then led her to the sorcerer. The plan Tharos had presented to her – as improbable as it sounded – must also be the goddess's will. Bren scratched at the dark outline of the jade disc sunk into her arm. If that had been his last act, she would do all in her power to make sure it was not in vain.

"When should we leave for Yestra?" she asked.

Tal had just taken a sip of his ale, and he nearly coughed it back up. "Bren!" he hissed, setting his drink down quickly so he wouldn't spill it. "Surely you aren't considering this madness?"

"What if that plan came from the Mother and Her daughters?" Bren told him, trying to make him understand. "The sorcerers of the Jade House are Nasai's representatives in this world. What if I am Her instrument?"

"The sorcerers are dead, Bren," he said, his tone almost like he was trying to explain something to a child. She found it more than a little infuriating. "We don't even know if that thing they put in your arm will work. And in the incredibly unlikely chance that you return from their empire with *dragon eggs*, what would you do with them? We know Velaschin can bond with dragons, but what about others? Perhaps the little monsters will break from their shells and fly off back across the sea to find their masters."

Bren reached out and gripped Tal's wrist. "Tharos thought the plan might work. And I've felt the Silver Mother guiding me ever since I lost my family. With Her at my side, it is possible. *I know it.*" She stared hard at him as she said this, desperately trying to make him understand. This would all be so much harder without him.

Tal hung his head, his expression troubled. Feeling guilty, she looked at Desian. The silver-haired boy had been staring sourly at Tal, but sensing her attention, he turned his gaze to her and crooked a smile.

"I thought I would have to convince you, shepherdess. I've been sitting here considering and discarding all manner of arguments. But it seems that's not necessary."

"Then you also think we should follow Tharos's plan?" she asked, though she already knew his answer.

He nodded emphatically. "I do. Though I won't claim we can expect the Mother's direct help. We in the House of Jade do not believe the goddess can so easily enter and affect the world, for there is a veil separating us from the divine. But you're right that Tharos would not have started us on this path if he did not think it had a chance of success, no matter how slim." He paused, frowning slightly. "The way forward will be difficult and fraught with danger. I will not lie about that."

"You would not lie?" snapped Tal, leaning across the table towards the boy. "The House of Jade is famous for the webs it spins. What you say cannot be trusted."

Desian responded to Tal's anger with a sneer. "The likelihood of Tharos's plan unfolding just as he hoped is vanishingly small. But he was willing to push forward because he saw no other way. I am being honest with Bren – tell me, what could I be lying about?"

Tal sat back in his chair, scowling. "There's always something with sorcerers. You know more than you're saying – I'd stake my life on it."

"Luckily, you don't have to stake *your* life," Desian replied sharply. "Tharos already gave his. And it is Bren who will risk everything."

"I will do it," Bren said quietly.

"Good," Desian said with a smile that for the first time did not seem feigned. "An oath, then, for the gaze of the goddess is turned upon us now. I can feel it." He put his hand in the center of the table. "I pledge myself body and soul to casting the Velaschin back into the sea. Whatever sacrifice is necessary, I will make it. For the Mother and Her daughters and the people of this land." When he had concluded, he glanced at Bren. She did not hesitate as she placed her hand over his and repeated what he had just said. To her surprise, before she'd even finished she felt another hand settle on hers.

"I won't swear to defeating the Velaschin," Tal said, "but I'll stand by you, Bren."

"You would leave Leris?" Bren asked, swallowing to try to hide how much his support meant to her.

The boy shrugged. "If the Ratman is loyal to the dragon lords, I'm not safe here. As soon as I poke my head up, I'll be dragged somewhere for questioning . . . and then they'll know you two survived as well."

"Truthfully, I do not know if they will keep pursuing us," Desian said slowly. "Perhaps the Huntress does not see me as much of a threat." His lips curled, his grin twisting into something darker. "Though that would be a mistake."

BREN HUNCHED in the shadow of the city walls, soaked by the cold rain falling from the slate sky. She supposed she should feel fortunate that the terrible weather was keeping almost everyone inside and that her drawn cowl would raise no suspicions on a day like this. Still, she felt miserable . . . though in truth, that had little to do with the chill seeping into her bones. She had wanted to return to her aunt's house and tell Heralia she was leaving Leris, but Desian and Tal had both balked at the idea. If the Ratman was in league with the Velaschin, then it would be known that the girl meeting with the sorcerer in the undercity was the same that had been searching for her family not long ago. This had made Bren fear for Heralia's safety, but Tal had convinced her that the Velaschin were trying to win over the heart of the city and would be reluctant to harm one of its beloved gardeners. Desian had also assured her that Velaschin sorcery would quickly determine Bren's aunt knew nothing about her rendezvous with the sorcerer. Bren still felt nervous, but she did understand that the risk of trying to meet with her aunt one final time was simply too great. Tal at least had said he would try to have a message passed to Heralia, letting her know that Bren was all right.

She straightened when she caught sight of a man leading a string of horses out of the city gates. Because of the rain, she couldn't be absolutely sure it was Tal, but he'd gone to retrieve Moon and procure mounts for Desian and himself, and the lead horse had the destrier's height. She jogged closer, wishing they'd thought of arranging a meeting place with a bit of shelter. The storm had seemingly come out of nowhere – one moment the sky had been an unbroken blue, and the next it had been filled with churning black clouds. Hopefully, this was not an omen of things to come.

The foreboding in her heart lifted slightly when she saw it was indeed Tal. His long dark hair was plastered to his head, but still he flashed a smile when he noticed her approaching.

"An auspicious start," he said, almost shouting to be heard over the hissing rain.

"I was just thinking the same," Bren replied, coming closer to pat Moon affectionately. The horse lowered his head so that she could scratch behind his ears, then chuffed a greeting that ended up spraying Bren with water.

"You cheeky monster," she cried, wiping at her face. Moon blinked his huge blue eyes, and Bren suspected he was well aware of what he'd just done. Perhaps this was his way of complaining about being left in the stables alone for so long.

"Where did you get the other horses?" Bren asked, giving Moon a playful slap on his flank.

"Their owners ended up stabbing each other over a game of knaves at *The Coronet*. No kin had turned up to claim what they'd left behind, and after hosting them in the stables for a month Gram Rhelga was willing to part with them for a reasonable price."

"It looks like you did a bit of shopping as well," Bren said, indicating the bulging saddle bags.

"The sorcerers of the Jade House apparently weren't lacking in funds. Desian gave me enough gold to buy a house in the Brocade. I don't think he has any sense of what things truly cost."

Bren frowned, staring back at the rain-shrouded gate. "I thought he said *he* was going to buy supplies."

"He told me he had other matters that needed attending to

before . . ." Tal's voice trailed away as he squinted into the mist. "Wait, is that him?"

It was indeed – Bren could tell just from the arrogant stride. It was strange, though, because he was coming towards the city, not out of it. Desian was ignoring the rain, and when he drew close Bren realized that it didn't look like his clothes were very wet at all.

Tal and Bren shared a glance, and she knew he was thinking the same as her. Where had he been? And what had he been doing?

Desian either read their minds or caught the look that had passed between them. "The Jade House rarely stays for long in one place," he said, raising his voice to be heard over the rain. "At the moment, it is outside the city walls."

"You said you were going to buy supplies," Bren said.

The silver-haired boy shrugged. "Such a mundane task is more suited for him," he said, jerking a thumb in Tal's direction. "I decided it would be better if I visited the House. Perhaps Tharos or one of the other masters slipped the Huntress's snares."

"And they didn't, or certainly they'd be here now," Bren said.

Desian nodded. "The House is empty, and I saw no traces of anyone else. It seems I am the last sorcerer in Leris. And because of this, I helped myself to a few of the more interesting items." He tilted his head towards the bulging satchel slung over his shoulder. Suddenly, he stiffened, letting out a hiss of surprise. "Is that one of the holy nthari? You said a paladin sheltered at your farmhouse – *did you take his horse*?"

Bren reached out to stroke Moon's silver mane protectively. "The paladin was dead. I was going to bring Moon to the Iron Daughter's temple." *Eventually*. The thought of giving up Moon made Bren feel sick.

"A paladin's horse . . ." Tal whispered, his eyes round with wonder.

Desian had recovered from his shock and was looking for something among the bags and blankets draped over Moon's back. "Where is his caparison?"

"His what?" Tal asked.

"His caparison," Desian repeated, the concern in his voice obvious. "A thick blanket stitched with the Silver Mother's sacred symbols. Where is it?"

"I left it at my house," Bren said, patting Moon's flank. "I didn't want anyone I met on the road to think I stole him."

The sorcerer growled in frustration. "Fire and ashes. Do you know what you've lost?"

"Not at all," Bren said defensively, bristling at the silver-eyed boy's tone.

"That caparison was an artifact of immense value," Desian almost snarled. "On the eve of the battle of Manoch Tir, powerful masters of the Jade House called down the moonlight of the Silver Mother and wove it into the barding and caparisons of all the nthari – the holy horses of Her paladins. The enchantment would grant protection against the breath of the Velaschin's dragons for a time to anyone who came into contact with the fabric." He breathed deep, clearly trying to bring his emotions under control. "But of course, you did not know that. How could you?"

A numbing wave of surprise had washed through Bren at the sorcerer's words. The caparison was the reason she had survived the dragon flames – by touching it in the stables, the Silver Mother's grace had been extended to her as well.

"How is such a thing possible?" she murmured, remembering the feel of the smooth fabric under her fingers. It had felt just like a mundane – if expensive – piece of cloth.

"It was a great enchantment," Desian replied calmly, the brief squall of his anger apparently already having passed. "But in principle, only a more powerful incarnation of a spell all sorcerers know." He lifted his arms and turned his head to the sky, as if welcoming the rain.

Rain that was not touching him.

"You're not wet," Tal observed, and he sounded annoyed about this.

Desian flashed him one of his lopsided grins. "I am also a sorcerer, you know."

"A very young one," Tal muttered, rolling his eyes.

Desian snorted. "As of now, I am the most senior member of the House of Jade in the City of Roses, and I demand to be treated with respect, urchin."

Bren swung herself up into Moon's saddle, then sent the boys scrambling out of the way as she kicked the horse into a trot. "You two are lucky I'm here to remind you both who the real enemy is," she called back at them, shaking her head in exasperation.

It was going to be a long journey to Yestra.

13

———

The rain gradually slackened until it was little more than a prickling mist, and by the early afternoon it had vanished entirely. Cracks spread across the stony sky, and when the sun finally returned its arrival was heralded by a chorus of birds calling from the forest. If it wasn't for her soaked clothes, Bren would have thought the ride was quite pleasant, although she knew the day's warmth would eventually deal with that before they stopped for the evening.

Her companions remained silent even after the rain had abated. They seemed lost in thought, perhaps turning over the events of the last few days. The ambush by the Huntress and the descent into the undercity had already acquired a patina of unreality, like a vivid dream. She watched them for a while, Tal squirming as he sat awkwardly in his saddle, still very uncomfortable on his horse, and Desian straight-backed yet obviously at ease, the reins held loosely in his graceful hands. That was something she'd noticed back in the tavern as he'd held his cup – his hands were soft and unblemished, the nails perfectly trimmed. Not like her own, calloused from a life-time of farm chores, or Tal's, grubby and scarred. She would guess that Desian had come from wealth before he'd even entered the

House of Jade. He looked to be from the same caste as the nobles she'd seen at the Briar.

But he was also like the rest of them now. They each had lost everything – for Desian, it was the other sorcerers of the Jade House. Did he have another home to go back to somewhere else, perhaps a noble's manse? Bren doubted this, though she wasn't sure exactly why. And then Tal had lost his two best friends in the world, the boys he had grown up with on the streets of Leris. The possible betrayal by the Ratman must have also cut him deeply, as Tal had said he'd once looked up to the thief as a father. Then there was her own tragedy, still achingly fresh. Most days she persevered only by refusing to dwell on what had happened.

Bren's hands tightened on the reins. The Velaschin. They were the ones responsible for their sorrow; their actions had united the three of them in revenge. But not just on the ones who had personally swung the sword or commanded the dragons – no, the plan hatched by the Jade House hoped for nothing less than the utter defeat of the dragon lords. It was a dizzying, impossible dream, but the sorcerer Tharos had thought enough of it to sacrifice himself. Bren idly traced the mark on her arm, trying to decide if she could feel the jade disc beneath her skin. It truly did just look like a birthmark, but would the Velaschin be able to sense the sorcery Tharos had imbued in it when she entered the Winnowing?

And that would only be the first of many arduous steps on this path. Tharos had claimed that very few passed the second test and bonded with a dragon. Then, in the unlikely event she succeeded, she was supposed to travel to the empire across the sea and somehow earn enough trust to be allowed near where the dragons nested. She imagined herself fleeing through the streets of some foreign city with a sack filled with dragon eggs, headed for the harbor. Or would she be clinging to the back of her own dragon, the sea glittering below her as dark wings beat furiously in pursuit? Bren sighed and shook her head. The very idea seemed so preposterous that it was almost impossible to imagine. And yet that was what Tharos had envisioned. Her, a dragon rider. Absolute madness.

"I much prefer you," Bren murmured, leaning forward to scratch behind Moon's ears. The great horse turned his head to look at her sidelong, then snorted loudly. Perhaps forgiveness for their long separation would take a little time.

THE SKY HAD ALREADY DARKENED when they arrived at the first roadside inn, which had wisely been built a full day's ride from Leris. It was a sprawling, multistoried building of timber and packed earth, the windows aglow with welcoming light. Wagons and horses crowded the field outside, the sound of raised voices and laughter drifting from the propped-open doorway. Tal was grinning like a fool at the sight, and Bren's stomach rumbled at the thought of sitting down for a hot meal.

Desian seemed to take pleasure in shattering their good cheer. "We keep riding," he said in a tone that would not brook disagreement.

Tal's wide smile faltered, then returned after a moment. "Aha," he said knowingly. "You know a better place not far down the road."

"No," Desian replied curtly.

Tal gestured at the very inviting-looking inn. "Surely we're not going to ride straight through the night. We'll have to stop eventually."

"We will." The silver-haired sorcerer nodded at the tops of the trees rising ahead of them. "In that forest. We'll leave the road and find someplace away from prying eyes."

Tal frowned. "You think we're being hunted?"

Desian shrugged. "Truthfully, I doubt it. The Velaschin probably think any threat from the House of Jade ended in the undercity. And we hardly look the sort to topple an empire."

Tal shifted uncomfortably in his saddle – he was going to be sore tomorrow, Bren knew. The first few long rides were always the hardest. "Excellent. Then let us find a warm spot in the inn here and fill ourselves with food and ale."

"No. We make our own camp," insisted the boy.

Bren found Desian's tone infuriating. He had clearly already decided he was their leader.

"What if I also want to stop?" Bren interjected. They had nearly reached the inn, which had only grown more enticing as they'd approached. The smell of cooking meat was making her mouth water – she guessed it was wafting from around the back where they must have a barbecue pit dug, a common custom at eating houses in the Seven Valleys.

Desian shifted to face her. "I'm not worried about us being discovered by the Huntress or other Velaschin. Or even the color of your skin raising the ire of the locals. I want some privacy so we can start preparing you for the Winnowing."

"Preparing me?"

Desian sighed. "Do you think they just hand over dragon eggs to anyone? You'll have to pass a grueling test, and if you fail, everything will have been for naught."

They were past the inn now, and the sounds of revelry were fading. Tal was twisted around in the saddle, staring forlornly back at what they were leaving behind them.

"I thought you didn't know the manner of the test," Bren said, somewhat sullenly.

Desian hesitated. "We . . . don't entirely know," he finally admitted, and Bren suspected it truly pained the boy to admit his ignorance. "It's a closely guarded secret. Tharos spent some time trying to guess its nature by observing who had already become dragon riders. Martial ability was most common . . . but it was not universal. Some riders display little aptitude with swords . . . but there is always something that makes them remarkable. Usually, if it is not their strength, it is their mind. So there may be many ways to succeed during the trial."

"How do you expect *me* to succeed?" Bren asked in exasperation. "I'm anything but special."

Desian crooked that infuriating grin again. "That may be true. But while you claim not to be remarkable, I saw you in the undercity.

You fought an abomination from the beyond and lived. The living darkness would have devoured all of us if it wasn't for you."

Bren had to stop herself from glancing at the sword hanging among the saddlebags Moon carried. Did Desian realize it had been the spirit in the sword and not her? That without it, she hadn't been able to defeat a deserter from some lord's army who had probably been swinging a scythe before the war.

"If you can fight like that in the trials to come, you'll be a dragon rider," Desian said confidently.

Bren bit down on her lip, her insides twisting at what Desian was suggesting. She would need the spirit to have any chance . . . but could she risk inviting it inside her once again?

Before night had fully fallen they left the road and entered the forest. The surroundings reminded Bren of her first night after leaving the farm when she had rescued Tal from the soldiers, though the trees here were taller and broader, and there was less undergrowth to bother the horses. They rode until they came to a clearing covered with pine needles, and then Desian proclaimed it suitable by sliding from his horse and beginning to unpack their camping supplies.

Kindling was plentiful, and before long Tal had coaxed a fire to life. It wasn't as merry as an inn's common room, perhaps, but still it felt wonderful to relax with their backs against the trunks of trees and the night's chill kept at bay by the flames. Tal dispensed strips of salted meat and chunks of hard cheese from their supplies, and they shared a round loaf of black bread. It was a simple meal, but after their long day in the saddle, Bren couldn't imagine anything more satisfying.

When they had finished, Desian stood, brushing away the needles clinging to his trousers.

"Did you bring the practice swords?" he asked Tal.

Tal nodded, then went over to the horses. After rummaging

around in the saddlebags, he returned with a long, wrapped bundle and laid it on the ground.

Desian stepped closer and threw aside the cloth, revealing a pair of worn wooden swords. "These will do," he murmured, hefting one and testing its weight by cutting the air.

Tal collapsed once more against a tree, his gaze turning to Bren. She saw concern there, as if he was worried about what might happen next. She couldn't blame him.

"Here," Desian said, tossing the other sword to her. She caught it smoothly and immediately realized that this must be one of the Bright Company's training blades. It had the same weight and balance as the weapon her uncle had given her. She stood and sketched a quick pattern, enjoying the sense of familiarity. How much simpler her life had been when last she'd held such a sword.

Desian moved away from the fire and over to a patch of grass that wasn't veined with roots or covered in a layer of forest detritus. "Come on. I saw you in the undercity, but I want to find out the limits of your training. If you're well beyond me, then that's one less thing to worry about. At least it won't be your skill with arms that leads to failure during the Winnowing."

Bren stepped across from him, setting herself in one of the forms. She breathed deeply, trying to calm her racing heart. She just had to remember the lessons Merik had taught her. She'd practiced these patterns a hundred times before – she may have been defeated by the soldier back at the inn near the gallows, but she had just been dizzy from being struck in the head, and she hadn't been prepared . . .

Desian lunged, and their swords came together with a clatter. He shuffled forward, testing her with quick, precise strokes, and to her surprise, she caught each blow and turned it aside. After a moment, he drew back, frowning.

"What is it?" she asked, feeling exhilarated that she had survived the exchange without being touched.

He did not answer, instead coming at her again, firelight gleaming on the polished wooden blade. Bren yelped in pain as the sword struck her wrist, the worn hilt slipping from her numb fingers.

Desian retreated, lowering his sword until the point brushed the ground. Confusion was clear in his face. Hurriedly, she bent down to retrieve her sword, trying to ignore the pulsing ache in her wrist, and settled again into the form she was most comfortable with.

"What is the matter?" he asked, tapping the blade against his leg.

"What do you mean?" she replied, though she suspected she knew.

He raised his sword, pointing it at her. "When that thing was dragging me away in the undercity, I saw you fighting against the darkness. You moved untouched through a dozen of those grasping tendrils, each strike of your sword perfect. And yet now that skill has vanished. You're not entirely without training, but you're still very much a novice."

Bren swallowed, a flush creeping up her neck. She had been foolish to think that her time spent sparring with cattails in the meadow had prepared her to fight with a trained duelist.

"That wasn't her."

Desian looked at Tal. "Explain."

The boy glanced at her guiltily, as if he was sharing something over which he'd been sworn to secrecy.

"It was the sword." He nodded towards the sheathed blade dangling from Moon's saddle.

Desian pursed his lips, turning back to Bren. "That creature in the undercity was interested in that blade . . . and you said that it 'spoke' to you. I have to admit, I was recovering from what had happened and couldn't focus completely on your strange little back and forth with that bird-thing."

Bren swallowed, unsure what she should reveal. But this mad quest was doomed to failure if they couldn't trust each other. She had to tell the truth to the sorcerer. "There is a . . . a presence. A ghost. She can slip inside me and seize control of my body when I wield the sword. I am like a passenger at those times, helpless. It's terrible and frightening, and I never know if she will return control to me once she is finished."

Desian was staring intently at the sword now. He didn't look surprised for some reason – perhaps he had already suspected something like what she had just told him. "You're sure the spirit is female?"

Bren nodded. "Yes. She calls herself Ashika and claims to be a blademaiden of Old Gith."

Tal hissed in surprise at this. She hadn't told him what the ghost had said. Desian, however, only frowned.

"A blademaiden . . ." he murmured, his gaze distant.

"Forget about that," Bren said, slicing a pattern in the air to try to keep her aching wrist from stiffening. "I need to learn how to win battles without the ghost's help."

Desian ignored her, tossing his wooden blade onto the ground. He looked deep in thought as he walked across the clearing to where the horses were tied.

Bren lowered her practice sword. Had he decided she was a hopeless cause? Perhaps he was about to swing himself up into his saddle and ride away. But instead he gingerly lifted the pale sword from where it hung, turning it this way and that as if expecting to see some evidence of the spirit lurking within.

Oh, please don't do this, Bren thought as the silver-haired boy walked back to where they waited.

"We shouldn't risk this," Tal said, clenching his fists like he was about to fight Desian for possession of the sword.

Desian ignored Tal, his brow drawing down as he continued to stare at the ancient sword he held. He crouched and set the blade gently on the ground, then stood again and stepped back quickly.

"The Mother must have led you to this sword," he said softly. "She wanted you to have it."

"Or maybe that demon inside wants us to believe it is the Mother's will," Tal said, taking a menacing step towards Desian. "It's dangerous. I saw how it changed after it killed those soldiers . . . It drank their blood!"

The silver-eyed boy snorted, still not looking at Tal. "You know nothing."

"I know enough!" Tal replied, now only a few paces from Desian. "I already lost someone to Gith evil! I won't let Bren be taken as well!"

Desian whirled to face Tal, his jaw clenched and his dark eyes blazing. "It is a tool, like everything else imbued with power. A tool that we very much need right now, or she will *never* succeed in the Winnowing. There is no hope of her becoming a master swordswoman in the few weeks we have before the testing begins. Either we try to harness what is in that sword, or we abandon my master's plan and forsake the Mother."

He stepped closer to Tal, holding his gaze. They were nearly touching, the air crackling between them. Even the fire seemed to sense their rising agitation, leaping higher.

"Enough!" Bren cried, pushing herself between the two boys. "Stop acting like fools. What are you going to do, beat each other bloody on the first night of this journey? The Mother would weep to see you both right now."

Tal looked chagrined at her words, but Desian only curled his lip derisively.

"I know the dangers of the sword," Bren said softly to Tal before turning to Desian. "But he's also right. Maybe if I had five years to train in the Bright Company I'd be ready for this test. I don't. *We* don't." Her gaze slid to the sword lying in the grass, and she couldn't help but imagine that it was somehow listening. "I need the sword. I need the help of the ghost inside it. I will have to bring it with me into the Winnowing."

Desian coughed, his smile faltering. "We have a problem there."

"What?" Bren and Tal said in unison.

The sorcerer's apprentice sighed. "While we know little about the Velaschin's test, one thing we are certain of is that those who partake may not bring their own weapons or armor with them."

Bren frowned in confusion. "Then why are we even talking about this?"

"Because . . ." Desian began, then paused as if searching for the right words. "Because there still might be a way."

"How?" Tal asked suspiciously.

Desian ran a hand through his silver hair. "We'll have to strike a bargain."

THE NEXT DAY passed in an uncomfortable silence. Tal glowered at Desian as they rode, but the sorcerer's apprentice ignored him. Bren nudged Moon closer to the sorcerer's horse once, and she heard him muttering to himself as if he were carrying on a conversation with someone who wasn't there. He even sighed, sounding almost exasperated, and Bren couldn't help but wonder what was going on inside his head.

When they stopped for a midday meal, Desian retreated deeper into the woods with an ancient book under his arm. Bren followed after wolfing down her bread and found him seated among the roots of a great tree as he pored over the tome.

"What's that?" she asked, and with what seemed like effort he dragged his eyes from the pages.

"A book," he replied distractedly.

"I can see that," Bren said in some frustration. "But why are you reading it right now? What are you looking for?"

His brow furrowed, as if he was having trouble understanding what she had asked. "An answer to our problem," he finally said, sounding like his thoughts were very far away from these woods. "Now, please, I need to concentrate."

Sighing, Bren retreated. When she arrived back where Tal was waiting with the horses, she found him running his hand along the flank of his mare affectionately and whispering soft words.

"You've taken to riding quickly," Bren said, brushing out a few leaves that had become tangled in Moon's mane.

"I think it's hard not to fall in love with them," Tal replied, scratching his horse behind the ear. "They give so much without complaint, and they hide nothing from you."

Bren frowned. She thought she understood his message – they shouldn't give their trust so easily, especially to a sorcerer. Or was he referring to how Bren had kept what she knew about the sword from him?

"I've named her Dapple," Tal said. "For the spots on her coat. They remind me of what the forest floor looks like when the sunlight comes down through the branches."

"Dapple and Moon," Bren murmured, staring into the depths of her horse's blue eyes. "I wonder what Desian calls his."

Tal snorted. "He doesn't seem like the sort to even bother with a name. To him, a horse is just a tool. A means to an end."

Bren felt a little surge of annoyance. "Perhaps we should draw some lessons from him," she said, more sharply than she'd intended. "Maybe he is the only one of us who understands the seriousness of this moment and what is truly at stake. That we are not important when the scales need to be balanced . . . Our lives are like feathers when weighed against the fate of the kingdom."

She glanced at Tal and found him staring at her with his jaw clenched. He looked hurt, she thought guiltily, but also defiant.

"Not to me," he finally said as he turned away from her and resumed running his hand along Dapple, though this time more forcefully. "Kings and queens can take care of themselves. And they wouldn't be troubled by anything that happened to us, I can assure you."

"We have to try," Bren persisted, but he did not look at her. She waited a moment, but when it was clear he thought this conversation was over, she sighed and began examining Moon's hooves for stones. How could they follow this mad plan when she couldn't even keep their little band from fracturing?

"I HAVE IT."

Bren had almost fallen asleep, her back against a tree trunk, when the sorcerer's announcement dragged her fully awake. She blinked, trying to focus on Desian. He had emerged from where he'd retreated earlier, but with their fire little more than glowing embers, he was only a vague shadow set against the forest's deeper blackness.

"You have what?" Bren mumbled, rubbing her leg where a root had been pressing.

"What I was looking for." Desian stepped closer, and she could see his excitement. He held the great black tome he'd been reading earlier, cradling it almost like it was a child.

"And that is . . .?" Tal asked from his spot across the fire. He was sitting with his knees drawn up to his chest, staring at Desian warily.

The silver-haired boy brandished the book at them. "I knew this was one of the treasures I had to take. I could hear it calling to me." He was almost babbling, his words coming out in a tumbling rush. "The Masters of Leris's House kept it in a place of high honor, which meant it was forbidden to those who had not yet been initiated into the deeper mysteries." He paused as if overwhelmed by whatever he had just learned, his gaze becoming unfocused.

"Desian," Bren said sharply, and this brought the boy back to himself. He shook his head, crooking one of his infuriating grins.

"This is a spell book," the apprentice explained. "But not for the sorceries of the Jade House. Nothing in this grimoire was bequeathed by Nasai or her mother. No, the rituals and spells within are from an earlier, darker age."

"Old Gith," Tal intoned flatly. He stared daggers at Desian, but the sorcerer's apprentice ignored him.

"Older than Old Gith, as you know it," Desian corrected him. "You see, that ancient people embraced demon magic fairly late in their history. It elevated them and allowed for the wondrous creations we can see today, like their roads and fallen cities, but truly, that time was but a moment. Flaring bright for an instant before they were consumed."

"So that book does not deal with demons?" Bren asked.

Desian shook his head sharply. "No. Before the Gith were seduced by the lure of what lies beyond this world, they were very much focused on this one. They worshipped their ancestors and drew power from those who had come before. It was a kind of . . . spirit magic."

"Necromancy," Tal said, sounding even less thrilled after Desian's explanation. "Consorting with the dead isn't much of an improvement over demons."

"We can understand the dead," Desian countered. "They were once like us. Demons . . . even if they take forms we are familiar with, even if their promises and entreaties seem reasonable . . . they are fundamentally unknowable. They cannot be trusted, as the sorcerers of Old Gith discovered. The dead, though . . . the dead can be bargained with."

"But what does a spirit want?" Bren asked, already dreading the answer.

"Life," Desian said, his silver eyes drifting to the smoldering fire. "The souls of the dead hunger for what they remember. Food, drink, the warmth of those they loved. A taste of such things was often enough to bind a spirit to the sorcerer's purpose."

"And whose life does that thing in the sword want?" Tal countered, gesturing at Bren. "Hers?"

"We need help," Desian replied sharply. "Help that might be found here." He raised his arm, and suddenly he was holding the sword from the barrow, its pale blade gleaming in the semi-darkness.

Bren's heartbeat quickened. She remembered the voice in her head, the presence swelling to encompass her. Her flesh had no longer belonged to her. But as unsettling as that had been, it was true she had never sensed hate or anger emanating from the sword. It had saved them more than once.

"What are you proposing?" she asked.

Desian cut the air with the sword. "A spirit has been bound here. I have found a ritual in this book that should allow us to communicate with the ghost inside this sword . . . and break the binding that holds it. We can discover who it was, what it is capable of, and whether it will agree to be bound to something else . . . or someone else."

Bren swallowed, her throat suddenly dry. "But we can just talk first?" She ignored the hiss of disapproval from Tal's direction.

"Yes," Desian said, stooping and laying the sword gently down in the grass beside the dying fire. "I will recite the spell, and when I tell you to, come forward and take up the sword. If my attempt is successful, you should be able to speak with the spirit. Now, listen to me carefully. This sorcery I am attempting is very particular. I am not going to simply shove the spirit into your body – that very well might result in it pushing out your own soul. No, what I am hoping to do is *twine* your existences together, pressing the spirit into the depths of your being so far that it loses its own awareness – yet, if the sorcery takes hold, you will retain the skills it gained in life. Long ago, necromancers performed this magic so that great talents were preserved after death – the shaping of metal, for example, or the playing of instruments. It is dangerous, but if I succeed, you may gain the spirit's ability with a sword without having to contest with it for control of your body."

Bren nodded, slowly climbing to her feet. A nervous fear was thrumming in her, but she shoved it aside. Instead, she focused on memories of her mother singing while cooking dinner, her father tossing a laughing Helat into the air. She would bargain with anything that could help her punish the Velaschin for what they had done.

"Bren, please don't do this," Tal begged, but he made no move to try to stop them. His eyes were wide, his face ashen.

Desian stepped back from the fire, submerging himself once more in the shadows. Bren heard the crackle of an ancient binding and the rustle of parchment. "I will attempt the spell," the sorcerer said, and to Bren's surprise she thought she heard a nervous tremble in his words. Her own fear increased, but she did not ask him to stop.

He began to chant. The words were in no language she had ever heard before – truly, it did not sound like a language at all, just grating utterances. One moment Desian's voice was barely a whisper, and the next it swelled to an almost booming shout. Yet there was a pattern to it, a structure that suggested it was more than mere gibberish.

Goosebumps prickled her skin. Bren felt like there were eyes watching her, as if the incantation had drawn something's attention from far beyond the light. She gasped as the fire crackled and hissed, the flames clawing higher. A piece of kindling, surely? She waited for the fire to die down again, but it did not.

Motion out of the corner of her eye drew her gaze from the leaping flames. Tal had drawn his dagger and was brandishing it at the darkness, his eyes wide and terrified. Bren wanted to call out to him, to ask what he had seen, but she found herself unable to form words.

It was then that she saw them.

In the darkened tangle of the forest, shapes were moving. Shadows, blacker than the night, flitting at the edge of her perception . . . Was this her imagination? She felt dizzy, more than a little nauseous. The horses were strangely still, huddled against each other as if paralyzed by what was happening.

"Bren, take up the sword!" Desian's voice echoed like they were all standing at the bottom of a very deep well. She lurched forward, her steps clumsy, and nearly went reeling into the flames. It was so hard to concentrate through the throbbing in her head . . .

"Now, Bren! The sword!"

The sword. She bent down, her hand scrabbling among the pine needles for the hilt. It occurred to her that when Desian had screamed at her, the chanting that filled the clearing had continued unabated. But how could that be?

Her fingers closed around the bronze pommel. The pale radiance of the blade had faded, like after it had drunk the blood of those soldiers at the inn, and now the metal resembled ceramic . . . or bone fresh-pulled from a corpse . . . or maggots crawling in a festering wound . . .

Bren gasped as a cold tide rose, carrying her away on dark currents.

14

_____

Shadows writhed on stone.

Bren stood in a rough-hewn chamber facing a wall daubed with jagged red runes. From the stillness, she sensed that she must be far underground, deep in the womb of the earth. Flames crackled behind her, and beneath the acrid smell of burning there was a mustiness that suggested an age had passed since this place had been sealed away and forgotten. A reverberation was welling up from below, echoed by the pulsing of her own blood. Was that a great drum being struck? Or the heartbeat of a terrible monster?

Where was the forest? Where were Tal and Desian? She still held the bronze hilt of the sword, its tip nearly brushing the hard-packed earth beneath her boots.

"Turn around."

The voice was deep and so strangely accented that for a moment Bren couldn't understand what had been said. Cold panic washed through her, and she raised her sword into a guard position as she turned.

Bren gasped.

A granite throne hunched behind her, flanked by smoldering

braziers. Beyond this puddle of light stretched a great and terrible darkness, the floor and ceiling swallowed by an endless black maw. A woman sprawled in the chair – it looked similar to the one in the Gith barrow, though not nearly so weathered – and her leg was flung over an armrest, her head tilted as she regarded Bren. She was long-limbed and broad-shouldered, and Bren suspected she would have overtopped her by a head or more if she rose from her throne. Dark red curls fell past her shoulders, and her eyes were the blue-black color of a lake at twilight. She wore armor, fur-trimmed hide that left her legs and arms bare, and a circlet of reddish metal on her brow. A necklace of long, curving claws interspersed with chunks of amber gleamed in the flickering light. Her lips were pursed, as if she had judged Bren and found her wanting.

"Who . . . who are you?" Bren asked, not lowering her sword.

The woman frowned. "We've met before, lass," she finally said, her leg slipping from the stone armrest as she sat forward.

"Ashika," Bren said, glancing down at the sword she held.

"Aye. Blademaiden of the First People, chieftain of the Green River tribe. Slayer of tusked stalkers and the great bear Nunega." Her hand drifted up to touch the largest of the claws resting against her pale skin.

"You're a ghost," Bren said, her gaze flicking to the sword she held. "You haunt this blade."

The woman watched her for a long moment. Then she sat back, her fingers curling around the ends of the armrests.

"At first I thought you were just another dream," she murmured softly, closing her eyes. "Yet then I tasted their blood, so hot and sweet. And I knew."

"Knew what?" Bren whispered.

The woman's twilight eyes snapped open. "What I was. What the graycloaks had done to me." She was silent for a moment, her brow furrowed. Then she reached towards Bren. Her nails were painted black, and a bracelet of rough-cut red stones encircled her wrist.

"Give me Banevak. Give me my sword."

Bren glanced down at the blade in her hand. The verdigris that had covered the bronze hilt was gone, and the sword looked like it had just been pulled from the forge.

"Banevak," Bren said slowly. It must have been her imagination, but she thought she felt the sword twitch in her hand.

"Aye," the red-haired woman said, leaning forward. She did not rise, but she was visibly straining towards the sword, a yearning in her indigo eyes. "The Duskbringer. It was my mother's sword and her mother's before that. The history of my people is written in the blood it has spilled."

"The Gith," Bren murmured. She tightened her hold on the hilt as she felt it squirm again, almost as if the sword was desperate to go to the woman.

"Those that became the Gith were once a hundred different tribes," Ashika said, frustration in her face as she stared at the blade. "All we shared in common were the stories of the mother bear Jegatha and how she found the first men and women nestled among the roots of the Great Tree. During my time we were as wont to murder each other as grant welcome in our halls."

"I was told the Gith were a mighty empire, united by demon-magic," Bren said, realizing with a sinking sense of unease that she had taken a step closer to where the woman sat, as if pulled along by the sword.

The blademaiden shook her head vehemently, making the bits of bone woven into her hair clink. "You speak of the Black Mountain tribe and what came later, after my death. They were my kin's enemies."

"You fought them?" Bren asked, then drew in a breath when she realized she had taken another involuntary step forward.

"I killed them," the woman replied sharply. "Banevak drank deep."

Bren's arm lifted of its own accord, extending the sword towards where the blademaiden's arm was still outstretched. She resisted this compulsion with all her will, causing the pale blade to waver.

"Yet it was not enough," the woman continued. Her hand was also shaking, her face gleaming with sweat. Bren could hear the strain in her voice, but she continued speaking calmly. "The graycloaks of the Black Mountain tribe delved beneath their clan hold and found something that had been hidden. A door to the beyond, where Others dwelled."

The woman's hand brushed the sword, her fingers closing around the pale metal. Bren was expecting blood, but even though she could feel the strength with which the woman was gripping the blade, nothing flowed forth. In shock, she released the hilt, surrendering the sword and stumbling back a step.

Despite what Bren had feared, the woman did not leap to cut her down. Instead, Ashika drew the sword closer, her other hand finding the hilt. Then she sank back once more into the stone chair, her expression almost blissful.

The blademaiden stayed that way for a long while, staring straight ahead with unblinking eyes. Was she dead? Had she fallen into a trance? The darkness had grown thicker, the flames in the braziers subsiding. Bren peered into the depths of the chamber, fighting against her rising panic. How could she get out of here? If she walked out into the blackness, would she be lost forever?

"You desire something," the woman finally said, her voice thick. Bren jumped, startled by the sudden noise. "Else you would not have braved this place."

"Y-yes," Bren stammered. "Your help."

The woman's lip curled. "To kill your enemies."

"Yes. No."

"I offered that once before," Ashika said, almost accusingly. "You stood beside the man who murdered your family, and I offered to cut him down. You refused."

"I was frightened," Bren whispered.

The spirit's mouth twisted further in disdain. "Would the future be any different, lass? If your enemies knelt before you now with heads bowed, could you swing the sword?"

"Yes," Bren said, trying to sound confident. "I'm sure of it."

"I am not," the woman replied, shaking her head. "You are not a warrior, at least not yet. You are a sapling, still green. Yet if you truly believe your will has sufficiently hardened, take Banevak up again. When the thrill of battle makes blood pound in your veins, I will awaken and offer you my strength. It is my purpose."

"Your purpose?" Bren whispered, her mouth dry.

"Aye. I did not consent to the ritual of my tribe's graycloaks, but I understand why they did it. We were at war with the Black Mountain, and my strength was still needed, even though I had fallen. And so they called my spirit back from the High Halls and bound me to the sword of my ancestors."

"Then . . . all I need to do is call on you?"

"Much of the time I sleep, and sometimes I do not know what are dreams and what are not. But when I taste your anger . . . your fear . . . then it is like the clotting webs are pulled away."

The woman had laid the sword across her lap and was staring into the depths of the blade. She looked troubled by something she saw in the metal.

"There is more," Bren said in a rush, trying to draw Ashika's attention from the sword. "A problem."

The woman said nothing, but she looked up from the blade, staring at Bren once more.

"I will be tested. A trial of strength and skill. And if I pass, I will have a chance at a great revenge against the ones who killed my family. I *must* succeed. But I will not be allowed to bring this sword – or any sword – into the testing ground. And without your strength, I will almost certainly fail."

The woman suddenly stood, and Bren took an instinctive step backwards. "Do you know what you are asking, lass?" she asked, her voice hard.

"Yes," Bren murmured, though in truth she did not.

"You dangle freedom before me," the woman said, scowling. "You are inviting me into your flesh, are you not? You are fortunate, child. Any other bound spirit would accept your offer at once. Foolish, foolish girl."

"Then you cannot help me?"

The woman reversed the sword, driving it point-first into the floor.

Bren winced, expecting it to shatter, but with a ringing shriek the metal slid a hand-span into the stone. Ashika released the hilt, and the sword remained standing upright, quivering slightly.

"The temptation once inside you to live again, to feel the sun on my face and the breeze in my hair . . ." There was a hunger in her eyes, a desperate yearning. "I have hunted down those of my tribe seized by spirits. There was a man possessed by the soul of his father. The fool thought the affections of blood would keep him safe, but it is hard to resist the chance of escaping this cold and lonely place . . ."

The woman waved her hand, as if dismissing Bren. "No. Go back to the world of the living, lass. Do not put this temptation before me."

Bren swallowed, but she did not turn away. Instead, she stepped closer, and the woman looked up in surprise. "Help me," she pleaded.

The woman's eyes narrowed. "Were you not listening? I do not trust myself. There is a chance my soul could devour yours."

Bren reached out, her fingers closing around Ashika's forearm. She'd been expecting something cold and clammy, corpse-like, but the blademaiden's flesh was warm. The surprise in the woman's face became something more like alarm at being touched, but she did not jerk her arm away.

"I will take that chance," Bren said fervently, holding the spirit's gaze. "If I do not, then my people are doomed. My goddess is doomed."

The woman tilted her head slightly, as if she had just noticed something for the first time. "Your people . . . you are from the Red Lands tribe. I see it now – you have their hair, their skin."

Bren frowned. "No. I grew up a child of the Seven Valleys in the kingdom of Felaesia, but my parents were Velaschin, from across the sea."

"Velaschin," Ashika said slowly, rolling the word around in her mouth. Vel'a-schin. People from the Red Lands, in the old tongue."

Surprised, Bren let go of the ghost. "What are you talking about?"

The blademaiden's gaze had drifted beyond Bren, looking at something only she could see. "That was what they called the eastern forests. The Red Lands, for when the leaves burned bright during autumn." Her voice sounded like it was coming from very far away.

"Who did? The Gith tribe you speak of?"

Ashika's eyes snapped back to her. "Are the wars of the past still being waged? Is it possible? I spoke with the shadow of the Trickster in that dark place, but I thought him to be but a wandering ghost."

"I don't know," Bren said uncertainly, feeling adrift on strange currents.

The warrior woman raised her arm towards Bren, opening her hand. "I need to understand. This is the bargain I put before you, Brenna of the Seven Valleys: I will lend you my strength and my skill, and in return, you shall help me discover if my enemies have survived. Such a reward is worth the risk."

Bren blinked in surprise at the condition the blademaiden had laid down. Surely whatever enemies Ashika had once fought were dead and dust ages ago. Still, she hesitated before extending her own arm to meet Ashika's waiting hand. Was this a trap?

Knowing she had to take this chance, Bren pushed aside her doubts and clasped the blademaiden's forearm once more. The red-haired woman shook her head slightly, then gripped the hilt of the ancient sword with her other hand and pulled it smoothly from the stone. Bren's heart quickened as Ashika flourished it, but she did not pull away.

"Blood shall seal our pact – it has power even here," the ghost said and quickly sliced her palm with the edge of the pale blade. Blood welled from the cut, though it flowed slowly, almost like honey, and in the low light it looked far more black than red.

The blademaiden laid the cool metal against Bren's open palm. The blood that had been there a moment ago was now gone, as if the sword had swallowed it. A voice inside her that sounded like Tal was screaming for her to jerk her hand back, that this bargain would cost her soul or her life or her freedom, but Bren ignored it and held her hand as steadily as she could. The edge slid along her skin, opening a gash in her hand.

There was pain, but less than she was expecting. Redness

bloomed, and then blood filled her palm. Bren forced her hand open, drops pattering against the stone.

"Seal the pact," Ashika commanded, and Bren met her hand halfway, their palms pressing together. She gasped as the coldness flowing from the spirit mingled with the warmth pulsing from her own wound.

"It is done," Ashika said, stepping away and lowering her arm. Bren also stumbled back a step, her head whirling. She felt like she was going to be sick.

"Take the sword, lass," Ashika continued, and Bren realized to her surprise that the warrior woman was no longer holding the blade. It was in *her* hand, somehow, the grip sticky. "Banevak is still mighty, even if . . . even if . . ." A tremor passed across her face, what looked to be a spasm of pain.

"Are you all right?" Bren cried just before the spirit doubled over and vomited blackness onto the stone. Ashika looked up at Bren with wide, almost fearful eyes and then collapsed into her throne, clutching at her stomach.

"This feels wrong," the blademaiden hissed. "Something tries . . . to swallow me. What sorcery is this?"

"Ashika?" Bren murmured, unsure what she should do.

It was then that she noticed the chill had not left her hand. Where Ashika's blood had mingled with her own, a spot of icy coldness had persisted, and now frozen tendrils traveled up her arm, through her veins. Bren moaned, falling to her knees, the sword clattering beside her. She clawed at the serpents slithering under her skin as they wrapped themselves around her heart, and she fell forward, gasping for breath. Bren tried to scream, but nothing emerged except a bone-dry rattle, and when she raised her head she saw Ashika was slumped on the throne, her limbs dangling slack, empty twilight eyes staring at nothing.

15

A croaking woke her.

Bren cracked gummy eyes and found herself staring up at red leaves flushed with morning light. Shapes flitted among the branches, and a dog-sized lizard clung to a trunk watching her with slitted eyes. Bren held its beady black gaze as her awareness slowly returned, and at this challenge, the lizard flared its neck frill and loosed a more aggressive hiss. Roots were pressing against her back, but someone had taken some care to make her comfortable – a blanket was draped over her, and her head was pillowed on something soft. With effort, she sat up, fighting through her aching stiffness.

"Welcome back," Tal said, tossing aside his own blanket as he rose to his feet.

Bren licked dry lips, blinking as she looked around blearily. The clearing was much as she remembered, though the fire was now just mounded ash. And Desian . . . Desian was sprawled on his back among the pine needles, the ancient book lying open beside him.

"Is he dead?" Bren managed as Tal knelt beside her with a water flask. She took it from him with hands that felt strangely clumsy, then drank deep.

"No," Tal quickly answered. "He's still breathing. But I wasn't about to get too close after last night."

Bren handed back the flask, feeling its contents settle in her empty stomach. "What happened?"

Tal swallowed, his gaze going to the forest. "There were things out there, among the trees. They were moving strangely, almost like a dance. Then Desian told you to take up the sword, and when you reached down and gripped the handle, you collapsed. I thought you were dead. I wanted to run to you, but I couldn't lift a finger, and the chanting got louder and louder until the ground was shaking." He let out a shuddering breath. "I've never felt so helpless. It was like when you wake up in the morning, but you're still half-asleep, and you can't speak or move, yet you can still sense what's around you." Tal managed a shaky smile. "So that was my night. Trapped in a nightmare with demons dancing among the trees while the sorcerer stood over you swaying and chanting. After what felt like forever, you twitched, and then Desian dropped the book and tumbled to the ground. All of a sudden I could move again, and the things in the forest were gone."

Bren's gaze drifted to the trees, remembering those writhing shadows.

A moan came from behind her, and they both started. She turned around and saw it was just Desian, his arms and legs weakly moving in the grass. The sorcerer sat up, putting his hand to his brow.

"Gods above and below, my head hurts," he slurred.

"I also don't feel so great," Bren replied.

Grimacing, Desian pushed himself to his feet. He stood there, swaying unsteadily, his gaze slowly traveling around the clearing until it alighted on the open book near his feet. Then he hissed in dismay and crouched down, gingerly closing the tome after brushing the pages clean. "Why did you leave the grimoire like this?" he asked sharply. "If it had rained, it might have been ruined. Such a loss would be incalculable."

Tal snorted. "That probably would have been for the best."

"Fool," Desian muttered, gathering up the book almost tenderly and holding it to his chest.

"The only fool here is the one consorting with dark spirits," Tal shot back. "I was certain our souls would be devoured by those things in the forest."

"But that did not happen," Desian replied tartly, stalking across the clearing to slip the book back into his saddlebag. The horse shied away, as if it sensed some remnant of last night's madness clinging to him. Bren was surprised Moon hadn't bolted, but she supposed the sorcery had also held the horses fast, just as it had Tal. She felt a stab of guilt – the night must have been absolutely terrifying. Moon had no doubt survived some harrowing moments as a paladin's destrier, but perhaps none like this.

Desian finished putting away the book and turned to face Bren. "Did it work?"

She hesitated for a moment, then shrugged. "I don't know."

"But you spoke with the spirit?" the silver-haired boy pressed.

Her memories of the barrow were hazy and growing more insubstantial by the moment. "I went somewhere underground. A dark place, but there were flames . . . and a woman in a stone chair. She looked . . . barbaric. Primitive. She wore furs and was draped in bones."

Desian was staring at her intently. "What did she say? Who was she?"

Bren frowned, struggling to remember. "She was a warrior, the leader of a tribe. She said she was Gith, but that her enemies were also Gith."

"Perhaps she speaks of the Warring Clans period," Desian mused. "There's almost no record of that age – writing as we know it had yet to be developed, and it was centuries before the oral histories recounting that time were put down. It was a mythic time of heroes and monsters, but those old stories can give us some insight into what the Gith had been like before they were united. Many tribes, all striving for dominance. This warrior woman must have been a champion or chieftain of one of them."

"She was both, I think," Bren murmured. "We spoke . . . but much of what she said I can't remember. She . . . agreed to help me, I think."

"You think?" Tal exclaimed, sounding alarmed. "You don't remember? Are you really Bren, or are we talking to the spirit right now?"

"It's me," Bren replied, sharper than she'd intended. "I can prove it if you want me to describe everything we've been through . . . including the *several* times the ghost in the sword has saved our lives."

Desian rummaged in his saddlebags and drew forth the two wooden training swords again. He tossed one onto the ground near her, then walked over to a patch of grass clear of rocks or roots.

"We need to see if anything has changed. Did the spirit abandon the sword and enter you? Was the spell successful, and can you call upon its fighting skills when needed?" He rolled his neck and winced, still obviously very stiff.

"Now?" Bren asked, the thought of moving making her body ache all the more.

Desian cut a quick pattern in the air. "Come on."

Groaning, Bren climbed to her feet and scooped up the other practice sword. She didn't feel any different or sense any great reservoir of skill that hadn't been there previously. Perhaps what had happened last night had been some sort of hallucination. She approached Desian and settled into the first guard position her uncle had taught her, raising her sword.

No . . . this wasn't right. Usually, she kept most of her weight on her back foot so she could lunge with greater strength, but this time she was spreading it evenly. And she was up more on the balls of her feet, which had always struck her as too tiring to maintain. Desian must have noticed her distraction as he chose that moment to attack, lunging forward.

She parried it. The movement was instinctual, like she had done it countless times before. With almost casual ease, she took advantage of his overextension and stepped inside his guard, then thumped his belly with the flat of her sword. He let out a *woof* of pained surprise as she continued her movement, whirling around to face him as he stumbled a few steps back. When he raised his gaze to meet hers, his eyes were wide.

"You couldn't do that yesterday," he said.

"I . . . no, you're right," Bren murmured, staring at the wooden sword in her hand. It felt so right, so natural.

"Is the ghost in your head?" Tal asked, sounding worried. She supposed she should be as well . . . but it didn't feel like something else was puppeting her. It was as if she had suddenly become a master swordswoman.

Bren turned within herself, searching for the presence she had felt before. "No. If the ghost is in me, it's being quiet."

"Oh, it's in you," Desian said, setting himself in a stance again. "You are not the warrior you were. The spirit has given you something of itself, which means the sorcery was a success."

"But did she know what would happen?" Bren said quietly, straining once more to remember what promises she had made to the dead blademaiden. The look on Ashika's face after they had sealed their pact with blood swam up out of the murk. Desian's sorcery had done something to her . . . hurt her. Bren had stolen Ashika's skill while locking the blademaiden away deep inside. That was what Desian had hoped would happen, but Bren still felt a twinge of guilt. Ashika had agreed to help her, and Bren had betrayed her.

Desian shuffled forward with the careful steps of an experienced duelist, then leaped at her with a quickness that would have shocked her not long ago. A rapid clatter of wood followed, ending when Bren sent the sorcerer's wooden sword flying into the bushes. Desian stepped back, rubbing his hand where she'd rapped his knuckles, his silver eyes studying her appraisingly.

"Whatever bargain you struck, it seems to be worth it," he said as he bent to retrieve the practice sword. "I know swordsmen who have trained for decades who could not disarm me so easily. This spirit's skill has certainly not been dulled during its long imprisonment."

"What if it wants her soul?" Tal asked, his arms crossed tightly over his chest. His disapproval was palpable and leavened with no small amount of fear.

Something swam up from the depths of her memory. "I remember," Bren said slowly, her gaze going to where the pale blade was half-buried in dark green pine needles. "I think the spirit offered to help me fight the Velaschin if I agreed to look for her old enemies."

Tal snorted, looking unconvinced. "That makes little sense. The tomb where we found that sword was ancient. Whatever enemies it had must be dust by now."

Desian seemed to be taking what she'd claimed more seriously. His lips were pursed, his silver eyes hooded. "Did the ghost say who they were? These enemies she wants you to search for?"

Bren concentrated, but it was like trying to grasp hold of a dream as it evaporated in the morning light. "No," she finally said. "But I think they were another tribe of Gith."

Desian nodded at this, relaxing slightly. "Just an old grudge, then. I suppose it's depressing to know that even in death we can't let go of such pettiness." He stepped forward and held out his hand to take the practice sword from her. "We should leave. Yestra is far, and the summer solstice is fast approaching. We must get you there before the Winnowing starts."

16

B ren had dreaded the journey east because they would be going directly towards the maw of the Velaschin army devouring the realm, but to her great surprise the way was remarkably free of dangers. It was as the older dragon rider had told her in the Briar's bailey: the Velaschin legions were not here to pillage but to conquer, and they did not want to rule over a resentful, desolate kingdom. Most of the local lords of the lands they passed through had, like the Duke of Thorns, bent the knee with alacrity once the queen's army had been scattered. They did pass one striking exception perched on a hill overlooking the Gith road they were traveling along, the ruin of what had once been a massive fortress, shattered walls blackened and ribbons of smoke rising from still-smoldering rubble. A farm they stopped at nearby to trade for fresh meat and milk told them that the castle had belonged to an old, stubborn baron who had cursed the Velaschin army from his battlements moments before being consumed by searing darkness expelled by the monstrous black dragon ridden by the Velaschin commander. The farmer had shuddered as he told this tale, which had been relayed to him by a small group of warriors who had fled the fortress before it was destroyed, but he had also admitted that the fortnight since the invaders had first entered these lands had been otherwise peaceful – the greatest danger, in truth, were the bands of broken men who had deserted their liege lords . . . such as the ones who had told him of their baron's folly and then made off with his prize sow and a dozen chickens.

At the inns they stayed in, they heard similar tales. The Velaschin officers were aloof and stern, but they paid for the room and meals with good silver coins, if oddly stamped, and the soldiers camped in the fields outside town did not bother the young women or quarrel with the young men. The discipline they displayed was admirable, more than a few folks admitted grudgingly. Bren bit her lip to keep from telling them about what the dragon lords had done to her farm and her innocent family. Not that they would have believed her, with her pale skin and dark hair. Then again, perhaps the responses they received to their questions were influenced by her resemblance to their new overlords.

Desian had insisted on staying in the finest accommodations available, paying for suites usually reserved for nobility and dining on venison or pheasant, accompanied always by copious amounts of goldenwine. This sort of luxury was completely unknown to Bren – the beds were so stuffed with goose feathers it felt like she was sleeping on a cloud, and the food dusted with spices she'd never encountered before, such as burning pepper, bitter hyssop, and sweet, pungent cinnamon. The dinners were so rich that she suffered from stomach pangs, and so she began refusing the portions Desian offered and instead eating the simplest fare available, usually a coarse black bread and stew that had been prepared for the poorest patrons.

During these dinners, she tried to find out what she could about the silver-eyed boy. He looked no older than her or Tal, but he seemed to have lived so much more: he was clearly worldly, familiar with many of the lands they passed through and accustomed to the finest things in life. His skill with a sword was also noteworthy – she suspected he had trained with a blade for many years, surprising since he must also have spent a great deal of time studying the secrets of the Jade House. When she asked him about his past he deflected her questions, refusing to divulge anything beyond that he had been given over to the sorcerers as a babe and had served Nasai in many cities along the Flowering Coast. He had even been to Yestra, though at that time the Velaschin had been confined to a single island in the lagoon, a trade mission from where they'd dispatched caravans carrying their exotic goods westward. Desian spoke of how those first visitors had shown little interest in the rest of the kingdom, rarely interacting with the local people and seemingly aloof from the politics of Felaesia. It had been a great surprise when their fleet had suddenly appeared on the horizon, dragons circling above sleek black warships.

The mention of Yestra had piqued Tal's interest, and Desian had smoothly turned to describing the City of Lotuses. Bren suspected he had seized this chance to lead them away from talk of his own past, but she hadn't pressed him further because she was also curious about their destination. Yestra was held to be almost as mysterious as the far western lands beyond the Crimson Dominion, and Bren remembered listening raptly as a child to the old storytellers of her village describe its mist-shrouded islands and masked revelries. Desian did not indulge in any of the more fantastical tales, like about the Eyeless who could peer into the souls of men or the hundred singing consorts of the caliphant – instead, the boy described the port in a far more prosaic manner. Yestra was composed of more than a hundred islands of varying sizes in a lagoon fed by the brackish waters of the Cull, the great eastern sea that had been thought to be uncrossable until the Velaschin had first appeared two decades ago. For much of the year a damp and cold mist rolled off those endless swells, clotting the stone streets and slithering beneath arched bridges. This was where Yestra's reputation for mystery and magic came from, Desian explained, but the Jade House in the City of Lotuses had been no more powerful than the chapters in Chalice or Malai. And now the sorcerers that had inhabited those mist-haunted islands were believed to be all dead, the very first victims of Velaschin aggression.

"What about the caliphant?" Tal had asked, interrupting Desian's recounting of how the dragon lords had deployed assassins like the Huntress to murder the chosen of Nasai just before the arrival of their fleet.

The sorcerer had scowled into his goldenwine before draining his cup. "The current caliphant is nothing like his forebears. They were master schemers, and as the historian Aeschaptys once famously penned, 'ferociously intelligent and unencumbered by the morality of their lessers'. Some were even whispered to be dabblers in sorcery, though I can assure you that Yestra's Jade House believed those rumors to be false. More likely, the lattice of spies and informants the old caliphants had woven into the city led many to believe they commanded otherworldly powers. But the current boy who sits the Seasworn Throne is even more pathetic than that idiot Duke of Thorns. He allowed the Velaschin to gather their strength right under his nose while putting on extravagant fetes, draining the treasury his ancestors had filled to bursting. They let him live, the last I heard, but he is nothing more than their puppet now." Desian had motioned brusquely for the tavern's serving girl to refill his cup. "Our lords have grown fat and comfortable ever since the old king united the Flowering Coast. Gone are the great men who jostled for glory and preeminence. We have become hollowed out by corruption and avarice." He had rubbed his chin thoughtfully as the girl tipped out the last of the bottle, drops glittering like specks of gold as they fell. "I wonder if the Velaschin knew of our weakness before their traders arrived in Yestra. That would suggest they had been scouting Felaesia for quite some time, watching as it slowly weakened." His grip had tightened about his cup, but he hadn't taken a drink. Instead, his silver eyes had gone to Bren. "But troubled times forge great men and women. And nothing tempers like dragon fire. Perhaps once we throw these bastards back into the sea, our land and people will be reborn, stronger and more glorious."

His words had touched something in Bren, and she'd found herself raising her watered ale towards the sorcerer. "They do not know what is coming," she had said, her other hand closing around her silver amulet.

The corner of Desian's mouth had lifted, and he had mirrored her gesture with his goldenwine. "No, they most certainly do not."

As they drew closer to Yestra, the air and sky changed, late-summer warmth giving way to a deepening chill, while the untrammeled blue above faded to a colorless gray. Bren was fine, as her father's cloak was good, thick wool meant to keep shepherds comfortable during the cold months when biting winds swept down from the Snowspears, and Desian had wisely procured for himself somewhere a fine dark coat trimmed with white fur, but Tal had evidently not been expecting such a drastic change and was soon clearly suffering in his thin tunic and trousers. Bren suspected that Desian had known very well what the weather would be like as they neared the coast and had intentionally chosen not to warn Tal. It was the sort of small pettiness Bren had come to expect from the sorcerer – though, in truth, if the situation were reversed, Tal would have done the same to him. Their dislike for each other had not softened during the journey, and Bren sometimes felt like she was a mother trying to keep the peace between squabbling siblings.

"You can wear my cloak for a while if you want," Bren offered, nudging Moon to come up alongside Tal's dappled horse. The fog that had risen to swallow the road not long after they had left last night's inn was clammy and wet, and she'd been watching Tal shiver for quite some time.

"I'm f-fine," he replied through chattering teeth, rubbing at his arms. "Just need for the sun to burn away this mist."

"You might be waiting a while for that," Desian called back from where he was riding a little ahead of them. "We're close to Scabtown, I can smell it."

"Scabtown?" Bren asked, taking an exploratory sniff. She couldn't smell anything except for leaves and wood rotting in the dampness. The trees hemming the Gith road had been steadily dwindling in size and number, but there was still plenty of moldering detritus covering the forest floor. Bren had wondered if the wet climate kept fires from regularly cleaning out what had accumulated.

"It's the only part of the city on the mainland," Desian replied. "Though most citizens refuse to consider the dwellers of Scabtown as proper Yestrians. The main docks that are used to ferry goods and travelers to the islands are there, and a rather rough little town has grown up around them."

"Will we see some big ships?" Bren asked, peering into the murk and hoping to see the shadows of great masts. Her uncle had told her of the mighty carracks the Velaschins had used to traverse the Cull – he'd said some were so large that their entire village could have sheltered below deck. Bren's mood darkened at the memory. That had been years ago, when the Velaschin were still thought to be merely strange, sea-faring traders from distant lands.

Desian shook his head. "Only barges and small boats frequent these docks. True ocean-worthy ships moor in the harbors on the Isle of Laughing Children and the Isle of Lost Shadows, depending on whether they're here to trade or indulge in Yestra's famed night pleasures."

"Well, the first thing we need to do is buy some warmer clothes," Bren said. Something occurred to her, and she turned to rummage around in her saddlebags, then handed one of the blankets they used when sleeping outside to Tal. He accepted it gratefully, nodding in thanks. "On which isle can we do that?"

Desian loosed a long-suffering sigh. "I will take him to a shop I know on the Isle of Broken Swords. That's where we will be staying. You, of course, will go elsewhere."

"What?" Bren cried, her hands tightening on the reins. "I thought we would all be together?"

"Tharos gleaned what he could about this Winnowing while forming his plan, and while it might be different when conducted on this side of the Cull, back in the Velaschin empire those competing to bond with a hatchling are sequestered away together. It is quite possible we will part ways in Scabtown and not see each other again until the Winnowing is finished. You will be on your own . . . except, of course, for the spirit."

Bren sat back in her saddle, a numbness separate from the feeling brought on by the terrible weather beginning to spread through her. She would be alone? The hopes of the Silver Mother rested on just her and a ghost? She swallowed, trying to tamp down her rising panic. Desian might be annoying and arrogant, but he was also knowledgeable and skilled in so many things, and his faith in what they were doing was really the only reason she thought this plan had any chance of success.

"You can do this, Bren," Tal said quietly, apparently having noticed her inner turmoil. She glanced over and was surprised by the calm confidence in his dark eyes. "I know it." The boy crooked a smile, and for the first time in a long while he looked something other than miserable. "No matter how hard things get, just remember that it can't be nearly as terrible as having to wait for your return with only *that* one for company." He pointed emphatically at the back of Desian's silver head.

"I heard that!" Desian shouted at them, and Bren had to stifle a giggle as Tal stuck out his tongue at the sorcerer.

Despite what Desian had said, in the end she heard Scabtown before she smelled it. Raised voices carried to them through the mist, accompanied by the clang of metal and the braying of animals. The woods had vanished, replaced by empty moors unfurling into the whiteness, and recessed within this bleakness she could glimpse simple wooden structures and the hunched shadows of their inhabitants.

"Not much space on the islands for the truly poor," Desian explained as they passed a pair of hollow-eyed children in ragged clothes picking weeds by the wayside. "The ones here survive on Yestra's scraps and by selling what they can scavenge from the land."

The number of crude huts and lean-tos grew as they continued on, sprouting on either side of the road like mushrooms from filth. They'd left the black stone of the Gith road some time ago, and now their horses were slogging along a muddy trail that did not seem like it could possibly lead to one of the greatest cities of the Flowering Coast. Still, Bren was expecting to arrive at some huge gate or doorway that marked the real entrance to Scabtown, but instead the buildings simply grew closer together, with some swelling to include a second story. They were only built of wood and looked haphazardly constructed, but this did indeed appear more like a real settlement, with hand-painted signs hanging over some doorways and even a few smoking fire pits where men were selling some scrawny little lizards blackened to a crisp and threaded on sticks.

The cries of seabirds rose above Scabtown's clamor, and now Bren smelled what she assumed must be the sea – sharp and salty but with the distinct aroma of rotten eggs. Desian must have seen her wrinkling her nose as he breathed in deep and then leaned close to her to be heard over the sounds of the little town.

"Ah, must be low tide."

Bren had no idea what that meant, but before she could ask, they reached the end of the road and the answer became obvious. Docks of varying lengths thrust out from the edge of Scabtown into a great expanse of water that vanished into the mist. Hummocks of gray-brown earth breached the surface here and there, and Bren could tell from the coloration of the shore in its upper reaches that the sea sometimes climbed much higher. Another time, she might have been interested in going down to explore what the retreating water had exposed, but right now her senses were being overwhelmed by the frantic activity on the docks. Men rushed this way and that, carrying bales and rolling barrels and loading crates onto wide, flat-bottomed boats under the supervision of overseers. Grubby boys and girls scurried underfoot, some playing and others looking like they had been set to tasks that required little hands and quick feet.

Desian slid from his saddle, then had to jump out of the way as a mangy dog scampered past chased by a pack of laughing urchins.

"But . . . where is Yestra?" Tal murmured, staring in confusion at the chaos roiling the docks. It looked to Bren like what was revealed when one dug up an insect mound.

"It's out there," Desian said, nodding towards the calm gray waters. "That's where all this is going. Takes a lot to keep the city fed and supplied."

Bren peered into the murk, and she thought she could indeed sense something vast lurking there, hidden in the fog.

"Out of the way!" bellowed a swarthy man covered in intricate red tattoos as he strode past them carrying what looked like a small mast balanced on his shoulder. Tal had to duck to avoid being brained by the length of wood, and Desian's silver eyes flashed in anger.

"Let's move," Bren said, leading Moon away from the bustle. Desian grunted in annoyance, but he followed her to a quieter corner of the docks filled with barrels stamped with a snake eating its own tail.

"They don't seem particularly troubled to be under the Velaschin's thumbs," Tal murmured as he watched the tumult.

"Common folk don't care very much who sits the throne," Bren replied, rooting in her saddlebag for carrots to give the horses, "so long as they have food on their plates and walls to protect their families. We saw that in Leris. And the dragon lords clearly understand how to win the hearts of the people."

"Just wait until they start burning the daughter's houses," Desian said bitterly. "They came for the sorcerers first, and no one cared . . . if they even knew what was happening to us. But the chosen of Nasai were what they feared, and the heathens will turn to the Mother and her other children soon enough. And then we'll see if the promise of full bellies is a fair exchange for their immortal souls."

Bren bit her lip, knowing that the answer she was about to give would only further irritate the sorcerer. Instead, she decided to change the topic to something they needed to discuss now that they had arrived . . . though she had been dreading this conversation.

"What do we do now?" she asked, stroking the side of Moon's face as he crunched on the carrot she had given him.

The annoyance in Desian's face softened. "Here is where we part.

I saw some guardsmen wearing the lotus of Yestra – they are supposed to be keeping an eye on things here, but they seemed far more interested in a game of knucklebones. I'm certain that there is a Velaschin who has been put in charge, as the docks are simply too important for keeping the city fat and content, so you should go to those guards and ask to see their superior. I doubt the Winnowing will mean very much to them, but once they get a good look at you, they'll trip over themselves to help. Then I assume you'll be taken to wherever the egg is to see if you truly have the potential to bond with the dragon inside."

"And the thing Tharos put in my arm is to make sure I at least pass that test," Bren said, glancing at the faint discoloration on her arm. It had faded since Tharos had first magicked it under her flesh, but the feeling of something strange and unnatural lodged inside her had only grown.

"Yes, and you will," Desian said confidently. "That much I can assure you. But whether you triumph in the one that comes after . . ." He glanced at her, and for a moment, Bren saw what he usually kept very well hidden beneath his arrogant and glib exterior. The sorcerer was worried, and that made her even more nervous.

"And we just wait for her?" Tal asked, his frustration plain. "There's nothing we can do to help?"

"It is in Bren's hands now," Desian replied, his confident expression returning. "And the Silver Mother's, of course."

"Can I take Moon with me?" Bren doubted the horse could assist her in her trials, but his mere presence was a pillar of strength she could lean against if the doubts gnawing at her grew too severe.

"I believe it's best if your horse comes with us," Desian replied. "Paladin's steeds are not like other horses, and traces of the Silver Mother's grace clings to them. It's possible that a Velaschin like the Huntress or one of their warlocks might recognize Her touch, and I don't know how you would explain that away."

Bren had been stroking her horse's mane, and now her hand tightened around the silvery hair. As if he sensed her distress and wanted to calm her, Moon butted his head gently against her shoulder.

"Tal and I will wait for you at *The Windblown Inn* on the Isle of Broken Swords. Can you remember those names?"

Bren nodded mutely, still dazed from the realization that she couldn't even take Moon with her. She would be completely alone again, for the first time since that terrible night she'd crawled from the ruin of her farmhouse.

"Good," Desian continued. "Whatever happens during the Winnowing, come find us after." When he finished speaking he continued staring at her, and Bren quickly realized that he meant for her to say her goodbyes and leave *now*. It all felt so sudden; she wasn't ready . . . but when *would* she be ready? Never. So she should just go before she had the chance to doubt what she was doing.

Bren turned away from the two boys and busied herself with untying her travel bag from Moon's saddle, hoping they couldn't tell how unsteadied she was. Her hand hovered over the hilt of the barrow sword, unsure whether she should bring it. Desian had said he thought no weapons would be allowed into the Winnowing . . .

"Take the sword," the sorcerer said, evidently noticing her hesitation. "It may be useful in some way, even though the spirit inside is now gone."

Gone into me. Such a strange, unreal thought. But at least she wouldn't be alone . . . maybe ever again.

No, she most definitely shouldn't dwell on *that* right now.

Trying her best to push aside her doubts, Bren unhooked the sword from where it hung and buckled it around her waist. Had she felt a little pang of excitement as the weight settled at her side? And had it come from her or the ghost of the Gith blademaiden? What if—

"Oh," she squeaked as Tal suddenly came to stand in front of her, putting his hands on her shoulders.

"You can do this, Bren," he said, and the absolute faith she heard in his voice almost made her shiver in relief.

"Thank you," she whispered, and she meant it.

"And if you need any help, try to send a message," he added, holding her gaze to demonstrate how serious he was.

"Just don't lead them back to us," Desian said quickly. "The Velaschin would very much like to get their hands on me."

"I'll be careful," Bren promised, probably a little too brusquely, but she was trying not to show how much Tal's support had meant to her. She busied herself with preparing to go, then placed her hands on either side of Moon's head and touched brows with him.

"Be safe," she said, and the horse *whuffed* in reply. Then she squared her shoulders and without looking back plunged into the swirling activity of the docks. She made her way directly towards the guardsmen wearing the lotus-livery of Yestra, wiping her face of a few stray tears as she pushed through the crowd. They were slouched against the wall of an ancient building, staring intently at where a few rough-looking men were tossing bones in the shadows. One of them glanced towards her when she arrived, then waved dismissively as he returned his attention to the game.

"Go away, whelp," he drawled. "We're not here to find the thieves that stole your coin purse."

"I want you to take me to your commander," Bren said, trying to infuse this request with as much authority as she could muster.

Both guardsmen turned, as did most of the men throwing dice. The one who had spoken to her curled his lip in disdain. "Look, *girl*," he began, but his words died in his throat as she reached up and pulled back her cowl.

"I've come for the Winnowing," she said, allowing herself no small amount of satisfaction at the sudden panic she saw in the guardsmen's faces.

17

"Who are you, really?"

"Brenna Gelindotter, as I said. From the Seven Valleys."

The pale Velaschin man seated across from her in the rowboat narrowed his beady eyes. "But from which of the families? Varyxes? Karth?"

Bren sighed and turned her head to look out over the choppy water. They were passing close enough to an island that it was more than just a shadow recessed in the mist, facades of carved green stone emerging from the murk. She closed her eyes, trying to replenish her rapidly diminishing store of patience.

"I'm not from one of these families you keep talking about."

"Then you are not truly Blooded!" the officious man said triumphantly. "And thus, you are wasting my time when I am well behind on my ledgers."

Bren groaned, rubbing at her temple to forestall the headache she felt coming on. "Once again, I am an orphan raised in these lands. I have never been to Velasch. But I met a dragon rider in Leris, and he believed me to be Blooded." *Whatever that truly means.*

"Agiz ben-Ahzan," the man said, and Bren could hear the wary disbelief in his voice.

"Yes. And he said I should come to Yestra for the Winnowing. That I deserved the chance to claim a dragon for myself."

The man sniffed, adjusting the frilled and now damp sleeves of his strangely cut frock. To Bren his clothes looked vaguely like something the rich ladies at the Briar might have worn, but she had come to understand that this was some sort of uniform for those in his trade. He'd called himself a clerk of the Tavernik Guild, and as he'd been poring over reams of paper covered with tiny numbers when she'd been brought to him in one of the warehouses near the dock, she supposed he was an administrator responsible for keeping count of the goods passing through Scabtown. He'd been incensed at being interrupted, but a mention of the Winnowing had drained all the blood from his face. Apparently, the mere chance she was indeed truly Blooded had necessitated him personally escorting her to the island where the trials would occur.

"If you are Blooded, you came from one of the families. Even the boatman here knows *that*." The Velaschin gestured at the gnarled little man straining at the oars, who stared back at him gormlessly, watery eyes blank. "Well, maybe *he* doesn't. But *he* does," the clerk amended, now indicating the Velaschin warrior standing at the bow in intricate black armor. The soldier straightened when he noticed he was now the center of attention, though he did not confirm or deny this claim.

"He's from your empire," Bren said tiredly. "I am not. I know almost nothing about your people."

The man sniffed again, plucking at his sleeves aggressively. "*Your* people? Your people as well, or so you say. How can you even entertain the idea of participating in the Winnowing?" He shook his tonsured head in disgust.

"Agiz ben-Ahzan—"

"Yes, Agiz ben-Ahzan," the man said testily, interrupting her. "His name is the only reason I'm even bringing you to the testing grounds.

And when the Sisters turn you away, don't expect me to return you to the docks. You can make your own way back."

"Fine," Bren said, crossing her arms and pointedly turning away from the man. She heard him sniff yet again, but apparently he had also decided he'd had enough of this exchange, as he finally lapsed into silence.

Instead, she watched the islands slide past, bewildered by the strangeness of this city. It was like Yestra had been shattered into hundreds of different shards or perhaps was in the process of sinking beneath the sea. Some of the rocky fragments were barely large enough for a single building, while others looked like they could contain her entire village with room to spare. These more impressive islands rivaled Scabtown in size, great lanterns that glowed like moons in the mist guiding crafts to their docks. Every ferry and barge and rowboat like Bren was in now also had a lantern dangling from its upraised prow, likely because without such a light the risk of collision would be too great. She thought it was only a little past midday, but the mist made it impossible to tell. Bren had also noticed that there were no ships large enough to sail on the sea moving between the islands – she assumed that was because the lagoon must be quite shallow.

Something large flapped through the fog above their heads, and Bren wondered if it was just a seabird or a messenger bird like the one that this Velaschin official had released before their departure. After writing out a message on a tiny scroll, he'd taken her to a rookery grafted onto the side of the warehouse where dozens of long-necked gray birds had been nesting. An old man, his face slicked by burn scars, had tied the message to a leg of one of those birds and then released it, and it had vanished honking into the murk. Bren thought this was a clever way to pass information quickly between the city's scattered islands, though she wondered if the birds ever went missing along their routes.

The question whether their bird had arrived safely was answered when the swirling mists parted to reveal the island they were approaching. A wide pier thrust far out into the lagoon, and waiting at its end for their little boat were a dozen or so figures shrouded in gray robes, hoods drawn down and hands tucked into long, loose sleeves. If the Velaschin official had not hurriedly risen to bow in their direction – which rocked the rowboat alarmingly and made Bren clutch at the side – then she might have thought they were strange statues set to greet visitors to what must be an island of some importance. Great shapes loomed behind these figures, bulked deep within the mist, and Bren could vaguely make out a huge dome and a trio of slender minarets. These buildings were larger than any she had seen on the other islands, and because of the lack of activity on the docks she had to assume this was not a place the common folk of Yestra frequented.

The old oarsman leaped up with surprising agility as their boat bumped against the docks and hurriedly tied it to a piling. Bren noticed he made an effort to not so much as glance in the direction of the silent figures standing nearby, and before she had even stood up in the boat he had already returned to his place at the oars with his gaze fixed on the knotted wood between his feet. The tonsured Velaschin official crossed over onto the docks far more awkwardly, then offered another deep bow with his hands pressed together. He also kept his eyes lowered, and Bren could see the pronounced apple in his throat bobbing up and down nervously like he was swallowing back whatever words he wanted to say. Bren followed him onto the island, though she did not attempt the same formal greeting. Instead, she nodded slightly in the Seven Valley way when one came upon strangers in the fields or woods, her hands open at her sides.

"So it is true. A prodigal daughter returns." The voice was cracked by age but strong, and when the figure that had spoken reached up to draw back her cowl Bren was not surprised to see that the woman's face was deeply lined. Her eyes were still unclouded though, dark and shrewd, and Bren felt a little like a mouse under a hawk's gaze. She was also one of the largest women Bren had ever seen despite her many years, her once-broad shoulders now hunched.

"I am not a daughter of Velasch," Bren said, lifting her chin to show she would not be intimidated. "I was raised in the west. My name is Brenna."

"And yet you come to us with a request to join the Winnowing," the imposing crone continued, withdrawing a crooked and claw-like hand from the depths of a dagged sleeve. Her fingers were closed tightly around something, but Bren couldn't tell what it was.

"I met a dragon rider in Leris. He told me I was Blooded and that I should come here to claim my birthright."

"Your birthright," the old woman muttered, shaking her head. "Agiz has always been a sentimental fool. Only he would encourage a girl who knows nothing of our ways to compete for a hatchling. A child reared by our enemies, no less!" She must have noticed Bren's surprise when she said the dragon rider's name, because she smiled sourly before continuing. "Yes, we know of your meeting in the City of Roses. The Old Drake sent a message to the temple that he had discovered a Velaschin with the old blood. We have been expecting you." The old woman raised her hand and unfolded her fingers, showing what was nestled in the center of her palm. It looked like a tiny shard of bone, maybe a vertebra, ancient and pitted.

"Sister Jaleska," the crone said, and one of the shrouded figures behind her stepped forward. "You will be this one's aide during the trials."

"Yes, Abbess Baya," the figure murmured in a voice that sounded surprisingly young. With quick steps, she approached the old woman and held out her cupped hands, her head lowered respectfully. "It will be as you desire."

The old woman did not look at her subordinate as she passed over the piece of bone, continuing to stare at Bren with her raptor gaze. "You are an outsider, girl, and you will never pass the trials to come. The Winnowing is a cleansing flame that consumes the weak and ill-prepared – only a true child of Velasch raised in one of the families will ever ride a dragon. But I know the old laws better than anyone. You shall have your chance, even if it is folly. And afterwards . . . who knows, perhaps a place can be found for you in the empire, if you are lucky." With that pronouncement the old woman turned and began striding away with a vigor that belied her age. Most of the shrouded figures turned to follow her, save for the girl who had been charged with preparing Bren for what was to come. She watched her fellows vanish into the mists, then glanced at the fragment of bone in her hand before finally looking to Bren. As she did this, she pulled back her cowl, revealing rounded cheeks and hair the color of late-summer straw.

"You can go," she said, and for a moment, Bren thought the girl was talking to her. Then she heard a frantic clattering as the Velaschin clerk who had brought her here untied the rope from the piling and scrambled back into the rowboat. Bren opened her mouth to say farewell, but the words died in her throat when she realized the man and the guardsman still standing at the prow were trying their best not to look at her as the oarsman pushed the boat away from the docks. Soon they were also swallowed by the fog, leaving Bren alone with the girl.

Who was staring at her in unabashed interest, her hands on her hips and head cocked to one side. "Hello," she said. "I'm Jaleska. Did you say your name was Brenna?"

"Call me Bren."

The girl's eyes brightened. "Oh! Bren, then. A great pleasure to meet you!"

Bren blinked in surprise. The cheery friendliness of the girl was in stark contrast to everyone else she had met this morning.

"And the same to you," Bren replied, expecting the girl to start leading her somewhere, or at least explain what she should do now. When that did not happen, she looked around uncertainly. The mist was encroaching where they stood on the docks, tendrils slithering closer like great pale snakes. Bren rubbed at her arms, trying to banish the creeping chill.

"You must be cold," Jaleska said. "I was born in the foothills of the Wraiths, so I'm used to fog thick as mallar soup. Dancing with ghosts, my mum used to call this weather, the Endless save her soul."

Bren blinked at her, struggling to understand what she'd just said.

Her accent was far more pronounced than any of the previous Velaschin she had spoken to, a tumble of strangely rolled syllables.

"Let's get you inside," Jaleska said amiably, motioning for Bren to follow her. "It's a bit of a walk to the testing grounds." She spun on her heels with a lightness that seemed incongruous with the somber robes she wore, roiling the mist as she plunged ahead.

Bren hurried to catch up. "I'm sorry, but where are you taking me? And who are you?"

The girl glanced at her askance. "I told you my name."

"Yes, Jaleska," Bren said, suppressing a sigh. "I mean, what are you? Why were you waiting for me?"

"I am a Sister in the Temple Draconium, of course," she said slowly, as if talking to a simpleton. "Who else would be meeting you on the docks? Surely you didn't think you'd just wander around until you found the other aspirants?"

Bren swallowed back her rising frustration. The girl was several years younger than she was, and obviously not accustomed to conversing with those completely ignorant in the ways of her people. Bren sighed, focusing on her surroundings rather than this annoying conversation. The avenue they were walking down was broad and tree-lined, the branches arching overhead dripping with vegetation. Once again, Bren was struck by the emptiness of this place, especially after the bustle of Scabtown. Perhaps this girl would be a bit more forthcoming about her new home.

"Where are we? Why are there no other people here?"

Jaleska reached up to brush her fingers through a clump of hanging moss. "There are others here! Lots of them. But this is a big island. It's where the plays were held."

"The ... plays?"

"Yes! The tragedies and comedies and epics. During festival days, the caliphant would invite his people here to watch the performances. It was open to every freeborn in the city, or so I was told. They'd come and watch the actors in their masks, and there would also be dances and tumbling and maybe even some magic." Jaleska's tone was wistful, as if she regretted never getting to see what she was describing. "After Lord Bessam Karth took the city, he gave this island over to the Temple Draconium. Now it's just us Sisters here. Oh, and the other aspirants, of course."

The trees standing sentinel abruptly ended, the avenue they followed emptying into a large plaza. To their right and left, other roads of similar width led off into the murk, but across from them a huge structure bulked, and it was perhaps the largest she had ever seen outside of the Briar. It didn't look like any other building she'd encountered before – the walls were windowless, the only entrance a massive archway that looked large enough for a dozen riders to pass through side by side. Huge scenes were carved into the façade, though the details were difficult to discern through the fog.

"The Odeum," Jaleska told her, a note of awe creeping into her voice. "Thousands could go inside to watch the plays. There's even a viewing box for the caliphant and his courtesans made completely out of onyx and silver. And if you look down from the highest benches..."

Jaleska kept talking, but what she was saying faded into irrelevance. Bren's breathing quickened, and she had to press her hand to her suddenly tight chest. Something invisible had emerged from the mist to wash over her like a wave. She felt like she was drowning, a flood of something cold and terrible forcing its way down her throat to pool in her stomach. It was an aching sorrow that hurt so much it made her want to lie down right here on the cobbled stone of the plaza and curl up in sadness with her tail tucked beneath her, just as she used to sleep with the Lady...

"Bren! Bren!"

She surfaced from these smothering thoughts, looking around blearily as if just coming awake. The Velaschin girl was shaking her arm, her round face creased with concern.

"What?" Bren murmured thickly, trying to understand what had just happened. Already the tide that had washed over her was receding, but in its absence she felt hollowed out, like it had taken something with her.

"I don't know! You just stopped walking and started shaking! I thought you were going to faint!"

"I'm all right," Bren whispered. "I don't know what came over me."

No, that wasn't entirely true. She'd felt like this before, on the night she'd crawled out from under the ruin of her house . . . with dirt under her fingernails as she scooped earth from the hole where she would bury her mother . . . the feel of burned flesh and bone, even though she tried her best to swaddle the remains tightly inside the blanket . . . it was that same sadness that swallowed every shred of her being and left nothing behind but a cold and desolate emptiness. But why was she feeling this again now? Why would—

"Ash and flame."

There was something alarming about the way Jaleska breathed these words – heavy with awe and surprise and not a small amount of fear. Bren struggled out from beneath the strange miasma that had settled over her, trying to understand what was the matter. The Velaschin girl was staring open-mouthed past Bren in the direction of what she had called the Odeum; Bren turned towards the entrance, and her attention was drawn by movement above the great archway.

Something huge lifted itself over the top of the wall. A paralyzing fear swept through Bren as the great shadow pushed itself through the clotting fog, revealing a monstrous head – dark blue scales, yellow eyes with irises of burning orange, wisps of mist clinging to curving horns. A serpentine neck twisted as its gaze swept the plaza below until finally settling on the intruders. It was a dragon, but larger than any other Bren had seen, easily half again as large as the great black beast that had flown over Leris to perch atop the Briar.

Bren had been in the presence of dragons before, but this time was different. This time she could feel the power of its attention as it focused on her, the awesome will behind that blazing gaze. This was no dumb beast, as she had once told Tal. There was a deepness within those eyes, an abyss that threatened to swallow her. She felt herself being drawn in, and the terrible sadness rose again, stronger than before.

She fell forward into the darkness.

WHEN BREN WOKE, she found herself staring into clouded blue eyes set in a nest of wrinkles. Bushy white eyebrows rose as the face that had been almost pressed against her own drew back.

"She returns to us!" cried the old man, clapping his hands together. He was dressed in robes of purest white, a golden circlet resting on his brow.

"What happened?" Bren slurred, looking around as she struggled into a sitting position on a mound of pillows. They were inside a large tent, the fabric spreading above her infused with a pale glow. This was not the only light, as a buttery radiance spilled from a strange metal contraption in the center of the tent, some kind of lantern with shapes cut into its sides. The cheerful, plump-cheeked girl who had met her at the docks had been fiddling with the device, and now she hurriedly snapped something closed and approached Bren. The other furniture in the room was just as strange, rounded chairs of burnished red wood and a low divan covered with brightly colored cushions.

"You collapsed, my dear," the old man told her, coming closer again to rest the back of his hand on her forehead. "Overwhelmed by your first close encounter with one of our dragons."

Not my first encounter, Bren almost said, but then she decided to keep that to herself. The less the Velaschin knew about her, the better.

"I sent for a doctor once we got you comfortable," Jaleska said, coming to crouch near her. Bren found the concern she saw in the girl's face somewhat surprising, given that they had just met. "Luckily, a patrol came by to investigate what had caught Mist's attention. I don't think I could have wrestled you into this tent on my own. You're heavier than you look!" She scooted closer, eyes bright. "How do you feel? What happened back there?"

"I . . . don't know," Bren murmured, touching the side of her temple. She could still feel a fading echo of the sensation that had overwhelmed her. "There was this great black sadness, and it seemed to come out of nowhere."

Jaleska and the doctor shared a glance, something passing between them.

"What?" Bren asked, surprised that they seemed almost excited.

"Well," the doctor said, smiling gently. "I think we know what this is. And it's nothing serious."

"It's actually quite auspicious," Jaleska assured her with a pleased smile.

"Oh, really?" Bren replied sourly, rubbing at her still-aching head.

"Indeed," the girl said, turning back to the doctor, who looked to be preparing to depart. "Thank you for coming so quickly. I'm sorry it wasn't really necessary. This is my first aspirant, and I guess I'm just nervous."

The old man paused in his gathering of various herbs and bottles strewn across a table and waved his hand dismissively. "It's nothing, Sister. I understand completely. One can't be too careful with these things."

Jaleska bowed her head with her hands pressed together in what must have been a gesture of thanks. The white-robed doctor acknowledged this with a nod, then closed his now-bulging bag and departed the tent.

"So you're saying what happened to me was a good thing?" Bren asked after the flaps had rustled closed.

"Yes! It bodes well for the hatchling responding in your presence. You clearly are Blooded – Mist was drawn by your arrival, and you sensed what she was feeling."

Bren frowned. "What she was feeling? Do you mean that . . . that sadness?" She shuddered. "It was awful."

"She lost her rider," Jaleska explained, standing and going over to the strange lantern again. A metal flask was positioned on top of the device, and she took it down and poured its steaming contents into a cup. "It was a tragedy. Vera ben-Ahzan was a great hero, and we all mourned when we learned of her death."

"What happened?" Bren asked, accepting the cup when Jaleska

returned to her side. It was the most beautiful object she'd ever held, small and white and patterned with red dragonflies in flight. It was also very hot, so she quickly put it down on the side table next to her.

"An arrow," Jaleska said with a sigh. "Just terribly unlucky. The battle was over and she'd brought Mist down to speak with General Varyxes, and no one suspected there was an archer still hidden in the trees."

Bren sank back into the mounded pillows. She'd felt the dragon's sorrow. It hadn't been her own, even though it had seemed so familiar. She'd feared that some barrier she'd built had been breached, that without Tal and Moon and even Desian around to fill the emptiness yawning inside her she would tumble into that pit. Bren shook her head to banish the last lingering shreds of her headache. She had a purpose, a very important purpose. She needed to focus . . . and also to understand more about what had happened.

"Try the kefa," Jaleska said, indicating the cup Bren had set down. "Everyone drinks it in Velasch, but it doesn't seem to exist on this side of the sea."

Bren licked her lips, suddenly realizing how thirsty she was, and then under Jaleska's apprehensive gaze she gingerly picked up the beautiful little cup and tentatively sipped the black liquid within.

"Sages," she muttered, wrinkling her nose as she hurriedly set it down again. "It's so bitter."

"Are you sure you're truly Velaschin?" Jaleska asked, looking crestfallen. "I thought for sure you'd love kefa. We have it every meal after we're old enough to stop drinking our mother's milk."

"Well, that's why you like it," Bren said, trying to swallow the last dregs of bitterness in her mouth.

"I just thought we'd be the same," Jaleska continued wistfully. "Even though you were raised in these lands."

That reminded Bren of a question that had been gnawing at her for quite some time. "But we are the same in many ways. For one, you use our language, though you speak it strangely. How is that possible when your people come from so far away?"

"You speak *our* language strangely," Jaleska said, sounding slightly miffed. "We spoke it first."

"That's impossible," Bren said, shaking her head. "We have always lived in these lands. Our history is ancient. A trader from the Crimson Dominion once came to our village, and when he was asked how he knew our tongue, he told our Keeper that in all the old dominions of Gith it was the same. In truth, it is their language that we speak."

Jaleska bit down on her lip, as if she wanted to say something but was uncertain whether she should. Finally she sighed, looking like she had reached a decision. "We have been told not to make it common knowledge, but you clearly are of our blood. You are Velaschin, although a great wrong was done to you when you were abandoned, and so I believe I can share with you our secrets." She blew out her plump cheeks, casting a quick glance at the tent flap. "We Velaschin are the rightful owners of these lands, what you call the Flowering Coast. Long ago, we raised great stone cities and hunted in the deep forests. And then a people came from the west wielding terrible sorcery. The Gith and their demons enslaved us, and we were dispersed throughout their empire. Even after centuries had passed, though, we still held tight to our old ways. And then during the great rebellion, we threw off our shackles and joined the war. After it was over, we wanted nothing more than to return to our ancient lands, a desire we had kept close to our hearts for many long centuries." Jaleska's mouth twisted bitterly. "But others had settled in our home. They refused to give back what was rightfully ours, and though we were strong, we were too few, and an evil sorcerer arose, a man named Kalenith—"

"The Sage of Pearls," Bren blurted in surprise. "You're talking about the greatest hero of the Coast. He cast the last of the demons from these shores." Her voice faltered as she realized the implications of what she was saying.

Jaleska snorted. "Demons? We had suffered and bled more than any others to defeat those who consorted with demons. Kalenith had in truth allied himself with the last of the demons still free in this land. She had taught him the dark secrets that gave him power—"

"The Silver Mother?" Bren said incredulously, unable to keep herself from interrupting Jaleska again. "She took pity on a poor fisherman when his people were being slaughtered and gifted him the strength to save these lands from tyranny. *Your* tyranny, if what you say is true."

"It is true," Jaleska replied heatedly. "Though not how *you're* telling it. Every Velaschin learns this story. Our lands were stolen from us a second time, and we were driven into the sea, cast adrift on the Cull to die. And many did die from thirst and the dangers of the deep waters. Finally, our ships found land, a place where we could make a new home. But we never stopped dreaming about where we had come from . . . and when we would return."

After this pronouncement, Jaleska crossed her arms tightly over her chest and glared at Bren defiantly, as if daring her to challenge these claims. The urge to argue with this girl over her ridiculously wrong assertions was strong, and if she was feeling better Bren might have given in to her indignation. But Jaleska had treated her well so far and had cared for her after she had fainted, so grudgingly Bren decided to leave the girl to her delusions.

"And here you are," Bren said instead.

"Yes, at long last," Jaleska replied, the flush that had crept into her face draining away when she realized Bren wasn't about to argue more. Now she looked embarrassed, and she stood hurriedly, smoothing out her robes. "I should let you rest. It's almost evening time, and you've had a trying day. Servants will come soon with your supper, and if you need anything, you can ring the bell and someone will attend to you." She gestured towards the tent entrance, and Bren noticed for the first time that a bell hung beside the flap. Her belongings were also piled beside the wall, including her travel bag and the pale sword in its green-leather scabbard. Seeing the blade brought a quick surge of relief, and she wondered uneasily if that had come from her or the ghost she had invited into herself.

"Try the kefa again," Jaleska suggested, her hands now kneading the silver hem of her robes. "It really will make you feel better."

"I will," Bren promised, forcing a smile. The girl might have been raised to believe all those horrible lies, but she clearly wasn't a wicked person. Just misguided.

"All right then, I'll see you on the morrow. Bright and early. We have to go to the egg to make sure you're really Blooded." She hesitated and then added quickly, "I'm sure that you are, given what happened earlier. But there is an official way to do things."

"I understand. Good night, Jaleska."

Some of the nervousness left the girl's face when Bren said her name, and she flashed a dimpled smile before leaving the tent.

After she had gone, Bren closed her eyes and allowed herself to sink fully into the wonderfully soft pillows. Her hand slipped beneath her shirt to rest upon the cool metal of the Silver Mother's amulet. *I know You are here with me*, she thought, *and I will make You proud.*

BREN DRIFTED off to sleep for a while, and when she woke she knew night had fallen, for the fabric hanging above her bed was now dark. A muted glow still leaked from the metal contraption on the table, filling the tent's interior with vague, shadowy shapes. The pain in her temple had subsided, but her head still felt musty, like it had been stuffed with wet wool. After some effort she managed to extricate herself from the morass of mounded pillows and stand, rolling her neck to work out a crick that was bothering her. The beds they had stayed at while on their way to Yestra had also been soft, but in a different way, feather-stuffed mattresses instead of this unstable heap of cushions. It was strange how such a simple thing could seem so exotic and strange – once again, she was reminded of how different the Velaschin were from her own people.

Her throat was dry, and when she couldn't find any water, Bren risked another sip of the drink Jaleska had tried several times to foist on her. The cup was where she had left it, and someone had come in and left a plate of piled flatbreads beside it, along with a small bowl filled with brown goop. The taste of the kefa nearly made her gag – as bad as it had tasted hot, when cold it was even more disgusting. She would have to request some water or she'd die of thirst before she could even attempt the Winnowing. Her gaze drifted to the bell hanging on the rope near the entrance. She suspected it was too deep in the night to ring it without disturbing others, but perhaps it was not as late as she feared. A quick look outside should tell her this much.

Her cloak had been carefully folded and set atop her travel bag, and she scooped it up and settled it over her shoulders. At once she felt more comfortable, the familiarity of its weight and smell helping to steady her. It was still damp from the mist earlier, and this reminded her of when her father would come in from the moors on gray and rainy days, lugging a satchel of peat moss.

That memory immediately made her feel guilty. Here she was, enjoying the hospitality of the people who had murdered her family, conversing amicably with a girl who spoke so blithely about the invasion of her homeland. She should not forget why she was here. Vengeance for her family and the salvation of the Silver Mother. The Velaschin were brutal conquerors, and their dragons threatened the lives of all she loved. Jaleska was her enemy, no matter how sweet and innocent the girl appeared.

Bren pulled aside the tent flap and stepped out into the night. It was not what she was expecting. Her pavilion was perched on a hummock of grass rising from what looked to be an expanse of shallow water. She didn't think it was very deep because sprays of reeds and cat-o'-nine-tails emerged from the depths here and there in small clumps, and the surface was mostly covered by a great swath of pale white lotuses. They glowed ghost-like in the light of the Silver Mother – the goddess rode high and full in the sky, almost as if in a rebuke to the claims Jaleska had made earlier. The thick mist that had clotted Yestra since their arrival had utterly dissipated, taking with it every last shred of cloud in the sky. Stars blazed and the daughters gleamed, the night so bright that Bren could clearly see where she had been brought.

Her little island in this lake or lagoon was only one of many. Each had a tent that looked like hers, rounded with a peaked roof, and while a few shared the same flickering heartbeat of light most were merely shadows set into the night. It must be very late, perhaps even the darkest hour before the dawn, as the only sounds were an incessant peeping rising from the water's edge and the mournful trilling of a distant bird. Bridges of white stone linked this archipelago of small islands, curving and graceful and arched high enough that Bren suspected small boats could easily pass beneath. There were two such links connecting her hummock with others, but those tents showed no signs of life. They might be empty, or perhaps their occupants were fast asleep. She briefly considered exploring a little bit but then discarded that idea – Jaleska had not told her that she was confined to her island, but she found it likely that the Velaschin would not want her wandering about. Bren swallowed back the dryness in her throat. Even if servants were still awake and could hear her bell, she supposed she shouldn't disturb whoever was staying in these tents. The other aspirants for the Winnowing, she had to assume. All here to claim a dragon so that one day they could take part in the conquest of faraway lands, spread terror on dark wings, and burn innocents who only wished to defend their hearths and homes.

Bren's hands tightened into fists, her anger rising. She lifted her gaze to the Silver Mother; the night was so clear the wounds inflicted by the demon Maliskaith looked freshly gouged, dark furrows on Her gleaming face. It was right and good that the Mother filled the sky this night, that She was not hiding from the invaders who wished to destroy Her. Bren drew strength from this knowledge, that while the Velaschin might rule the sky, the heavens beyond were still the domain of the Mother and Her daughters. She had banished demons from these shores before and would do so again . . . and Bren would be an instrument of Her will.

With a last, contemptuous look at the shadowed islands of her rivals, Bren turned back to her tent.

18

B ren awoke to a terrible clanging. She sat up, blinking away the remnants of her dreams as she struggled to focus on the source of the clamor. Jaleska stood at the entrance to her tent, ringing the bell with what looked like an almost sadistic enthusiasm, already having tied back the flaps to let the morning light pour inside.

"Wake up, aspirant," Jaleska said cheerily. "We are expected at the temple. Here, I brought you the robes you must wear." She stepped forward and laid a square of folded white cloth on the same table that held the kefa she'd tried to press on Bren the day before. Jaleska's eyebrows rose when she noticed the cup was still almost full, and she made a *tsking* sound, as if disappointed.

"Couldn't you have just said something to wake me up?" Bren grumbled, tossing aside her blanket and climbing from the bed of piled cushions.

"I tried!" Jaleska cried, her hands on her hips. "You sleep like the dead. Also, you snore terribly."

"I do not!"

"You do," Jaleska assured her. "You'd never have lasted in the novice halls. Someone would have smothered you with a pillow."

"I don't snore," Bren muttered, going over to the table and snatching up the robes. Quickly, she shrugged out of her tunic and trousers – mud-spattered and stiff from the sweat of many days of hard riding, they badly needed a wash. Jaleska must have caught a whiff as well, as Bren saw her wrinkle her nose just before losing sight of her as she pulled on the plain white robes. The fabric felt cool and smooth against her skin, and despite the lack of embroidery Bren sensed that this was the finest garment she had ever worn.

"Servants will clean your clothes," Jaleska said. "Or burn them and find you new ones."

"Don't do that," Bren told her, frowning when she realized Jaleska was staring at her in distaste.

"What?" she asked, then realization dawned, and her hand went to the amulet around her neck. "Oh."

"You'll have to take that off," Jaleska said flatly. "Or the abbot will yell at both of us. I know you were raised in these lands, and that symbol must mean a lot to you . . . but all Velaschin hate that demon."

"Goddess," Bren corrected her quietly, but she took off her mother's amulet and placed it carefully in her bag. While she did this, she silently chided herself – how could she be so foolish? She should have hidden the talisman as soon as Jaleska had told her what her people thought of the Silver Mother. She had to be more careful.

Jaleska frowned. "You must understand you'll never be allowed to claim a dragon if you are open about your beliefs," she said, and as she stepped closer Bren was surprised to see how serious she looked. "This isn't just your great chance. It's mine as well. If you succeed in the Winnowing, I'll be your handmaiden, and to be the handmaiden of a dragon rider is the dream of every girl when she swears her first oath to the temple." She reached out and gripped Bren's arm tightly, her eyes imploring. "Please. Don't ruin this for both of us."

"It belonged to my mother," Bren said softly, gently pulling her arm from Jaleska's grasp. "I don't really care about the Silver Mother – after all, she let my family die." The lie tasted bitter in her mouth, and she hoped no flush darkened her cheeks. "But it is a keepsake to remind me of them."

Relief filled Jaleska's face, and she smiled. "Oh, good. I understand – we Velaschin honor our families as well. Just don't show anyone, all right?"

"All right," Bren replied quietly. An uneasy silence stretched between them for a few heartbeats until it was interrupted by Bren's stomach growling.

Jaleska's eyes flicked to the pile of flatbread on the table. "You didn't eat supper last night?"

"I wasn't hungry then," Bren said. "But now I could eat a horse."

Jaleska held up a hand to stop her before she could reach for the plate of bread. "I should have informed you," she told her apologetically. "You must go before the fledgling on an empty stomach."

"What? Why is that?"

Jaleska's expression grew pained, as if she was truly sorry for denying Bren her breakfast. "Your experience yesterday may have been a little intense, but it was not unique. The Blooded can sometimes suffer when they are first brought into the presence of a dragon, and it is even more pronounced with their eggs. The fledglings inside have not yet learned how to control their minds, and this can bring on sudden sickness in aspirants. You will not make a good impression on the abbot and abbess by throwing up in their presence."

Bren frowned but stepped back from the table. Days of eating well in the taverns along the road to Yestra had apparently spoiled her, as her stomach grumbled again at the thought of skipping its morning meal.

"I'll have a feast brought here for when we finish," Jaleska assured her, dimples appearing as she smiled brightly.

"Let's get it over with, then," Bren sighed. "Do I need to bring anything else?"

"No," the Velaschin girl said with a firm shake of her head. "You cannot bring anything with you into the temple, not even any rings or other jewelry." She made a show of looking Bren up and down and then nodded, satisfied.

Bren resisted the urge to glance at the slightly discolored patch of skin that covered the jade disc. She was almost sure after her experience yesterday with the great blue dragon that the fledgling in the egg would respond to her, but the thing Tharos had put in her arm should make it a certainty. Perhaps the disc was the real reason she had drawn the attention of the dragon yesterday.

"Follow me," Jaleska commanded, then turned and exited the tent. Bren followed with a last, wishful glance at the pale sword. She had quickly grown accustomed to having the blade at her side and the sense of comfort it provided.

But no matter. This morning should be merely a formality – and anyway, the presence that had made her so dangerous with the sword in her hand now resided in her and not the blade. If she was forced to fight, Bren was certain she would not be alone.

The day outside was so sharp and bright that it almost seemed impossible this was the same mist-choked city they had arrived at yesterday. It was like Yestra had shrugged off a shroud it had been wearing and revealed itself for the first time. The humped islands with their colorful pavilions marched away in every direction until finally reaching hulking buildings of gray stone or the sea. Last night the lotuses clotting the water within this archipelago of small islands had looked almost spectral in the moonlight, but in the morning it was clear they were real. The flowers floated so thickly in places that a white road seemed to extend unbroken between a few of the islands.

"What was this place before the Velaschin arrived?" Bren asked as Jaleska led her towards a thin, arching bridge.

"It was where the caliphant kept his hundred consorts," the girl replied, running her fingers along a railing beautifully carved to resemble twining flowers. "I heard he'd visit a different island every night and that the other courtesans were expected to stand outside and sing until he left." She snorted in derision. "You barbarians have some strange customs."

Bren ignored this comment. While crossing the bridge, her attention had been drawn to one of the closer islands, where a girl with flaming red hair was fiddling with the string of a great black bow down by the water's edge. She had set up a makeshift target a hundred paces away on the opposite bank of another island, a chair identical to the one in Bren's pavilion with a small cushion propped on its seat. A half-dozen arrows were sunk point-first into the soft earth beside the girl, and Bren slowed before coming to a halt at the bridge's arched midpoint to watch what was about to happen.

She was not disappointed. When the girl had finished checking the string, she tucked a stray red curl behind her ear and spent a moment staring across the lotus-speckled water. Then in one smooth motion, she reached down for an arrow, drew it back, and sent it arcing towards the chair. It plunged into the center of the cushion, pinning it to the wood, and before the feathers that had erupted had even settled another arrow *thunked* directly beside the first. In moments, the pillow bristled like a pincushion, every arrow having found its mark. Despite the focus such a feat must have required, the girl must have known she was being watched as she turned smoothly towards the bridge where Bren stood before the last arrow had reached its target. The girl brushed back another red curl that had squirmed free and raised her hand in greeting. Bren mirrored the gesture, and then the girl shouldered her bow and turned away, making towards the bridge that linked her island to the one where she had set up her target.

"Seris," Jaleska said from behind Bren. "She's almost as much of a scandal as you are."

"She's not from your land?" Bren asked, finding it hard to look away from the girl. Her fiery red hair looked familiar . . . where had she seen its like before? A hazy memory rose of Ashika sprawled on a stone throne, one of her legs thrown over an armrest. Her hair had been red as well, hadn't it?

"Oh, she is from my land," Jaleska said. "She's a kalishwoman, from the Kalish Marches. There are no better archers in Velasch, and every army has a cohort of their bowmen. No, the reason the hornet's nest started buzzing with gossip is because the fledgling responded to her when she went before the egg. You see, kalishwomen have no connection with the four great houses. Apparently it was a family legend that her mother had been seduced by a wandering scion of one of the families, but no one else had put much credence in the tale until Seris demanded her right to go before the egg and prove the truth of it. To be frank, I'm not sure if the disdain some feel towards her is because she's a bastard or because she's a dirty kalishwoman from the poorest corner of the empire." Something like pride entered her voice, and Bren turned back to the girl in surprise. Jaleska blushed, as if flustered by showing such emotion. "She's the favorite among the other novices," Jaleska explained quickly. "Most of us girls come from humble places, small villages or the city's low quarter. The other aspirants all have great names and grow up in wealth. Seris, though – she was just a soldier in the empire and now she might end up a dragon rider."

"And are you still hoping she succeeds?" Bren asked, making Jaleska's flush deepen.

"No, of course not. Maybe before yesterday, but since the abbess called my name I want nothing more than for you to triumph in the Winnowing. Our fates are entangled now. If you ascend, I will be at your side."

Bren grunted at this, uncertain what she should say in response. It was strange to think that someone so important as a handmaiden would be assigned by that old abbess's whim. And what would happen to Jaleska if the plans of the Jade House bore fruit and Bren managed to steal away a clutch of dragon eggs? Would she be punished, maybe even put to death? The thought was disturbing. Well, no point in thinking about that until she triumphed in the trials to come.

"What *is* the Winnowing?" Bren asked, finally stepping back from the stone-flower balustrade and starting to descend the curving bridge.

"I can't say," Jaleska said as she fell in beside her. "And not because I've been commanded to be silent. It's a secret closely guarded by the warlocks of Velasch and the nobles who have partici-pated, but I do know its form changes often, and no two Winnowings are exactly the same. It is a competition, of course, and the winner is most often extremely skilled in battle. It's why the children of the great houses train constantly from the time they can hold a sword."

"So it is a contest of arms," Bren said, trying not to show how much this pleased her. If it came down to sword fighting, she had the utmost confidence in the spirit of the blademaiden.

"Maybe," Jaleska replied vaguely, batting at a dragonfly that was hovering around her head. "There's more to it than just fighting, though. The winners always show great strength of mind and a deep cunning. And that's because you need more than just a good sword arm to bond with a dragon, or they will bend you to their will."

They passed onto another island, skirting its tent without seeing anyone who might be in residence, then started upon another of the graceful bridges. Bren could now guess where they were headed, as beyond the linked chain of islands rose an impressive white-stone building adorned by a gleaming pink dome. None of the other aspirants were visible, although a few dark-armored Velaschin were scattered about standing guard.

"Do people die during the Winnowing?" Bren asked, remembering the arrows striking into the chair's wood.

"It's rare," Jaleska assured her, ignoring the respectful nod one of the guardsmen gave her as they passed. "Almost all the martial members of the four great families will compete for a dragon when they are on the threshold of adulthood, and if the competition was too deadly, many mothers would refuse to let their children participate. Tragedies happen, but every precaution is taken."

Bren squinted into the brilliant blue sky, half wondering if she hadn't woken up in a completely alien city. It was incredible how different it all seemed without that shroud of mist. "What are these families you keep talking about?"

Jaleska came to an abrupt halt, turning to her with wide eyes. "You don't know about the families?"

Bren sighed, rolling her eyes. "Always pretend I know nothing."

The girl shook her head in amazement, the bangs of her straw-colored hair swinging. "I'm sorry, I just keep forgetting how ignorant you are of my people. Of *our* people." Her brow creased, as if she was trying to decide where to begin. "Well, I suppose you could say the families *are* Velasch. Karth, Regast, Varyxes, and Ahzan. Only those born with their blood can bond with dragons. If the fledgling stirs in your presence, it means you are Blooded and that one of your ancestors had been born into the families. If I were to guess, I would think maybe Karth. They were the ones first charged twenty years ago by the throne with settling in Yestra and establishing trade with the cities and kingdoms of this land. Perhaps your mother or father crossed the sea on a black-bellied Karth ship."

"Karth . . ." Bren murmured, testing out the feel of this strange name. Was that her family? Her *true* family? No, her true family was under a cairn beside the ruin of her house. She shoved that thought aside, shaking her head. "What makes their blood special? Why can't anyone else bond with dragons?"

"You're asking for a history lesson," Jaleska said with a sigh. "And I'm no lorekeeper. But we're all told the story when young – though to be honest, I don't know how much of it is truth and how much is fable. My mam always said that tales grow in the telling. Maybe only the warlocks know what really happened all those years ago – it's said they keep a record of everything that happened locked within their Red Tower." A shadow crossed her face, as if the mere mention of these warlocks was enough to disturb her. "No matter. I can tell you what the lorekeeper told us as we huddled around his feet back in our homestead. You see, after the demon queen drove us from these shores, we sailed for a month and a day over the trackless waters of the Cull. Nearly half our ships were lost to storms or beasts of the deep before we finally saw the gray peaks of the Wraiths rising on the horizon. It was a new land, one untouched by men, but it was not empty. Terrible monsters dwelled in the forests and caves, and also a race of one-eyed, savage giants that we came to call the gnul. They were brutal killers and eaters of men, but they were not animals. No, they may have draped themselves in the fur of giant creatures and had not yet learned how to grow wheat or build houses, but they still had a cruel and terrible cunning. If our people had not been so exhausted from their long and terrible journey they would have sailed away. But they knew the chance of finding another land so suitable was very unlikely. This was a rich land, with good dark soil and fresh water and great herds of animals that quickly bowed their horned heads to the yoke, as if they remembered such service in the distant past. The gnul were merciless, though, and my people huddled behind the stone walls they had hurriedly built and prayed for deliverance. And when the gods did not answer, they burned the idols and cast out the priests to be devoured. That is why there are no gods anymore in Velasch."

"But I was asking about the families," Bren reminded her. Jaleska had claimed not to be a spinner of stories, but she seemed to have warmed rather quickly to the role and wandered far from the main thread.

"I'm just getting to that," the girl told her, a little testily. "Have patience. You have to set the table before you can eat, as my mam used to say."

Bren couldn't help but smile at her tone. "My mother said something similar."

"Hearth wisdom must span the seas," Jaleska said with a sniff, sounding slightly mollified. "Now, where was I? Oh, yes – the gnul. It was a dark time for my people, and it seemed like all they had found in this new land was their doom. In desperation, a young warrior and three companions journeyed north along the coast into the cold sea where the great ice clashed and the sun stayed sleeping for days at a time. They were searching for a refuge from the monsters of the south, but all they found were endless white wastes and a great range of snow-sheathed mountains that dwarfed the Wraiths. The warrior's companions wanted to turn back, but he knew this was their only hope of salvation. Perhaps they could find a valley sheltered from the frozen winds and hunt what game could be found in this desolation." Jaleska's voice had taken on a sing-song cadence, and Bren suspected she was reciting something she had heard many times before. "But they found no green-touched valley. Instead, they found a city."

"Truly?" Bren exclaimed. "How could anyone build a city in such a place?"

"It was a dead city," Jaleska continued, unperturbed by the inter-ruption. "And not built by the hands of man. Its size would have more suited the gnul if those creatures had been capable of shaping stone. The warrior and his companions spoke of mighty edifices sunk in snow and ice, with soaring doorways entering into vast, empty halls. They found no writing, no carvings depicting the ancient builders, no remnants of their labors outside of these great buildings."

"You have a poet's soul," Bren murmured, imagining this strange and abandoned city locked in endless winter.

Jaleska colored at Bren's praise. "These are the lorekeeper's words," she reminded her. "And I must have listened a hundred times as a child." Then she cleared her throat and continued. "Again, the companions wanted to turn away. But the brave warrior was not frightened by this city, and he pushed deeper, hoping to find some-thing he could bring back to his people. Which he did, in the ruin of a mighty building shattered by some terrible blow. A great chasm had split the ground there, warm air billowing up from the darkness below, and nestled in the walls of this crack, he found Velasch's salva-tion. At first he thought they were merely great smooth stones made hot by this underground wind, but then he saw movement inside and realized they were huge eggs and that something still lived within their shells. He surely must have feared that their mother was still close by, but soon it became apparent that many ages had passed since the eggs had been laid, even though the creatures inside had somehow still survived."

"These were the first dragons, then?"

Jaleska nodded. "Twelve eggs they chipped from the rock and hauled across the snow to their small boat. And as the gnawing ice thickened, they returned south to the besieged holdfast they had left behind."

Bren had a strong suspicion that something was being left out of this tale. "Why did they take the eggs?"

"Because these four companions were the first to experience a bond with a fledgling dragon. They had felt the minds inside the eggs and knew this was something that could reshape the world. And years later, after the eggs hatched and the dragons were grown, they did. The gnul had reclaimed nearly all their old lands by this time, with the tattered remnants of our people hiding from their wrath, but when the dragons were unleashed they hunted the gnul like great raptors feasting on animals in the meadows. Just as we could not stand before the might of the giants, they in turn had no defense against claws and flame. The gnul all perished, and the dream of Velasch was rekindled."

Bren surfaced from the story as Jaleska finally fell silent. They had crossed a dozen bridges, the number of lotuses beneath each arching span dwindling as they drew closer to the sea and the pink-domed building. "Those four companions . . . did they found these four families?"

Jaleska nodded, looking pleased by Bren's insight. "Indeed. The Velaschin had once been slaves to the Gith, but in the years since their revolt certain families had risen to power. The arrival of dragons upended the old order. It was found that only those born from the blood of the ones who had braved the dead city could bond with a dragon. And so their descendants replaced the old nobles. That warrior who had led the expedition north married the old king's daughter, but when he sat the throne he ruled under his own name, which had been of no importance before his great deeds. And the Regast family still rules the Velaschin a thousand years later, the line unbroken despite rebellion and famine and war."

"Rebellion?"

"The families can be . . . competitive. Sometimes for centuries there is peace between the great houses, but then some ambitious lord rises up who thinks the hierarchy should be re-ordered. A Varyxes sat the throne during one such period of troubles, the Black Tyrant. Rode a shadow dragon larger than any other in history, bigger even than Mist, the great storm dragon we saw yesterday. But every time the realm convulses, the Regasts return when it finally settles again. The only thing more intolerable than not ruling for the three other families is the thought that they might be ruled over by one of their rivals." Jaleska paused as she stepped off the last and broadest bridge and swept out her arms to indicate the huge building rising before them, its soaring dome blushed a deep pink in the morning light. "And here we are. The Temple Draconium in Yestra. Once the home of the caliphant, now used by my sacred order." Beyond the palace, the sea glittered, crowded with islands and small boats.

"A temple?" Bren said as they approached massive bronze doors embossed with all manner of sea creatures, crabs and fish and many-armed beasts she did not recognize. "I thought you said the Velaschin turned away from their gods."

"We did," Jaleska answered, making a gesture to the guards flanking the great door. One of them bowed deep and then brought the end of his halberd down hard on the marble platform. At the ringing strike, the great doors slowly began to swing inward. "We call it a temple, but we do not worship anything. Well, I suppose in a sense we worship the dragons. My Sisters care for them when they are sick or aged, we keep their eggs warm and safe, and some of us – if we are very lucky – become handmaidens to riders, making sure their dragons are fed and clean and comfortable. Oh, and we help conduct each Winnowing when a fledgling is about to hatch."

Bren's breath caught in her throat when the opening doors revealed the interior of the building. It was a vast circular space, great pillars of pink stone ringing the room and rising to the edges of the dome's underside, which was painted with an extraordinarily detailed and colorful representation of Yestra. Islands bristling with buildings emerged from a stormy sea filled with all manner of vessels and monsters. In the center of this room tiered steps rose up to a platform where an ornate tripod holding a shallow silver basin was perched gleaming in the light slanting down from high windows. And in that basin was the egg.

At first Bren thought it was a part of the wide silver bowl, as it had a similar metallic sheen, but as they drew closer to the dais she realized the color was not the same, instead a mottled gray-blue. And was that a shadow she saw curled inside, darkening the shell?

"Father, Mother," Jaleska murmured respectfully, ducking her head as a pair of figures in gray robes emerged from behind a pillar.

Bren recognized the large older woman from the docks, but she'd never seen the ancient man before – he was the twisted reflection of the abbess, hunched and wizened and so small his head might not even have reached Bren's shoulder. His dark eyes were the same as the crone's, though, dark and sharp and predatory. They were not the only ones in the huge chamber, as Bren glimpsed men standing stiffly at attention in the shadowed gallery between the pillars and the outer wall, their armor enameled a deep blood-red. Unlike the other Velaschin soldiers she'd seen, the helms of these warriors were closed and lacked ornamentation, with only a thin slit for their eyes. Bren even considered that they might be statues because they were completely covered in plate and she couldn't see the slightest movement.

She was so distracted by the guards that she did not notice the old man had drawn close to her until his claw-like hand shot out and grabbed her chin. Startled, she pulled back a step, and a ragged fingernail scratched her cheek. Bren tensed, preparing to retreat further if he came at her again. Was this a madman?

No, those glittering eyes were far too shrewd. And he did not pursue her – instead, his thin lips twisted into a sneer as he glanced up at the towering abbess.

"She has the Karth cheekbones," he rasped. "I'd recognize them anywhere. Sharp enough to cut bread."

The abbess's stern expression did not waver. "It is as I told you, Father. On the streets of Velasch, they would only have to look at her to know she is Blooded."

"I wonder how many others like her are scattered about these lands," the old man mused, peering at Bren intently as he made a slow, shuffling circuit around her. She turned with him, ready to leap away if he tried to touch her again.

"Given her age, we might be able to discern her lineage," the abbess said. "There were only so many of the Blooded who accompanied Bessam when he first came to this city."

Bren's attention went to the old woman. "You're speaking of my mother or father?"

"Perhaps both," croaked the old man. "Your blood looks as pure as fresh snow."

"We would have heard if a trueborn child had been lost," the abbess countered. "No, the Karth blood is so strong it must have overwhelmed whatever thin stock her mother provided."

"You are sure it was her father who was Velaschin?" the abbot asked, which elicited a snort from the old woman.

"Of course. How could you imagine otherwise?"

Bren's initial shock at being accosted was quickly fading, replaced by a growing anger. How dare they talk about her as if she was just an object of curiosity?

"My parents came from the Seven Valleys," she said with as much force as she could muster.

"The Seven Valleys?" the abbot said in an amused tone, looking at the old woman questioningly.

"A simple land to the west, so far as I understand," she replied. "Small villages of mostly farmers and shepherds. The closest city is Leris."

"Interesting. Perhaps a chance encounter in the City of Roses—"

"Stop talking like I'm not standing right here," Bren snapped, and she heard a strangled gasp from Jaleska. These two must usually command more respect than she was willing to give them.

And yet her outburst had only deepened the amusement visible in the old man's face. "She certainly has the Karth temper,"

"Some would say their insolence," added the woman.

"Quiet, Mother Baya, or you will get us in trouble," the old man replied, but he was chuckling. He clasped his gnarled hands in front of his gray robes. "And enough gossip. Let us see if she is indeed what she appears to be." His head turned towards the center of the room and the egg set atop the dais. "Come, girl. Approach, and we shall see if the fledgling recognizes you."

Bren glanced at Jaleska uncertainly. Did he just want her to climb those steps? Should she try to speak to the dragon? "Go on," whispered the girl. "They will know if you are Blooded by what happens."

Bren supposed there was no point in putting it off any longer.

Either she would formally become one of the aspirants and secure her place in the Winnowing, or she would find Tal and Desian on the Isle of Broken Swords and tell them that the mad plan of the sorcerers had failed.

She wasn't sure which outcome she preferred.

Taking a deep breath, Bren squared her shoulders and strode towards the tiered dais. As she neared the bottom step, she realized that this had been the audience chamber of the caliphant before the Velaschin had seized control of the city. A throne must have stood where the egg now loomed, courtiers and sycophants jostling below as they tried to catch the Mistlord's eye. Now this great space was quiet as a tomb, the only sound her boots scuffing the marble floor, but she could imagine laughter and the hum of many voices and the skirling sounds of lutes played by minstrels recessed in the alcoves . . .

Wait. Bren slowed, her pulse quickening. It almost seemed like she could indeed hear voices at the very edge of her perception – nothing intelligible, more like a vague susurration that rose and fell with the cadence of speech. Was it coming from the egg? Or some-where else? Her arm . . . her arm was tingling where the jade disc had been sunk into her flesh. Had the birthmark that had appeared there suddenly darkened? Bren swallowed, forcing herself to look away from the spot.

Something invisible struck her as soon as she stepped onto the first step. Bren staggered, momentarily dizzied as a flood of strange emotions washed over her. It wasn't like she'd experienced before, either the intense sorrow she'd felt flowing out of the great blue dragon or the anger and disdain radiating from the green and red dragons perched on the Briar – no, this was a jumble of feelings that she struggled to name or even understand. But these sensations were most definitely emanating from the gray-blue egg set in the silver basin above her, and they strengthened as she placed her foot on the second step. Bren shook her head, trying to clear it. If the fledgling's emotions continued to swell at this pace, she doubted she could reach the top of the dais without fainting. The thoughts were so powerful, so raw. So alien.

And the voices she had heard earlier were growing louder, becoming clearer. It was a chant, she suddenly realized, in a language she did not know. There was a taste on her tongue, bitter and vile, but she did not know if it had been brought on by the dragon's unformed emotions or the profane chanting echoing within her.

Another step. There was a roaring in her ears now, and the disc burned white-hot beneath her skin.

The shadow in the egg grew more distinct as she ascended, a curled shape beneath the metallic gray-blue luster of the shell.

And then she was at the top, though she did not remember climbing the last few steps. The broad and shallow basin curved before her, and the egg . . . the egg . . . it was so beautiful.

Bren raised her arm. She thought someone somewhere was shouting at her, but the voice was muted, swallowed by the chanting that was reaching some kind of crescendo . . .

Her fingertips brushed the shell, and the shadow inside spasmed violently. Bren gasped and drew back her hand, the voices inside her vanishing even as the swirling emotions emanating from the egg strengthened, battering her mind as the intelligence behind them became aware of her . . .

The shell cracked. Bren stared at the sudden imperfection in shock, waiting for it to spread and then the shadow inside to burst forth . . . but it did not widen any further as she swayed unsteadily atop the dais.

She could sense the attention of the dragon inside the egg; it was completely focused on her, sending strange, curious tendrils slipping into her mind to explore, to try to understand . . .

Pounding footsteps swelled as someone heavy rushed up the steps behind her, and then an arm sheathed in red plate went around her waist, pulling her away from the cracked egg. The tendrils that had been trying to latch onto something inside her lost their grip and disappeared, leaving a cold absence.

She was being dragged down the steps, and in a daze she saw red-armored guardsmen and the old abbot and abbess, their faces flushed from shouting. A little ways behind them, Jaleska had sunk to her knees on the marble, her eyes wide and fearful, her hand over her mouth. What was the problem? Bren wanted to ask her, but her thoughts were growing sluggish, and her tongue was thick in her mouth. A numbness rolled over her as the strength fled her body. And then there was only darkness.

19

When Bren opened her eyes, she found she was back in her tent sunk deep in a mound of pillows and swaddled in a silken blanket. The tent was flooded with a deep bronze light, and she guessed it must be late afternoon. Grimacing with the effort, she extricated her arm from where it had been bound tight against her side and pulled aside the blanket. It slid off her with a rasping hiss as she sat up, pouring over the edge of her bed to puddle on the ground.

"Oh! You're awake!" Jaleska cried, leaping up from where she had been slumped in one of the red-wood chairs.

"How long have I slept?" Bren asked, shaking her head slightly to clear it of the last clinging vestiges of sleep.

"It's still the same day," Jaleska said, hurrying over to put a pinch of what looked like dried petals in the metal contraption on the table. Something must have still been smoldering in its depths, because almost immediately the air was filled with a smell sweet, floral scent. "Which is an improvement, I suppose! Last time you were out all night."

Bren kneaded her temple, annoyed that she had yet again succumbed to whatever horrible thing emanated from dragons.

"How can I bond with something that knocks me unconscious every time it notices me?"

Jaleska crossed the tent again and rang the bell hanging by the entrance. Moments later a young servant with pale, sharp-boned Velaschin features slipped inside and bowed with his hands clasped in front of his chest.

"She's ready for her bath," Jaleska told him, and the boy nodded. Before he vanished again, he cast a quick glance at Bren and the wary interest she saw in his eyes surprised her.

"A bath?" Bren repeated dubiously. She didn't want a bath – she wanted to sink back into her nest of pillows and sleep some more.

"Yes," Jaleska said matter-of-factly. "You smell terrible."

Bren lifted her arm and sniffed experimentally. This was true. It had been days since she'd last scrubbed herself in a river, and she'd been less than thorough at the time, as Desian and Tal had been waiting to take their own turns. She felt a pang in her chest thinking of her two companions – hopefully they hadn't strangled each other yet.

"And don't be too concerned about what happened when you went before the dragons," Jaleska continued, busying herself by picking up and folding the blanket Bren had thrown aside. "Some Blooded respond more strongly than others, and you are not unique." A flicker of something Bren couldn't quite place passed across her face. "The *hatchling's* response to your presence, though . . . that was more than a little unusual."

Bren remembered the egg shivering as the shadow inside had thrown itself against the walls, sending cracks spiderwebbing across the surface. She resisted the urge to look at the spot on her arm where the sorcerer's disk was hidden, keeping her face carefully blank. "What do you mean?"

Jaleska pursed her lips, and for the first time Bren noticed how haggard she looked. The last few days had evidently been draining for her as well. "Usually when a Blooded approaches a dragon still inside its egg a slight stirring is expected. The reason both the abbot and abbess of the temple were there was because if this movement is very slight, one might catch what the other misses. But the hatchling's behavior this time was . . . unprecedented."

Bren affected what she hoped was an innocent expression. Apparently, Tharos's sorcery had worked all too well. "And what does that mean?"

Jaleska sighed. "That we can no longer use the temple's predictions about this hatching. The abbot was certain the dragon would not emerge until after the summer solstice, still nearly a fortnight away. Now, though . . . the dragon is alert and restive. It could hatch at any time, and so we must conduct the Winnowing as soon as possible."

A coldness stole into Bren. "How soon?"

"The Winnowing will be held in three days. The abbess wanted it even sooner, but some of the Blooded must be warned so they can hurry here in time. Until then, the temple will try to soothe the hatchling so that it does not arrive too early."

Three days. Was she ready? Would she *ever* be ready?

A commotion from the tent's entrance drew Bren's attention. Three servants were wrestling a huge wooden tub through the flap, steaming water slopping over its sides.

"Oh, good," Jaleska said, clapping her hands together. "Put it there."

With grunts of effort the servants lowered the tub into the middle of the tent, then bobbed their heads and scurried outside again.

"Come on, let's get you in," the girl commanded, offering her open hand. Bren accepted and allowed Jaleska to pull her from the mounded cushions. Her legs wobbled briefly, but all in all she felt better than after her earlier interaction with the adult dragon. She hesitated, unsure whether Jaleska expected her to undress immediately, but given how the girl was looking at her, she guessed that the Velaschin did not stand on modesty in such situations. Bren shrugged out of her robes, then carefully stepped into the tub and lowered herself into the warm water.

Bren gasped – the water was hot enough to prickle her skin, but far from uncomfortable. Purple and pink petals had been scattered across the surface, imparting a floral aroma that made Bren think of the City of Roses. She shivered, feeling the sweat and grime of days spent traveling slough from her body, and with a twinge of embarrassment she saw the water was starting to cloud with filth. She had indeed needed a bath.

Jaleska crouched beside the tub, her rosy red cheeks already starting to glisten from the rising steam. She had found a sponge somewhere, and she dunked it in the water, then wrung it out and motioned for Bren to incline her head so she could wash the back of her neck.

"So we don't have much time before the Winnowing," Jaleska said as she scrubbed vigorously. Bren had to restrain herself from sighing in pleasure as the rough surface of the sponge abraded her skin. "And before the trials begin, I must instruct you on all matters that a potential dragon rider should know." The sponge paused, as if Jaleska had suddenly been struck by the full weight of what she had just said. When she spoke again, she sounded sadly resigned to her fate. "Which I suppose is nearly everything. So where should we begin?"

Bren's knowledge of dragons and Velasch would have barely filled a thimble. She knew so little, she realized, that she did not even know what she didn't know.

"I've noticed that the dragons do not all look the same. Some are larger than others, some have more spines or lack front limbs, and I've seen all different shades of scales. Are there different kinds of dragons, just as how the people of Velasch or the Dominion look different from those on the Flowering Coast?"

The scouring resumed as the sponge moved on to her shoulders and upper back. "Oh, yes. Though unlike men who only resemble their ancestors, a dragon's clutch is more random. A dragon like Mist might give birth to a forest or marsh hatchling, for example, instead of another storm dragon."

"So no one knows what sort of dragon is inside the egg in the caliphant's palace?"

"I heard the abbot say it's almost certainly a greater dragon," Jaleska replied, pausing to wet the sponge again. "Which would mean it is either a storm, shadow, river, ash, or sun dragon. Greater dragons are larger and stronger and live far longer. They are also much rarer than the lesser dragons, which are mountain, forest, blood, marsh, sand, and ice."

Bren splashed water on her face, then ran her wet fingers through her hair. Or tried to – the number of matted snarls made her wince in disgust. The abbess must have thought she was half-feral. "Are they called these names because of where they are found?"

The Sister shook her head. "All dragons are hatched in temples and dwell in the aeries," Jaleska told her, gently pulling Bren backwards so that most of her hair was submerged before beginning to patiently tease out the tangles. "No, they were named thus because of the color of their scales and what they can breathe forth. Sand dragons, for example, can produce a blast of extremely hot and dry air, while ice dragons expel a frozen gust of wind laced with sharp shards of ice."

"Which ones can create flames?" Bren asked, her thoughts returning to that terrible night.

"That is most common. Forest, mountain, ash, and sun dragons all expel fire, though each breed is different. The sun dragon's breath is nearly molten, while the ash's is a torrent of black flames mixed with cinder. All dragons save the river can breathe forth something. That breed is different for several reasons, for it is long and sinuous like a snake and can swim much better than the others. River dragons are also far gentler than their brethren and spend most of their lives underwater, coiled at the bottom of lakes."

Bren sank deeper into the tub as she slowly digested this new knowledge. She had noticed that there were different breeds of dragons, but she'd had no inkling how varied they actually were. She found her thoughts returning to what Jaleska had said about the river dragon.

"You said some dragons are gentle? But don't they all fight in the war?"

Jaleska had moved beside her so she could scrub Bren's arms, and her straight, straw-colored hair swung back and forth as she shook her head. "No. Not all dragons have the temperament for battle. They are complex creatures, just like people. But river dragons are the only kind that never are ridden into battle. They have no breath to use as a weapon, nor do they have claws. River dragons are coveted by the high-born girls who are not martial and they are often gifted to them. It is possible to tell from the shape of the shadow if the hatchling inside a shell is a river dragon, so they are never claimed during a Winnowing."

"Is that common? This gifting of dragons?"

Jaleska hesitated for a moment, then shrugged. "I don't know. It is supposed to only happen with river dragons, as they are not violent creatures, and the Winnowing selects for the fiercest. But there is a suspicion that some Winnowings are . . . not entirely fair. Otherwise, why would the children of the most powerful almost invariably be the ones who succeed? The heads of the houses would have us believe, I suppose, that their sons and daughters are simply superior through birth or training . . . but I'm not so sure. Most believe that the aspirants conspire to see a chosen one triumph. As in, the lesser members of each family strive to ensure that it is the one favored by their family who wins."

Bren frowned. This was the first she'd heard that the Winnowing might not be an equitable competition. Would she be competing against entire families? That would make things far more difficult. "And what about this time?"

Jaleska's expression became pained. "I don't know. We're far from Velasch, and there aren't many high born Blooded on this side of the Cull . . . but there will still be several in this Winnowing. Most prominent is the son of Bessam Karth, the governor of Yestra and the man the emperor charged with conquering these lands. Many in the temple believe it is a foregone conclusion that Zair Karth will triumph and claim Mist's hatchling."

"He is a skilled warrior?"

Jaleska nodded. "He has been preparing under the best tutors in Velasch all his life for this moment. It is said he was trained by a sword dancer from the Gray Redoubt and that he was invited to join their order if he fails in the Winnowing, a very rare honor for those born outside their walls."

That meant nothing to Bren, but it had clearly impressed Jaleska. Still, she doubted this Zair would be a match for the spirit inside her.

"You'll see him soon, I'm sure," Jaleska said, lifting Bren's arm from the water to reach an area that hadn't yet been scrubbed clean.

"What do you mean?" Bren asked, turning her head to stare at the girl in confusion.

"There's to be a feast in two days, on the eve of the Winnowing. All the aspirants will be there, so you can take the measure of each other before the trial officially commences. I hear that many of them are very interested to meet you."

20

B ren had decided she didn't like the sea.

She clung to the side of the small boat as its prow pushed through the choppy swells, grimacing miserably every time the cold spray soaked her heavy woolen cloak. Water had already pooled ankle-deep in the boat, and to avoid ruining her boots, she was being forced to keep her feet propped up on the plank across from her, right beside the grizzled old man straining at the oars.

"The Isle of Broken Swords," the sailor growled in a voice that sounded rusty from disuse. Bren hadn't seen him turn his head to see the shadows swelling in the mists, and she wondered how he'd known they were so close to arriving. The fog had returned with a vengeance today, and for most of this journey she'd feared they had lost their way and were rowing out into the open ocean. It was so thick that she was still amazed the sailor had seen the lantern Jaleska had lit on the docks to signal someone wanted passage from the caliphant's island. She supposed there must be many boats out in the lagoon waiting for just such an opportunity.

"Thank you," Bren said, squinting past the sailor at the vague shapes emerging from the mist.

"Three venmarks," the man said, drawing the oars in and dropping them with a splash in the water that had collected at the bottom of the boat. He held out a weathered hand, and after fumbling in the pockets of her cloak Bren dropped the copper coins into his palm. With a grunt that almost sounded pleased, the sailor rubbed his thumb across the surface of each of the venmarks, then flipped open the lid of a battered tin box beside him and tossed them inside with a clink.

Jaleska had told her that as a Velaschin she could insist on free passage between the islands, but Bren preferred to pay others for their labor. It wasn't really her money, anyway, instead having been drawn from the sum Desian had given her before they'd parted ways.

Their boat was drifting between jetties bustling with far more activity than anywhere else she'd seen in the city save Scabtown – dockhands were unloading crates overflowing with vegetables from a wide-bottomed barge as shrieking children scampered underfoot, and a trio of sailors with the dusky skin and bright garb of southerners were sitting on the edge of the wharf fishing with rods of golden wood. One of these men grinned at her as their boat slid past, his teeth startlingly white. He doffed his cap in her direction, flourishing its iridescent feather.

"Stay away from them," grumbled the sailor, scowling. "Azakani, Umber Isles folk. Can be trusted about as much as a cat in a fishmonger's cart."

"I'll be careful," Bren replied, oddly touched by the old man's concern. She thought that would be the extent of his warnings, but after a moment he continued.

"Best keep that up," he said gruffly, indicating the cowl of her cloak with a gnarled finger. "Not everyone here loves your kind."

Bren raised her hood, and he grunted in satisfaction before picking up the oars again and using them to guide the boat towards one of the jetty pilings.

She wondered just how dangerous this trip truly was. Jaleska had been aghast when Bren had told her that she wanted to explore the city proper, insisting that all manner of thieves and cutthroats prowled the mist-shrouded streets, but Bren had assumed she was being overly dramatic. Now she wasn't so sure . . . or perhaps the real danger – as the sailor had implied – was exploring the city with the pale skin of a Velaschin. Still, she badly wanted to see her friends. She had to share with Desian what she'd learned of the Winnowing, and Tal . . . Tal she just missed terribly.

The boat bumped against the piling, and the old sailor rose and brought the dangling rope ladder closer to her. With a final grateful smile, she hauled herself up onto the dock, then had to jump back as a sailor rolling a barrel nearly collided with her.

"Careful, lassie," he snapped, and she muttered an apology before turning back to the boat that had brought her here. The sailor had already pushed away and was bent again to his oars.

Bren sighed – she had meant to ask if he would wait for her here, but it had slipped her mind with all the distractions. Her gaze drifted to where the Azakani had been fishing, and to her dismay she saw that the one who had smiled at her was sauntering in her direction, his thumbs hooked into his bright red sash.

Turning her back to him in what she thought was very pointedly a dismissal, Bren began to stride down the length of the jetty towards the city proper. Surely, this would be a clear enough indication that she did not want to be bothered. Surely, he wouldn't chase after someone who obviously didn't want to—

"Beautiful girl, a moment."

Bren gritted her teeth and quickened her pace. The voice had come from just behind her, the cadence rich and almost musical.

"Degas wishes to speak; do not worry, his intentions are as pure as the home waters. Please, girl."

Bren ignored the entreaties, though she was not surprised when the sailor slipped in front of her, walking backwards so that she could again see that gleaming smile he must believe was charming. She did not slow and was grudgingly impressed when he somehow gracefully avoided several piles of coiled rope and a length of broken wood without looking where he was going.

"Perhaps this girl wants to wish for luck while ringing the broken bells? Or drink from the Archon's Fountain, a gift from the Crimson Dominion?" He leered and waggled his eyebrows suggestively. "Or perhaps the girl wishes to sample the fine wares in the House of Silken Dreams? Degas can escort you to all these wondrous places. There is no better guide on the Isle of Broken Swords, Degas can promise you that."

Bren raised her arm to shoo the young man away, but then hesitated. Her gaze went past him to the great stone buildings crowding the island – would it really be wiser to simply wander about in the hopes of stumbling upon where Desian and Tal were staying?

The Azakani pounced, noticing her indecision. "A young Velaschin girl must need a guide to this strange and exotic city, yes? Let Degas escort you; many would attest to his knowledge of this city."

"*The Windblown Inn,*" Bren said, coming to a halt and crossing her arms tightly over her chest. "Do you know it? My friends are staying there."

The Azakani clapped his hands together, his face brightening even further. "Of course! As fine an establishment as can be found in Yestra. This girl must be blessed with rich friends!"

"How much for directions, then?" Bren asked with a sigh, trying to give the impression that she couldn't care less if this fellow helped her or not.

The Azakani waved his hand, as if to dismiss her question as ridiculous. "You misunderstand Degas. What help this man can give is free."

"You're too kind," Bren said flatly, cocking an eyebrow.

"Degas is, it is true," the Azakani admitted, placing his hand over his chest and bowing slightly. "But it is my nature."

"*Hmm,*" Bren murmured, but the man seemed not to notice her skepticism.

"Then follow Degas; I will bring the beautiful lady to the inn." He winked at her, then turned sharply on his heel and began to march down the last little length of the dock before it joined with the island proper.

Unsure whether she was making a mistake, Bren hurried to follow. Would he take her to a dark alley where his friends were waiting with daggers drawn? Or lead her deep enough into the island that she was well and truly lost and then demand some exorbitant sum to bring her out again? For some reason, she didn't think so. She knew she might just be naïve, but there was something about this fellow that seemed trustworthy to her . . . or at the very least not dangerous.

She studied him as he led her under the arch of jagged metal – all manner of broken swords welded together, she realized – that marked the entrance to the main avenue leading further into the island. His clothes were dyed bright, but now that she was closer Bren could see that the hems of the sleeves were frayed and the fabric was peppered with more than a few holes. The metal she had seen glinting in his ears and around his wrist looked to her like bronze or copper rather than gold, and his shoes were on the verge of falling apart. He may have waved away payment, but he could clearly use the coin. Bren frowned. There was something here she did not understand. She thought back to what she knew of the Azakani, but it was all traveler's tales and stories told by the elders around the fire. They were the seafaring folk of the Umber Isles, the archipelago at the very southern end of the Flowering Coast, and she doubted they ever had had much cause to visit the Seven Valleys. The Azakani were portrayed as wanderers who sought out adventure, and in more than a few tales, they seduced maidens and stole them away to live on their painted boats in the southern seas. Bren resolved that would not happen to her, no matter how charming this Degas turned out to be.

"Is the girl a trader?" he asked, jolting her from her thoughts.

"No," Bren replied, drawing down her cowl as they started on the narrow cobbled streets. The buildings looming over her seemed to be carved whole from great chunks of gray-green stone, glistening wetly from the rain earlier this morning. Yestrians must rise late, as there were few abroad this early, and she did not see any Velaschin. The conquerors must be restricting themselves to certain islands – good for Desian, if he wanted to stay out of sight, but if anyone peered closely at her they might wonder why she had come here.

"The girl does not look like a soldier," Degas continued, seemingly unaware of her attempts to stay hidden. "Though she wears a sword, this man sees. Still, a little young for the army, yes?"

"Yes," Bren murmured, turning her head away from a group of women clustered around a blanket where fresh-caught fish had been laid out. "I'm not a soldier. Truly, I'm not even Velaschin."

Degas twisted around to stare at her in surprise, and Bren chided herself for giving away too much information.

"I grew up in the west, near Leris. I was a foundling."

Degas nodded sagely, as if this explained everything. "And the girl wishes to discover her people. This man understands."

"It's not really . . ." Bren began, but then hesitated. "Yes, you're right, I suppose."

"It is a shame for Degas, though," the Azakani continued with a wistful sigh. "Long has this man wished to make friends with one from across the eastern ocean. It is the great dream of this man and his brothers to be the first of the Salt Folk to see the distant shores where the dragons dwell." He smiled ruefully, removing his elaborate hat and plucking at its ridiculous feather. "This man had hoped the girl would perhaps render some assistance in the future to secure work on a ship when it returns across the trackless water. Ah, well. Fortune does not turn her face on Degas today. Perhaps tomorrow."

Bren was trying to think of what she could say to raise his spirits when he suddenly gestured grandly at a stately building that was even more impressive than its surrounding brethren, the gray-green stone carved with intricate flourishes.

"*The Windblown Inn*, my new Velaschin-yet-not-Velaschin friend."

It certainly looked like the sort of inn Desian would choose. "Thank you," she said, turning to the Azakani.

Degas noticed her hand drifting towards her coin pouch and shook his head emphatically. "No, no," he said, flourishing his cap at her again. "To learn the name of this pretty girl would be enough payment for this man. And perhaps a promise that she will remember his."

"I'm Bren," she replied before she could even consider whether telling him was truly a good idea.

"Bren," Degas said, somehow making her name – which she'd always thought to be rather dull – sound almost exotic. "This man hopes we meet again." Then with another pearly smile he settled his ridiculous cap on his head and turned away from her. She watched him until he'd vanished where the crooked street jagged around another imposing building.

What a strange fellow. With a shrug, Bren pushed through the door to the inn and found herself in a sprawling common room filled with tables of heavy black wood. Ornately fashioned metal sconces were fixed to the walls, but their number was insufficient to illuminate the huge space, leaving much of it draped in shadow. Only one of the tables was occupied this early in the morning, and it looked like the men sitting around it hadn't yet retired from the previous night's revels. Bottles and scraps of food cluttered its surface, and three of the foppish-looking fellows slouching around it were staring blearily at the cards they held in their hands. The fourth raised his head from where it had been pillowed on his arms, and then he straightened with a gasp.

Tal.

The others around the table barely stirred as the boy stood, though one scowled as the sudden movement knocked over the pile of coins precariously stacked in front of him.

"Bren!" Tal cried, hurrying across the common room. "You're back!"

"I am," she said with a smile. It was good to see him, but he smelled like he had washed himself with wine.

Tal blinked bloodshot eyes, as if something had just occurred to him. "Then . . . that means you weren't selected? The hatchling didn't recognize you?" He sounded more hopeful than disappointed.

"No, it did," she whispered, lowering her voice even though the fops Tal had been sitting with seemed almost dead to the world. "The Winnowing will occur in a few days, and I am to participate."

Tal blanched, his face paling. "What? But it wasn't supposed to happen until the summer solstice!"

"Things changed," she told him, looking around the room to make sure she hadn't missed the sorcerer. "I need to talk to Desian. I've found out some things. It's not a fair competition, Tal."

The expression on his face suggested that of course he knew that already. "Well, yes, you're carrying around the ghost of a great warrior—"

"No," Bren said in exasperation, "I mean others will have advantages as well. There is a favorite who is expected to win, and I've been told the dice have been loaded in his favor."

"Oh. So you're worried about someone else also cheating?" He said this loud enough that a few around the table he'd been sitting at turned in their direction. One even glanced at the cards he was holding with a guilty expression.

Bren rolled her eyes, pulling Tal out of the common area and into the darkened foyer, where a wide wooden staircase ascended to the inn's second floor.

"I want to know if Desian can help me. Where is he?"

"In his room," Tal replied, then after a moment added, "I think."

"You think?"

"I haven't seen him since we arrived days ago," Tal muttered. "He secured the finest room for himself and then disappeared inside. He won't answer when I knock – the only reason I know he's still there are the weird noises."

"What kind of noises?"

"Thumps and banging. Once I swear it sounded like a hawk was inside screaming. The owner of the inn seems surprisingly unconcerned – I think maybe he's used to hosting members of Yestra's Jade House. Either that or the pile of gold Desian dumped in his lap has convinced him to ignore any strangeness."

Bren jerked her chin in the direction of the common room. "So that is what you've been up to while I've been gone? Drinking and gambling?"

Tal's cheeks colored. "What else was I supposed to do? Sit in my room and worry about you?"

Bren sighed, rubbing at her face. "I'm sorry, I'm just . . . the last few days have been very hard."

"I understand," Tal said, putting a hand on her shoulder. "Come on, I'll take you to Desian's room. It's on the topmost floor."

Bren followed him up, her boots sinking into the thick runner covering the stairs. The interior of the inn seemed to exude age and wealth, from the ancient, well-polished wood everywhere to the craftsmanship of the newels, delicately carved to resemble the heads of snarling wolves. There was a smell as well, musty but faintly spiced with a hint of far-away lands. It was the sort of place sorcerers would frequent, Bren decided – mysterious and ancient and shadowy. She wondered why the Velaschin were not watching this inn if they were hunting the servants of Nasai.

Or perhaps they were. That thought made her fingers tighten on the well-polished banister. Perhaps one of the fops downstairs was in the employ of the invaders . . .

"This one," Tal said, pulling her away from her thoughts. He had stopped on the third-floor landing and was indicating a door that looked markedly grander than any they had yet passed. She stepped closer and put her ear to the wood, but she couldn't hear anything.

"Could he be sleeping?" she asked, to which Tal shrugged.

"Perhaps. Usually, the noises come late at night. But he'll want to see you, I'm sure. After you left us at the docks of Scabtown he was very agitated – I think he's been hiding how nervous he truly was about this mad plan."

"That would make two of us," Bren murmured, and then after a moment's hesitation she rapped loudly on the door.

"It's Bren. I want to t—" Before she could finish, the door was flung open, and Bren jumped back a step with a yelp of surprise. Desian must have been waiting just on the other side. His face was haggard, darkened by circles under his eyes and the pale shadow of a silver beard.

"You failed?" he asked curtly, his jaw visibly clenching.

Bren gathered herself and stepped forward. "I did not, and the Winnowing is imminent."

Desian grunted, his face softening somewhat. "Good." He moved aside to let her in. "Come, you must tell me everything. And why you're here – if you were followed, everything might be ruined."

"I wasn't followed," Bren said as she stepped inside. "I would know." She paused just beyond the threshold, unnerved by what Desian had done to his room. Strange, jagged symbols had been painted on the walls in red paint, and there was a bitter smell that reminded her of the mugwort tea her mother used to brew.

"Would you now?" Desian countered, his tone snide. "Were you brought to the inn by a rather charming Azakani fellow?"

Bren glanced at him sharply, and the sorcerer smiled without humor.

"There are many hidden servants in this city. Hopefully, you did not draw the attention of one who reports to the warlocks of Velasch. Coming here was foolish."

"Don't speak to her like that," Tal said angrily. He began to follow them into the room but then stopped abruptly, as if he'd walked into an invisible barrier. "Let me in," he growled, placing his palm against whatever was blocking his way.

"No," Desian said, and then with a curt gesture the door swung shut, leaving Tal outside. Bren heard a muffled curse and then the sound of something striking the wood hard.

Desian turned away from the door as if dismissing the irate boy outside and crossed the room to where a strange little statue squatted on the table beside his bed. A bed that had clearly never been slept in, Bren noted.

"Desian! Open this door right now!" Tal shouted, but Desian ignored him, muttering under his breath as he stroked the bulbous head of the idol, which looked like a disgusting amalgamation of frog and fish and man.

Bren watched the sorcerer warily, unsure what he was doing. She thought it might be some sort of sorcery, as the hairs on her arms had lifted ever since he'd started whispering to the statue.

"Go downstairs!" she called out to Tal. "I'll see you in a little while."

The bottom of the door shivered as the boy kicked it again hard, but then she heard his cursing growing fainter.

Bren crossed her arms and glared at Desian. "You don't have to be so cruel to him."

The sorcerer stopped his murmuring and turned from the statue to stare at Bren with a look of utter exasperation. "He hates me for what I am. And the thief is a danger." He held up his hand when Bren opened her mouth to dispute this. "No, I do not mean he would hurt us . . . intentionally. But he is careless, and if he said the wrong thing to the wrong person . . . He is a liability, Bren."

"He won't say anything," Bren huffed, but she did wonder again about the extravagantly attired young bravos he'd been drinking with downstairs.

"Let us pray to the Mother you're right," Desian said, then threw himself into the room's only chair, a monstrosity of black wood that looked like it would be at home in the solar of a great manse. He motioned for her to sit on the edge of his bed, then let out a long sigh, pinching the bridge of his nose like he was trying to ward away a headache. "I do realize he is important to you," he said tiredly. "But you must recognize, Bren, that we have a very important task. A task ordained by the Silver Mother Herself. Tal does not offer anything that can help complete it. It would be best for everyone if he went somewhere else – back to Leris, perhaps. It would be safer for him, certainly. For if we make even the slightest misstep, then we are all dead – you must know this. Why should he share such a risk?"

Bren frowned. The sorcerer's words had the ring of truth, as much as she would have preferred otherwise. She might have tried to muster some rebuttal, but Desian suddenly leaned forward, his fingers steepled.

"Now, tell me everything that's happened."

~

DESIAN SHOWED little reaction as Bren described the events of the last few days, up until she arrived at what had happened in the caliphant's palace. Then he allowed himself a triumphant smile, and some tension that she hadn't realized he'd been holding seemed to seep away.

"So Tharos was correct," he said in excitement. "The old buzzard's little trick actually worked."

"It worked too well," Bren replied, annoyed for some reason that the silver-haired boy would refer to his former companion so disrespectfully. "The egg cracked. The Winnowing is the day after tomorrow, and I don't think I'm ready."

Desian waved her words away. "You're as ready as you can be. It is the other aspirants who will be unsteadied – possibly some of them now cannot even arrive in Yestra in time for the trials." He rubbed his hands together gleefully. "No, this is good. If there are others who have planned some sort of subterfuge, we might have disrupted their machinations."

"The handmaiden assigned to me told me such plots exist. That the Winnowing is not a fair competition."

Desian rolled his silver eyes, as if what she'd just claimed was obvious. "Of course. A dragon is far too valuable a prize to expect integrity. But you have an edge that should be the equal of any other. Tell me, can you sense the spirit? Does it speak to you? I would think not, if the spell I bound it with remains strong."

Bren shook her head. "No. To be honest, I forget she's there most of the time."

A flicker of concern passed across Desian's sharp-featured face. "Perhaps we should find a place to spar and see if you still retain the spirit's skills. This will all be for naught if you are left alone during the Winnowing."

Bren nodded at the sorcerer's suggestion – she had already considered doing exactly that. In truth, it was one of the reasons she had sought out Desian today, for if the blademaiden's spirit had abandoned her or dissipated into nothing, then she wanted to know this before the trial commenced. It would be a very unwelcome surprise to realize only then that she was on her own against Velaschin who had trained their entire lives for that moment.

Bren looked around the cluttered room, noticing for the first time that more of the strange designs had been painted on the floor, and in places where lines converged, candles had been melted down into lumps of wax.

"And where could we draw swords? Not here, certainly."

Desian tilted his head towards the door. "Outside. Enough blades have been drawn in the alleys of this island that it's unlikely anyone would raise an eyebrow. This is the Isle of Broken Swords, after all. Every night, the bravos of Yestra come here to drink and gamble and settle ridiculous grudges." He frowned, his gaze also wandering his room. "I wonder though if I dare leave my work unattended . . ."

"What *are* you doing here?" Bren asked, finally unable to contain her curiosity.

"He's been trying to send a message."

Cold surprise washed through Bren at the sound of this new voice. She whirled to face where it had come from, rising from the bed with her hand on the hilt of her sword.

A man reclined in the frame of the room's one large window, his back against the sill and his arm resting on a knee he'd drawn up nearly to his chest. His other leg was stretched out the length of the ledge, his black boot pressed up against the far side. He looked like he'd been lounging there for some time, but that was of course impossible. She was certain the window had been shut when she'd entered the room.

Desian leapt to his feet, his eyes narrowed. "You!" he snapped, sounding less than pleased to see the intruder. "What are *you* doing here?"

The man crooked a smile, uncoiling his long body as he slipped down from the window's ledge. He was tall and gaunt, his loose dark clothes so ragged that strips of cloth fluttered in the cold wind slipping in through the open window. For a moment Bren thought he was Velaschin because of his pale complexion and the black hair that reached past his shoulders, but then she realized that she'd never seen skin like his before – it was as perfectly smooth and unblemished as a fresh-laid egg. And his eyes . . . Bren flinched when they settled on her, gold surrounding slitted irises of absolute darkness.

"I heard you crying out into the void, Desian. No one else was answering, so I thought I'd stop by and see if I can render any assistance." He sauntered slowly across the room, and Bren felt a stab of fear when Desian took a step backwards, putting space between himself and this stranger.

"We don't need your help, Garith," the sorcerer muttered, his eyes flicking to the statue on the table.

The man seemed to sense the tension in the room and stopped his approach, then spread his arms wide as if to show he held nothing dangerous. His fingers were unnaturally thin and long, Bren realized, almost as if they boasted an extra joint below the knuckles. It was a disquieting sight, especially when coupled with his strange cat-eyes.

He did not look entirely human.

"I think you should take help where you can find it, Crowbringer. There is no one left in the city to answer your entreaties. They are all dead or imprisoned in the shadow cells. The Velaschin hounds are thorough."

Desian ran a hand through his silver hair as he took a deep breath, and this seemed to help him regain his composure. "And how have they not caught *you* yet?"

The man Desian had called Garith shrugged sharp-boned shoulders. "I know they can feel me. The slightest of breezes in the dark, a whisper in the shadows. But if I could remain free of Nasai's shackles for so long, these crude warlocks have no chance of binding me."

Desian folded his arms tightly across his chest and stared at the stranger in undisguised annoyance. "Truly, Garith, what are you doing here?"

The man's gaze wandered slowly around the room, pausing briefly on the frog-thing statue and the packs piled beside the bed.

"You've brought objects of power into my city. Things I haven't smelled for centuries. You never would have risked doing this if the situation was not truly desperate."

"Of course things are desperate!" Desian snapped, his self-control slipping again. "The Silver Mother Herself is threatened! In Yestra and Leris and Farlden the Jade Houses have already fallen. If the Velaschin advance continues at the same pace, in another year the entire Flowering Coast will be cleansed of the Mother's light!"

Garith appeared unaffected by the sorcerer's agitation. He clasped spidery fingers behind his back and began to meander around the room, investigating a battered length of wood leaning against the wall and then an ancient tome lying open on the bed – Bren suspected this was the same book that Desian had used to bind the Gith spirit inside her. When he came close to the bed, Bren made to move further away, but he fixed her with his golden eyes, and she felt her limbs go rigid.

"And what do we have here, Desian?" His perfectly smooth brow furrowed as he approached her. She wanted to scramble away from this creature, but the force of his will held her frozen.

"Nothing," Desian said, almost sullenly. "Just a Velaschin spy I am using to help find the missing sorcerers."

"No," Garith said, making a slow circuit of Bren before stopping directly in front of her, his face only a hand-span away. The gold in his eyes seemed to move sluggishly, like it was flowing liquid.

"No, there is something unexpected here. Two souls sharing the same body, but one is sleeping, insensate. Trapped. An old, old presence with a flavor I haven't tasted since this city was young. How interesting." Bren shivered when his long fingers brushed the spot on her arm where the jade disc was hidden. Then he turned to Desian, and Bren gasped as the spell that was holding her was severed. "Your schemes are always so intricate, Crowbringer. I shall enjoy watching this one unfold, I think."

"Just stay out of my way," Desian said, his hands clenched at his sides.

Garith offered another of his lopsided smiles as he began to back away. "Oh, you won't even know I'm there," he promised just before his legs bumped against the window ledge. Bren wasn't sure what she'd expected to happen next, but it wasn't this – the creature laughed as he tumbled backwards in a flutter of black rags, toppling out of the open window. The laughter vanished, replaced by a guttural croaking, and a moment later Bren glimpsed dark wings churning the air as a massive raven soared away on the wind.

No one spoke for a good while following the strange creature's abrupt departure. Bren was at a loss for words, and Desian was visibly fuming, staring balefully after the bird until it was swallowed by the gray sky. Finally he took a deep breath, clearly trying to master his emotions, and turned towards Bren with a rueful expression.

"Well, at least we know the spirit is still inside you."

"How could he tell?" Bren blurted, feeling like she was waking from a dream. "And *who* was that?"

"*What* might be a better choice of words," Desian said, crossing the room to investigate his bags, as if he was afraid the sorcerer had somehow pilfered them from afar. "Garith Shadowborn, the Raven Lord. He's been a thorn in the side of Nasai and the Jade Houses for centuries. He's a trickster. A rogue. No one knows what he wants . . . or if he wants anything at all, beyond his own entertainment." Desian pulled an ancient book of cracked red leather from one of his packs and spent a quick moment leafing through its pages. Then he grunted in satisfaction and motioned for her to approach. When Bren did, she saw that on the faded vellum had been sketched a thin man in a ragged cloak, most of his face hidden beneath a broad-brimmed hat. Under this illustration, someone had written *The Raven Lord* in a spidery, archaic script.

"But how is that possible?" Bren whispered, her gaze lingering on the figure's crooked smile, the same one she had seen just moments ago in the flesh.

Desian snapped the book shut and returned it to the pack. "There are many powers in this world, Bren. Great and small, ancient and newborn. The sorcerers of the Jade Houses, the warlocks of Velasch, the heuromancers of the Crimson Dominion, the artificers of

Zenovia . . . we all hold our guttering candles aloft and claim that we have illuminated the truth of the eternal mysteries, but this is only hubris. In the great dark spaces beyond our little circles of light lurk things we mortals cannot understand. Garith is one such being. Was he a man once? I don't know. I think not. But I *do* know that he is no friend of the Silver Mother . . . though I suspect the dragon lords will find him just as infuriating as She does."

"So he will not oppose us?" Bren asked softly, shivering as she remembered the feel of his clammy fingers.

"I don't believe so," Desian answered with a shrug, "but I doubt anyone knows the mind of the Raven Lord."

"He knew you. It sounded like there was a history . . . but you can't be much older than me."

Desian snorted. "I suppose you could say I'm precocious. While you were counting sheep I was traveling up and down the Flowering Coast learning from the elders of the Jade Houses. They were preparing me for something great . . . but none of them could have imagined that I would have to be the Silver Mother's instrument in these desperate times."

Bren frowned. There had been something in the sorcerer's face before he had answered, a glance like he was calculating what he should say in order to placate her. He was trying to lead her away from something he didn't want to discuss.

"You're not telling me the whole truth," she said, moving closer to Desian. An anger was rising in her she hadn't expected, and her menacing tone had apparently also surprised the silver-haired boy as he took a quick step backwards, grimacing in confusion.

"You know what you need to know," he said, somewhat defensively. "Any more endangers everything."

Bren took another threatening step towards Desian, her anger flaring hotter. "I know that your schemes need me. That there's no other who can claim the hatchling. It's my life that is being risked! I should be told everything!"

The sorcerer had retreated further from her, his face showing a mixture of surprise and outrage and maybe even a hint of fear, but then his expression hardened into something else, his eyes narrowing.

"Which one are you?" he asked suddenly, tilting his chin up defiantly.

"What do you mean?"

"Are you Bren . . . or the other one?"

She sneered. "I'm me, of course. I'm . . ." Bren hesitated, blinking. Why was she arguing with Desian, even trying to make him fear her? This wasn't something she would normally do, was it? Where was this anger coming from?

Desian had recovered from his initial surprise, and he drew himself up. "Garith was right. The ghost is still inside you, and though it may be buried deep, aspects of it are seeping into your personality. The Bren I know would not have lost her temper so easily." He ran his fingers through his silver hair. "I suggest you save this aggression for the Winnowing."

The fires that had been burning in her breast just moments ago had now subsided, leaving behind a cold emptiness. Was Desian right? Or had she simply had enough of being a piece in whatever game the sorcerer was playing?

He lies.

Bren just barely kept herself from gasping in surprise as the familiar voice spoke in her mind. Despite her best efforts, Desian must have seen something in her face, as his brows drew down in consternation.

"What is it? What is the matter?"

"Nothing," Bren murmured, swallowing hard. "I think I'm just tired. It's been a difficult few days."

The sorcerer nodded, though he still looked suspicious. "You need rest if the Winnowing is to begin soon. Return to the island and prepare yourself, Bren. The Silver Mother needs you – if you fail, there is little hope of stopping the Velaschin."

"I understand," Bren said softly, turning back to the door. She felt unsteady as she crossed the room, bile creeping into her throat. Had that been her imagination? Was she going crazy? It had been similar to when Ashika had been trapped in the sword, but there was a subtle difference – before, the voice had seemed to slither into her mind from the outside, and this time it had echoed up from a deep place inside her. Which would make sense, she supposed. But where was it now?

Bren nodded farewell to Desian once she reached the corridor outside; it looked like the sorcerer was debating saying something more to her, but she shut the door before he could decide. She stood there, staring at the whorls in the black wood in front of her, then hissed as quietly as possible through clenched teeth: "Where have you been?"

Lost in mists. I wandered through an endless murk, sometimes glimpsing shadows from long ago.

Bren tried to calm her racing heart. The feeling of having someone else awake and inside her was unsettling. She backed away from the door, then slowly started descending the stairs, her hand tightly gripping the banister.

"But why have you returned now?" she whispered.

There was a raven. It landed on my shoulder and told me to follow. Then it flew away, and I did.

"Garith." Somehow, when the creature had gazed into her eyes he had awoken the spirit inside her. Had he done it on purpose? For what reason?

I do not know.

Bren's hand slipped from the balustrade. "You can hear my thoughts?"

Aye. As you can hear mine.

Bren grimaced. The idea that her thoughts were no longer private was disturbing . . . but in some ways, it might be for the best. Otherwise, those around her would think she was a madwoman for talking out loud to herself.

Bren concentrated, trying to direct her next thoughts at the presence in her head. *How do you know he lies?*

The response came without the slightest hesitation. *Because he is a shaman. A graycloak. They always lie.*

Bren reached the bottom of the stairs. She glanced into the common room and saw that Tal was now sitting slumped at the table by himself, his drinking companions having dragged themselves off to bed, or perhaps a livelier establishment. He surged unsteadily to his feet when he noticed her and rushed across the room, knocking over a chair in his haste.

"Are you all right? What is he doing up there?" he asked, grabbing hold of her arm as if to reassure himself that she was real.

"I don't know for certain," she said, struggling to focus on Tal and not the presence in her head. "I think he was trying to send a message to other sorcerers."

Tal frowned, clearly not pleased with the idea. "Do you think it will work? I don't want to deal with any more of *them*."

Wise lad.

For a moment, Bren feared Tal had just heard the voice as well. Concern was etched in his face, and his grip on her arm tightened. "Are you all right? You look like you've seen a ghost."

Heard, not seen, Bren thought, and there was something like a snort in the recesses of her mind.

"What did Desian say to you? Did he try to scare you with talk of you being the Silver Mother's hope? It's not true, you know. Gods can't die." He leaned in closer, and she winced at the alcohol on his breath. "We can leave right now and never look back. Moon is out in the stable. We can go down to the docks and find someone who will take us to Scabtown. Then we can ride anywhere we want, even far away from the Flowering Coast. I've always wanted to see the thorned towers of the Dominion. We can leave them all behind, Bren – the dragons and sorcerers and goddesses."

Wise, yet also a coward.

"Don't call him that," Bren hissed in anger under her breath, and Tal drew back from her in surprise.

"What was that?"

"Nothing," Bren said hurriedly, reaching out for him. "Sorry." She tried to smile, though it felt forced. "Tal, I have to do this. For my family and all the other families that have suffered. If by bringing dragons back to our people I can save lives, perhaps spare a city from being consumed by flames . . . I have to try."

Tal nodded glumly. "I understand," he said, his eyes downcast. His hand went into his pocket, and when he drew it forth again a soft radiance leaked from between his fingers. "Here," he said, unfolding her fingers and dropping the glowing stone into her palm. "Take this. It's helped me out of a lot of difficult situations. Maybe it can do the same for you."

A tightness filled Bren's throat. "I can't, Tal," she said, trying to return the pebble. "It's from your mother—"

"I want you to have it," he said before she could finish. "Just think of light when you hold it, and that will summon its magic."

Bren hesitated, but then she slipped the cool stone into her pocket. Tal nodded when she did this, and she thought she saw some mix of relief and resolve in his face. He must feel helpless, she realized, sending her away and unable to offer any aid during the Winnowing. Now he'd given her his most valuable possession – there was no greater sacrifice or help he could provide.

"Thank you," Bren said, wrapping him in a tight embrace. "I won't lose it."

He sagged into her. "I know. You can give it back after."

She let go of him and stepped back. "I'll be off, then. Next time you see me, I'll have a dragon."

That elicited a grin and a rueful shake of his head. "I'm excited to meet it. Him? Her? Do dragons even have genders?"

"Of course they do," Bren said with a sigh, turning to the inn's entrance. "I think so, anyway."

She left without looking back, afraid Tal might see the tears in her eyes. She imagined she could feel the weight of the pebble in her pocket – such a small thing, but heavy with Tal's concern for her.

Outside, she skirted the elaborate façade of *The Windblown Inn* until she found a cobbled path leading behind the building. It emptied into a courtyard filled with a smaller stone structure that looked like it might once have been a house for servants, but now had been hollowed out and converted into a stable. Where the door had once stood a larger opening had been made with a sliding gate, and straw was heaped about this entrance. The interior was divided into stalls, all of which were empty save for the last. Moon looked like he had been expecting her, and his tail swished back and forth in greeting.

"I've missed you, too," Bren said, grabbing a handful of oats from a barrel just inside the entrance.

Moon *whuffed* an agreement, then lowered his head and began eating out of her hand. His eyes stayed fixed on her, deep and blue and knowing.

"It's almost over, Moon," she whispered, scratching him behind his ear. "For better or for worse."

21

Flames danced with shadows under the horned moon.

Blood pounded in her veins in time with the drums, the sound of palms striking taut buffalo skin. Pipes skirled, moaning like lost spirits as they twined with the thick column of smoke rising into the night.

The others celebrated, drinking mead from tusks as they danced around the great fire, sweat-slicked and giddy with the day's victory. A league to the west, the warriors of the Black Mountain tribe lay like leaves in autumn, scattered across the killing field on the edge of the great forest. They had thought themselves invulnerable, accompanied by one of their unholy shamans. But even the graycloaks of the mountain could not stop arrows when they fell like rain and the threshing swords of her tribesmen after they had burst from the prairie holes where they had hidden like the great serpents of the plains.

Ashika breathed deep of the sweet smoke, running her finger along the pale metal that lay across her lap. Banevak had feasted; her father had been avenged. She had taken six lives, including the shaman who had spat curses at her through bloody lips as she twisted the sword inside his guts. She should have felt satisfaction watching the blackness leak from the graycloak's eyes as the life left his body, but instead she was troubled. She had glimpsed something else inside that man for the briefest of moments. A thing. An evil. It had seen her and marked her, and she knew it would remember.

It would come for her again, wearing the skin of another.

Ashika watched her tribesmen, her heart heavy. There had been rumors that a darkness had seeped into the western lands, welling up from cracks beneath the Black Mountain. And today she had seen it, felt its hate and hunger. It gnawed at her still.

"Blademaiden!"

A man lurched towards her, his grinning face red from drink. His hand was extended to where she sat cross-legged at the very edge of the light, inviting her to join the revels.

"Come! This is your victory! Dance with the spirits to thank them for their help!"

Ashika stared at the outstretched hand. She knew this man. Chaebu, son of the hunter Jerth. Handsome and young. This had been his first battle, and the excitement of the day and the strong sorghum wine were carrying him along like a boat on a swift-rushing river. Sober, he never would have dared approach her. She was a blademaiden, married to her sword, the protector of the tribe. Three hundred heartbeats were her responsibility, and the danger had not yet passed. She knew it. She felt it. She had seen it.

When she did not move to take his hand, his expression faltered, and he blinked like he was just returning to himself. He swallowed, then ducked his head in respect and withdrew back to where the others danced.

He would find another woman tonight; she was sure of it. Blood always ran hot after battle. But she did not envy that girl. She had sworn her soul to a single purpose, and until her tribe was safe, she would not indulge in any pleasure of the flesh.

She stroked the ancient metal that lay across her knees, thinking again of what she had seen as the shaman's life had fled on shadowed wings.

BREN OPENED her eyes to darkness. She lay on mounded cushions, swaddled in a light blanket. For a moment, she was confused about where she was and what had happened. Her skin still felt a fading warmth like she had been close to a fire, and there was an ache in her sword arm she knew came from swinging a blade too much. But she hadn't practiced her forms yesterday. She had gone to see Desian on the Isle of Broken Swords. She'd met that strange sorcerer Garith, and now . . . and now . . .

She closed her eyes, considering what she had just dreamed. It was still so sharp, so vivid. Like something summoned from the depths of memory, not cobbled together from the events of the day before.

Aye. It was from my past, on the eve of the great war between the tribes.

Bren grimaced. It was so strange to feel another presence inside her, to hear a voice that was not her own. Was this what it was like to be mad? Was she mad?

A dry chuckle echoed in her head. *Perhaps you are. You did invite me inside you.*

This wasn't what Desian said would happen, Bren thought. *He said I would be able to draw upon your skills, but you would be . . . quiet.*

Never trust a shaman, Ashika replied. *A valuable lesson and one I learned as well. Do you think I wanted to be bound forever to my sword? It was supposed to last only until our enemies were defeated.*

And that tribe you fought has been gone for a thousand years, the one that became the Gith. Bren felt a swell of pity for the blademaiden. She had touched Ashika's mind, her memories. She'd sensed her care for her people, how much she'd been willing to sacrifice to keep them safe. It was not pleasant, in truth, this sharing of souls. It was very unnatural to feel Ashika inside her, to be privy to those private moments of her past. It was . . . a violation, in a way.

Perhaps we could return to Desian. He could perform the sorcery again, put you back to sleep . . .

You need me, the voice said in a manner that brooked no dissent. *And not just my sword-skills. This test is fast approaching, and you need my guidance. After it is finished, we shall cleave our souls apart. Yet for now, I will help you. And also . . . I want to learn more about this new world.*

Why? Surely everything you cared about is long gone.

A moment's pause, as if Ashika was hesitant to share the reason . . . or perhaps, Bren supposed, her bluntness had touched a nerve. *Because I believe the reason I stayed wedded to Banevak might not be simply because of some flaw in the sorcery of my tribe's shamans. Perhaps my war never ended. Perhaps whatever the Black Mountain graycloaks welcomed into our world persists to this day.*

22

————

"I feel ridiculous," Bren muttered as Jaleska stepped back and looked her up and down approvingly.

"You look striking," the girl insisted, holding up the silver-framed hand mirror she'd brought into the tent with the ceremonial clothes.

Bren winced – it was worse than she'd imagined. The layers of heavy brocade Jaleska had draped her in were all dyed different colors, resulting in an outfit that seemed at war with itself. Long crimson sleeves vanished into the arms of a tunic the same dark blue as the sky before a summer storm, which clashed spectacularly with both the bright green scarf hanging about her neck and the gray belt that cinched her garishly bright yellow leggings. It was true – she looked utterly ridiculous.

Jaleska noticed the face she was making while looking at herself in the mirror and sighed. "Well, if it's any consolation, everyone else is going to be dressed the same. It's tradition."

"It's tradition to look like a jester on the eve of the Winnowing?"

The Sister of the Temple Draconium rolled her eyes. "No. The clothes are supposed to honor the ten species of dragons that may be claimed during a Winnowing. Each one is represented by a color you are wearing."

"And what about this?" Bren asked, indicating the round pearly buckle that secured her belt.

"River dragons," Jaleska told her, approaching again to toss one end of the emerald scarf over Bren's shoulder jauntily. "They have iridescent scales, like the inside of an oyster's shell. They're beautiful." She stepped back, looking Bren up and down critically, then smiled in obvious satisfaction. "Like you."

Now it was Bren's turn to snort and roll her eyes. "This better not be some elaborate joke. If I show up to the dinner and everyone else is dressed in white robes, I'm going to strangle you when I get back."

We look foolish.

You are not even really wearing these clothes, Bren replied testily to the voice in her head.

Jaleska placed her hands over her heart and briefly closed her eyes in what Bren could only assume was some sort of Velaschin promise. Then she went to the tent's entrance and pulled the flap open, gesturing grandly for Bren to precede her out into the cool night. "After you, aspirant."

LIT TORCHES HAD BEEN SET upon the arched bridges, forming blazing pathways that led deeper into the island. As Bren followed Jaleska across the first one, she thought she saw through the smoky haze a pair of shadows upon another bridge, and she felt a pang of nervousness. Tonight she would finally meet her competition in the Winnowing, all Velaschins born and bred who had been preparing for this moment their whole lives. Would they know she was different, an outsider? She suspected they all had heard the story of the dragon egg fracturing in the caliphant's palace and knew who had caused the trials to be moved forward from the summer solstice.

For once Jaleska was silent as she led Bren over the bridges, her head bowed and her hands hidden in the sleeves of her long robes.

This more than anything unnerved Bren – she had become very accustomed to the girl's constant chatter, and to have her so quiet now impressed upon Bren the solemnity of the occasion. This was the ceremonial commencement of the Winnowing, the moment when all the aspirants could take the measure of their rivals. Bren found her palms were clammy with a cold sweat despite the heat from the torches lining their way.

When they arrived at the start of the last and largest bridge, this one guarded by a pair of red-armored warriors holding halberds, Jaleska turned back to Bren. She kept her gaze fixed on the stone path in front of her, and when she spoke, her voice had the formal inflections of a prepared speech. "I leave you now, aspirant. Go forth and meet your brethren on this the eve of the great trials." Then she shuffled forward, her head still bowed, though as she passed Bren she whispered quickly, "Good luck. Don't let them intimidate you."

Bren wanted to ask what she meant by this, but Jaleska clearly had no intention of staying to answer questions. Her part in this night must have ended.

Bren turned over those final words as she started on this bridge, which was broader and arched much higher than the ones they had already crossed. Intimidate her? She'd confronted demons and delved into haunted barrows – how could others her own age possibly prove intimidating? Of course, Jaleska didn't know everything that had happened to bring her to this moment. If she had, she would have probably run to tell her masters that this Velaschin foundling was far more than she appeared.

When she crested the highest section of the bridge Bren glimpsed her destination. It was the largest islet she'd yet seen on this archipelago, though most of it was only a flat and inky black field on this starless night. A dozen torch-lit roads like the one she had followed terminated here like spokes converging in the center of a wheel, and then illuminated pathways wended the rest of the way to the island's middle where a great bonfire blazed. At this distance she could just make out the shape of tents and long tables, and around them silhouetted by the glow of the flames moved many small figures.

The others.

Steeling herself, Bren started to descend from the bridge.

It was not what she had been expecting.

When the abbess and the Sisters of the Temple Draconium had awaited Bren at the docks, they had done so in solemn and dignified silence. She'd felt the same heavy weight when she'd approached the egg in the caliphant's palace – an almost spiritual awe, as if she was being watched and judged by some higher power. Bren had assumed this moment would be much the same, with somber aspirants sharing a final meal together before the start of the trials.

But the scene she found when she finally reached the dinner could not have been any more different. It looked more like a festival day in the Seven Valleys, such as the Night of the Three Sisters, when everyone in her village danced and celebrated in raucous good cheer. Long trencher tables had been set up around the huge central bonfire, groaning under the weight of a feast unlike any she had ever seen before. Suckling pigs with skin lacquered bronze were surrounded by platters of crisped capons slathered in sauce, and there were mounds of elaborate pastries garnished with small bright fruits and flowers. Open pavilions surrounded these tables, and Bren glimpsed minstrels playing strange stringed instruments. Servants in simple gray tunics were bringing more dishes from the darkness beyond the firelight and refilling the many great golden decanters scattered about the tables. The help was easy enough to differentiate from the aspirants because – as Jaleska had promised – the Velaschin nobles in attendance were dressed just as ridiculously as Bren.

Every summer a troop of performers would pass through the Seven Valleys, acrobats and singers and thespians, setting up camp in meadows and inviting villagers to experience the spectacles they offered for a venmark or two. The most popular of these acts among the children was always the pantaloons, fools dressed in motley who bumbled about hilariously. Their outfits had always elicited guffaws as soon as they appeared . . . and it looked to Bren like she had stumbled upon the beginning of one such massive performance.

Velaschin about her age were everywhere, milling about as they drank and feasted and conversed loud enough that the playing of the minstrels was nearly drowned out. They were all dressed in variations of the same many-colored outfit as Bren, though some wore elaborate gowns streaked with hues that also represented the different breeds of dragon, while others had donned tunics and trousers. Bren found herself relieved that Jaleska had realized what style she would be far more comfortable wearing. Having to squeeze into one of those high-waisted dresses would have made this night far, far worse.

What most surprised her about this swirling revelry was that she had expected the aspirants to be wary of each other, restrained in their behavior as they tried to take the measure of their rivals. Instead, they seemed completely at ease, as if this was a gathering of old friends. Which perhaps it was. After all, they were almost all drawn from the same four noble families. They had likely been encountering each other at parties and hunts and formal events since they were children.

Bren slipped between the tents encircling the feast and skirted a knot of carousing aspirants – each with a fluted glass in hand – as she made her way over to the closest table. Her stomach twisted at the aromas rising from the mounds of glistening meat and heaps of pastries. She had been too nervous earlier to eat much, only picking at the lunch Jaleska had delivered. Now she found her hunger kindled by the sumptuous sights and smells, and even though she had told herself she wasn't going to indulge too much she tore a leg from a crisped hen and stripped it bare in a few large bites.

One leg turned into two, then three. After days of flatbread and strange sauces, the taste of good honest meat dripping with juices was overwhelming. Also, focusing on the food was a welcome distraction.

"Are they not feeding you?"

Bren slowed her chewing and swallowed guiltily. She turned to find a red-haired serving girl in a dark gray tunic watching her with a faintly disgusted expression. Bren wiped at her greasy mouth self-consciously, surprised that the servers would be so brazen.

The girl frowned, then picked up a half-full goblet of some dark liquid from the table beside her and took a sip. Bren blinked in confusion. Surely *this* behavior was not allowed . . .

Wait.

Bren's gaze lingered on the girl's red hair and the profusion of freckles on her pale face. She had been a hundred paces away at the time, but Bren thought she knew this girl. It was the archer who had been shooting arrows across the islands into a chair. What had Jaleska said her name was?

"Where are your clothes?" Bren asked.

The girl grunted in what sounded like annoyance. "My clothes? I'm wearing them, aren't I?"

Bren felt her face flush. "No. I mean, why aren't you wearing the dragon colors?"

The girl took another drink, swishing it around her mouth before swallowing. Then she looked Bren up and down, her expression critical.

"Because they look ridiculous."

Oh, I like her.

Bren opened her mouth to retort, but then closed it a moment later. She scowled, glancing down at the outfit Jaleska had told her she had to wear. "You're right."

The girl grunted again, and this time it sounded like an agreement. She plucked a golden grape from a bowl and popped it into her mouth, chewing slowly.

"I'm Seris," the girl said, clapping a hand to her chest.

"Bren," she replied, mirroring the gesture.

Seris gave her a crooked grin. "You just greeted me like you are in the legions."

Another wave of tingling embarrassment swept over Bren. "I'm not."

"I know. You're the foundling. The one who cracked the egg."

"I . . ." Bren considered trying to explain what had happened, but finally just shrugged. "Yes."

"*Hm*," Seris said, eating another grape. "You've caused quite the stir. I'm grateful, I have to admit. All their attention would probably be on me if it wasn't for you."

"You're not like the rest of them," Bren said, and though it wasn't a question, Seris still nodded.

"Aye. I hate them."

Bren frowned at her honesty. "Then why are you here? If you claim the hatchling, you'll have to become one of them, yes?"

Seris snorted. "You know, I saw you a few days ago. You were being led around by one of the Sisters. Did she tell you about me?"

Bren nodded. "She did. She said you are common born."

Seris's gaze sharpened. "She's right, but I'm not ashamed. My mum was out in the moors gathering bloodmoss, and this dragon rider spied her and flew down to have his fun. I was born nine months later. Even on the marches, a lot of folk didn't believe her, but it was the reason I went and joined the army as soon as I could. Always hoped I'd find out who my da was and spit in his face for what he did."

Bren swallowed. "I'm sorry."

Seris shrugged and plucked another grape, though this time she began carefully peeling the skin away to reveal the flesh within. "From what I hear, we might have much in common."

"I didn't know my birth parents. I was found in the forest as a babe."

"Wouldn't be surprised if the same thing happened to your mum as happened to mine," Seris said with more than a trace of bitterness. She swept out her hand to encompass the Velaschin nobles. "They take what they want. If you're not Blooded, you're just a thing to them. I don't think they know what to do about me now, to be honest. None of them believed I truly shared their precious blood until the dragon in the egg took notice of me. And I'm not sure if I'd even have been given the chance if the abbot hadn't been so certain I was lying." She pulled on a red curl hanging down beside her face. "I look like a kalishwoman through and through. And they like to think their blood is so pure it would cleanse any muddy peasant blood it meets."

"They said something similar to me," Bren said quietly, remembering the conversation with the abbot and abbess.

"But you resemble the very image of a Karth," Seris said, her lip curling as she sipped from her goblet. "There really should be no doubt about where *you* come from. Now, whether you are a true Velaschin and should be allowed in the Winnowing ... that's a debate even I've heard, and I try to avoid ever talking with *them*." She raised her cup, again indicating the nobles. As Bren's focus was drawn to the others, she suddenly realized that more than a few of them were also paying attention to her and Seris. Mostly it was quick glances cast in their direction, but a few were staring boldly as they swirled their cups, their expressions opaque.

"Yes," Seris murmured, reaching for another grape, "they are very interested in us. But I think they mostly want to know what you in particular are capable of."

"I'm a nobody," Bren said softly. "I was a shepherdess."

"A shepherdess who met the Old Drake and cracked a dragon egg," Seris said with a shake of her head. "You're a mystery, and that worries them. In many ways, these trials were already scripted long ago – they knew each other's capabilities and had schemed for how to win the game. The factions were already settled, the pieces all placed."

Bren frowned, glancing at Seris. The girl's freckled face was now flushed by drink, but her blue eyes were still sharp as she watched the other Velaschin with disdain. "Factions?" Bren asked. "You mean the different families?"

Seris sneered, waving her goblet again at the nobles, though this time more dismissively. "You can see, can't you? There's almost no mingling between them."

And then what the girl was talking about became clear to her. The Velaschin nobles in their garish finery were not a single swirling crowd – no, they were clustered together in distinct groupings, commonalities obvious within each of these gatherings that she hadn't noticed at first. In one they were mostly large and thickset, with prominent jaws and deep-set eyes, but closer to the bonfire the Velaschin were taller and willowy, and more than a few had streaks of copper in their hair like lightning strikes on a dark night.

"Those are the Varyxes," Seris said, indicating the more brutish Velaschin. "Famed for being gentle giants or cruel monsters. I've heard that back in the empire many of the greatest scholars come from that house, but here they're more likely to be drawn from the army. I've seen several of them up high on their horses barking orders – never actually spoken with any, of course, since their station is so far above mine. The high general in this campaign is a Varyxes, and he's earned his reputation as a merciless warrior." Seris's gaze unfocused as she stared at something only she could see. "I've watched him fight. He gives no quarter."

Bren could now see the resemblance between the sneering, scarred warlord at the ceremony in the Briar and these nobles – none were as large or fearsome as he had been, but they were also all decades younger.

"And them?" Bren asked, nodding at the contingent of tall and thin Velaschin.

"Ahzan. I heard you've met the most famous scion of their house, Agiz ben-Ahzan. The Old Drake."

Bren nodded absently, her gaze drawn to a girl with more copper than black in her hair. The rest of her cohort seemed to move around her, as if she was their center.

"Merith Ahzan," Seris said, a slight edge to her voice. "If anyone other than Zair is going to claim the hatchling, it is expected to be her. But it will be difficult to overcome the Karth strength in numbers."

"And that's them?" Bren said, turning towards the largest knot of Velaschin.

Seris grunted in agreement. "Of course. And it must be like looking in a fractured mirror for you."

Bren frowned, but she was right. With their high cheekbones, deep black hair, and pale skin the Karths did indeed look like her ... and also like the dragon rider who had given the command to destroy her house. It was no wonder the abbot had been so certain which of the Velaschin houses her mother or father had come from.

Something twisted inside Bren when she thought about how a warrior who very likely shared her blood had been responsible for murdering her adopted family. Grimacing, she forced herself to turn away from the Karths.

"And the fourth?" she asked, her voice tight. "Where's the last house?"

Seris made a show of looking around and then shrugged. "Regast, the imperial house. I've heard there aren't many of them here. Emperor Fariz prefers to keep his relatives close by, and they are by far the smallest of the four houses. I'm sure they have at least a few in the Winnowing, but I don't know who. Perhaps they're ... oh."

Bren glanced at the red-haired girl and saw that her brow had drawn down in concern as she watched the swirling revelry.

Slowly, Seris set her goblet down on the edge of the table, then drew herself up straighter. "You've drawn some attention, shepherdess," she said out of the corner of her mouth, and though she was clearly trying to look relaxed and confident, her fingers were playing nervously with the sleeve of her tunic.

Bren followed where she was looking and saw that a tall boy had emerged from the Karths. He was broad-shouldered but still lean, and his movements had a fluidity that stood out among the sea of awkward adolescents. He had the look of someone who had trained for many years to move with precision and grace. It was a swordsman's gait, Bren realized, light and balanced.

This must be Zair Karth.

Despite the stir his departure had caused, no other Karths followed the boy as he approached the trestle table where Seris and Bren waited.

This boy could have been trained by a blademaiden.

Bren startled at the spirit's sudden intrusion, and Seris glanced curiously in her direction. It was easy to forget that Ashika's presence was inside her, always watching, even if she usually kept silent.

He is one to be wary of.

Bren had already reached that conclusion. There was an air of arrogance surrounding the Karth boy that reminded her of Desian, amusement in his dark eyes as he sauntered closer. But his smile was surprisingly warm and open.

"Greetings," he said when he stood before them, then flourished a deep bow. "I am Zair Karth, first son of Bessam Karth, the magistrate of this city as appointed by the Crimson Throne of Velasch. I am honored to meet you, Brenna." He reached for her hand, and before she understood what he was doing, he lowered his face to brush his lips against her knuckles.

"Hello," Bren said softly, again feeling foolish in her extravagant clothes. Like Seris, Zair was clad in simple black trousers and a tunic woven of some expensive-looking fabric, with the only ornamentation a tiny silver sword pinned to his left breast.

"Lord Karth," Seris said stiffly, clapping a closed fist to her chest, but the dark-haired boy ignored her.

"You are the very image of my cousin," the boy said with a slight shake of his head. "It is remarkable. You know, when I first heard that a lost Karth girl had been found in the wilds of this land I could not believe it. And yet . . . it is impossible to deny that now after seeing you standing here. Come, you must tell me your story."

Bren shifted uncertainly. "My story?"

Zair plucked a grape from the bunch Seris had been picking at and peeled it with quick, precise movements. "Yes. There's quite a bit of curiosity about where you came from."

Seris had taken a step back, watching this exchange carefully. She looked tense, Bren thought, as if Zair's closeness had put her on edge.

"I was a foundling," Bren said. "My mother stumbled upon me in the woods while she was gathering herbs. I was still a babe, and I remember nothing."

"There were no bodies?" Zair asked, his eyes bright with interest. "No evidence of an ambush?"

"My mother said there was no sign of anyone else. I was in a basket, swaddled in simple white cloth. No one knew where I had come from – I doubt a Velaschin had ever even visited the Seven Valleys before that day."

Zair furrowed his brow as he considered this. "It doesn't make much sense. My family does not abandon our own. Even if you were an unwanted child, my father would have insisted you be raised in the House."

Bren shrugged helplessly. "There was nothing to suggest where my birth family had gone or why they'd left me."

Zair considered this for a moment and then flashed her such a dazzling smile that she was taken aback. "Well, you have found your way here. The pull of the Blood is indeed strong, as my father says. You were in Leris? And the Old Drake noticed you?"

Bren nodded, relieved that Zair had leaped over the events that had brought her to the City of Roses. She truly did not want to explain what had happened to her family, because she didn't trust herself not to stammer over the lies she'd have to tell.

"Fortunate timing, with the Winnowing approaching. I do not put much stock in fate or provenance, but if I did it, would be easy to believe a higher power is orchestrating events."

Bren hoped she wasn't flushing. Had he somehow guessed that the Silver Mother had pushed Bren onto this path? If he truly had such suspicions, surely she would be in a torture chamber right now. And Zair was smiling as if he had just made an off-hand, inconsequential remark.

She stiffened as he reached out to put his hand on her shoulder, but he did not seem to notice her discomfort.

"Come, you should meet the others from our House. They are all very interested in you."

With a quick glance of apology at Seris, Bren allowed Zair to guide her away from the feast tables and towards the contingent of Karths, all of whom were indeed watching them with avid interest. Her last glimpse of Seris was the girl pursing her lips in annoyance, but Bren wasn't sure if that was because Bren was abandoning her or perhaps something to do with how Zair had ignored her . . . as if she was not even worthy of his notice.

She would try to apologize later, but right now she had to prepare herself. The faces of the youths she was approaching gleamed in the firelight, their dark eyes glittering. She saw none of the friendliness that Zair had shown her, only measuring stares and closed expressions. Bren's palms were slicked by cold sweat, her pulse rising. This was like out of a nightmare.

"Alyia! Malisk! Come greet our cousin!"

Two of the youths stepped forward. One was a girl, small and slight and surpassingly beautiful, the Karth features perfectly balanced, the other a boy whose face was so long and his cheeks so high and sharp he almost looked otherworldly. An odd scar covered his left cheek, a ragged circle with a cross in the center, and Bren wondered how he had come to bear such a mark.

"I'm Bren," she said, trying to ignore the coldness crawling across her skin from being the center of attention.

"You cracked the dragon egg," the scarred boy said, and it wasn't a question.

"I . . . yes," Bren replied haltingly.

The girl arched a perfect eyebrow, the edge of her lips rising in something that resembled a smile. "We should thank you. Several Varyxes scions were with the army's vanguard and won't be able to return in time for the Winnowing. House Karth's chances of claiming the hatchling strengthened significantly when the abbot decreed the trials would be moved up." She brushed back a lock of midnight hair. "My name is Alyia, and I am the second daughter of Farin Karth."

"My father's brother," Zair interjected. "Alyia is ranked second for our House among those that are here. And Malisk is her half-brother."

"A half-year older than me, but he's a bastard," the girl said lightly. "His mother worked in the kitchens. You both should get along well."

The scarred boy snorted at this, the first crack in his cold façade. Bren hadn't noticed even the slightest flicker when Alyia had so blithely shared his past – apparently, he was well-conditioned to accept his place in the family.

"I do not know for certain if I am truly one of you," Bren said. "A Karth, I mean."

"You are," Zair assured her. "There is no doubt in my mind. And after the trial is finished, I shall find a place for you in our House. Perhaps you could even be groomed to be a magistrate in these lands – surely you would be a better choice to govern the City of Roses than whoever my father has planned to install."

Bren could only stare at Zair, stunned by how casually he had just offered Leris to her. She had spent much of her life just dreaming of visiting the city, and now she could be its ruler? Was he jesting?

"Your father has probably promised that plum to someone else," Alyia said, clearly amused by Bren's reaction.

Zair waved her words away. "Perhaps, perhaps. But my father is always going on about how if we want to rule these lands we need to make a bridge between us and those who live here. Bren might be just what we have been looking for."

A grunt focused her attention on the scarred boy. "You don't even know if she wants to be part of the family," Malisk drawled, scratching at the strange symbol carved into his cheek.

"Why wouldn't she?" Zair asked, his brow drawn down like he couldn't conceive of any answer to this question.

"Perhaps she wants to claim the hatchling herself," the boy said, his gaze settling on Bren. She shivered, unnerved by the emptiness behind his eyes.

Zair blinked in confusion, as if he hadn't even considered this possibility. Then he also turned to Bren, and he almost looked apologetic for what Malisk had just stated.

"Surely not. You don't really imagine yourself a dragon rider, do you?"

Bren frowned. "I don't understand. That's why we're all here, yes?"

A ripple of subdued laughter passed through the crowd of Velaschin nobles.

Zair shook his head, grinning as if she had just said something ridiculous. "Well, yes. According to the rules of the Winnowing, any aspirant may in the end claim the hatchling. But what is most important is that the dragon bonds with a Karth . . . and thus is kept away from the other houses. For that reason a champion has already been chosen, and the will of everyone here is dedicated to seeing them triumph."

"And that would be . . . you?" Bren asked, though she was certain she already knew the answer.

"Of course," Zair said lightly. "I am the son of Bessam Karth, and I am the finest swordsman in the trials. I deserve to join my cousins in the Second Wing. It is my destiny."

The smugness of his smile was beginning to grate on Bren. "And if you fail in the Winnowing?"

He waved his hand dismissively towards the other Karth youths. "Then Alyia would be next. Of course, not Malisk, given his rather sordid history. I suppose if the unimaginable happens and we both fail, then the rest here can fight it out among themselves." His expression suddenly hardened, but the iron she'd glimpsed in his face vanished as quickly as it had appeared. "But I will not fail. It is impossible. So Bren, will you swear to support me in the Winnowing, and by doing so bind yourself to the House of Karth?"

"No."

Ha.

Zair's confident expression collapsed into shock. The beautiful girl beside him snorted in laughter, casting a glance over at her scarred half-brother as if to say, *'I told you so.'* The rest of the Karth clan muttered and shifted uncertainly.

Rage clouded Zair's face, and for the first time he did not remind her of the dragon rider who had taken so much from Bren. He looked like an angry little boy, ready to stamp his feet or break his toys after being denied something he thought he deserved.

He took a step towards her, his hands balled into fists . . . and then grimaced, staggering.

Bren felt it as well, a sharp keening that made her gasp. Through the haze that had suddenly descended she saw the sensation sweep through all the Karths, blood draining from their faces as they winced in pain.

Something comes!

I know, Bren said to the voice in her head as she stumbled away from the others, cries of panic rising behind her. She looked up just as the Silver Mother and her daughters vanished, swallowed by a vast black shape. Wind buffeted her, nearly knocking her to the ground, and most of the flames scattered about the feast were instantly extinguished. Even the bonfire guttered, almost going out before strengthening again. Then the shadow came once more, and as the dragon passed over her, it was accompanied by a sorrow so intense the breath was driven from Bren. The feeling subsided as quickly as it had come when the dragon flew on, but she could see how its presence affected the others – the Velaschin cowered as the beast soared over them, clutching at their heads. The dragon banked, spiraling higher in the sky, and then with a tremendous crack that made every hair on Bren's body stand on end, a sword stroke of lightning split the sky, exploding from a great maw that was illuminated in a sudden brilliant flash. Bren fell to her knees, her vision consumed by white light. Screams of pain and surprise sounded, and she realized her own voice had joined this chorus.

And then it was gone, the pressure in her head dwindling. She cracked her eyes open, trying to blink away the floating white islands in her vision. Around her, tables had been overturned by the passage of the dragon, food and wine spilling across the grass. Seris was one of the few other aspirants still on her feet, and her head was turned to watch the dwindling patch of utter darkness as it soared away. White-robed Sisters of the Temple Draconium had appeared out of nowhere, rushing about to check on the fallen nobles. One was hurrying towards her, but Bren waved her away and pushed herself upright. She swayed, still unsteadied by the intensity of the sadness the dragon had pressed down from above, though this alien emotion was now draining from Bren like water from a broken cup.

So, that is the kind of monster you wish to claim? What madness.

At that moment, Bren did not disagree.

23

"It was all highly unusual," Jaleska said as she poured Bren a cup of steaming kefa and placed it on the silver tray she had brought into the tent. She looked haggard in the early morning light filtering through the fabric, as if she had barely slept the night before. "Dragons simply do not visit the aspirants like Mist did last night. She seems to be taking a quite unusual interest in this Winnowing."

Bren sat up among the mounded cushions and stretched her arms. Her stomach grumbled, reminding her that she'd partaken in very little of the food before the dragon had disrupted the feast. "But it's her hatchling. It makes sense she cares about who will claim it."

"Dragons don't, typically," Jaleska said as she placed the eating utensils beside the dishes. "Once the Temple Draconium takes the egg away, most mother dragons seem to forget they even laid it until they meet the hatchling again after the Winnowing is concluded. And yet she caused such chaos on the eve of the trial. It's all very odd." She blew out her plump cheeks. "One of the other Sisters heard the abbess talking about this, and she said that grief makes all creatures do strange things. Mist has still not recovered from losing her rider."

"Dragons feel sadness about such things?"

Jaleska nodded. "Indeed. When death severs the bond it is extremely traumatic for both dragons and riders. Some dragons turn wild, flying beyond the boundaries of the empire. Others return to the aeries and spend the rest of their lives in mourning. Mist, it seems, has not yet decided what she will do."

Bren slipped from the bed and padded across the tent to where Jaleska had arranged her breakfast. Like nearly every other morning it was a bowl of glistening red-and-purple vegetables mixed with small chunks of meat and a pile of warm bread. At first Bren had found the flavors disconcerting, but they had quickly won her over, and several times she had literally licked the bowl clean. Even the kefa had grown on her.

"Where will the Winnowing take place?" Bren asked through a mouthful of the spicy vegetables and bread.

Jaleska paused in her reorganization of the cushions where Bren slept. "Here."

Bren swallowed some of the bitter drink, looking around the interior of the tent in confusion. "What do you mean?"

"This is where you will embark on your trial," Jaleska continued, settling a blanket across the bed with far more care than she typically took.

Bren frowned. She had been expecting to be led back to the field where the feast had been laid out the night before – surely, if all the aspirants were going to take part, they needed a large open space for whatever competition would decide who would bond with the hatchling.

"How—" Bren began, but she was interrupted by a gasp from Jaleska as the tent flap rustled and a young man in heavily embroidered robes stepped inside. On a chain around his neck dangled an hourglass, half of the white sand already pooled at the bottom, and he was carrying a wicker basket filled with what appeared to be dried fronds.

"Hazin?" Jaleska blurted, sounding surprised. "What are you doing?"

"I'm here to begin the Winnowing," the man said, his wide eyes settling on Bren. He looked even more nervous than Jaleska, and as he started to cross the tent he stumbled, his foot catching on a corner of a rug.

Jaleska made a noise deep in her throat that sounded heavy with disbelief. "Shouldn't a real warlock perform the ritual?"

The young man drew himself up with as much dignity as he could muster, given that he had nearly tripped and fallen a moment ago. "I'll have you know I am an acolyte of the third circle and very close to earning my amulet." He hesitated and then sighed deeply. "And there simply aren't enough masters in the city for all the aspirants. But don't worry, all the great sorceries for the Winnowing have already been woven. I am just tasked with opening the door." He attempted what Bren suspected was supposed to be a reassuring smile.

Jaleska made a grunt of displeasure. "Well, you're early. She hasn't even had her breakfast yet."

"Eat, eat," the young warlock urged Bren as he bustled over to where she sat and placed his basket on the table. "It will take me a short while to prepare." He began whistling cheerily as he pulled out the withered fronds, making a pile beside the metal contraption that served as a lamp at night. Bren eyed the yellowed leaves dubiously – what role could they possibly play in the Winnowing? She had been expecting a contest of arms, some sort of tournament or competition. Instead, a boy who was not yet a warlock had brought her clippings her aunt might have gathered while pruning the gardens of Leris.

Bren tried another bite of the vegetables, but now they tasted like ashes in her mouth. The hunger that had driven her from the bed had almost completely dissipated, replaced by a gnawing nervousness. What was going on?

"You should eat what you can," Jaleska murmured, coming to stand beside Bren. Her lips were pursed, and she was watching the young warlock's preparations with some suspicion. He had now wrestled the awkward device onto the floor and was in the process of moving all the fronds beside it.

"I'm not hungry," Bren answered, pushing herself away from the table and standing.

"Finished?" the man said brightly, fiddling with a small hatch at the bottom of the contraption. It popped open, and Bren gave a little hiss of surprise as a small green flame suddenly appeared on the tip of his finger. With a wink in her direction, he slipped the fire inside the device and the bottom began to glow as something inside ignited. Then he withdrew his finger, closed the hatch, and made a show of blowing out the flames.

Jaleska shifted in obvious annoyance. "Stop trying to impress us, Hazin," she muttered.

"It's all part of the ritual," he assured her, peering within the contraption at what he had started within. A faint green luminescence had begun to spill from the wide mouth at the top, and it strengthened until spectral jade flames emerged to lick the air. Satisfied by what he had conjured, the young warlock glanced at a tiny hourglass on the chain around his neck and then nodded.

"We're still early. If there are any other preparations you'd like to make, now is the time."

Bren fought back the strong urge to hurl one of the bed cushions at him. "How can I prepare if I don't know what is going to happen?"

Hazin spread his arms wide, looking very satisfied with himself. "You may ask."

Gritting her teeth, Bren gestured at the fronds piled on the table. "Are they part of the Winnowing?"

The warlock nodded sagely. "Indeed. When I place them in the zulkir lantern, the trial will begin."

"And what *is* that trial?" Bren asked, now not trying to hide her exasperation.

Hazin raised his eyebrows at this question. "Why, to find the egg, of course. The first aspirant to touch the shell will bond with the dragon."

Bren took a deep breath. That made sense. Burning leaves was a strange way to start the Winnowing, but she supposed there was some reason or other that this had become the ceremonial commencement of the trial. The Seven Valleys had its fair share of odd traditions as well. Bren sat on the edge of her bed of cushions, watching the sand trickle through the hourglass and willing for it to go faster.

Why was it necessary for a shaman to come here?

She flinched in surprise as the voice swelled, but Jaleska and Hazin were far too distracted to notice her sudden movement. *I don't know.*

Bren could sense the suspicion radiating from the presence within her.

Guard yourself well, the voice grumbled, but it offered nothing further as the three of them watched the sand run down. When there were just a few grains left, the warlock clapped his hands together and scooped up some of the yellowed fronds. Carefully and quickly, he ripped them into smaller pieces, discarding the thick stems.

"And it begins," he said with another wink before dumping the shreds of leaves into the metal contraption's open top. The jade flames reached higher, devouring the offering as the warlock leaped back, his eyes bright with excitement.

"Come!" he cried, beckoning towards Jaleska. "With me, Sister. We must leave now."

"What do I do?" Bren asked nervously as a hazy green smoke began to issue forth.

"Sit down," Hazin commanded her, motioning to a cushion that Jaleska had set on the floor of the tent. "When the smoke clears, the Winnowing begins." His voice was muffled, as he'd produced a cloth from somewhere and was holding it over his mouth. Beside him, Jaleska was using her long sleeve to keep from breathing in the smoke.

"Good luck!" the Sister cried as Hazin herded her towards the tent's entrance. "Claim a dragon for us!"

Then she was pulled through the flap, and Bren was alone. Eyes watering, she made her way over to the silken pillow Jaleska had set a few paces from what Hazin had called the zulkir lantern and settled down cross-legged. The smoke now looked more like mist, long green serpents crawling over the side of the contraption before slithering away when they touched the floor. The haze quickly thickened, and Bren could barely make out the vague silhouettes of the furniture in the tent. Then even these were swallowed completely. Her heart flailing, she coughed, struggling not to rush in a panic towards the entrance to breathe the fresh air outside. A wave of dizziness washed over her, and bile crept up her throat. She must have moved without realizing because she was suddenly no longer sitting on the cushion. The grass beneath her strangely felt far more lush than a moment ago, and Bren frowned, trying to make sense of this. When the smoke finally began to clear, she gasped in surprise.

The tent was gone. As was the bed, the table, and the metal device. A brilliant purple sky threaded with thin gray clouds arched above her, and floating in this vastness were what looked to be chunks of earth torn from the ground. On several of these flying islands were crumbling ruins, the jagged remains of towers and sundered archways dripping with vegetation. She stared dumbfounded at the strange sights above her, and then she forced her gaze away to what sprawled below her.

Slowly, wondering if this was all some illusion conjured by the smoke, Bren climbed to her feet. Thick grass was under boots she had no recollection of putting on. The white aspirant robes she'd been wearing were gone, replaced by a dark tunic and trousers. Had she fallen asleep and been moved here? It didn't look like she was in Yestra anymore. She stood on top of a grassy hill spotted with yellow flowers, the side sloping down in front of her bereft of any trees or shrubs. And at the bottom . . . Bren couldn't believe what she was seeing. Great stone walls battered by age rose from the meadow below, veined by thick vines. From her perspective standing high above she could see that there were more walls beyond the first, laid out to form twisting passages that unraveled into the distance, all open and exposed to the sky.

It was a labyrinth so large she couldn't see beyond it. This great maze filled her vision to the horizon, a mad profusion of stone and brick, its walls rising several times the height of a man. There were other things she couldn't quite make out deep inside the labyrinth: odd constructions of smooth dark stone and huge trees with spreading branches heavy with shimmering silver leaves. And at the bottom of the hill was an entrance into this vast warren flanked by statues of helmed warriors, their stone spears crossed. Beyond these guardians, the way was shadowed by the high walls rising on either side. She knew without any doubt that this was the test she had to pass, that somewhere in that maze was the egg Hazin had told her she must find. But how had she been transported here? And what was this place?

A warrior must know her surroundings.

"What?" Bren murmured numbly, still staring in dazed shock at what lay beyond the entrance.

Look around, child.

Bren pulled her gaze away from the maze, turning to her left. Another hill rose beside the one where she was standing, but it was not empty; instead, a massive wall of brambles almost completely obstructed her view, and this barrier extended down the hill until it met the outer wall of the maze below. To her right was the same, although the brambles did not quite reach the stone, leaving a gap large enough to pass through.

"It looks like there are two ways we could go," Bren said, eyeing that opening. "If we don't like the look of this entrance. And there might be others elsewhere."

Good. You are thinking clearly. If this place was built by shamans, it shall be riddled with traps and trickery. The best way inside may not be the most obvious.

Bren began to descend the hill, trying her best to stay alert to any danger. "However we proceed, we must be care—oh!" She stumbled as her foot struck something hard that had been hidden in the long grass. It was a piece of lacquered red leather, intricately wrought with writhing serpents. When she reached down, she saw that there was a second one that looked exactly the same beside it. Both were hollow and about the length of her forearm.

A vambrace. Merik had arrived at the farm one summer day

when the Bright Company had been passing nearby, and Bren had begged to examine every piece of the armor he'd been wearing. His vambraces had been steel and hinged to cover the elbow and part of the upper arm as well, but these would serve the same function, she supposed, even if they were not metal. Bren picked them up, turning them over in confusion. What were they doing just lying here in the grass?

I think they are meant for you.

Bren frowned at the thought. Why would she be dumped outside a labyrinth with only a pair of bracers? But still she slipped her hands inside and pulled them up until they settled snugly on her arms.

These are suited for an archer, protection for when one pulls a bow. Look around. Perhaps something else has been left for you.

"There," Bren said when she caught sight of a length of polished gray wood lying in the grass. A bow, and beside it was a quiver of black-fletched arrows.

"I don't suppose you're as good an archer as you are a swordswoman," Bren asked as she retrieved the bow and quiver.

She could almost hear Ashika's mental snort. *Bows are not an honorable weapon for battle. You should be able to look your enemy in the eye when you take their life.* There was a small pause, and then the voice continued in her head, almost grudgingly. *Yet it is true I was a fair hunter in my youth.*

Bren nocked an arrow and pulled it back, testing the draw. It slid smoothly, as if the string had been freshly waxed. "You're certainly better than me, then. My father showed me how to shoot after I pestered him for days, but I never hit a single target. It was much harder than I thought, and after that I decided my future in the Company would be in the infantry."

My skill should guide your draw, Ashika said inside her. *If I under-stand our . . . situation.*

She shouldered the bow, considering this. Desian's sorcery had buried Ashika deep inside her but had allowed Bren to borrow the blademaiden's skills. Now that the ghost was awake again, would Bren have to allow her to control her body like when she had inhabited the sword? She hoped not. Those moments locked in deadly battle but unable to move her own limbs had been terrifying.

"So what do we do now?" Bren asked, shielding her eyes from the bright sun as she gazed out over the overgrown labyrinth. A flock of some large black birds burst from the branches of one of the large silver-leafed trees and surged into the sky.

If this is a test, what you are looking for must lie at the center of that maze. Why else would they send you here?

"I know," Bren said with a heavy sigh. "I suppose I'm just delaying the inevitable. I can't say I'm looking forward to going in there."

Fear is good. Fear is caution. Yet fear should not keep you from doing what needs to be done.

"My uncle's words," Bren said as she descended the grassy slope towards the statue-flanked entrance to the maze.

You were holding Banevak when you said them, and so I heard. There is wisdom in his words.

"It can't be too dangerous in there," Bren reasoned, adjusting the leather vambraces so that they fit better on her forearms. "Jaleska told me that few aspirants die during the Winnowing. Perhaps we are just supposed to beat the others to the center of the maze."

If that is so, we need to hurry.

"Agreed," Bren replied, breaking into a jog. If this test was merely one of speed, whatever advantages she had with the blademaiden's spirit inside her would be useless. But if the warlocks had given her a weapon at the beginning of the trial likely they meant for her to use it.

She reached the base of the hill, and the great crumbling walls loomed over her, covered with thick vines and buckled in places where knotted little trees were growing from the stone itself. As she approached, she imagined she could feel the attention of the helmed warriors, and her skin prickled. Or perhaps there was another pair of eyes on her . . .

Movement made Bren turn her head towards the gap between the barrier of brambles and the outermost wall of the labyrinth. A heavyset boy dressed the same as her was struggling to extricate himself from the thorns that had snagged his tunic as he attempted to pass through the narrow opening. He held a short, broad-bladed sword, and he was hacking away at the prickly branches, but either the edge was very dull, or the brambles were made of tougher stuff than they appeared. Finally, he gave a snarl of frustration and ripped himself free, in the process tearing his tunic.

"Greetings," Bren called out as the boy began to hurry in her direction, red-faced and panting. He looked like one of the Varyxes, though he lacked the solidity she had come to expect from that family – soft rather than hard, awkward instead of graceful. What had Seris said? The Varyxes were either warriors or scholars? This one certainly seemed more the latter, just from the way he was holding his sword.

"I'm Bren," she said, unsure whether to attempt one of the Velaschin greetings she'd learned over the last few days or simply nod in the Seven Valley way. Then, before she could decide, the boy swung his sword at her.

It was an awkward strike, off-balance, and if Bren had even imagined the boy would attack her so brazenly she could have easily sidestepped the clumsy blow. But it was so unexpected that she was caught completely flat-footed, and only by lurching away was she able to avoid being disemboweled. She toppled over, the wind rushing out of her as she landed flat on her back. For a heartbeat she stared up at the purple sky with its filaments of gray clouds in disbelief, and then her view was blocked by the large boy as he came to loom over her.

Move!

The command exploded in her head, and the paralyzing shock dissipated. She rolled to the side as the boy squealed like a pig and his sword stabbed into the ground where she'd been lying a moment ago. Bren scrambled to her feet and hurriedly backed away from the boy, who pulled the blade from the earth with a grunt of effort. He looked at her wild-eyed, his face red from exertion, and then extended the sword in her direction. The tip trembled, as if he was struggling to hold it up.

The boy is more afraid than you. He's no warrior.

"That sword still looks sharp, though," Bren said, casting about for the bow she'd lost when she'd flung herself away from the boy's attack. It was lying a few paces behind him in the grass, along with the quiver of arrows.

"Maybe I can get around him," Bren said, starting to shuffle in a wide circle around the outstretched sword.

"Who are you talking to?" the boy yelled, sounding almost panicked as he lunged at her with a half-hearted thrust of the sword. Bren skipped back a few more steps, keeping a safe distance between her and the shaking blade.

"Oh, so now you talk," she said, continuing to maneuver around the boy in the direction of the bow. What she was going to do when she got to it, she wasn't sure – knock him over the head? Threaten him with an arrow?

"You're that bastard!" the boy cried, jabbing at her again. "The Karth girl! The one who cracked the egg!"

"I don't think that's reason enough to kill me," Bren replied, holding the boy's wide, frightened eyes with what she hoped looked like calm confidence.

The boy's fat face twisted in disbelief at her words. "This is the Winnowing!"

Bren had drawn close enough to her fallen weapons that she risked dashing in their direction, and she heard the boy's heavy steps pounding the ground as he charged after her. She scooped the bow and quiver from the grass, ripping an arrow free and nocking it as she turned. It certainly did seem like she was drawing upon Ashika's skills, but she couldn't dwell on this realization as the boy was almost upon her, his blade flashing in the sun. Without even thinking about what she was doing, Bren released the arrow. The hiss of it slicing through the air abruptly ended as it plunged with a meaty thunk just below the boy's collarbone, and the force of the impact made him spin partway around, the sword flying from his hand. He collapsed with a cry that sounded more shocked than pained, his finger scrabbling at the shaft sunk in his body.

"I'm sorry," Bren said, surprised by what she had just done. It had all happened so fast.

Finish him, Ashika said, and there was no hint of compassion in this command.

"I don't want to kill him," Bren replied, lowering the bow. The boy was thrashing now, his breathing wet and ragged as he tried to pull the arrow free.

The boy is dead anyway, the blademaiden continued, and with a sinking sensation Bren realized she was probably right. The boy's frantic movements were growing weaker, and blood had started to seep from the corner of his mouth. He coughed, vomiting up a wash of red.

Bren slowly raised the bow again. She truly didn't want to hear that sound again of metal entering flesh, but this would be mercy. Better a clean death than this suffering. She set another arrow and pulled it back, focusing on where she thought the boy's heart should be. That would be the fastest, yes? Her father had always talked about heart-kills with his hunting friends, how quickly they made life flee the body of the deer or rabbit. But what if she missed? Her own fingers were shaking, she realized, and she took a deep breath to steady herself, closing her eyes.

When she opened them, she found the boy slumped in the grass, his wide eyes staring at nothing. With a shudder she let the tension leave the string, blinking back tears. Why did she care? The boy had tried to kill her. But he had just been so pathetic, so scared. Surely his family must have known this would happen when trained warriors like Zair Karth were also entering the trials. What had they been thinking? Bren looked away, sickened by the sight of the dead boy. Her gaze was drawn to the massive stone warriors at the entrance to the maze. The mouth of one was twisted into a sardonic grin, as if amused by what it had just witnessed.

"Is that what you wanted to see?" Bren muttered, tossing down the bow in disgust.

If every dragon rider has undergone a trial like this, it is no wonder they are capable of terrible acts. And if you should wish to claim the hatchling, you must harden yourself. This will not be the only life you must take.

Bren scowled at Ashika's words, even though she recognized the truth in them. If she was going to survive this madness, she would almost certainly have to kill again. The thought made her even more nauseous. How cruel were the Velaschin to sacrifice their own children to find the strongest and most vicious? She pulled her gaze from the smirking statue, forcing herself to look at the dead boy again.

And found the body had disappeared.

"How . . . where?" she stammered, glancing around to make sure that the boy hadn't somehow returned to life and crawled away. Slowly she approached where he had fallen, and as she grew closer she saw at least some evidence that he had indeed been real and not some strange illusion. In the middle of a swatch of flattened grass lay a finely tooled red leather belt and a sheath clasped by a bronze buckle shaped into a dragon's head. It looked to have been made by the same craftsman and out of the same material as the bracers she had found on the hill. Bren crouched beside the still-fastened belt, eyeing it like it was a snake that might lunge at her.

Was the boy ever truly real?

Bren gingerly picked up the belt, examining it carefully for any hint as to its provenance.

"I think so," she murmured, unhooking the clasp that made the metal dragon's jaws hinge wide. "What he said, what he did . . . I think he was also dropped into this place alone and frightened."

Where is he now?

"Perhaps gone back?" Bren answered absently as she settled the belt around her waist and cinched it tight, then snapped the buckle shut. "Perhaps death is not final here. Perhaps when aspirants perish they are returned to where they came from."

Ashika was silent, as if mulling over what Bren had said. *Then is this real?* she finally asked.

Bren ran her fingers along the serpentine designs incised into the belt's leather, feeling the smoothness imparted by the lacquer. She raised her face, squinting into the purple sky as the breeze suddenly strengthened, stirring her unbound hair. "It seems real. There are stones under my feet and an ache in my back from throwing myself to the ground."

Sorcery, the voice in her head growled in disgust, and Bren had to agree . . . although she took some small comfort that the boy might not truly have died by her hand. She wanted to believe that.

"So we cannot die here?"

I do not think assuming that would be wise.

"True," Bren agreed, then stiffened as something else caught her eye.

Oh. Now that is fortuitous. The ancestors smile upon us.

"Indeed," she murmured, keeping her gaze fixed on the sword the boy had dropped, afraid that if she looked away it might also vanish. Slowly Bren reached down, her hand closing around the leather-wrapped hilt.

"It feels well-balanced," she said, hefting the sword and slashing the air in a quick pattern. It was heavier than Bren had recently grown accustomed to, with a short, broad blade more similar to the thrusting swords wielded in the tight infantry formations of the Bright Company. But it was still familiar, as this was the style of sword her uncle had given her to train with.

It is not Banevak Ashika said, *yet it will do.*

Unsurprisingly, the blade slid perfectly into the sheath at her side. Just like the bracers she'd found with the bow, the sword was meant to be paired with this belt. She wondered if every aspirant had been gifted a weapon. She assumed so, although it seemed quite random. That boy had clearly undergone very little training with a sword, and even if Ashika had some skill with a bow, it was not her preferred weapon.

Bren rubbed the bronze pommel at her side with her thumb. Now that the blademaiden had gained a blade, her chances of success had increased dramatically.

With a new confidence in her step, Bren approached the entrance to the labyrinth.

24

I f this place had truly been conjured by the Velaschin warlocks then Bren was in awe of their capabilities. Crumbling walls rose around her, mottled by vegetation and riven where monstrous vines slithered through the masonry. The branching passageways bent and twisted, contorting in ways she rarely antici-pated, several times leading her to dead ends and forcing her to retrace her steps. It reminded her of the mad design of the undercity below Leris, and she couldn't help but wonder if this maze – assuming it had not been woven whole-cloth from Velaschin sorcery – had been built by the Gith long ago and only been repurposed to serve as the staging ground for the trials. Every aspect certainly seemed ancient enough. The features of the statues she sometimes passed had been gnawed by time, and everything seemed to be in the process of being devoured by nature. Gnarled trees with grasping, serpentine roots had grown up inside the corridors, and Bren was forced in places to hack through the tangle.

The labyrinth thrummed with life. Clouds of glittering insects rose as she waded through waist-high fronds. Lizards the length of her forearm watched her from where they clung to the walls, skit-tering into cracks as she drew closer. Flying creatures that looked like winged snakes occasionally undulated through the sky, moving between the huge, silver-leafed trees thrusting up from deeper within the maze. She had arrived at the trunk of one of these behemoths not long after entering the maze – it had been so wide she'd thought it would have taken more than a dozen men to encircle it with linked arms, the bark pitted and scarred. With a wary eye on the dense, shimmering foliage above her – she could only guess what dwelled up there with the winged serpents – Bren had ascended to the lowest branches, just high enough that she could peer over the surrounding walls. Her heart had fallen when she'd seen the countless corridors squirming into the distance. Behind her, she could just make out the bramble-bounded hill where she'd awoken, but in the other directions the labyrinth vanished into a ruddy haze. Whatever this place was, she could see the passage of time in the darkening of the sky.

Bren had climbed back down dejected but not defeated. She had to assume that the other aspirants had also been deposited on hills ringing the maze, and if that was true they faced the same challenges. She would not reach the center – or wherever the egg was hidden – before the day ended, which meant she should find a safe place to hunker down for the night. She doubted she would be able to sleep, but her aching legs would certainly appreciate the rest. Perhaps it would be wiser to press on, but the thought of blundering about in the darkness made her nervous. She'd already tripped over the bones of an animal hidden beneath the fronds, and even though from its teeth it hadn't looked to be a meat-eater, she also doubted it had died of old age.

Food and water were another concern. Her stomach had begun to complain as she slogged through the knee-high fronds choking the passageways, and she wished she'd forced herself to finish the breakfast Jaleska had laid out that morning. The clotting humidity of the air in the labyrinth and the lushness of the vegetation suggested that rain was an inevitability, but still she watched the sky nervously. She knew she could suffer through many days without food – and if worse came to worst, those lizards climbing the walls would have at least a little meat on their bones – but water was another matter entirely.

So she felt some relief when she happened upon a pool fed by a waterfall trickling through a gap in one of the walls. The space it filled was wide and circular, with several corridors radiating outwards, and it seemed that someone else had thought this a good place to rest because a lean-to of branches lashed together with vines and covered with yellowed fronds had been constructed at the water's edge. Bren approached the structure warily with her hand on the hilt of her sword, but the interior was empty except for a heap of fronds that might have once served as a bed. They were so desiccated that she thought she'd prefer to sleep on the ground, but that was a decision to make later.

If others have been here some time ago, does that mean the shamans of Velasch always use this place for their trials?

This was a thought she'd been turning over for quite some time, but evidently Ashika's insight into her mind had its limits. Bren shrugged at the spirit's question, which she realized a moment later was a ridiculous reaction to a voice in her head.

"I don't know," she said as she exited the lean-to. The pool was only a few steps away, and aside from the ripples spreading out from the waterfall it was calm and clear enough to see strands of green rippling beneath the surface. Bren crouched down and cupped a handful of water, bringing it to her lips. She hesitated for a moment before tasting, but in the end decided that the dangers of dehydration outweighed the possibility of disease. It tasted as cool and fresh and pure as the streams that used to run down to the high meadows in spring, carrying snowmelt from the upper slopes of the Snowspears.

A chunk of masonry that looked to have been pulled from the walls had been placed beside the water, and with a sigh that released at least a little of the tension that she'd been carrying around Bren allowed herself to sit. The sky had darkened further, swallowing the clouds, replaced by pinpricks of emerald light.

"Why are the stars green?" she murmured, shivering as she slid her feet into the pool. The abrasions and scrapes she'd accumulated since entering the maze prickled in the cool water, but the sensation was pleasant.

They are not our stars.

Bren grunted at this, searching the evening sky for any hint of the Silver Mother or her daughters, but for the first time in her life, none of the moons were visible.

"Do you think I should stay here tonight?"

Ashika's response was a moment in coming, as if she had to consider carefully her answer. *You are thirsty and tired. We do not know what dangers lurk in the labyrinth, and though we risk allowing another aspirant to push deeper into this place, I would suggest we should rest here. We do not know if there will be shelter or water elsewhere.*

Bren turned back to the little hut, which was being devoured by the darkness as night descended. "All right."

IN THE FADING LIGHT, she ventured into the nearby passageways to gather an armful of fresh fronds, then cleaned out the lean-to and placed down this new bedding. There was no covering for the entrance, so she situated herself against the far wall facing the opening and kept her sword nearby – if anything appeared, she would be ready to confront it with steel in her hand. By the time she finished, the last red rays of day had vanished, and a night blacker than she had ever experienced had settled over the labyrinth. The light of the emerald stars speckling the sky did not reach the world below, and Bren was grateful that Ashika had convinced her to camp here for the night. The thought of pressing on into the unknown in absolute darkness made her shudder. Instead, she lay on her side with her back to the far wall and watched the inky blackness outside the entrance, her fingers curled around the hilt of her sword. She thought that sleep would be impossible, but eventually her bone-deep exhaustion proved too much to resist. Her dreams were strange, scenes of blood-red forests and fur-clad tribesmen under an endless sky. Breath misting the air as she led battered refugees through a winter-choked mountain pass while being chased by unnatural howls. They were drawing closer, and soon she would have to turn and face them, or the Black Mountain graycloak's abominations would descend upon the wounded and old struggling in the snow ...

Bren jerked awake. Her fingers felt stiff and cold from holding the sword hilt, but that wasn't what had brought her back. She held her breath, listening intently. There was a sound coming from outside, something soft and rhythmic. For a moment she entertained the hope that it was the wind rising and falling, perhaps rustling the vegetation as it wended its way through the maze. Or maybe it was the mournful cry of some strange bird or water creature. But as she lay there holding her breath, Bren became more and more certain it wasn't any of those things. It sounded – strangely enough – like a child sobbing.

She sat up as quietly as possible, bringing her sword into her lap. It could be a trap, an attempt to draw her out of this lean-to for an ambush. Anything was possible, because she truly had no idea what things dwelled in this place or how the other aspirants would conduct themselves during the trial. There could be a half-dozen of them out there with weapons poised, waiting for her to emerge into the night.

Bren breathed out slowly, trying to steady her nerves. *What do you think?*

The response was almost dismissive. **With a sword in our hand, there is little we should fear.**

Bren wished she shared Ashika's confidence. Then again, she doubted she would have any chance of succeeding in these trials if she hid from the sound of a crying child. Rising to her feet, Bren crept through the lean-to's opening and out into the humid night.

She had been expecting complete darkness, but the light of the stars had strengthened while she slept. The pool shimmered with a gray-green patina, and the vines climbing the walls were etched against the deeper blackness of the stone. Glowing insects swarmed her head, and she dispersed them with a wave of her hand.

The sobbing was louder now and clearly emanating from a spray of reeds rising near the banks of the pool. Adjusting her grip on the sword, Bren crept closer. Despite her best effort to stay silent, something crackled under her feet, and the crying abruptly ceased. Still, there was no rustling from the reeds she was approaching or any shiver of movement, so she had to assume whatever was hiding in there had hunkered down.

Perhaps you should thrust your sword in and see what squeals.

Bren would have sighed if she wasn't trying to be quiet.

And what if it is a child?

Ashika gave what Bren could only describe as a mental snort. *You remember this is a competition, yes? Everyone else here is a rival you must overcome to claim the dragon.*

That doesn't mean we have to kill everyone. The warlock said the Winnowing will end when we touch the shell.

Ashika's exasperation was palpable across the bond they shared, but the spirit said nothing else.

Bren was only an arm's length away now from the clump of reeds, and she slowly reached out and pulled the closest stalks aside. A faint green radiance crawled along the blade as she raised it between herself and whatever lurked within.

Apparently she was not the only one who could see the gleaming metal.

"Please!" squeaked a voice, hoarse from fear. "Don't hurt me!" All Bren could see was a huddled shadow. It did not leap at her or make any threatening movements, but still she kept her sword up.

"Who are you?" she hissed, trying to sound intimidating.

"Jerym!" A boy's name. The voice sounded so young she thought that otherwise she wouldn't have known the child's gender.

"What are you doing?" she asked, finally lowering her sword. She simply couldn't believe the boy's obvious terror was false.

There was a moment of silence, and Bren assumed he was considering what he should say.

"Hiding," the shadow finally admitted.

"Well, I found you," Bren said. "You might as well come out and join me in my shelter."

Another pause, longer this time. "You're not going to stab me?"

"If I wanted to stab you, I would have done it already," Bren said. "Come on, come with me."

She stepped back, attempting to appear less threatening. Slowly the shadowed shape unfolded as the boy climbed to his feet. He was much shorter than her, barely coming to her shoulder.

"How old are you?"

The boy sniffled, raising his arm to wipe at a face she couldn't see clearly. "My twelfth nameday was last month," he said, sounding miserable.

Bren frowned in surprise. Jaleska had told her all aspirants had to be at least fifteen years old. Or perhaps this child was not competing in the trials? Bren sighed, then motioned for the boy to follow her. Despite the darkness he must have seen her do this because she heard his crunching steps as she made her way back to the lean-to. She ducked inside the entrance and stood against the far wall to watch him enter. He did so tentatively, as if still afraid she was going to skewer him with her sword.

"You made this?" he asked.

"I found it," she replied, then settled herself cross-legged on the fronds she had strewn across the floor. "Go ahead, sit."

The shadowed boy sank down, and Bren thought she saw his shoulders sag in relief.

"Thank you," he said earnestly. "This has all been worse than any nightmare."

"You're an aspirant?"

A shiver of movement that might have been a nod. "Of course. And you must be as well. What's your name?"

"Bren."

"That's a strange name," the boy said. He sounded like he was growing more relaxed by the moment, his words coming faster. "Wait . . . are you the orphan girl? The one who was born in these lands?"

"I am."

"I suppose that's why you didn't stab me."

"What do you mean?"

The boy sighed. "If you were a Karth, you'd happily have cut off my head and carried it around like a trophy to show to all your horrid cousins. They hate my family. And the others aren't any friendlier."

"Your family?"

"I'm a Regast," Jerym replied, almost nervously, as if he were afraid of what her reaction might be. "My mother is Seliana Regast."

Bren leaned against the wall of piled branches, vines digging into her back. Regast. She knew that name. She remembered the story Jaleska had told her of the boy who had ventured north and found the first dragon eggs. A boy who had become the emperor of Velasch.

This child was a member of the imperial family.

Someone of his blood had ordered this conquest . . . and had dispatched the dragon riders who had killed her family. She should feel anger, but all she could see was a scared, shivering child. Still, it was a shock to know whom she was sharing this little hut with.

"You probably don't know my mother since you weren't born in Velasch," Jerym continued, oblivious in the darkness to the emotions that had been playing out across her face. "She's Emperor Fariz's younger sister."

"You're the emperor's nephew," Bren intoned, feeling like if she hadn't been sagging against the wall already she would have had to sit down.

"Yes," Jerym said. "Although it didn't save me earlier."

"What do you mean?" Bren asked, shaking her head as she tried to clear it.

"Yesterday a girl tried to *kill* me," Jerym whispered fiercely, as if afraid someone else might be listening. "It was madness! The warlock burned those leaves in my tent, and when the smoke cleared, I was sitting on a hill looking out over this place with an iron pike that weighed nearly as much as me lying in the grass. There was an entrance into the maze, so I wandered down to take a look—"

"Did you take the pike?"

Jerym shook his head sharply. "No! I'm a student, not a warrior! I wouldn't have known what to do with the thing, and it was much too heavy, anyway." He paused for a moment, as if reliving the events of yesterday. "I wish I had taken it, though. Maybe the other aspirant wouldn't have attacked me."

Bren shifted, leaning forward. It sounded exactly like what had happened to her.

"There was this great wall of thorns rising up, and it was so high I couldn't see what was beside me. But there was a gap down near the entrance to the labyrinth, and when I got to the bottom of the hill, this girl – I think she was a Karth, but I'm not certain, as her hair was a little lighter than yours – this girl burst out from the brambles like she had been waiting to ambush me. And she was swinging an ax! She almost took my head off!" Jerym's voice had risen to a fever pitch, but now he lapsed into silence again. "I'd never met her, and she wanted to murder me!"

"But she didn't," Bren said quietly.

"Not for lack of effort," Jerym replied, his words edged with bitterness. "I stumbled and fell, and she buried the ax-head in the ground a span from my head. While she was trying to pull it free, I jumped up and ran into the maze, and I didn't stop running until I collapsed."

"Someone attacked me as well when I arrived here," Bren said, her grip tightening on the hilt of her sword. "a boy from the family that all look like ogres."

"Varyxes," Jerym said, and she heard a hint of amusement in his voice.

"Yes."

"And what happened?" he pressed. She could sense him shifting excitedly in the dark, as if he was leaning closer. "Did you run away, too?"

"I killed him."

The shadow froze, and Bren was sure if she could see his face his eyes would be wide with surprise.

"I didn't want to," she said quickly, suddenly afraid that he might dash from the shelter. "He was trying to kill me."

Jerym was quiet for another long moment. "I understand," he finally murmured. "And it's not like he's really dead."

Bren's heart lightened a little. "Truly?"

"I believe so," the boy said, though she could hear the uncertainty in his voice. "I mean, aspirants die during every Winnowing, but usually only a few. My mother knew I would not claim the hatchling, but still she agreed to let me take part. She never would have bowed to the governor's wishes if she thought there was a chance I wouldn't return. I suspect . . . I suspect this is all some sort of dream and that when we die here, we return to the caliphant's island in Yestra."

"I had hoped the same," Bren said, "but this all seems so real."

"It does," the boy agreed. "That's why I don't want anyone chopping me with an ax, even if it's the best way out of here. Better to hide and wait until someone else reaches the egg, and then presumably the rest of us will get to go back as well."

Bren shifted, stretching out her legs and laying the sword beside her. She was certain now that this boy was no threat to her. "Why are you here, then, if you knew you had no chance of winning?"

"It was the governor," the boy said, his distaste obvious. "That Bessam Karth. He said that all the families must be represented at every Winnowing. It is a tradition that stretches back to the birth of the empire. But there aren't many Regasts on this side of the sea – my uncle likes to keep his family close. He didn't even want my mother to come here, and she had to beg to be allowed to join the expedition."

"She is a soldier?"

"Ha!" Jerym's sudden laughter startled Bren. "Oh my, no. My mother hates battles and blood and such things. But that doesn't mean she's not brave. She's a naturalist. An explorer. It was she who recorded the different tribes of garthik dwelling in the caves under the Wraiths. And last winter, she went north by reindeer and sled to see the glacier where the ice worms tunnel. We came here to catalog the animals of this new world – or old world in truth, I suppose – and bring back specimens to Velasch."

"You're a scholar as well, then?"

"I'm studying to be one," Jerym said quickly. "I won't be able to swear my oath to the Peregrine Society until my sixteenth name day. But it is my dream to wear their ring." He sighed deeply. "Not to be a dragon rider. Yes, it's true dragons are fascinating creatures, but almost all of them are used as tools of war. And I have absolutely no interest in such things."

That, at least, made Bren feel a little better. And if she understood the title correctly, a naturalist studied plants and animals. Her own mother had been fascinated by everything that lived in the Seven Valleys and had often brought Bren into the woods to hunt for rare mushrooms and herbs that could be used to remedy ailments.

"How are you an aspirant if you are so young?"

"Governor Karth got a special dispensation from the Temple Draconium to allow me to join," the boy said with a heavy sigh. "Apparently, it was more important for one of the Regasts to be here than to honor the traditional age requirement."

Bren frowned, rubbing at her face. Her exhaustion was starting to return, the excitement of the boy's appearance draining away. If the sharpness of the stars and the deepness of the night were any indications, morning was still a long way off. "Are you tired?"

"Yes," Jerym admitted. "I spent much of yesterday running, afraid there was a crazed girl chasing me with an ax. I didn't even stop to gather any of the specimens I noticed. My mother would be so disappointed."

"I think she would prefer you to stay in one piece," Bren told him wryly.

"You don't know my mother," Jerym said, and she couldn't tell if he was making a jest or not.

"Well, we should try to get some rest," Bren said. "There's no telling what will happen tomorrow, but I'm sure we will need our strength."

"Are you . . . are you saying we should travel together?" The boy's words were tentative. Hopeful.

Bren pursed her lips. That had just slipped out. She truly didn't need a companion, especially one that was young and weak and couldn't fight. She needed to press on quickly to conquer this labyrinth and claim the hatchling, not spend her time protecting a helpless child. But sitting across from him in the dark and knowing how terrified he had been before she'd found him, Bren knew she couldn't abandon him to the other aspirants or whatever else lurked in the maze.

"You can come with me if you want," Bren said. "Though perhaps it would be best for you to hide here, where there's water and shelter. All the other aspirants will be pushing on to the center of the labyrinth – you could just wait until one of us finds the egg, and then, as you said, you'll likely be returned to Yestra."

"I'll come with you," Jerym said without hesitation.

The child will only slow you down.

Ashika's sudden emergence surprised her – Bren hadn't felt her presence since waking. The blademaiden's spirit must have been watching and listening, and now felt compelled to share her opinion on this matter.

A companion would be useful. One can keep watch while the other sleeps. And if he's truly knowledgeable about plants and animals he may be able to figure out what is safe to eat here. Even if this place is some strange sort of dream, there's an emptiness getting bigger in my belly. I'll have to eat sooner or later.

Ashika did not offer up any counterarguments to this, so Bren assumed she must have grudgingly agreed.

"We'll sleep here tonight, and when it's light enough to travel we'll press on."

"Together?" the boy said nervously, as if afraid he had misunderstood what she was saying.

"Together."

25

When Bren awoke the next morning, the boy was gone. She lay there in the hazy light spilling into the shelter and stared at the spot across from her where she remembered him curling up last night. Had it all been a dream, some phantasm conjured by the same magic that had brought her here?

It was no dream.

Good to know, Bren answered the voice, pushing herself stiffly to her feet and brushing away clinging bits of leaves and dirt. Despite her best efforts to create a comfortable bed, she still felt like she'd slept on stone. A soreness had seeped deep into her body, and her muscles and feet ached from all the walking she'd done the day before. She was hungry, too. Starving. The hollowness in her stomach she'd gone to bed with had widened into an abyss.

She froze when she heard a noise from outside the shelter. Slowly, she reached down and picked up her sword, then as quietly as possible crept through the listing entrance. Brightness assaulted her, and she blinked to try to clear her vision. A breeze was rippling the surface of the pool, and something leaped from a clump of reeds into the water with a splash. In the purple sky, one of the overgrown floating islands had drifted closer, its crumbling stone spires wreathed with iron-colored clouds.

"Bren!"

She whirled around to find a slight boy with golden hair wading through a patch of waist-high fronds while cradling something to his chest. He smiled when their eyes met, though he did glance uncertainly at the sword she had instinctively raised.

"Good morning," he said as he emerged from the vegetation. His face was flushed and sweaty, but he looked pleased with himself as he dumped his burden in the grass near her feet.

"Jerym," she said, just to make sure, and she knew she was right when he didn't look at her in confusion.

"I'm sorry if I woke you," he said as he crouched down beside what he had brought and began sifting through the pile. It looked like a rather varied collection of foraged things, mostly roots and red berries.

"It's all right," Bren said, lowering herself next to him. "I was hoping to wake up with the sun. I must have been more exhausted than I thought."

"Well, I did disturb you last night," the boy said, scooping up a handful of the plump berries and offering them to her. "Hopefully this makes up for it. I found these."

Bren stared at the fruit skeptically. She had spent much of her childhood in the woods and knew that eating strange berries was a terrible idea.

He is trying to poison us.

Oh, be quiet.

The boy was staring at her in anticipation.

"Are you sure they're safe?" she asked, even as a pang went through her stomach. They did look delicious.

Jerym popped one into his mouth and then spoke through his chewing. "Almost certain. Do you see how soft and inviting these are? They are that way to entice animals to eat them and spread their seeds. Poisonous berries are usually hard and smooth and a brighter shade of red to warn away those that might feed on them." He lifted his hand a little higher, shaking the berries in front of her face. "I found the same ones yesterday and ate quite a few and didn't die."

Against her better judgement, Bren plucked one of the largest and most seductive of the berries and carefully placed it in her mouth. It exploded in a flood of sweet juice, and she almost moaned with pleasure.

"Eat as much as you want," Jerym told her as she hastily grabbed a few more. "They're all over the place here. And other kinds as well, though I haven't tried them yet." He glanced down at what else he had deposited in the grass. Much of it looked like a tangle of brown encrusted with dirt. "We can't just rely on berries, though. These roots look exactly like something we eat back in Velasch. Most of the plants here are unknown to me, but I'm fairly certain these are something I'm familiar with." He reached into the knotted mess and drew out a single twisting strand, then spent a few moments carefully brushing it clean. "It would make sense that the warlocks would put some things to eat that we Velaschins know about. Nobody wants the aspirants resorting to cannibalism, I think."

"No, surely no one wants that," Bren murmured as she poked through what the boy had gathered in search of more berries. She would be shocked if the gnarled little roots were anywhere near as appetizing.

Undeterred, Jerym finished cleaning the root and stuck one end in his mouth, then, with some effort, ripped away a piece. "Not bad," he said, though he was chewing with some difficulty.

"You learned all this from your mother?" Bren asked as she watched him struggling to swallow.

He shook his head, looking relieved when he finally managed to get it down. "Tutors, mostly. My mother was far too busy. Though I learned quite a bit as her assistant on this scientific expedition."

Scientific expedition. Bren frowned at that choice of word. The Velaschin weren't here to discover new roots and birds. They had come to conquer with fire and sword.

Jerym must have seen something in her face. "You don't like the berries?"

"No, no," she replied, turning to squint up at the great floating ruin in the sky so he wouldn't see her expression. Something large and winged darted between two crumbling towers, and Bren wondered if there were more dragons in this place than just the hatchling in the shell. Though this creature was much thinner and more serpentine than the dragons she had seen so far, more like the winged snakes she'd glimpsed earlier.

Jerym had fallen silent, and when she finally looked at him again she found he was staring at her rather intently. "I want to thank you, Bren," he said, and the earnestness of his tone surprised her. "For offering to let me travel with you. I never imagined I would be forced to participate in a Winnowing. I know I'm not of any use in a fight. But I'll help you claim the hatchling any way I can."

Bren traced the design incised into her leather vambrace as she studied the boy. "Why would you want to do that?" she asked, honestly curious.

"Because you're not like the rest of them," the boy said, waving his hand towards the pockmarked walls of the labyrinth. "The scions of the families. They're raised to be vicious and arrogant and violent. Most of them have trained to be warriors since they could hold a sword. They want to be the sharp spearhead of the empire's armies, and they will do whatever it takes to claim a dragon and bring glory to their name." His voice had risen as he spoke, but he sounded more sad than angry. "If anyone else had found me last night, they wouldn't have hesitated. They'd have struck me down, and maybe I'd truly be dead or maybe I'd be back in Yestra . . . I know they wouldn't care either way. But you . . . you did not. You shared your shelter, even fell asleep while I was only a few steps away. You truly trusted me. And you offered to let me travel with you." He shook his head. "I'll do whatever I can to help you claim the hatchling, because you are the kind of person who *should* be a rider. The riders speak loudly of honor and chivalry, but I've seen how they behave. You deserve a dragon, not them." Jerym lapsed into silence, looking almost embarrassed by this outburst.

Bren stared at him for a long moment, digesting all he had said.

The skin on her arm where the sorcerer of the Jade House had sunk the disc itched, as if to remind her why she was truly here. She swallowed, trying to ignore the prickling sensation.

"I will get you back to Yestra," she promised. "No one will hurt you while you're with me."

~

EXPLORING the labyrinth with Jerym made for a far different experience. Yesterday she had given the strange plants and insects she passed a wide berth, wary of what she did not know, but Jerym approached each new discovery like a child waking to his whittle-gifts on midsummer morn. A string of black-petaled flowers growing from a length of broken wood elicited cries of excitement, and he plucked one of the blossoms and placed it into the pocket of his trousers. When they stopped for a rest later, he pulled out a handful of crumpled flowers, desiccated insects, and several small bones, spreading each out on a flat rock to examine them. Bren could sense Ashika's disdain, but she refrained from commenting on the boy's collection – after all, this experience must be traumatizing for one so young and helpless, and she appreciated whatever helped him forget the fact that there were many others out there prepared to murder him because he was a small obstacle on their path to becoming a dragon rider.

"This reminds me of a specimen my mother once showed me," Jerym said, holding up a sprig that to Bren's eyes looked much like every other curling little tendril she'd seen in the forests near her home. "But that was from the islands in the Shattered Sea, far to the south of Velasch. It grew on vines that could move on their own like a snake, and according to the sailor who brought it back, it could even *eat* people. My mother said she had scoffed at the story at first, but when she examined the plant more closely, she'd noticed it shared much in common with an animal's muscle."

"You can tell it's the same?" Bren asked, eyeing the sprig skeptically.

Jerym shrugged, looking faintly embarrassed. "I'm not absolutely certain, but there are strong similarities, such as the variegation of its leaves. It's really quite unique and I remember it well."

That was a word Bren did not know, but before she could ask further questions Jerym turned, his gaze slowly traveling over the crumbling, vegetation-choked walls rising around them to linger on the gnarled trees growing out from between the stones and a large web shimmering iridescent in the light. "I just want to know where we are. Did the warlocks create all of this from their imagination? Or did they populate this place from things pulled from elsewhere? Is it possible that we are in an entirely different world?" He fell silent, as if dazed by this thought. "My mother would do anything to spend a month cataloging the specimens in this place."

"She must have come here," Bren said, hefting a jagged little black rock that looked possibly volcanic and then throwing it at the web suspended high above them. "Don't all the high nobles take part in this Winnowing?"

"Only the martial ones," Jerym quickly corrected her. "Though aside from a few royal princesses who are given the opportunity to bond with river dragons, every other hatchling is won during these trials. And unless an aspirant is ruthless and a skilled fighter, they have almost no chance of success." His expression had grown progressively more miserable as he explained this to Bren, as if being reminded of how much he did not belong here. "It is a shame that dragons are claimed by only the most violent. Surely they have more potential uses than merely being creatures of war."

This one had very little use to his tribe. No wonder they were content to send him here.

Oh, be quiet, Bren replied to the voice in her head. *A boy's worth is not just determined by how well he swings a sword.*

If more of your people knew how to swing a sword, perhaps the Velaschin would not have found this conquest so easy.

They had dragons; it wouldn't have mattered if every farmer and smith had been trained by the weapon masters of the Bright Company.

"Bren?" Jerym said, and she returned to herself with a shake of her head. "Are you all right?"

"I'm fine," she said gruffly, realizing she must have been staring at nothing while conversing with the ghost inside her. "Come on, gather your things. We should keep moving."

THE AMETHYST MIDDAY light had darkened to indigo by the time Bren next called a halt. The trek to that point in the day had been largely unremarkable – a few times they had reached dead ends and had to retrace their steps, and once they'd been startled when they turned a corner and been confronted by a collection of stone monsters in various threatening poses, but those statues had been so eroded by time that their features had long since been lost. They'd drunk from a spring bubbling up from the center of an ancient mosaic sunk into the ground, and around midday finished the last of the berries Jerym had gathered that morning. Bren even tried one of the roots and found it every bit as inedible as she suspected, though after some effort she had choked at least part of it down. The boy had wanted to spend some time replenishing their stores, but the berries seemed so plentiful that Bren had asked him to wait until they camped for the evening. Still, while she sat on a chunk of fallen masonry and massaged her sore legs, Jerym went to wander about poking through the bushes clustered against the base of the walls.

You need to move faster. The boy is slowing you down.

I wouldn't have anything to eat if it weren't for him. He's useful.

She sensed something like an annoyed sigh from the presence inside her. *If you truly desire revenge for what befell your family, you must set aside this compassion. Or it will kill you.*

"Bren..."

Jerym's tone returned her abruptly to the labyrinth. She blinked, looking around, and found him standing at the entrance to one of the passageways leading away from where they'd stopped to rest.

"What is it?" she asked, rising and craning her head to try to see what he'd noticed.

"I'm not sure," he said slowly. "Maybe it's nothing." But he did not turn away as if it was truly nothing, and she hurried over to stand beside him. She frowned, examining the crumbling, lichen-scarred walls draped with vines. To her eye, it looked the same as every other passage they'd gone down.

"Do you see that hole?" he asked, pointing high up on the wall where a few of the great bricks had apparently fallen away, leaving behind a shadowed gap. Several of the long vines were dangling down from there as if growing from the darkness.

"I do," Bren replied, peering into that hole. She expected to see a shiver of movement, as Jerym must have noticed some animal or bird nesting inside. "What do you—"

She snapped her mouth shut, whirling around to stare back the way they'd come. Jerym heard it too, as he reached out to grip her arm tightly, his nails digging into her skin.

Voices. There were voices behind them, coming closer.

Bren glanced at Jerym in alarm and found him already looking at her with wide eyes.

"Hide," she hissed, hurrying to where the vegetation grew particularly thick against the wall. Thorns plucked at her, but she did not allow herself to make a sound – the voices were louder now, perhaps just around the bend of the passage they had come from earlier. Jerym squirmed beside her in the tight space, and together they hunkered down, peering out through the tangle.

"If I know the Karths, they'll have pushed on through the night." It was a boy's voice, loud and arrogant, and it carried to them just before a trio of youths appeared. Two were boys and the other a girl, though it took Bren a moment to realize this because the girl was as heavyset as her companions – all three were tall and broad, with sloping shoulders and barely visible necks. One carried a polearm he was using as a walking stick, a crested helm squashed on his large head, while another had a spear slung across his back. The girl had no visible weapons, though a bulging pouch was tied at her waist.

Varyxes. Bren felt a stab of guilt thinking of the boy she had killed at the maze's entrance. No doubt he had been some cousin of theirs.

"Tire themselves out, won't they?" growled the other boy. "My da said you can't just rush through the Winnowing. It unfolds at its own time, like a flower."

"Like a flower," the girl said in a wheezy, mocking tone. "You been reading your brother's terrible poetry again, Gervs?"

The Varyxes with the too-small helm gave a braying laugh, and the other boy scowled, then punched him in the arm.

"Slow and steady, my da said," the aggrieved boy continued sullenly. "And that's how he got his dragon. None of your das ever won a Winnowing, so maybe you should just shut up and listen."

The girl raised her hand for quiet, and for a moment Bren thought she had caught a glimpse of them hiding in the bushes. But her eyes passed over them without stopping as she slowly turned, her gaze instead lingering on the entrances to the three other passageways that emptied into this space. "So, which one this time? Either of you have a good feeling about a direction?"

The boy with the spear ran thick fingers through his mess of black hair. "I dunno. Last time we went right, it ended in that dead-end with all those skeletons. I'm thinking left this time."

"Left sounds good," the other boy agreed, then cleared his throat and spat. "I just hope we find more of those mushrooms. I'm starving."

"Left it is, then," the girl said, and she started in the direction of one of the passages. Bren flinched as Jerym jabbed her with his elbow, and she turned to find him staring at her meaningfully.

What? She mouthed, but he only shook his head sharply and shifted to watch the three Varyxes scions as they left the larger space and entered the passage. When they were no longer visible he started to emerge from the bramble, but Bren caught his arm.

"Wait," she whispered. "Let's make sure they don't double back to try a different way."

To her surprise, Jerym shook himself free of her grip. "I have to see," he said before pushing his way through the thorned branches.

"Jerym!" she hissed, but he ignored her, and with a muttered curse Tal had taught her – which would have shocked her mother – Bren followed him. By the time she also had extricated herself from the grasping tangle Jerym was crouched low and hurrying in the direction the other aspirants had disappeared.

The boy is mad, Ashika murmured in her mind. *Perhaps it would be best if you let him go. And then take a different passage away from here.*

Bren ignored the ghost's advice and dashed as quietly as possible after Jerym. He had stopped just outside the passageway's entrance and was peering around the cracked stone wall, and she gave him a sharp little jab in the shoulder when she arrived beside him.

"What do you think—" she whispered angrily, but he cut her off with a finger to his lips and a head-movement indicating the three Varyxes, who were proceeding down the passage engaged in the same loud conversation as earlier. They were passing beneath the large hole she had noticed earlier high up on the wall, and she realized suddenly that was what Jerym was staring at so intently.

The three Varyxes aspirants were so engrossed with their argument that they didn't see what was happening until it was too late.

Bren did, and she couldn't hold back a gasp of surprise as several of the long vines dangling down the side of the wall suddenly twitched and began to move, slithering like serpents over the stone. These were the vines that disappeared into the hole, Bren realized, and in the darkness above she thought she saw the movement of something huge. She clutched at Jerym's arm again, but this time not to try to keep him from rushing forward – he looked as aghast as she felt, his face pale as fresh milk.

The closest of the slithering vines lifted from the wall, extending towards the oblivious Varyxes. One last little snatch of their conversation floated to her, something about someone's da, and then the vine slipped around the helmed boy's neck and squeezed. He gurgled in shock, clawing frantically at the green limb as the other two turned to look at him in dumbfounded surprise. Their moment of shock cost them as vines looped around their legs and constricted, sending them tumbling to the ground. The pain and terror in their screams made her tighten her grip on Jerym's arm, but he didn't seem to notice – he was staring wide-eyed at what was happening, though to her surprise his expression was more akin to avid interest.

He wanted to see this.

Bren pulled at him, but he resisted. "No, just a moment," Jerym murmured. "I have to memorize every detail . . . for the sketches later."

"Sketches?" Bren repeated, panic making her voice shrill.

"Yes," Jerym said. "Mother would be so disappointed if I left out anything."

Bren's every instinct was telling her to flee, but she forced herself to stay beside Jerym – though she did look around to make sure no vine-snakes were slithering up silently behind them.

"It's so strong," Jerym said, and when she turned back she saw that the three aspirants had reached the wall and were being dragged thrashing upwards. The one with the vine around his neck had gone limp, though she wasn't sure if he was dead or had just fainted from lack of air. The other two were now dangling upside down, their hands scrabbling at the crumbling wall as they were being pulled higher. Occasionally they grasped a root or chunk of stone, but the strength of the vines was inexorable and immediately their grip was ripped away.

Up on the wall came another stirring in the darkness.

"Oh, saints and sages," Bren whispered hoarsely as the thing – a huge maw with concentric rings of glittering teeth spiraling down its throat – finally emerged into the light. The vines some sort of tendrils sprouting from the thin circle of flesh surrounding its gaping mouth.

With some effort Bren tore her gaze away from the almost hypnotic pattern formed by the monster's rows of teeth. She turned to Jerym, resolved on insisting that they flee . . . only to find that he was no longer beside her. The boy had moved away while she was staring up at the abomination and was now creeping past the wall where it laired, his eyes fixed on the ground as if searching for something.

"Jerym!" she hissed, though her voice was swallowed by the screams from above. Against her better judgement she dashed after him, her hand on her sword hilt. "What are you doing?" she asked in incredulous anger when she drew close enough that he could hear her. A sudden change in the tenor of the panicked cries above made her look up just in time to see one of the Varyxes boys disappear halfway into the monster's maw. The huge jaws snapped shut like a trap, and then a severed arm tumbled free. Bren stared in shock as the limb rebounded off the bricks, passed through the skeletal branches of a stunted tree growing from the wall, then landed near them with a heavy, wet thunk that made her gorge rise. A moment later it faded away into nothing, as if it had never been.

"We have to go *now*," she said, shaking Jerym roughly. He had been loitering at the base of the wall, poking through tufts of grass.

"Aha!" he cried, finally plucking whatever he had been searching for from the ground. Bren only got a glimpse before he closed his hand around it – whatever it was, it wasn't very big. Then he squinted upwards to where the monster was stuffing the lower half of the dismembered boy into its mouth while the Varyxes girl screamed and the other boy dangled limply.

"Yes, let's go," Jerym said before starting to run down the passage. Bren cursed again and followed, searching the walls ahead of them for any more holes which might be hiding more of these monsters. She couldn't see any, and after they'd turned enough corners that they could no longer hear any screams – though Bren wasn't certain if that was because they were far enough away or if the creature had finished devouring the aspirants – they stopped, doubled over and gasping for breath.

"Well, that was—"

Jerym never finished what he was about to say, as Bren shoved him so hard that he went sprawling.

"What were you *thinking*?" she cried, looming over him with her hands balled into fists. "You could have gotten us both killed! Eaten!"

Jerym propped himself up on his elbows with a hurt expression. Then he raised his clenched hand and opened it, showing what he had found on the ground beneath the monster's lair. It was a curling green tendril, a near-exact duplicate of the sprig he had shown her earlier.

"I was right," he said. "That monster is native to the islands of the Shattered Sea. I'm sure of it now."

Bren threw up her hands and snorted in disgust. "Who cares where the beast is from? The only important thing is that it doesn't *eat* us!"

Jerym slowly stood, brushing himself off. "But now we know a little bit more about this place," he said with a sniff.

The boy does make some sense, the voice in her head suddenly interjected, sounding almost grudging. *More knowledge of this place could aid in our survival.*

Bren ground her teeth, still furious.

"It was distracted," Jerym continued, more than a little defensively. "I had taken account of its arms, and they had all retracted when the others were grabbed. I knew we could pass by if we seized the chance . . . and that we might not get another. If that was the way we wanted to go, we had to proceed while it was"—he paused, swallowing hard—"consuming them."

Bren forced her anger to dissipate. Then she sighed. "In the future, you must let me know when you're planning on doing something so risky." The day suddenly darkened, and she raised her gaze to the indigo sky. One of the floating islands had eclipsed the sinking sun, and its tumbled ruins were now limned by purple witchlight.

"I will," Jerym promised, and she could hear his gratitude that she was not going to leave him behind over this.

"All right, then," she said, wincing at the brightness as the edge of the sun passed from behind the island. "And we should look for shelter before it gets too late. I definitely don't want to sleep in the open now."

∽

"I don't know about this," Jerym said, staring uncertainly up at the massive shadow blotting out most of the late evening sky.

Bren ducked under a root that had lifted from the ground to form an archway. She slid her palm along its length as she passed beneath and found that it was as hard and smooth as polished stone. Many other roots spread out from the base of the massive gnarled trunk, rippling the earth and bursting through the closest walls. Bren couldn't fathom how many years it must have taken for this tree to grow to such enormous heights and cause this sort of devastation to the surrounding labyrinth.

"Well, do you want to sleep outside?" Bren asked, picking her way carefully over the buckled stone and nest of treacherous roots. "Because I haven't seen any better places to shelter, have you?"

"No," Jerym admitted grudgingly. "But as a naturalist, if I was going to try to collect specimens this is where I would come first. All sorts of creatures must inhabit this tree."

Bren knew the boy was right, but after watching that thing pluck the Varyxes aspirants up, she had no desire to spend the night under the walls. "We'll shelter in the roots, someplace we can wedge ourselves with something at our back and then take turns watching to make sure nothing comes out of the night."

"What about climbing up into the branches?" Jerym asked, pointing at one of the lowest-hanging limbs. It wasn't even the largest, and still it looked like a horse could have ridden down its length.

"Do you want to risk rolling off in your sleep?" Bren asked, and Jerym shook his head. That wasn't her real fear, though – Bren had been watching those long winged serpents darting between the crags and towers of the islands floating in the sky, and she truly did not want to leave them exposed to things that might swoop down from above. Also, while she trusted herself to climb the knobby bark, she wasn't sure if Jerym had the arm strength to haul himself up.

"Come on," she said, punching him lightly on the shoulder to try to dislodge his skepticism. "We'll be fine. I have a sword, and I'm quite good at stabbing things. You can use all that book learning to figure out how to keep us safe."

"All right," he finally said softly, but in the dwindling light she saw his nervousness as he stared at the twisting mass of roots. She had to admit that in the dark it did sort of look like the bones of some monstrous, many-armed sea beast that had washed up on a desolate shore. Still, he followed her as she pressed deeper into the tangle. Bren tried to act confident, but she did keep her hand on the hilt of her sword, and she couldn't restrain a small gasp when something small and furred bounded away from them through the grass. She glanced at Jerym to see if he'd noticed her agitation, but he was staring after the small creature with interest.

"I'm almost certain that was a lamiat," he said in surprise. "They live in the forests near Velasch. Harmless and delicious, we eat them cooked on sticks during the husking festival." She saw him lick his lips, as if imagining the taste of meat and crisped skin. The thought also made her own stomach twist – only so many berries and roots could be consumed before the body demanded something else.

"We can try to catch one tomorrow," she promised him, staring at the patch of shadows where the lamiat had vanished.

He turned to her, his eyes now bright with excitement. "This is good, though. It means I can start trusting my knowledge of the plants here, that they are indeed the same as from back home. We'll have many more options for food come tomorrow."

"Good," Bren said with a smile. She appreciated anything that helped distract the boy from the dangers they were facing. "And I think we've found our house for the night," she said, sweeping her arm out grandly to indicate a large hollow formed by coils of roots. There was more than enough room for them both to sleep, and they would be protected on three sides, the bottom of one of the tree's largest tendrils forming a roof so nothing could ambush them from above. She ducked inside and tossed her bow and quiver in the corner, then let out a sigh of contentment as she also threw herself on the mossy ground.

"Cozy, don't you think?"

"It will do," Jerym said, joining her in the space. He sniffed the air, then wrinkled his nose. "I do think something else has slept here recently."

"We'll take turns staying awake," Bren assured him, beginning to massage the muscles in her aching legs. "You can be first while there's still a little bit of light. Just make sure to wake me when you're about to fall asleep."

26

Her dreams were terrible. Tendrils wrapped her limbs, pulling her slowly but relentlessly towards a gaping black maw filled with curving fangs. She struggled, but the grip only tightened further until the bones in her arms and legs creaked from the tremendous pressure and she felt her body begin to split apart. She screamed and pleaded and sobbed as the mouth swelled larger and larger until it blotted out everything else and then her head was drawn into the humid darkness, where the thing's hot, rasping breath billowed up from its gullet, the smell of rotten meat washing over her. She whimpered, expecting the jaws to snap shut and her spine to be crushed beneath those huge teeth, but the mouth closed with agonizing slowness. And when the fangs finally reached her neck, they suddenly paused, sharp and cold against her skin.

"Do not move, shepherdess."

Bren jerked awake. A shadow loomed over her in the closeness of the little hollow where they'd camped, its voice low and threatening. The feel of the monster's teeth against her neck had not vanished, and Bren realized with a surge of fear that a blade was pressed to her throat.

"Let her talk." This was a different voice, and it sounded like it had come from outside their shelter. It was also familiar.

Zair Karth.

The sensation of the metal against her skin disappeared, and Bren turned her head slightly in the direction where the second voice had come from. Outside the entrance formed by the roots, a ghostly dawn had crept into the sky, painting the world in shades of charcoal and bone. Zair Karth reclined in a crook made by a twisting root, one knee drawn up to his chest. Before him on the hard-packed earth knelt Jerym, his head bowed and his shoulders slumped. The boy turned his face slightly so that their eyes met, and anger overwhelmed her fear – his cheek and jaw were a mottled purple, blood dripping down his chin from a split lip. The look he gave her was one of shame and terror, but he made no sound, not even a whimper.

Bide your time. If he wants to talk, we shall have an opening. And this one will gloat – I know his kind. Be ready.

"Too afraid to fight me?" Bren spat. The sight of the bruises covering Jerym made her yearn for the chance to wipe away Zair's smirk. The young boy was harmless and no threat to any of them. "Leave him alone, *sword dancer.*"

Zair grinned at her words, then leaned forward and cuffed Jerym on the back of the head. The boy gave a sharp cry of pain and fell forward into the dirt. Before he could rise, Zair stood and placed his foot on Jerym's back, pinning him to the ground.

"It's such a rare treat to have a Regast grovel in front of me. Usually I have to bow and scrape before *them.*" He stepped forward, and Jerym gave another squeak of pain as Zair's full weight pressed down on him. "It's truly pathetic that this little worm was the only member of the imperial family who could join the Winnowing. The emperor commanded this invasion, but then left its conduct entirely to my father. A true leader would have traveled to these shores to personally command the reconquest of our ancient homeland."

Zair ducked down, peering into the shadowed interior of the hollow. "Bring her out," he commanded, and the shadow leaning over her roughly grabbed her by the shoulders and pulled her into the gray morning. She was not surprised at all when she saw the ragged circular scar marring the face of the one who had put the blade to her neck. Malisk.

Not yet, the voice in her head warned as she started to tense in preparation for throwing herself at Zair.

Out of the corner of her eye Bren noticed another Karth keeping watch among the tangle of roots. He had a rounder face than his fellows but the same cruel eyes and arrogant sneer. The bow Bren had found when she'd first been deposited in this place was slung over his shoulder – she remembered Jerym taking it outside when he'd gone to keep watch. Since it was morning and he had never woken her, he must have fallen asleep during his watch last night. She must have been absolutely exhausted to sleep through all that had happened.

Bren looked for anyone else, but it seemed to be just the three Karth boys. She snuck a quick glance at where they'd sheltered, making sure she could see the pommel of her sword poking out from under the piles of leaves where she'd hidden it. Could she lunge for it if Malisk turned away? Maybe, but she didn't know how good the third Karth boy was with that bow. For all she knew, he could be an expert shot and an arrow would find her before her hand even touched the hilt.

"Where's your sister?" Bren asked Malisk as the Karth bastard took a step away from her, brandishing a curving dagger.

"I don't know," he said, his eyes narrowing. "Have you seen her? She was supposed to meet us here at the tree."

"Quiet!" Zair barked, and the scarred boy flinched like he expected his cousin to strike him.

They knew about this tree? How?

Both Seris and Jaleska said the Winnowing wasn't fair, Bren thought in reply to Ashika. *That the high nobility have advantages others do not.*

Pathetic, Ashika mentally sneered. *A sign of their society's rot, to claim the trial is equal for all but then to put their thumb on the scales so blatantly. I . . . I . . .*

Ashika? It felt like the presence in her head was dwindling, the voice growing fainter. Bren fought to hold back her rising panic – this was not the time to lose the blademaiden's help, but as she quested for the spirit inside she encountered an echoing absence.

Zair sauntered closer, his hand resting lightly on the decorative pommel of the sword at his side. To Bren the blade looked nothing like the other, more utilitarian weapons she'd seen in the labyrinth so far. Had it been brought into the Winnowing from outside? How much help had Zair been given?

"You're probably wondering why we haven't cut off your head yet," Zair said, looking her up and down in obvious disdain. "Send you back to wallow in your failure and consider what might have been. Brenna Karth, governess of Leris and mistress of the seven midden heaps. Instead, you'll return to being nothing."

"Better nothing than a braying ass," she replied, and the coldness in his dark eyes deepened.

"I'm curious," Zair continued, and she could tell he was having trouble keeping his tone light. "And my father is curious. Who exactly are you? Which of my uncles put you in some washer girl's belly?" He jerked his chin in the direction of Malisk. "He could be your brother, you know. Though his father usually admits to his indiscretions." The scarred boy snorted at this, running his finger along the edge of his dagger. Bren had no doubt that he would not hesitate to cut her throat even if he suspected they were indeed siblings.

"I told you, I don't know," Bren said tightly.

"Yes, you said that," Zair replied with a sigh. "But I feel you are holding something back. A secret. I can see it in your eyes." With a flourish he drew his sword, and Bren saw that the blade was gleaming obsidian. She hissed as he turned back to Jerym and placed the curving tip in the center of the boy's back.

"We *can* die here, you know," Zair said. "If the heart is pierced. Any other death and we will return to our tents in Yestra, unscathed save for a pounding headache and a crushing sense of failure. But if we die with something lodged in our heart . . ." He must have pushed down slightly, because Jerym gasped. "Then we are truly dead. Every

Winnowing several aspirants meet this fate, and if it happens to you two . . . ah, well, a pity. At least one of you will be missed." He pressed harder, and Jerym's hands scrabbled in the dirt.

From somewhere nearby came a cry of pain and terror. Zair jumped back a step and lifted his sword from Jerym, looking about in bewilderment. The other two Karths seemed just as surprised, peering into the tangle of huge roots that bounded the clearing.

"Was that her?" Malisk said. "It sounded like her!" Bren could hear his fear and guessed he must be talking about his half-sister.

"Stay where you are," Zair said, turning to the Karth boy with the bow. "Baehez. Go see who that was. If it's Alyia and she's in trouble, whistle twice and I'll come running. If it's anyone not of the family put an arrow in them."

Bren could see the fear in the boy's face, but he nodded and disappeared into the tree roots and shoulder-high shrubs, headed in the direction of the scream. For a moment they all watched the leaves and branches shiver from his passing, and then Zair turned back to her.

"You must be wondering why you're not already back in Yestra, bastard. Your refusal of my offer in front of my family was . . . embarrassing."

Bren shrugged. "I assume you just want to gloat."

Zair flashed her the same smile she had seen at the feast. At the time, she had thought it charming. Now she saw what had always been behind it.

"That as well. But I also need to know more about you. The whole . . . complexion of my family could change based on that truth."

Bren sneered. "I'm not talking to you."

Zair shook his head. "I think you will. You see, you share some of our family's traits – you're obviously resourceful and proud, and you do not bow to those who, through mere chance, have been placed higher than you. All this I can respect. But I also see some weaknesses that would have been cut away if you'd grown up alongside me." He lifted his sword, pointing it at the still-prone Jerym. "You have compassion. This boy is useless, yet you allow him to accompany you during the trial. Worse than useless – he is slowing you down, damaging your chances of claiming the hatchling. And so I think you will tell me everything I want to know. Because otherwise I will carve this child's heart from his chest and spit it upon my blade, and then I will tell his mother after this is all over that it was the barbaric foundling who did it to her beloved little boy." Zair's condescending smirk returned as he took a step closer to the whimpering Jerym. He crouched down beside the boy, stroking Jerym's hair almost tenderly. "Do you hear that, whelp? And do you remember how your mother treated my father when she first arrived in—"

Bren whirled and lunged for the entrance of the little hollow. Her fingers scrabbled in the dry leaves, closing around the hilt of her sword, and then she sprang back to her feet brandishing the blade. She had been expecting Malisk to charge her with his long dagger, but her sudden movement had so surprised him that he hadn't even moved.

Zair slowly rose – though not before shoving Jerym's face down hard into the earth – and lifted his own glistening black sword. But not towards Bren. The blade gleamed as he raised it over his head, catching a ray of morning light that had broken through the gray sky. He was really going to bring it down on Jerym, she realized in horror. Was he telling the truth about heart-kills? There was no way she could cross the distance fast enough to stop him, especially with Malisk in her way . . .

"You did this, peasant," Zair snarled, and then he brought the sword down . . . but his swing faltered halfway as a figure stepped from the foliage.

"Complete that stroke and you're dead." The words were uttered so casually the speaker might have been commenting on the weather.

Seris. The red-haired archer had an arrow nocked and aimed at Zair. The bow she was holding was the same one the other Karth boy had carried into the snarl of roots and branches only a few moments ago.

"The kalishwoman," Zair said, and Bren had to respect his composure.

"The kalishwoman," Seris repeated blandly. "Now step away from the boy."

"Would you really shoot me, lowlander? A high lord? Would you dare?"

Seris shrugged. "If you don't step back, you can find out. I think you know I won't miss if I do let this arrow fly."

"March filth," growled Malisk, and he took a threatening step towards the freckled girl, his long dagger raised.

Seris didn't hesitate. She shifted her aim and released the arrow, and before it had even found its mark she swiveled back to Zair, reaching for another shaft. Malisk gave a cry that sounded more surprised than pained, her shot striking him in the shoulder and spinning him half around before he tumbled to the ground in a heap.

Zair bared his teeth, but the red-haired girl stilled him from lunging at her with the flatness of her gaze. "I could have put that in his neck or dead center in that scar on his cheek, but instead I chose just above his collarbone. Think about that."

"The sword dancers taught me to catch arrows," Zair said, but Bren saw some of his coiled tautness begin to unwind, as if he had taken Seris's measure and decided not to try his luck.

"Well, you're holding a sword already. That leaves you with one free hand. Do you think you can reach me before I loose two arrows? Or can you catch more than one arrow with the same hand? Now *that* would be impressive."

"You wench! You *shot* me!" Malisk was writhing on the ground, his hand clutching at the shaft buried in his shoulder. "Ah, it hurts! It *hurts!*"

"Quiet!" Zair snapped, his eyes still fixed on Seris. "At least for a moment, pretend you really are a Karth."

"It hurts . . ." Malisk said again, but this time more of a quiet whine, and then he began whimpering as he rocked back and forth.

"What happened to Baehez?" asked Zair, ignoring the scarred boy's mewling.

Seris's face remained almost completely blank, but Bren thought she saw the edges of her lips twitch. "I don't know. I found this bow just lying around. Very careless, if you ask me."

Zair's mouth twisted. "Kalishwoman, listen. I am the first-born son of Bessam Karth, the man who rules these lands and commands your very legion. I demand you lower that arrow and leave us now."

Seris lifted an eyebrow, but the hand holding back her draw did not waver in the slightest.

"All right, then," Zair continued, his tone suddenly shifting from imperious to ingratiating. "It is a negotiation. You are an archer, yes? In the first army's cohort? Surely your village needs gold. Your family."

"You think you can sway me with talk of family?" Seris asked, her voice flat.

Zair seemed to realize he'd made a mistake. "Your mother's family, I mean. You must have brothers and sisters, grandparents . . . You could build them a great roundhouse, make your blood one of the lords of the moors."

"My blood," Seris said with an edge of bitterness. "That's why I'm here, isn't it? Because of my blood. You offer to give me what should be rightfully mine anyway, yes?"

Zair's mouth opened and closed, but he had no answer for this.

"Go," Seris commanded, motioning with the nocked arrow towards the roots behind Zair. "Take your rude friend. And you'll find the other one sleeping about a hundred paces from here. Sorry about the lump on his head."

The anger in Zair's eyes could have ignited kindling, but slowly he slid his obsidian sword into its sheath. He went to where Malisk was sprawled out panting heavily – blood had darkened the left side of his cousin's tunic, and the scarred boy gasped sharply as Zair gripped him roughly under his arms and began dragging him away.

"This isn't over, bastard," Zair spat at Bren just before he disappeared into the surrounding tangle.

"It hasn't even begun," Seris murmured, so quietly that Bren barely heard. Then she crooked a smile and lowered the bow.

Bren hurried over to where Jerym was struggling to his feet and helped him stand. The boy looked at her wild-eyed, like he was shocked to discover himself alive.

"I hate him," he said in a dazed voice. "He's always been a bully."

"So you two have a history?" Seris asked. Bren noticed she hadn't stopped staring at the spot where the Karths had disappeared.

Jerym reached around to try to touch the spot on his back where Zair had pressed the point of his sword. He shuddered when he drew back his hand and saw the blood coating his fingertips.

"Here, let me," Bren said and pulled up the back of his tunic to examine the wound. It wasn't deep, but she knew it must hurt, especially if he was not accustomed to such injuries. "It's shallow and should stop bleeding on its own soon. You'll be fine."

"Thank you," Jerym said, then turned to Seris and bowed with a pained wince. "And thank you. I'm in your debt, kalishwoman."

"Call me Seris," the red-haired girl said, then whirled around and lifted her bow as something crackled in the nearby bushes. "We should move, put some distance between us and Zair. As soon as he feels he has an advantage, he'll come after us."

Bren nodded. "Do you have a suggestion on which way to go?"

Seris pursed her lips, then pointed at a crumbled section of the labyrinth wall. "I came from that way."

"We entered from over there," Bren said, nodding towards where they'd last seen the Karths.

"Then we should go the opposite," Seris said, turning to stare up at the massive silver-leafed tree. "There must be another passage on the other side of this trunk."

"Lead on," Bren told her, and without another word the red-haired girl shouldered her bow and began picking her way over the monstrous roots.

SERIS SET a punishing pace and did not stop to rest until the sun was high overhead in the violet sky. She hadn't spoken since they'd left the massive tree, and Bren wondered if she was considering dashing ahead into the twisting passageways and leaving them to fend for themselves. Even if she did choose such a course, Bren would still be grateful for what the red-haired girl had done. It would have been very unlikely that she and Jerym could have survived their encounter with the Karths without her help.

But she did not abandon them, and when they stumbled upon an archway of some smooth, nacreous stone she halted and began rummaging around in a belt pouch while waiting for Bren and Jerym to catch up.

"We can rest in the shade here," she said through a mouthful of whatever she had pulled forth. Berries like Jerym had foraged, Bren thought, but she couldn't be sure.

The boy groaned in relief and found a spot in the shadow of the arch, gingerly leaning his back against one of the supports. Bren was more hesitant, cautiously approaching the strange construction and laying her palm against its surface. It was cool to the touch despite the hot day, and it might have been her imagination but she thought she felt a slight vibration welling up from within.

Seris went over to a wall where a trickle of water flowed from high up. She cupped a handful and slurped some, then splashed the rest on her face.

"How do you know the water is clean?" Bren asked, squinting dubiously at where the water was emerging from within a crack near the top.

Seris shrugged. "I don't. But I refuse to believe that the warlocks who made this dream-place would go through all this trouble to conduct the Winnowing only to have it decided by who did and did not drink tainted water."

"That's a good point," Bren admitted and went to where another patch of the wall was darkened by water from above. Pushing aside her squeamishness, Bren pooled some in her palm and sucked it down. She hadn't realized how much her lips had cracked and how dry her throat had become until that first swallow, and then she brought her mouth to the wall and drank greedily from the stone.

"You should have some," she said to Jerym after taking her fill and turning back to where he was still slumped against the arch. He nodded but clearly could not muster the strength to join her quite yet.

"You didn't answer my question from earlier," Seris said, also addressing Jerym. "I asked if you knew Zair."

The boy sighed as he began to root through his own supply of berries and scavenged things. "Oh, I know him well. Every Day of Deliverance and Winter Tiding, his father would come from the Karth seat at Stormguard because my uncle insisted that the high lords celebrate at the palace to try to keep the bonds between the families from fraying." He shook his head with a rueful grin. "It didn't often work. I remember Leithe ben-Ahzan coming to blows in the great hall with Harin ben-Varyxes over the affection of some girl. Leithe lost three fingers and always had trouble controlling his dragon afterwards. And Zair . . . Zair and his cronies would always make a point to seek out the smallest and quietest and throw us in a fountain or pinch our ears until we cried. He was the reason I started hiding deep in the library on feast days. Zair was never much one for books."

"Who *are* you?" Seris asked, and something in her voice made Bren glance at her sharply. She was staring at Jerym, her face having gone very still.

Jerym struggled to his feet and offered another bow. "I'm sorry I didn't introduce myself earlier. My name is Jerym Regast, and I am the son of Seliana Regast."

"The emperor is your uncle," Seris murmured numbly. From her tone it sounded to Bren like this knowledge had upset her.

Jerym clearly didn't notice anything was amiss. "Yes. Though I can't promise he'd even care very much if he heard how Zair has treated me."

"Of course he wouldn't," Seris said with a scowl, then turned and stalked over to where yellow creepers veined a section of the wall, folding her arms as she began studying them with a strange intensity.

"What is it?" Bren asked as she came up beside Seris, her voice pitched low enough that Jerym couldn't hear.

For a moment the red-haired girl was silent, as if considering what to tell Bren, and then turned with storm-blue eyes blazing. "He's a Regast," she said simply, as if this explained it.

"You . . . don't like your emperor?" Bren asked, surprised. How could someone serve in the legions if they hated the imperial family?

"It was a Regast who raped my mother," Seris said, her voice low but seething with fury. Then she turned and strode away, over to where a chunk of that same iridescent stone as the arch rose up from the tall grass. She sat heavily, facing away from them.

Jerym seemed to have finally realized something was wrong, and he glanced towards Bren in confusion.

Bren thought back to what Seris had told her at the feast on the eve of the Winnowing. She had said a dragon rider had found her mother out alone in the marches, and that she had joined the legions when she'd gotten older – and also joined these trials – to try to prove the truth of what had happened that day.

But Jerym of course had absolutely nothing to do with that crime. Bren approached Seris again and stood beside her, though the red-haired girl did not acknowledge her arrival.

"He's a good boy," Bren said. "Innocent."

Too innocent.

Ashika! Bren thought as she felt the return of the presence in her mind. *Where did you go? What happened?*

I . . . don't know, the blademaiden said, her spectral voice sounding dazed. *I tumbled once more into the mists. Or no, they rose up to swallow me. One moment I saw you being threatened by the arrogant boy, and then I was lost again. What happened? How did you escape? And that is the archer girl from the feast, is it not?*

It is, and I'll tell you later what happened. We—

"What is wrong with you?"

Bren returned to herself with a start and found that Seris had twisted around on the chunk of shining stone to stare at her.

"I'm sorry," Bren said with a shake of her head. "My mind was elsewhere."

Seris cocked an eyebrow, her gaze skeptical. "Something more important to think about right now?"

"No, no . . . " Bren began, struggling to come up with any reason to explain her distraction. "Did you say something?" she finally finished lamely.

"I said that none of them are innocent," Seris muttered with a bitterness that surprised Bren. "Every member of the four families has lived their life in great luxury and ease, all made possible by the toil of others. On the marches we gather bloodmoss and Scagen's Tears to meet the quota the emperor sets, and his demands are so high that there is only a tiny amount every year left over to sell. It is hard, backbreaking work. Have you seen the sores that open up from a season of wading through the swamps? They fester and leak a vileness that smells like rotten corpses. The Emperor's Blessing, we call it. After a decade or two, every mossgrubber has lost a limb or finger to the Blessing's rot. It's why so many of us leave to join the legions. We send our pay home, the grubbers gather what the marches provides, but still many bellies cry out in hunger while the cold winds lash our roundhouses." Her eyes grew more distant, as if she was reliving a memory. "The traders that come after the emperor's collectors pay a pittance for the Tears. But I saw in Velasch how much the eating houses charge for them. A kalish child could eat for a month with what the city folk spend on a single bite."

"That's not Jerym's fault. He is not responsible for this injustice."

"He is a leech, like all the other Blooded. *You* must be sickened to see your land oppressed by the dragon lords. My lands are as well, as are all the lands of the empire outside the city. The marches, the hollows in the foothills of the Wraiths, the people of the plains."

"And yet you partake in the Winnowing," Bren said, finally allowing her annoyance to creep into her tone. "*You* conquer this land for them. *You* brought death and ruin to my home."

"Your home," Seris said, her eyes narrowing as if she'd finally heard what she was waiting for. "You hate them as much as I do, don't you? You must. Have you lost a loved one to the war? Why are *you* here, shepherdess?"

Careful, Ashika warned. *We do not know her.*

Bren clenched her jaw. She wanted badly to share with Seris what she truly thought of the Velaschins and their dragons, though of course she would not tell of the mission entrusted to her by the sorcerers of the Jade House. The girl clearly despised the noble families ... but did she despise the empire?

Bren bit her tongue. The risk was too great – for all she knew, the warlocks of Velasch might have some arcane way of watching and listening to the aspirants during the trials.

"Why am I here?" Bren snapped. "I'm here because I have *nothing*."

Seris flinched, the intensity of this admission seemingly taking her aback.

The truth, yet it reveals little even as it satisfies. Bren could sense Ashika's approval.

"I want the hatchling because it would give me purpose. I am not of the families, and I will not serve to further their ends. But a dragon ... a dragon would let me shape my own destiny."

Seris watched her for a long moment with pursed lips, as if considering what Bren had just said. Then she brushed a red curl away from her face and crooked a humorless grin. "Well, I came to this city to prove a crime was committed, and as soon as the hatchling stirred in its egg my claims were shown to be true. To be honest, I'm not certain why I stayed to take part in the Winnowing. I don't want a dragon like my father was riding on the day he spied my mother. I suppose I could have walked away, rejoined the legions, secure in the knowledge that they now have to acknowledge what happened to my mother. But now I can see a purpose – to deny the great families. To ensure the dragon is claimed by someone who will not bend to their desires. I love my people and my land, but we deserve to be free of the Blooded's yoke." She tilted her head to one side as she regarded Bren. "Do you share that sentiment?"

Bren hesitated for the briefest of moments before nodding.

"Good," Seris said, then abruptly stood. "Then I will help you reach the center of this maze." She looked over to where Jerym was still watching them with a wary expression. "But do not ask me to show kindness to the Regast boy. He is my enemy . . . as he should be yours."

27

The composition of their surroundings began to change as they pushed deeper and deeper into the labyrinth. Crumbling gray stone overgrown with vegetation gave way to what seemed to be less ancient walls of the same strangely nacreous substance that they'd already encountered scattered throughout the maze. To Bren, it reminded her of a sea-thing's shell that her mother had kept in her small box of most treasured possessions. This made her wonder if this part of the labyrinth was organic in nature, but that idea made her uncomfortable and so she did her best to forget that she had even imagined such a thing was possible.

Seris rarely walked with them – she claimed it was because she had some experience scouting when she was in the legions, but Bren guessed that she simply did not want to be near Jerym. Instead, she ranged ahead and behind, investigating the myriad branching paths and keeping a lookout for any danger. Bren had told her about the many-armed monster that had snatched up the Varyxes aspirants, and Seris made sure that they avoided any passages with large, dark gaps high up in their walls.

Jerym walked beside Bren, but since the encounter with the Karths he had become far more reserved and displayed little of the curiosity that had previously sent him scurrying off to examine patches of mushrooms or flowering vines. Bren wasn't sure if this was because of his brush with death, or if his new behavior was because of Seris's clear dislike. Bren tried to drag him out of the shadow he'd fallen under a few times with questions about his mother's work and some oddities they'd stumbled across in the maze, but he merely shrugged or mumbled a brief response before turning away. Only once did he display some of his old excitement, and that was when they had crossed a narrow bridge arching over a chasm. Wisps of noxious yellow mist rose from the depths, and Bren had half-expected some monster to reach up and pluck them from the narrow span as they shuffled across. She'd been forced to drag Jerym away from the edge, as otherwise the boy might have fallen in trying to see what was below.

It was not long after this crossing that Seris rushed up to them breathing hard, her face flushed. Bren's hand had immediately gone to the sword at her side, but she didn't see anything pursuing the girl.

"Others," Seris said, gesturing back the way they had come. She had been scouting behind them, making sure they weren't being followed.

"Hunting us?" Bren asked, peering past her.

"I don't think so," Seris said, finally catching her breath. "They just went over the chasm. Six of them, all Ahzan aspirants. The favorite of their house is with them – Merith. Or at least one that looks like her, a girl with hair that's almost entirely copper with just a single streak of black."

Bren remembered Seris pointing out the Ahzan daughter at the feast. She had been tall and thin but not particularly imposing. "You said she was the most likely among the aspirants to claim the hatchling after Zair. Why?"

Seris motioned for them to keep moving down the passageway, and she set a brisk pace. "It's because of the rumors swirling about her. I've heard it whispered that she's umbrari."

"That can't be true!" Jerym exclaimed, then nearly stumbled over his own feet. Bren had to catch his arm to keep from sprawling on the iridescent tiles. "Merith, a shadow-weaver?"

"It's just a rumor," Seris hastened to reply, apparently forgetting in the heat of the moment that she was avoiding speaking with the Regast scion.

"Of course it's a rumor," Jerym continued. "No one knows who belongs to that order."

"What are umbrari?" Bren asked, annoyed once again by her ignorance.

"Assassins," Seris said, unshouldering her bow as she glanced behind them. "Warlocks."

"That's . . . not entirely true," Jerym said, his tone suggesting he was a bit nervous to contradict Seris, though her attention was so focused elsewhere that she didn't seem to care. "The umbrari is a group that cuts across the families. I have no idea if its members are recruited or born into it, only that it is so secret that no one outside their order knows who belongs."

"I'm just repeating what I've heard in the legions," Seris said defensively. "Merith's father has been traveling with the army. He's often in counsel with General Varyxes and Vanoc ben-Karth, which is strange since he holds no official rank. That's what gave birth to these whisperings. And he's quite close with his daughter."

Bren helped Jerym scramble over a chunk of fallen masonry. "What do these umbrari want?"

The boy patted her arm in thanks as he shrugged at her question. "I don't know. But over the years they've been blamed for poisonings, unrest, even the great fire that burned the Library of Desdomel, where the oldest books from before the crossing of the Cull had been stored."

Bren frowned, suddenly realizing that in their hurried flight they'd entered a new section of the labyrinth. The space was open, but it looked as though once it had been just as cluttered with twisting corridors as the rest, but now low mounds of rubble marked where walls had stood. And in the center of this expanse was what looked like a massive building that had collapsed inward. Seris had once again taken the lead in this new place, dashing across the cleared ground to hunker briefly behind one of those piles of shattered stone, her gaze fixed back the way they'd come.

After they'd joined her, Bren turned once more to Jerym. "Why does your uncle not root out these umbrari?"

The golden-haired boy was peeking out from between two tumbled slabs and didn't look at her when he answered. "Many think the umbrari and the throne have some sort of accord. They support my family, and in turn the emperor helps further their agenda." He frowned, and then admitted grudgingly, "It would make sense for there to be umbrari assisting the legions in the conquest. But that doesn't mean Merith or her father truly belong to the order."

"It's said the umbrari killed the Black Tyrant," Seris said. "He was found in his bed with a dagger in his heart the day after he destroyed the western marches. We kalish had refused to recognize his claim and he arrived at the head of a flight of dragons. For that reason, the march folk don't fear the shadow-weavers, for whatever game they are playing is with the families, not us. Let them kill each other."

Bren wanted to ask more about this secret society but a slight trembling suddenly distracted her, as though the ground had shivered ever so slightly. "Did you feel that?" she asked, but Jerym only glanced at her in confusion. Seris was completely focused on the passage they had taken here; she had rested an arrow loosely against the bowstring, clearly intending to nock it if the aspirants appeared.

"Once they arrive, I want you both to duck down," Seris said. "And for the Endless's sake, be quiet. If they haven't noticed our trail yet, I think they'll go right past us without being none the wiser. And then we can take a different route out of here."

Another tiny shiver welled up from below, and a fist-sized rock tumbled down the side of the pile where they were hiding. "You must have felt that, right?" Bren asked again. "Are those earthquakes?"

Jerym had noticed it this time as well, and he looked around in surprise. "It could be . . ." he began, but before he could finish his voice trailed away.

Bren glanced over to find him staring wide-eyed at something behind them. His mouth was working like he wanted to scream, but nothing was escaping.

Bren turned, coldness pooling in her stomach.

At first she didn't see it. Jerym was staring at the collapsed building in the center of this space – no, Bren suddenly realized that it had never truly been a structure of any sort. It was merely a haphazard pile of heaped stones, probably gathered from the remnants of the demolished walls. But whatever had made this mound must have been massive, as some of the chunks were as large as horses . . . the way the stones were set had created a shadowed interior, and with growing unease Bren realized that something was moving inside that space.

Something vast.

"They're here!" hissed Seris, her voice sharp but pitched low. "I don't think they were following us . . . Wait, something's wrong. They're pointing and yelling. What is it?"

"Turn around slowly," Bren whispered hoarsely.

She heard the archer shift, then a strangled gasp. "What in the demon-spawn hells is *that*?" Seris breathed.

It moved forward, out of the darkness and into the light.

The first thing she saw clearly was its fingers curled around the ragged edge of the opening – each as long and as thick as a piglet, the great nails cracked and yellowing. Then the fingers tightened against the stone, pulling the creature's vast bulk from the shadows.

Someone screamed in terror, but Bren wasn't sure if it was Jerym or Seris or even herself. She had never imagined that she would ever encounter a monster more imposing than a dragon, but this . . . this *thing* was somehow even worse. It looked like an enormous, hairy man with long arms and sloping shoulders. It wore no clothes, its sex dangling from a matted thatch of dark fur, though around its neck it had a necklace of skulls – some human, others tined like a deer, and there was even the long, fang-filled snout of what looked like a devil-lizard. Its head was what was most dissimilar to a man's, lumpy and bulbous, with a lantern jaw protruding beneath a squashed nose.

But that was not the strangest feature of this thing.

In the center of its forehead was a single great eye, much larger than a closed fist.

And it was focused on them.

"Gnul!" she heard Jerym moan beside her, and then there was the twang of a bowstring as Seris released her arrow. It carved a glittering arc through the morning light, seemingly destined for the monster's impossibly huge eye. Hope briefly pushed aside her fear, for surely Seris could not miss such a target, and once the monster was blinded they could escape . . .

An eyelid crashed down like a falling portcullis, and the arrow rebounded off hard, gnarled skin, different in appearance from what covered the rest of its body. A defense for what would have been the most vulnerable part of the creature, Bren guessed.

The eyelid flicked back up, a pupil the color of dried blood finding them again. And the giant roared, massive jaw hinging wide as great fists pounded its hairy chest.

"Run!" screamed Seris, and Bren did not need any further encouragement. She grabbed Jerym by the arm and dragged the stumbling boy after Seris as the archer sprinted away from the monster.

When the ground began to quake she knew it was after them. The great pounding strides must have devoured the distance in moments because suddenly the world darkened as a great shadow enveloped them. Bren braced herself for the blow that must be imminent, expecting all her bones to be shattered and her body to be mashed into a pulp.

But it did not come. Instead, the monster roared again, and Bren risked a glance behind her. The giant still loomed over them blotting out the sun, but its attention had shifted. Its head had twisted almost completely around, and its eye was looking across the ruined landscape at a pair of Ahzan aspirants who had clambered up onto one of the rubble piles. Both had bows, and as Bren watched in open-mouthed astonishment they drew and fired, sending arrows hissing through the air to strike the monster, one high in its back and the other just below its ear. Apparently the monster's flesh was softer than its eyelid, as two other arrows were jutting from among the rolls of fat in its neck like the spines of a porcupine. The giant swiped at these irritants with a meaty paw, tearing them loose, and then bellowed as it charged towards the archers.

Its speed shocked Bren, but the Ahzan aspirants were already scrambling down the mound of broken stone and running for the entrance to the passage where they had come from. One of the two archers was a girl with copper hair marred by a single streak of deepest black, and remembering Seris's description she assumed this must be Merith, first among the Ahzan faction.

"Come on!" Bren screamed, yanking a frozen Jerym to get him moving again and then putting her head down to sprint for one of the other corridors leading into the labyrinth. Seris was already there when they arrived, and before following her Bren glanced over her shoulder – the mountainous creature was on the other side of this rubble-strewn space tearing chunks of stone from the walls as it desperately tried to get to where the Ahzan aspirants had fled.

She did not linger to see what happened next. Seris snarled something and pulled her down the passageway, and Bren in turn kept a tight grip on Jerym's arm. Somehow they all stayed upright as they careened through the corridors of the maze, though when they finally stopped in a random alcove Jerym collapsed gasping for breath. Seris sat heavily with her legs splayed, her lowered face hidden by a mess of red curls. Bren remained standing as she tried to massage the stitch out of her side. She was reminded of another frantic flight through the haunted corridors of Leris's undercity – though her companions were very different. She had been fleeing from the Velaschin then, and now they were at her side. Such strange twists her life had taken.

I prefer our current situation, Ashika interjected. *Much better here with the sun on our face than in the tunnels of that cursed place. And the enemy is flesh and blood, not some horror from the beyond.*

Bren let her agreement flow across the bond they shared, though she was too exhausted to engage the blademaiden in mental conversation.

Jerym was the first to break the silence. "I think that was a gnul," he said, staring at Bren with wide eyes.

"I'm sure of it," Seris agreed, climbing slowly to her feet. "I've seen that ugly face before."

Jerym snorted a laugh that sounded on the verge of being hysterical. "That's impossible. The gnul died out in our lands centuries ago."

"I didn't say it was still alive," Seris said, unlimbering her bow and testing the draw to make sure nothing had been damaged during their escape. "It was just the skull, kept in a place of honor in the r'Hatha clan roundhouse. They'd found it out in the bogs and dragged it back – the r'Hatha lorekeeper used to sit on its lower jaw and tell stories to us little ones when we visited." She glanced back the way they'd come, a shiver passing through her. "It frightened me even then, but I never truly appreciated how huge those monsters had been in life. I can understand why our forebears were nearly destroyed before Taivon Regast returned with the first dragons."

"But they're all dead!" Jerym insisted, sounding almost petulant. "I've seen their bones as well – the Peregrine Society has an almost intact skeleton in the room where the members take kefa."

"This place isn't real," Bren said, more sharply than she'd intended. "We have to stop thinking that it is. Our bodies must be back in Yestra. It's why we vanish when we take a killing blow here."

"Then how do I know you're not just in my mind?" Jerym muttered, somewhat defensively. "Maybe you're all just a dream I'm having." He gave a little yelp of pain as Seris bounced a rock off his shoulder.

"If this is indeed a dream, it's a shared dream," the kalishwoman said. "But as you claimed, death here must not be permanent. This place seems deadly, but I've been told the Winnowing is rarely fatal for the aspirants."

"I still don't want to be crushed by a monster like that," Bren muttered.

"I hope it was the only one in here," Jerym said with a shudder.

"Well, there might be more," Bren added, then frowned. "And I don't understand why you are so ignorant of this place. You are the emperor's nephew."

The look on Jerym's face when he turned towards her was almost exasperated. "Perhaps if I was one of my more martial cousins I'd know more. But I never entertained the idea that I'd take part, and I think my mother almost prides herself on how little she knows about the Winnowing. She is interested in far more important things. Although if she knew there were *gnul* here, she might have volunteered me herself."

"Does that mean you're going to go back there and start sketching that thing for her?" Bren asked.

"I never want to be anywhere near one of those monsters again," he told her, so earnestly that Bren actually smiled.

Seris snorted. "You don't have to worry about that – I think we'll see them coming next time. A giant is fairly difficult to hide if you know what to look for."

"There will be other dangers," Bren assured her.

"I know," Seris said, slinging her bow over her shoulder again. "Now come, no more tongue-wagging. We should find a good place to camp before it gets dark."

WHEN THEY FINALLY STOPPED AGAIN THE islands floating above them had nearly been devoured by twilight, their jagged ruins and steep cliffs a deeper black against the darkening sky. The gloaming did not reach into this section of the labyrinth, as bell-capped mushrooms of all sizes grew in great abundance here, glowing with a spectral radiance. They sprouted from cracks in the walls and larger mushrooms that nearly came up to her waist covered the ground. The light was more than enough to push on through the night, and if Seris had had her way, Bren suspected that was what they would have done. But Jerym was swaying on his feet, and she knew they should rest at least for a while, lest their exhaustion leave them vulnerable to whatever danger they next encountered.

And so they found a mossy space in the center of a ring of the ghostly mushrooms and attempted to make themselves comfortable. Jerym wrestled off one of the great caps to use it as a pillow and Seris put her back to one of the sturdier stalks, laying her bow across her lap.

"I'll take the first watch," she said, arranging three of her black-fletched arrows within easy reach of her draw hand.

Bren nodded agreement, then began clearing a spot amongst the luminescent mushrooms. When she finally finished making a little burrow for herself she tried to curl up and will herself to sleep but despite the heaviness in her limbs her mind refused to rest. Jerym clearly had no such problem, and almost as soon as his head touched the spongy mushroom cap he started to snore softly. After listening to his reedy rumbling for a little while, Bren propped herself up on her elbows and looked over to Seris, only to find the archer was already staring at her with a troubled expression.

"Do you know what I can't figure out?" the kalishwoman asked, running her fingers along the smooth grain of her bow.

"Why they helped us."

Seris's eyes widened. "It must be bothering you as well, then."

"Yes," Bren replied, drawing her legs up to her chest and resting her chin on her knee. "They could have fled as soon as they entered the gnul's lair. Instead, they attacked it."

"They drew it away from us," Seris added. "And they must have known they could do little to harm such a monster. They risked their lives to save ours."

"That does not seem to be in the spirit of the Winnowing. Though I suppose you also came to our rescue."

"But I do not want to be a dragon rider," Seris said. "Merith, on the other hand . . . she has almost certainly been preparing her whole life to claim a hatchling."

"She must have been following orders," Bren guessed. "But whose?"

"Her family," Seris guessed. "You were sent here by the Old Drake, yes? He may not be the head of the family, but he is by far their most famous scion. Perhaps he instructed the Ahzan aspirants to help you."

"Maybe," Bren said uncertainly. "But I doubt it. Why would he care if I won the Winnowing? Surely he would prefer the hatchling go to his own family." Bren plucked the cap off a mushroom brushing up against her and crumbled it into softly glowing chunks.

"Then perhaps the umbrari have an interest in you, if she does truly belong to their order."

Bren shook her head. "That makes little sense." Her gaze drifted to Jerym, whose face had slackened in sleep. "What about him? He's important. Perhaps they were protecting him."

She regretted saying this as soon as it was out of her mouth. Seris's expression hardened, her jaw clenching. Bren chided herself for reminding the kalishwoman that Jerym was a Regast and the nephew of the emperor.

"The families are fierce rivals. I would think they'd be quite content to watch the imperial house fail."

Bren mulled this over for a little while, then shrugged. "I know almost nothing about the politics of your people."

Seris sighed. "I'm little better. We heard all sorts of rumors in the legions, but I can't claim to know which are true and which are false. I'm just a kalishwoman from the marches."

She is better than the rest of the aspirants we've met.

You like her, don't you?

I respect her. When that monster appeared, she did not freeze with fear. She is brave and skilled and has come here to prove an injustice was done to her family. She has a sense of duty that would satisfy a blade-maiden. It gives me hope these Velaschin are not all spoiled brats.

You're certainly right about that. She's no spoiled brat.

"Get some sleep," Seris said, pulling Bren from her conversation with the ghost in her head. "I'll be waking you soon enough to take my place."

"Not too soon, I hope," Bren replied, then stretched out in the moss with her head pillowed on her arm. The glow of the mushrooms leaked past her shut eyes, but she knew she wasn't going to stay awake long. And that was because she trusted the girl keeping watch. As she drifted towards sleep, Bren mumbled a quick prayer thanking the Silver Mother for leading Seris to them.

THE NEXT DAY their exploration of the labyrinth yielded several strange and wondrous sights, though thankfully little in the way of danger. One long and broad corridor was lined with great stone faces, and when they were about halfway down its length unusual sounds began to emanate from their lips. Seris hissed in surprise and aimed an arrow at the closest of the faces, but no threat materialized and Bren cautiously approached to bend her head and better hear what the faces were saying. It sounded almost like a chant in a language she had never heard before. Neither of her companions could understand either, though Jerym had thought he'd once heard his mother speaking a similar tongue when conversing with a trader from the islands of the Shattered Sea.

Not far beyond these faces, they came to a large door of dark metal set into a stone wall at the end of a twisting corridor. What might have once been a knob was situated in the middle of the door, though when Seris grasped that decaying lump it had crumbled away into rust. Bren thought they were going to have to retrace their way back to the last junction, but then Jerym noticed something hidden beneath a layer of gray-green patina, and after scraping this away a rune-covered wheel was discovered. It still turned, though with a shriek that put Bren's teeth on edge, and this was how they learned that there were in fact several circles of runes nested within each other, all of which could be manipulated independently.

After a few moments of fiddling with the odd contraption, Seris sighed in frustration and turned away. Jerym moved to follow her, but Bren stayed staring at the runes. A strange familiarity was tickling at the back of her mind, as if the symbols resembled something she had once known . . .

Turn that man so that he aligns with the one that looks like a bundle of wheat.

You recognize something?

Yes. No. Perhaps. Just do as I bid.

Bren stepped forward and rotated the runes as Ashika had requested.

"What is it?" Jerym asked from behind her, but she ignored him, waiting for the spirit to tell her more.

And now the aurochs. Bring them all into a line.

Bren found the symbol on the third and smallest wheel that resembled a bull and brought it into alignment with the others. Then she jumped back in surprise as a hollow clang sounded from beyond the door, and the wheel sank slowly into the metal to reveal a curving handle. Tentatively she grasped it, and the door swung inward as if on well-oiled hinges. On the other side was a corridor that looked indistinguishable from the one they currently stood in.

"You did it!" Jerym cried, grabbing her arm in excitement. "How did you know what to do?"

"I'm not sure," Bren replied, then turned inward to ask the same question to the ghost in her head.

Ashika?

Only the graycloaks learned all the rune sets, but I saw this one above the entrances to our halls.

Then this is the writing of your people?

Of the People. The Black Mountain tribe must have kept the old symbols after they conquered all the tribes and founded the city they came to call Gith.

Bren felt Jerym shaking her arm, but she was lost in her thoughts. She turned, taking in the labyrinth with new eyes. The Gith must have built this place, as they had built the labyrinth beneath Leris. She had thought this to be some illusion fashioned by the warlocks of Velaschin, but that must be incorrect – rather, this maze was something very old that had been repurposed for the Winnowing. But where had it come from?

She startled, returning to herself when Seris clapped her hard on the shoulder.

"Well done," the kalishwoman said as she started down the passage that had been revealed.

BREN WAS NOT surprised when they stumbled upon the statues. They were cracked gray stone instead of the pale, shining glowstone she had first encountered in the burrow of the Ratman, but otherwise they were identical. Animals with the heads of men and women, or men and women with the heads of animals. A stag's blank eyes gazed down on them from atop the strong, naked body of a youth. Beside this statue a woman's beautiful face – empty of any emotion – was perched atop the coils of a great stone snake.

"What are these?" Seris asked, reaching up to touch one of the stag-man's cracked tines.

Before Bren could say anything, Jerym spoke up, surprising her.

"The gods of the Gith," he said, giving the statue of a brutish, bear-headed man a wide berth. "I saw pictures like this once in a book my tutor showed me."

They were not my gods, Ashika muttered inside Bren's mind. *They were what the Black Mountain graycloaks found on the other side of the door. Though the shamans of my own tribe thought these were not their true forms . . . Just the shapes they assumed when they entered our world.*

"What are the gods of the Gith doing here?" Seris asked. Bren noticed she had unshouldered her bow and had an arrow nocked.

"My tutor also told me it is whispered that the warlocks of Velasch have preserved fragments of the Gith's ancient knowledge. Perhaps this place is something they made."

Seris cleared her throat loudly and spat in the direction of the strange, chimeric figures. "Out on the marches we still remember the old songs, the ones we Velaschins sang as slaves while being crushed under the heel of our Gith masters. What foolishness it would be to keep anything made by their demon-magic."

I agree.

The sorcerers of my people are the same, Bren thought, remembering the story Tal had told her about how his mother had been lost while trying to recreate a Gith ritual.

All shamans are the same, Ashika muttered, and Bren could sense her disgust. *They lust for power like a moth does a flame . . . And almost always share the same fate.*

"Bren . . ."

The tenor of Jerym's voice as he called her name pulled her attention back. He had wandered down the statue-lined passage and was hovering at the entrance of what looked to be a much larger space. Seris must have heard something in his tone as well because she hurried in his direction keeping her bow drawn.

Bren drew her sword and followed, her fingers settling into the hilt's unfamiliar grip. This was Ashika's influence, she supposed, preparing her for what was ahead . . . but nothing could have prepared her for what she found when she reached the others.

The next chamber was a hub like they had encountered many times before with passages spilling into it. Filling most of the room was a pool of thick black liquid, and something huge was half-submerged in this tarry substance. It looked at first glance like a boulder that was slowly sinking into the morass, but then Bren noticed that its surface was pebbled gray skin instead of stone. There was something familiar about its shape, the swells and contours of the thing's bulbous body.

Jerym realized it first. "It's a toad," he whispered.

"It's a monster," Seris said, just as softly. She had raised her bow and trained an arrow on the creature's head. Bren wasn't sure what that would do – it looked easily large enough to swallow them whole.

"Is it a statue?" Bren asked because she could see no movement. "Or is it dead?"

"I don't know," Seris replied, "but we should go back—"

A clang interrupted her. They whirled around to find that at the far end of the statue-lined corridor the metal door they'd passed through had swung shut. Bren quickly returned her attention to the toad-thing, but it showed no sign of having heard. Her suspicion that it wasn't alive strengthened.

"Come on," Seris said grimly, and then she led them back down the passage. This time, there was no handle or rune-scribed wheel sunk into the door, just smooth metal. The red-haired girl set down her bow and ran her fingertips along the thin seam separating the door from the stone, but she could find no purchase to pry it open. Finally, she stopped and stepped back, looking at Bren and Jerym with a helpless expression. Then they all turned once more to face the opening to the chamber with the giant toad-thing.

"Saints and Sages," Bren breathed in tired resignation, her gaze going to the violet sky with its floating islands.

"The door closing was very loud," Jerym ventured hopefully. "I bet we can sneak right past it to one of the other corridors without it even knowing we're there."

"I can put an arrow down its throat if it tries to eat us," Seris offered, taking up her bow again. "We have weapons – there's no reason we should be frightened of a giant frog."

What do you think we should do? Bren thought, turning inward.

The reply was almost dismissive. *I am the killer of the great bear Nunega. I do not fear toads.*

Bren sighed. "All right. We try to get to another passage." She glanced at Jerym to get his agreement, and the boy nodded nervously. "You stay close to me. I'll take the lead and keep my sword between us and that thing. Seris, you're behind Jerym. If that frog so much as twitches, send a few arrows its way before we run. Agreed?" Neither of her companions looked thrilled with the plan, but they offered no alternative, and after heaving a deep breath Bren led them down the corridor of Gith gods again and into the hub chamber. The oily black liquid nearly reached the walls, and Bren's shoulder brushed stone as they crept along the thin strip of dry ground ringing the pool.

Bren had made it nearly halfway to the next passage when Jerym gave a squeak of fear and began frantically hitting her back with his open palm. She had been fixated on the vine-draped entrance up ahead while also trying not to step in the oily sludge, but now with a sinking sensation in her stomach she glanced over at the hulking creature.

A great yellow eye had cracked open and was watching them.

Seris must have noticed this as well, as she gave a small, strangled cry of surprise and began swinging her bow up. Bren grabbed her arm to keep her from releasing the arrow she had nocked.

"What?" Seris asked, glancing at her in wild alarm.

"It hasn't done anything," Bren whispered fiercely, meeting and holding her eyes. "But if you stick an arrow in it, I'm fairly sure it will think we are enemies."

Seris grunted something unintelligible and wrenched her arm away from Bren, but she didn't send an arrow arcing out over the black pond.

"Let's just try to keep go—"

FRESH THINGS, NEW THINGS

The voice seemed to bubble up out of the dark liquid near their feet. Bren froze, cold fingers sliding along her spine.

LONG TIME THE DOOR DID NOT OPEN. BUT NOW IT HAS AND CLOSED AGAIN, LETTING IN THESE INTRUDERS TO OUR SANCTUM. WHAT ARE YOU?

"Don't say anything," Seris muttered, and Bren could see her bowstring start to bend as she drew back the arrow.

"We are aspirants," Jerym said loudly, which elicited an angry curse from the kalishwoman.

AS-PIR-ANTS, the voice said slowly, as if testing out a new word. **WE DO NOT KNOW THIS. ARE YOU GITH?**

"No," Jerym called back. "The Gith are gone. Dead. Our people are Velaschin."

VEL-AS-KIN. WE ARE CONFUSED. ARE YOU ASPIRANTS OR ARE YOU VELASCHIN?

Bren stirred nervously when the great toad raised its head out of the sludge and opened its wide maw. Something moved inside its mouth, long and sinuous.

"We are both," Jerym said.

YOU SMELL LIKE GITH. BUT SWEETER. OR PERHAPS TOO
LONG HAVE WE BEEN HERE. MEMORIES FADE.

"How . . . how long have you been here?" Jerym asked, and to
Bren's disbelief she realized he was moving his hand through the air
like he was practicing how he would draw this monster later.

MORE THAN A MOMENT AND LESS THAN AN ETERNITY.
TIME IS DIFFICULT TO PARSE IN THIS PLACE, AS IN ALL THE
FOLDINGS FARTHEST FROM THE CENTER.

"And . . . what are you doing?"

RUMINATING ON A TECHNIQUE OF WHICH WE HAVE
HEARD RUMORS. BUT THE SECRET ELUDES US. PERHAPS
WE BATHE IN THE WRONG EFFLUVIA.

Ashika's voice infringed upon Bren's thoughts. *This thing is a
demon, I am sure of it. It is not of our world.*

DEMON? WE KNOW THAT WORD; IT WAS SPOKEN IN HATE
AND ANGER BY SOME, IN AWE BY OTHERS. WE DO NOT LIKE
IT. WE PREFER WANDERER, FOR FAR HAVE WE WANDERED.

Cold surprise washed through Bren. It had heard Ashika.

"What is it talking about?" Seris said out of the side of her mouth.
"Is it mad? Should we run for the passage?"

"*Which* passage?" Bren hissed back, frantically trying to decide
the best route away from this place.

"Let's ask it," Jerym said, and Bren shared a look of alarm with
Seris.

"We can't trust—" Bren began, but Jerym had already taken a step
closer to the great toad, his toes nearly touching the oozing
blackness.

"Wanderer," he called out loudly, and Bren winced, "we seek the
middle of this maze. Do you know the way?"

A flash of movement distracted her as a winged snake that looked
to be a spawn of the much larger creatures she'd seen darting around
the floating islands swooped down from above, skimming over the
surface of the black pond like it had been drawn by the movement of
some prey. Before it could dive under the sludge, a long, whip-like

tongue exploded from the toad-thing's mouth and seized the flying serpent, then dragged it thrashing into its waiting maw. After a quick swallow it was like the snake had never been.

The look of horror on Seris's ashen face mirrored what Bren felt – were they far enough away to avoid the same fate? Because she greatly doubted she could dodge that tongue if the toad decided to discover if they did indeed taste sweet.

Jerym, on the other hand, looked fascinated by what had just transpired.

A MIDDLE? THERE IS NO MIDDLE TO THIS LABYRINTH.

The Gith must have made some sort of center, Ashika scoffed. *Otherwise why build this place?*

THE GITH DID NOT MAKE THIS PLACE. THEY APPROPRIATED IT FROM THE BUILDERS.

Jerym seemed confused by what the toad was saying – understandable, since he was not privy to what Ashika had said. "Then . . . you don't know which way we should go?" he shouted across the pond. The toad shifted slightly, though no ripples disturbed the blackness in which it crouched.

PERHAPS. SOMETHING IS DIFFERENT FROM BEFORE. THE WARP AND WEFT OF THIS FOLDING HAS BEEN FRAYED. SOMETHING HAS HAPPENED. IS HAPPENING.

Bren shared another look with her companions. What else but the Winnowing was occurring right now in this place?

"And where is that?" Jerym pressed, taking a quick step back from the edge of the pond as a bubble rose to the surface near his feet.

The toad did not move, but the vines climbing the wall on either side of one of the corridors suddenly began to writhe.

THIS WAY WILL TAKE YOU TO THE DISTURBANCE. WE SMELL A SWEETNESS WAFTING FROM THAT DIRECTION. IT SMELLS LIKE YOU.

Do not trust the demon, Ashika warned.

"I think we should go that way," Jerym said. "I don't know why it would lie to us."

"Perhaps its bigger and hungrier mother is down that passage,"

Seris replied mockingly. "What about you, Bren? Do we go in the direction the giant toad wants?"

Bren swallowed. Her instinct was certainly not to trust this thing, but when the vines surrounding that exit from this place had squirmed, she had felt something, an answering twinge in her arm where the jade disc had been buried. And if anything would know where the hatchling waited, it was the sorcerer's artifact.

"I say we go that way," she said, indicating the corridor where the vines were still weakly squirming.

"Two against one," Jerym said.

Ashika's voice swelled again in her head. *Do I not have a say in this as well?*

No, Bren replied. *You don't.*

Ashika lapsed into silence, radiating annoyance.

They all jumped as a deep thrumming emanated across the pond in rippling waves. It took Bren a moment to realize the toad-thing was laughing – and she suspected it was because of her dismissal of Ashika.

"Come on," Bren said, beginning to edge her way along the thin strip of ground towards the passage the toad had indicated. "We don't know how much time we have left."

To her surprise, both Seris and Jerym seemed reluctant to move – Seris's reasons were obvious enough, as she was plucking at her bowstring while staring at the toad suspiciously, but Jerym pulled away from her as she went to drag him forward.

"I want to know more about you, Wanderer, and also this place," the boy called out across the pond.

The toad-thing shifted again, and Bren thought it was staring at Jerym in newfound interest. **WHEN YOU RETURN ASPIRANT-VELASCHIN, WE SHALL TRADE KNOWLEDGE IN THE OLD WAYS.**

"Thank you," Jerym said before finally letting Bren pull him along.

"Stop talking to the monster," Seris grumbled, keeping her body turned to the toad-thing and her bowstring taut as she also moved to follow Bren.

THE PASSAGE BROADENED as they continued, and since the few side-corridors they passed were markedly smaller they kept to the main path. Seris walked backwards for quite some time watching the way they had come, apparently expecting the toad-thing to come bounding along in pursuit, but eventually she accepted that nothing was following. She still wore a troubled expression, and Bren was about to ask her what was wrong when she finally spoke.

"That was brave," she said, and Bren was surprised to realize her words were directed at Jerym.

"What was brave?" Jerym asked, looking over at her cautiously. He'd clearly gotten accustomed to her hostility, but the edge which Seris usually spoke with was gone.

"Treating with that thing. That monster. If you had not responded to its questions, I would have loosed an arrow, and who knows what might have happened then."

"Oh," Jerym said, his face coloring slightly. "After it talked, I knew it wasn't just an animal. And so it was probably just as curious about us as we were about it."

The corner of Seris's mouth lifted. "I wasn't curious."

"I was," Jerym replied. "And I still am. I don't think I'll really get the chance to go back and talk to it . . . but I wish I could. It is one of the few intelligent creatures I've ever heard of. My mother went on an expedition under the Wraiths to prove that the garthik are not simply beasts. She said they shape their caves with tools and use the glowing ichor of their spiders to draw the most startling images on the walls. And of course the gnul were also believed to have some cunning. But that toad back there . . . it would be only the second known species capable of communication with men."

Bren frowned. "Second? There is another one?"

"Well, dragons, of course."

That revelation startled Bren so badly she nearly tripped over her own feet. "Dragons can talk?"

"Not truly," the boy continued hurriedly. "They lack the proper organs in their throat to speak as we do, and they don't seem to fully understand the idea of language. But they are highly intelligent, especially the greater dragons. My mother's cousin Lady Rukhsa told me that they can push images and emotions into the minds of those they bond with. She said her river dragon Reed has the most beautiful personality. Can you imagine having something showing you what *they* can see inside *your* head?"

Bren could, of course. She wondered if she would be able to keep herself from going mad if she ended up with a dragon and a ghost inside her mind.

"Oh, and thank you for your kind words," Jerym said to Seris, glancing at her shyly. "I have always thought of myself as a coward, to be truthful."

Bren remembered the boy creeping closer to investigate the monster up on the wall as it devoured the Varyxes aspirants. "You're no coward – you are brave to the point of foolishness."

At this, Jerym blushed and looked away.

"Come on," Seris said, her pace quickening. "Let's see where that monster sent us."

28

If not for what the toad had said, Bren would have assumed they had indeed reached the very center of the labyrinth. The long corridor they traversed as the sun drifted across the sky eventually emptied into a vast, circular space, the walls curving away from them on either side to join again in the hazy distance.

"What happened here?" whispered Seris, shielding her eyes from the day's brightness.

The flat and stony ground speckled with tufts of yellow grass was marred by a large pit in the very center of this expanse. Bren wasn't sure of its depth but given how the earthy sides slanted inwards she thought the hole must descend at least several times the height of a man. Bren wondered what could possibly have put such a pockmark on the skin of this world.

That was not the only odd feature in this section of the labyrinth. A wall standing shoulder-high formed an arching barrier between where they stood and the rest of the great space. It almost looked like a kind of fortification, with crenellations that would not have been out of place atop a castle. This defensive barricade emerged from the wall to their right, then pushed a few dozen paces out before curving back to enter the wall on the other side. It certainly wasn't high enough to keep them from clambering over . . . but perhaps that wasn't its purpose at all.

"Look!" Jerym cried, pointing at something far away. Bren squinted at where he was indicating, then let out a hiss of surprise.

Almost directly across from them she saw a wall that looked the same, and visible between the gaps of its stone teeth staring back at them were other aspirants.

Lots of them.

"Who are they?" Jerym asked, rushing up to the edge of their battlements to try to get a better look.

"Get down!" Bren hissed, quickly pulling him down behind a merlon with her.

"Too late, they saw us," Seris said grimly, not bothering to hide herself. "And given their height and generally ogrish build, I'm certain they're Varyxes."

"What are they doing here?" Bren said, rising from her crouch. "Why are they waiting?"

"For us?" Jerym asked, peeking over the top of the fortification.

Bren put her elbows on the top of the stone fortification and leaned forward. "They couldn't know we were coming."

"Then perhaps the egg is here," Seris mused. "At the bottom of that pit?"

Bren frowned. "That also makes little sense. If the egg were down there, they'd surely have already claimed the hatchling."

"Every entrance along the walls is the same," Seris said, her gaze wandering along the length of the encircling wall. "They all have barricades. But why?"

"To defend," Bren said, guessing the most obvious answer.

"Which suggests we are supposed to stay here."

"The egg *must* be here," murmured Jerym, also looking around the huge open area. "And the hole is the only place it could be hidden."

"I'll go take a look," Bren said. "You two stay here behind the wall."

Seris snorted. "Why would we do that? I don't care if anyone seizes this sad little fortress we've found ourselves in. Besides, you'll need me to provide some cover. I can keep those lumbering oxen from rushing you."

"Give me your bow," Jerym asked Bren, holding out his hand. "I can help!"

Seris dismissed this idea with a sharp shake of her head. "I suspect you'd be as likely to plant an arrow in Bren's back as hit a Varyxes. Have you ever used a bow?"

"A few times. My father has taken me hunting before."

Seris raised her eyebrows, as if she hadn't been expecting this. "And did you hit anything?"

"A tree," Jerym admitted.

"I'll keep my bow," Bren told the boy, patting him on the shoulder. "But I appreciate your offer."

"When do you want to—" Seris said, but she broke off what she was saying and sighed when she realized Bren had already started climbing over the barricade.

"Now. Before it gets dark. I need light to see what's down in that hole."

"Fine," Seris muttered. "I'll keep a hundred paces behind you. Any farther and I won't be accurate enough to be much help."

Bren nodded, her gaze on the distant fortifications as she dropped to the cracked earth and started striding across the expanse, her boots kicking up dust between the patches of desiccated yellow grass. The Varyxes aspirants had noticed her approach by now and were rushing around in preparation. Bren hoped those she could see were most of their numbers – if they charged across the field a dozen strong, she didn't know what she'd do.

Run Ashika answered at once. *Even with my skill guiding your arm you would be overwhelmed.*

Then let's hope they don't have so many.

She let out a sigh of relief when only four aspirants emerged from behind their wall. It wasn't all of them – she could see two others that had stayed to protect their fortress – but they must have assumed that four against one with an archer lingering well behind Bren was good enough odds.

And in most instances, they probably would have been right.

Loose a few arrows when they come within range.

Bren sent a flicker of affirmation to the presence in her head. The pit was still several hundred paces away, but the Varyxes were closing fast so she unshouldered her bow and nocked an arrow, trying to judge how the slight breeze would alter her shot. She could see the enemy now: three young men and a woman, though they all shared the same stocky build. One of the boys carried no weapon – instead, he held only a tower shield nearly as big as he was, and the sight of it made Bren frown. It would be his duty to stop arrows, and with a shield that size it shouldn't be a very difficult task. The others all wielded heavy weapons, though they did not seem to be straining overmuch as they drew closer. One had a two-handed greatsword, another a double-bladed ax, and the girl held the handle of a morning star in one hand and the chain near its head in the other so that the spiked ball would not drag along the sere ground. Their passage was stirring up a cloud of yellow dust, so thick she couldn't see their faces clearly.

Bren drew back and loosed an arrow. This was a test of the wind, and she was not surprised when it went wide left.

But it also caused the Varyxes aspirants to slow and draw closer to the boy carrying the shield. That was good – she didn't want them to spread out and try to take her from three sides at once. Even the greatest warriors would struggle if surrounded, especially on this sort of open ground.

She let another arrow fly, and this time it flew true but the boy lifted the tower shield and it thunked solidly into the wood and stuck there quivering. They were also within Seris's range now, and another arrow buried itself beside Bren's in the shield as the boy rushed forward to protect the girl with the morning star. Bren got another shot off – though she had little hope of it getting past that shield – and then she tossed aside the bow and drew her sword. She breathed deep, settling into a stance drawn from Ashika's memory that was both unfamiliar and familiar.

The boy with the sword is the greatest threat, the blademaiden told her calmly. *See how he stays balanced despite how fast he moves? He has trained hard with such a heavy blade. Do not try to parry his blows, for he will tear your sword from your grip. Use your feet. Dance like a blademaiden, and wait for your chance. Yet do not forget the others.*

The ax-wielding boy charged her first, eliciting angry cries from the others, for they must have wanted to coordinate their attack. His first swing was ill-balanced, and Bren skipped backwards to let the wickedly curved head whistle past her. She might have been able to duck inside his guard and stab him there and then, but she didn't want to risk catching her sword in his flesh or clothes. She would have to choose her moment wisely she decided as she circled the boy to keep him between her and the others. He snarled and lunged again, and this time Bren side-stepped the blow while lashing out with her sword. The steel sliced through his tunic, and she felt the satisfying but slight resistance of flesh parting. He stumbled back holding his side, nearly dropping his ax. Bren wanted to press this advantage, but then the boy with the sword descended on her like an avalanche. His speed was shocking and she had no time to dodge, so Bren was forced to catch the strike with her own blade, which jarred her arm all the way up to her shoulder.

She let Ashika's instincts take over, bringing her sword up to meet another blow, then the next and the next. Bren sensed the girl with the morning star trying to find an opening, but her weapon was not suitable for such a task – she'd just as likely have sent the heavy spiked ball crashing into the other Varyxes if she tried to swing it – and so Bren allowed herself to focus completely on the swordsman. The expression on the boy's face had been sneeringly confident for the first few ringing exchanges, but as Bren found her footing and continued to turn aside his attacks she saw doubt creeping into his face. He was far stronger, but the blademaiden inside her knew how to angle her sword just perfectly so that the heavier blade slid off her steel, blunting the power behind each blow. And she was far, far more skilled. Bren grinned, realizing she had her opponent outmatched. She could see he knew it now as well, as he tried to disengage from her so that the girl with the morning star could enter the fray.

Bren did not allow that to happen. She seized the initiative, and though the boy managed to deflect her first swing his second parry was a heartbeat late, and she caught his sword arm with a downward chop. He bellowed in shock and pain as his hand was severed just above the wrist, but the scream ended abruptly as Bren slashed his throat. She whirled around, expecting to dodge the morning star, but instead found that the girl had dropped her weapon and was running back towards the Varyxes barricades. The shield-bearer was beside her, his tower shield raised high to try to stop any arrows from catching them as they fled.

He should not have worried, because Seris had turned her attention to easier prey. The ax-wielding boy Bren had wounded first had staggered away holding his side, and he must have been delirious from the pain because he was going in the completely wrong direction, straight towards where Seris crouched on one knee with her bow drawn. A moment later an arrow took him in the throat, and he finally let the ax he'd been dragging through the grass fall as he toppled over.

For the first time Bren witnessed a body disappear – it wasn't the gradual fading she had expected, with the flesh slowly growing insubstantial – no, the dead boy was there one moment, and then he wasn't. Only the ax remained behind, half-swallowed by a tuft of yellow grass. Bren glanced at the boy she had struck down and saw that his body had also been replaced by scuffed earth. He had left behind his sword, a serrated dagger, and a crudely stitched bag that looked like it had once been the bladder of some beast. All the things he had gathered during his time in the labyrinth, Bren guessed.

Do not dawdle! Ashika reprimanded her. *Pursue your foes and cut them down before they reach their sanctuary!*

Bren looked at the fleeing boy and girl. She imagined charging after them and thrusting her sword into their backs, the terrified, pained cries . . . her gaze went to the patch of dusty earth where the boy's hand had fallen moments ago. She closed her eyes, a wave of exhaustion and no small amount of nausea sweeping over her.

You told me you would not display weakness again, Ashika said, her tone accusing. *That you would do what was necessary.*

Those are not the ones who burned my family.

They will come for you once more.

And when they do and my life is threatened, I will defend myself! Bren replied with a strength that surprised even herself. The presence in her head seemed to recoil slightly at the force behind her thoughts.

When Ashika finally responded, the feelings flavoring her words were far more subdued. *So long as you accept the consequences.*

I do, Bren answered testily. *Now I have important things I must do.* She quickly plucked the saw-bladed knife and the makeshift bag from the ground – the massive sword was far too cumbersome, and she was certain neither Jerym nor Seris would be able to swing it – and then she jogged over to the pit to see what was hidden within.

Bren frowned when she reached the crumbling edge. There was nothing of any interest that she could see. It was not very deep – she could easily clamber down the steep, earthy slope and stand at the bottom if she wished. That would be foolish, of course, given that rival aspirants could arrive at any moment. All her advantages with a blade would be rendered useless if an enemy with a bow loomed above her.

She studied the sides, trying to understand how this pit had come to be. It looked to her from the color of the churned dirt that it had been dug recently . . . but if that was true, where had all the earth gone? The surrounding area was empty of any such piles. It was all so strange.

"Bren!" Seris cried, sounding panicked.

With a last searching look at the pit, Bren turned. The red-haired girl had gone halfway back to their wall before halting, and she was now gesturing emphatically in the direction of another entrance. Bren followed where she was pointing, then hissed in disappointment – the battlements fringing where that passage spilled into this space were now manned. A tall boy with jet-black hair stood on one of the merlons, his hand on the silver hilt of his dark sword. Zair. Beside him was another boy, strips of torn cloth wound around his shoulder, and a smaller, slighter girl. There were others as well, though Bren couldn't see them clearly.

The Karths had arrived.

Bren hurried over to retrieve the bow she'd dropped in the grass, then took off at a run towards where Seris and Jerym had already taken refuge behind their battlements. When she glanced over at Zair, she found that he hadn't moved – apparently, he preferred caution, and she wondered if he had witnessed her brief but brutal battle with the Varyxes aspirants. Or perhaps he was confident he could overrun them at any time. Whatever the reason, no one was pursuing Bren when she arrived sweaty and panting at the battlements where Seris and Jerym were waiting.

"How many do you think Zair has?" Seris asked as she offered her hand to help Bren over the wall.

"I don't know," Bren replied between gulping breaths. "But he's found more friends. I think I saw the girl he introduced at the feast as his cousin. The scarred boy Malisk's trueborn sister."

"Alyia," Jerym murmured. "She's even worse than he is."

"She's dangerous?" Bren asked, leaning against the stone and tossing the dagger she'd carried back from the fight into the grass at Jerym's feet. "Take that, by the way. You need some sort of protection."

"Alyia isn't a great swordswoman, to my knowledge," Jerym said, gingerly picking the dagger up by its handle like it was something distasteful or dangerous. "But she's much more clever. And deceitful. I remember she pretended to be my friend back in the palace on one of those Deliverance Day festivals, only to betray me to Zair and his awful friends when they came looking. The glee she took in seeing my surprise, and then later in what they did to me . . ." Jerym shook his head. "Honestly, as much as I abhor violence . . ." He brandished the dagger, holding it in the most awkward grip imaginable.

Seris rolled her eyes. "Just try not to stab one of us," she said, then looked out past the merlons again. "So what's in the pit? What did you see?"

"Nothing," Bren said with a shrug. "It's just a big hole. It looks freshly dug, though."

Seris frowned. "That's . . . odd. Why are we all here, then? It's almost like the labyrinth has funneled us to this place." Her eyes widened. "Do you think this is an arena? That we're supposed to fight each other until only one remains?"

"Perhaps," Bren said with little certainty. "I was told it was a competition to find the egg, not murder everyone else."

"What's in that?" Jerym asked, gesturing dangerously with his dagger at the bag Bren still held, and she jerked her hand back when the point came close to puncturing its leather. "Sorry," he said as Seris sighed loudly.

"Just be careful," Bren said, pulling aside a little flap of hide to reveal the bag's contents: acorns, berries, flint, and a carefully folded sheet of paper. She withdrew the parchment and spread it open – at first the knotted mess of intersecting lines and strange markings meant little to her, but as Jerym and Seris drew closer, the realization of what she was holding dawned.

"It's a map," she breathed. "A map of the labyrinth."

"They made a map?" Seris asked, peering over her shoulder.

"They didn't make this," Jerym answered, reaching out to pinch the corner of the paper, as if to reassure himself that it was real. "It's drawn in ink on sheepskin vellum. Look at the details and the fineness of the lines. This was made by an experienced mapmaker."

"They brought it into the labyrinth," Bren said, feeling a swell of righteous indignation at the unfairness. "That boy I fought must have been a high-born Varyxes scion, maybe their champion. They gave him this. Just like Zair was allowed to bring his obsidian sword into the trials, he was gifted this map."

"I'd bet Zair has a similar map," Seris muttered with a disgusted shake of her head. "And probably the Ahzan faction, as well. A great advantage for those most favored by their families."

"We must be here," Jerym said, pointing at a large open space among the labyrinth's tangled passages. A red circle had been drawn in that area . . . no, it was an oval, not a circle. An egg.

"So it *is* here," Bren murmured. "It must be. It's why the others have come as well."

"Then where is it?" Seris asked, going over to the wall again to peer out between the fortifications.

"It wasn't in that hole," Bren said. "I'm sure of it. Unless it's buried under the dirt somewhere."

Jerym was chewing on his lower lip, his gaze distant like he was lost deep in thought. "What if," he finally said, focusing again on the map, "the egg isn't here yet. But it's coming."

Bren frowned. "You mean the warlocks haven't placed it in the labyrinth? That they're waiting for all the factions to reach this location before they do?"

"I think it's in the labyrinth," Jerym continued slowly. "It just hasn't arrived yet."

Bren sighed. "Speak plainly. Where is the egg?"

To her surprise, Jerym tilted his face upwards and squinted into the wash of violet, then pointed at the closest of the floating sky-islands. It was one of the islands covered with ruins that were being devoured by thick vegetation, claws of green reaching up from below to engulf crumbling towers and arches. "That island has been getting closer and closer all day. I think it will pass directly over this place."

Bren contemplated the island's underbelly of rock and packed earth. Was it possible? Handing the map to Jerym, she went over to stand beside Seris and stared out at the pit. "You think it came from here."

"And now it's returning," Jerym agreed.

"Then what?" Seris asked. "We all run out to try to find the egg and kill each other?" She smiled sourly. "No wonder the dragon riders of the empire are such bastards."

"I don't think the island will come down to the ground until all the families are here," Jerym said. "It's waiting. The maze was part of the test, and some of the chaff has been separated—"

"And by 'separated' you mean eaten by monsters or stabbed to death by other aspirants," interrupted Bren.

Jerym grimaced. "Well, yes. The weak have been culled and now the strong will have the chance to prove their worth. It was never about being the first to solve the labyrinth. Everything has been leading up to this moment . . . a final Winnowing."

And so you were correct. It will be a bloodbath. No quarter shall be given by your rivals, this I know.

"Let us say you are right, Regast," Seris said, and Bren could hear the skepticism in her voice. "What do we do now?"

"We wait for the Ahzan," Jerym answered. "And try to stay alive. The Varyxes might mount another attack. Or the Karths. It would make sense to eliminate any rivals before the island arrives."

"I don't think the Varyxes would dare," Seris said, glancing over at Bren. "You fought like a sword dancer from the Gray Redoubt. The Karths, on the other hand . . ."

Bren unshouldered her bow and leaned it against the fortifications. "They won't be able to get close to the wall without being turned into pincushions. Someone just has to always be keeping watch so that they can't sneak up on us."

"I'm not worried about what happens during the day," Seris said, brushing back a red lock as she watched the island drift in a sky that had darkened noticeably since they'd reached this place. "But night is coming."

IT WAS Jerym who devised the idea for their defenses. As the day waned and the shadows cast by the labyrinth's walls lengthened, Bren and the Regast boy gathered the yellow grass and piled it in heaps not far beyond the wall. At first, Seris stood watch atop the fortifications as they labored to ensure the Varyxes and the Karth did not attempt an attack, but after a while she came down to help. Their rival aspirants seemed content to wait behind their own barricades, which lent support to Jerym's theory that they also believed the egg would eventually appear in this place. Bren was less certain that the hatchling was on one of the flying islands, but it did seem to her like the one he'd pointed out earlier had continued to drift closer.

When it was finally late enough that the far walls of the labyrinth were lost to darkness, Bren used the chunk of flint she'd taken from the Varyxes boy to kindle fires in the grass piles they'd made. These were not large bonfires – they'd only managed to gather so much grass, and some they kept in reserve to add as fuel – but they were strategically placed so that anyone approaching their wall would be illuminated.

Bren and Seris took turns staying awake through the night, sitting atop the wall's merlons with their bows across their laps. The decision to set the watch fires proved fortuitous, as a dense layer of clouds hid most of the stars and the floating island had now drawn so near that it blocked a fair swath of the sky. None of their rivals tried to sneak past the fires, but the night was not entirely uneventful – just before the sky lightened Bren heard something in the silence. Yelling, so faint that she'd thought it might be her imagination, and then the distinct sound of clashing metal. As quickly as it had started, it ended, and by the time morning had fully arrived, she had convinced herself that her ears had been playing tricks.

It was Jerym who realized they hadn't.

"Something is wrong at the Varyxes wall," he said while staring out across the expanse. He had his arms crossed on top of the wall and was resting his chin on his wrists as he chewed one of the fibrous roots, golden hair tousled from how he'd slept. He truly looked like a child, Bren thought as she came up alongside him and squinted, and not for the first time she felt a hot swell of anger that the Karth governor had insisted he join the Winnowing.

"What do you see?" she asked, shielding her eyes from the early-morning brightness.

"I'm not sure," he said slowly. "But don't they look ... different?"

Bren frowned. Now that the boy mentioned it, the far-away figures did seem to lack the Varyxes's characteristic bulk. They seemed thinner, slighter ...

"Those are Ahzan aspirants," Seris said as she appeared beside Bren, her red curls a disheveled mess.

"You're sure?" Bren asked, straining to see what they could.

"I am," Seris said confidently. "I have falcon eyes, as my grandfather used to say."

"So what happened?" Jerym asked, snapping the root he'd been gnawing on in half and offering a piece to Seris. She frowned skeptically, but still accepted it. That surprised Bren, but she had noticed the kalish girl's coldness towards Jerym had thawed quite a bit ever since the encounter with the toad-creature.

"I thought I heard something during the night," Bren said. "Screams. Metal clashing."

"So the Ahzan killed the remaining Varyxes aspirants," Seris mused before taking a tentative nibble of the gnarled root. Bren was expecting her to immediately spit it out, but she seemed to enjoy the taste. Perhaps it was still better than Velaschin army rations.

"Or drove them off," Bren suggested, though as she scanned the other labyrinth entrances she couldn't see anyone save for the Karths manning their own walls.

"Maybe they came up behind them," Jerym said. "The Varyxes might have been focused on the field because they knew the Karths were out here, and the Ahzan ambushed them."

"Whatever happened, it's good for us," Seris said.

Bren agreed – one fewer faction to deal with, and she had to admit that ever since Merith and her Ahzan companions had saved them from the gnul she'd thought of them as something less than enemies, if not exactly allies. She was sure that Zair would have gleefully watched them get mashed to a pulp by that monster if it had been the Karths who happened upon them at that time.

"It's going to pass right over," Jerym said. He was twisted around and staring up at the massive island that had snuck up on them during the night; it filled the sky, a great mass of rock and earth. From this angle she couldn't see much of the ruin she knew was perched atop it, just the jagged tops of a few shattered towers. The thick vegetation was evident in a green fringe around the edges of the island and the long vines dangling like wisps of a ragged beard. Bren wondered if this particular island could truly have been lifted from this barren place.

Together they watched in silence as the great shadow cast by the island crept closer, slowly devouring the labyrinth, and then with a final flash the sun slipped out of sight, darkness enveloping them. Bren startled as Jerym grabbed her arm, but then he just as quickly let go, his face flushed with embarrassment.

"It's all right," Bren told him, reaching out to slip her hand into his and give a comforting squeeze. She knew what had come over him, as she felt it as well – the thought of a small mountain hanging suspended directly over their heads by magic or some invisible force was terrifying. If just a small chunk sloughed away and came tumbling down they would be crushed flat.

Bren hadn't even realized she'd been holding her breath until they emerged from the shadow. Jerym disentangled their fingers and rushed to the wall to peer up at the island as it slowly moved away from them.

"Did you see any of those winged snakes?" he asked, almost babbling. "I saw them earlier darting around another of the islands. If they are from our world, they're not from anywhere near Velasch . . . at least so far as I know."

"I think you'll get your chance to search for them," Seris said. "That island is getting lower."

"You're right," Bren said, her pulse quickening. The island was indeed descending towards the ground, and it looked to her like it would settle into the pit scooped out of the field.

"My supposition is looking better and better," Jerym said with a nervous swallow.

"Your *what*?" Seris asked and then made a cutting motion with her hand when Jerym opened his mouth to answer. "Never mind, I don't care." She turned to Bren. "I think we have to assume the dragon is on that island. When it reaches the ground, the Karths and Ahzans and the Varyxes – if any of them survived – will try to be the first to reach the egg. We have to be ready to go."

"You two don't have to come," Bren told them, holding each of their gazes in turn. "Neither of you want to be dragon riders. I can't ask you to risk yourselves to help me claim the hatchling. You'll be safe here with everyone else rushing to the island."

Seris snorted, rolling her eyes. "I want nothing more than to help deny those spoiled brats."

"And I have to see what's there," Jerym said. "My mother would be aghast if I told her I passed on the chance to explore such a place." He paused, glancing at Bren as the color again rose in his cheeks. "Also, I don't want to be left alone."

"All right, then," Bren said, putting her hand on his shoulder. "But I want you to hide if you see any Karths. Let Seris and me handle them."

Jerym's fingers went to the hilt of the serrated dagger he'd shoved into his belt, but Bren shook her head firmly and he let his hand fall away, looking chagrined.

"They're getting ready," Seris said. Bren turned to see that the other aspirants had emerged from behind their walls – it looked to her like Zair and Merith had both gathered a half-dozen of their family members during their time in the labyrinth – better odds than she had feared, if she was being honest. Perhaps they could let those two factions fight first, and then she and Seris could deal with whoever survived.

"Then we should get ready, too," replied Bren, climbing on to the wall and offering a hand to Jerym. Seris joined them, somehow accomplishing this feat while still holding her bow. It seemed to Bren that they should leap down and start making their way towards the pit, but the sight of the massive hunk of earth slowly descending was so incredible that they could only watch in awed silence. And they weren't the only ones – the Karth and Ahzan aspirants also appeared to be waiting until the island settled before charging forward.

"There are more of them," Seris said, quickly checking her bowstring. "A lot more. So we go fast and try to beat them to the egg. I was told whoever finds it first and touches the shell wins the Winnowing. That is our goal."

I have to admit I was excited to cross swords with the boy who moves like a blademaiden.

I wouldn't be surprised if you still got your chance, Bren replied.

A tremble traveled up through the wall as the island touched the ground, its bulging base vanishing into the pit. The fit was far less than perfect, which was just more evidence – to go along with the lush vegetation covering the ruins – that this was not where this island had originated. The entire topside was canted slightly, and one of the crumbling towers pressed up against the edge of the island collapsed in a slow-moving avalanche, blocks of stone spilling across the yellow-grass field.

"With me!" Seris cried as a great haze of dust billowed up from the impact of the island arriving. She made a beckoning motion, then leaped down and started running.

Bren glanced at Jerym and saw the fear in his face, so she attempted a comforting smile and laid a hand on his shoulder. "You'll be fine," she said. "Soon this will all be over."

He breathed out shakily. "Come on, we have to hurry, or one of those bastards will win."

"Can't let that happen," Bren said with a wink before jumping from the wall. She heard a grunt and a thump as Jerym followed her, and then they were off, chasing the dark smudge that was Seris charging into the dust. For a moment Bren feared they would lose sight of her, but then the kalish girl stopped and waited for them to catch up.

"Protect yourself!" Seris cried just before the choking wave of grit washed over them all. Bren closed her eyes and pulled her tunic up to cover her mouth, and when the dust had abated a few moments later she found her companions coated in a layer of filth. Seris grimaced, running her hand through matted curls now more brown than red, and Jerym looked more like one of the Ratman's grimy charges than an imperial scion. Bren wanted nothing more than to scrub herself clean, but there was no time to waste, and with an unspoken agreement they resumed their run towards the looming ruins.

The area where the edges of the island had collided violently with the ground was a mess of jagged rock and upthrust earth, but it was still navigable, and soon they were scrambling up one side to the greenery above. It did grow steeper, and they had to use the roots from the trees as handholds to pull themselves up. Jerym lacked the arm strength to overcome the more treacherous sections, but Bren was always there to lend aid, and after a brief but strenuous climb they reached the top of the island together. They collapsed on the thick grass breathing hard, and while recovering Bren used this time to examine their new surroundings.

Not that she could see very far. The denseness of the vegetation was unlike anything she had seen before, even in the deepest and darkest depths of the forests of the Seven Valleys. The trees did not cluster overly thick – in truth, their gnarled, creeper-wrapped trunks were fairly far apart, but it was everything else filling the space between. Great sprays of spade-shaped fronds burst forth from the ground, warring with tangled bushes spotted with yellow, bell-shaped flowers, and vines dangled down from bowed branches in such profusion that they formed curtains veiling what lurked deeper in. There was life in far greater abundance than elsewhere in the labyrinth – brightly colored birds flitted between the trees, and a legion of hand-sized insects with iridescent wings hovered near Bren's head, as if intrigued by her sudden appearance. She waved to try to scatter them, but they only retreated for a few moments before returning. At least they didn't seem interested in feeding on her.

"Look at this," Jerym breathed in wonder, reaching out towards one of the buzzing insects. It danced away, but he did not seem disappointed. "There must be dozens of unknown species just in this little area. Can you believe it?" His eyes were wide. "Why have the warlocks never shared this with us? If my mother knew, she would have begged my uncle to let her explore this place."

"Perhaps that's why they haven't," Seris said, climbing to her feet and trying to brush the layer of dust and dirt from her clothes.

Bren heaved herself upright, staggering slightly as the blood rushing to her head made her dizzy. This seemed to excite the swarm, which darted in closer before she chased them away again with a sweep of her arm. "There's no time to dawdle," she said, pulling aside one of the vine-curtains. "We need to go quickly. The other aspirants are probably already on the island."

Seris straightened at that reminder, her gaze sharpening. "Lead on," she said, drawing an arrow and setting it to her bowstring.

Jerym made a disappointed sound, but he followed Bren as she started to push through the choking vegetation.

They had not gone very far before a sharp command from Ashika brought Bren to a sudden halt.

Stop.

"What is it?" hissed Seris from behind her, and Bren heard the creak of the kalishwoman's bow being readied.

"I don't know," Bren murmured, peering into the encroaching tangle.

What is it? she asked the ghost, echoing Seris.

Listen.

Bren focused on the sounds around her, but she heard only the wind whispering in the leaves overhead and a crackling as Jerym shifted his feet in the underbrush.

I hear nothing.

Exactly. The forest has suddenly quieted. Where are the birds that were chattering? The crying of the tree frogs? This sort of silence . . . it usually means only one thing.

And what is that? Bren asked though she feared she already knew the answer.

A predator.

"It's too quiet," Bren said, pitching her voice low enough that she hoped only her companions could hear. "Something might be near."

"Stalking us," Seris said in agreement, swiveling to aim an arrow back the way they had come. The path they had made through the forest had already disappeared, the vegetation returning to fill the gaps.

"Stalking is such an aggressive word. I think 'observing' is more appropriate."

Seris whirled around at the unexpected voice, aiming her arrow at a branch high above their heads. Bren could see snatches of black between the leaves, and then a shiver of movement as whoever it was descended to a slightly lower branch.

Bren prepared herself for anything, but that voice was familiar . . .

"You," she said flatly as the speaker moved out from behind the foliage, his ragged black cape fluttering as he squatted down to regard them.

The creature Desian had called Garith smiled toothily down at her, then doffed his broad-brimmed hat in greeting.

"Me!" he exclaimed. "And it is so good to meet you again, Bren."

"Who are you?" snarled Seris. "Answer quick, or I'll put this arrow in you."

Garith rocked back on his heels, clapping his hands in delight. "Oh! Such a fierce soul!" He shifted his attention to where Jerym was gaping up at him. "And this one! You've found a rabbit and a tiger, Brenna!"

"You know him?" Seris asked, the arrow she had drawn back still trained on the gaunt, grinning creature.

"His name is Garith," Bren said, throwing her shoulders back and putting her hand on the hilt of her sword. "He's some kind of sorcerer."

Not a sorcerer. Something else. He reminds me of things the Black Mountain graycloaks invited into our world . . . yet he is different, as well.

Garith had cocked his head to one side, listening to Ashika. "You are near the truth, spirit, but also very far away."

"What does he mean by 'spirit'?" Seris muttered, and Bren could hear beneath the forced steadiness in her voice a rising panic. The kalishwoman visibly swallowed, adjusting her grip on the shaft. Bren saw a slight trembling in her fingers, as if she was having trouble keeping herself from loosing the arrow.

"It's all right," Bren said, laying her hand gently on Seris's arm. "He's not a threat . . . I think."

"A threat?" Garith scoffed, fluttering his unnaturally long fingers as if to dismiss such a ridiculous suggestion. "To you all? Of course not."

"Then what are you doing here?" Bren called up to him, folding her arms across her chest.

The creature Desian had also named the Raven Lord rose smoothly to his feet on the narrow branch and spread his arms wide to encompass their surroundings. "I came to investigate this place! It is not every day a doorway opens in my city – I did not even know the dragon lords possessed any of the keys! And here I thought they had all been lost. And this is such a fascinating folding. The rules are different here, though I'm sure you've discovered that for yourselves."

"We can't die," Bren said.

Garith wagged a pale finger at Bren's assertion. "You can, Brenna. But it is true that in most instances your spirit will merely return to my beautiful city. The rules have been bent, you see, but not broken entirely."

Bren sighed. The longer they spent distracted by this creature, the more likely one of the other aspirants would claim the dragon first. "So you came here to explore. But I want to know why you're *here*, right now, talking to us."

Garith blinked his golden cat-eyes, as if surprised by this question. "Why, Brenna, don't be rude – I merely wanted to warn you about *that*." He pointed at something behind them, a sly grin crooking the corners of his too-wide mouth.

Brenna turned. The patch of dense forest Garith had indicated seemed empty of any dangers. There was just a large, misshapen tree, its trunk bulging with fuzzy growths and draped by vines. It looked like any number of other trees they had already passed . . .

Wait.

A shiver came high in the branches. Bren gripped her sword's hilt, peering intently where she'd thought she'd seen movement. But everything was still again, except for the leaves trembling in the faint breeze.

"Don't. Move."

The dread in Seris's voice made Bren's blood run cold. "You see something?" she hissed back, wanting to draw her sword but afraid the scrape of steel would draw the attention of whatever Seris had glimpsed.

"Look twenty paces up, the big branch with the yellow flowers."

Bren followed her instructions, but whatever it was still remained a mystery. Unless...

She drew in a sharp breath, her hold on her sword's hilt tightening. Coiled on the branch was a huge serpent, its scales perfectly matching the brownish green of the tree. As Bren watched it moved slightly, and she was sure its color also shifted so that it remained in perfect accordance with its surroundings. She couldn't tell exactly how big it was with the way its coils were piled, but its head looked larger than any man's. Easily large enough to swallow a child whole if the jaw could unhinge like other snakes she'd seen.

"Oh!" Jerym cried suddenly, startling Bren. "A snake! Can you see it? It's so big!"

He quieted as Seris cuffed him on the back of his head, but the damage had been done – the serpent seemed to realize it had been spotted, and it slithered to the edge of its perch. Something unfolded from its body – wings that flexed, then spread wide as the serpent lifted the front part of its body from the branch, rearing back.

The next moment seemed to last an eternity and less than an eye blink.

Seris released her arrow just as the snake lunged from the branch. The sudden movement was enough to throw off her shot, and the arrow flashed past harmlessly to sink into the gnarled trunk. Bren only noticed this peripherally, as she was focused on the uncoiling serpent soaring towards Jerym with fangs bared. He was rooted to the ground, too surprised to even scream or raise his hands.

Bren reacted on instinct. She surged towards him, ripping her sword free of its scabbard and slicing upwards in the same motion. A small shock traveled up her arms as her blade met the snake's neck just below its fringe of spines, then passed through scales and flesh and bone without stopping. The beast's head went flying as the bulk of its length continued on to slam into Jerym, sending him sprawling underneath writhing snake flesh and flailing wings.

"Ah!" he screamed, beating at the thrashing coils as blood sprayed from the stump where its head had been just a moment ago. Seris was the first to react, dropping her bow and with a grunt of effort heaving the thick body away from Jerym. It landed amongst the roots of a tree, still moving, though the spasms were subsiding as realization slowly seeped into the monster that it was dead. Bren fell to her knees beside Jerym, who was taking in gulping, panicked breaths, his face ashen where it wasn't painted in serpent blood.

"Are you hurt?" she cried, looking to see if any limbs had been twisted unnaturally by the weight of the snake's bulk. He turned to her with eyes wide. Blood covered him and soaked his tunic, but she didn't think it was his own. His lips moved, but she couldn't hear anything over the sound of the serpent's last convulsions in the underbrush. She lowered her ear to his mouth, gripping his arm tight to offer some reassurance that the danger had passed.

"He's gone," Jerym whispered, staring past her, and Bren turned to find that Garith had disappeared.

Bren tore a strip of cloth from her own clothes and used it to clean the boy's blood-spattered face. He blinked, trying to focus on her.

"Who was he?" Jerym asked, his words slightly slurred. He was in shock, Bren realized. She'd seen it before when she'd rescued Tal from the soldiers at the gallows.

Seris had disappeared into the undergrowth a moment ago, and now she emerged holding the serpent's severed head by one of its neck spines, then tossed it onto the grass near Bren. "It's a flying snake like the toad ate. But much bigger."

"Not as big as the ones I've seen flying around the islands from afar," Bren said, gently wiping away the last of the sticky, reddish-black blood from Jerym's face. She paused, squinting at the snake's head in surprise. "Are those feathers or scales?"

"Something in between," Seris said. "It looks as much bird as snake, and they can change color, so we need to be careful. Others could be hiding in any of these trees."

That seemed to penetrate Jerym's fog, because he sucked in his breath in fear, his gaze going to the canopy above their heads.

"I doubt they'll come for you when you're covered with their brother's blood," Bren assured him, though she had no idea if this was true.

"Who was that man?" Seris asked, nudging the feathered coils of the dead snake with her boot. "He knew you."

"We met once."

"You named him sorcerer. That's what the people of this land call warlocks."

Bren helped pull Jerym to his feet. He swayed a little, but then found his balance.

"I don't know what he is."

"But you know him. Why?"

Bren swallowed, her thoughts racing as she tried to think of an explanation that might make sense.

"He appeared when I first arrived in Yestra. He was interested in me, maybe because I had come for the Winnowing."

Seris gave her a measuring look. "So a sorcerer of Yestra has followed us into this place and now intercedes to save you. In the legion we tell stories of this realm's warlocks, these sorcerers of the Jade House. How they drink blood to grow strong and worship a demon goddess. I was at a battle where a dark mist was summoned that swallowed a whole cohort of Ghentish cavalry. Devoured them; only bones were left when the shadows cleared. I lost a friend that day, a boy from the marches. That was the work of those sorcerers. And now we have one following us? *Helping* us?"

"I don't know why," Bren said quickly.

Seris narrowed her eyes, as if she wasn't sure she believed this to be true. "If I see him again, I'm putting an arrow in his neck," she said, loud enough that Bren suspected she wasn't just talking to her.

"We should continue," Bren said. "The others must be on the island by now. If we don't hurry, then this whole terrible ordeal will have been for naught."

"Lead on, then," Seris said flatly, her gaze slowly traveling over the tangle of limbs and vines, her fingers so tight around her bow's grip that her knuckles had whitened.

29

Bren watched the branches carefully as she pushed through the thick undergrowth, but they encountered no more of those feathered snakes. Still, she breathed a sigh of relief when the trees began to thin and the edge of the forest appeared ahead. She would much rather be out in the open, far away from where the color-shifting serpents could ambush them from the trees that pressed oppressively close.

When they finally stumbled out of the woods they found themselves in the middle of a war.

"By the Endless!" Seris hissed, pulling Bren and Jerym back into the shadowed fringes of the forest.

A broken landscape of jagged rock and the shattered remains of buildings stretched in front of them, eventually washing up against a great ruin. And across this wasteland battle had been joined. A trio of dark-haired Karth aspirants hunkered behind a toppled pillar, and at least two were archers, the tops of their bows poking up above the stone. Across from them in the destroyed remnants of a small house two Ahzan had taken cover in the collapsing doorway. An attempt had been made to venture across the no-man's-land between these two forces, as she could see a double-bladed ax and a pair of pikes lying in the rubble, likely all that remained after their wielders had perished. One Ahzan aspirant still sprawled there, propped up against a chunk of stone with a gaping wound that had nearly cleaved his arm away. His face was deathly pale, but even from this distance Bren could tell that he was not yet a corpse; his mouth was opening and closing, though nothing but blood was coming out, and he was still gripping the hilt of a gore-streaked sword.

Bren couldn't see Zair or the copper haired Ahzan girl Merith. The family champions must have pressed on into the ruins and left their lessers here.

"It doesn't look like we can skirt the edges of this fight," Seris said, her expression almost pained. "Both sides will see us if we try to get to that building. And we'll be out in the open, easy pickings if they have any skill with those bows."

"I need to get there," Bren replied in frustration. "If Zair is already inside, he will soon find the egg."

"You could make a run for it," Jerym said softly. He looked much improved from the immediate aftermath of the snake ambush – his eyes were clearer, and the color had returned to his cheeks. "We could distract them, draw their attention away."

Seris frowned, running her fingers down the length of her bow. "Bren would be exposed for half a hundred heartbeats. More than enough time for them to realize what's happening and put an arrow in her back."

"I have to try," Bren said grimly, already planning her route across the rubble-strewn expanse. She unshouldered her bow and handed it to Jerym, along with her half-full quiver. He accepted both with wide eyes.

Seris sighed. "I suppose there's no other choice." She motioned for Jerym to follow her as she began to pick her away along the forest's edge. "Stay in the shadows," she said to the boy, and he hurried to follow her. "And you," she said, turning back to Bren, "good luck. Wait until we start firing before you run."

Bren nodded, taking a deep breath to try to calm her racing heart. It *would* be lucky if she made it to that central building, and she hated leaving her fate to chance. But she had little choice. She just had to hope none of the aspirants were accomplished marksmen. If one of them had the same skill as Seris, she'd likely end up like that poor Ahzan aspirant, dying slowly as her life leaked away . . . She blinked in surprise, for that boy had vanished, leaving behind only his bloodied sword.

And then the first pair of arrows arced from the tree line where Seris and Jerym had gone. Shouts of alarm went up from the Karth aspirants crouched behind the fallen pillar as they scrambled for safety – one arrow skipped off the stone near a raven-haired girl, while the other – fluttering like a dying duck – embedded itself in the ground a good thirty paces away. Bren was certain she knew who had fired which arrow. The Karths were scrambling as they tried to find better cover, yelling and pointing towards the forest.

Bren dashed from the trees. She did not run in a straight line, changing her direction every few steps to make it more difficult for any archer who had seen her to predict the route she would take.

Like the field mouse trying to avoid the hawk.

Bren agreed with the voice in her head, although she didn't much appreciate the comparison.

Time crawled as the distance slowly shrank between her and the stone steps leading up to the pillared entrance. She had almost convinced herself that no one would notice her when an arrow suddenly shattered against a chunk of stone so close by that she felt shards of wood prickle her legs. Bren forced herself to continue instead of running for the nearest cover or looking around to see where that arrow had come from, and after a few dozen more agonizing strides she reached the base of the steps and began the ascent. Another black-fletched arrow bounced off the stone near her, but her luck held and when she finally arrived at the top of the steps unscathed she threw herself behind one of the pillars. She stayed there with her back to the cracked stone for a few moments breathing hard, then risked a glance out at the scene below. To her relief, no one had followed her, and whoever had tried to strike her down had apparently already turned their attention to the other two factions. She couldn't see where Seris or Jerym had hidden, but from the occasional arrow lofting towards the trees she could roughly guess where they had taken cover.

There was no time to worry about them. Bren turned back to the interior of the building – it was a shadowy forest of pillars punctured by light stabbing down from gaping holes in the high ceiling. Dust glittered in these slanting columns, swirling as if recently disturbed. And yes, Bren could see many footsteps leading deeper into the structure and even a smear of what looked like fresh blood. When her gaze followed this trail, it led to the motionless body of a girl slumped against another pillar. Her head lolled, hiding her face, but from the long copper hair marred by a single shock of deepest black Bren knew who this must be. Merith had been stabbed in the belly, and an astonishing amount of blood darkened the surrounding stone. She must be dead, but then why hadn't her body—

A ragged cough echoed in the high hall, and Merith raised her head to stare straight at Bren. Her face was ghost-white, and it looked as if she was sitting in a pool of every drop of blood that had once been inside her.

This one is not long for this world, Ashika murmured in Bren's head. *Forget her and find the egg.*

"You," Merith rasped, showing red-stained teeth in what might have been an attempt at a smile.

"Me," Bren said, approaching the dying girl warily. She peered into the pillars marching into the distance, knowing she had no time to waste . . . and yet something made her linger.

"Did Zair do this?" she asked, staring at the gaping wound in Merith's midsection. Some of her entrails had spilled out and lay glistening in her lap.

The girl tilted her head to one side to regard Bren. She was showing impressive control, given how much agony she must be in.

"Who else?" Merith said, wincing as a ripple of pain passed across her face. "The bastard has wanted to stab me for years." She jerked her chin slightly in the direction indicated by the footsteps in the dust. "Go. Stop him from getting a dragon."

"Why do you care?" Bren asked. "Why did you save me from the monster? Why do you want me to succeed?"

Another spasm passed across Merith's face. When she spoke again, her halting voice was almost too faint to hear. "Why . . . do you think . . . I was helping *you*?" She bared her teeth in a bloody grimace, hissing in pain. "See you . . . on the other side," she managed in a faltering whisper, and then her head fell forward again. A heartbeat later she was gone, leaving behind only dark stains on the stone floor, an eddy of dust rushing in to fill the space where she had been.

How many of these Velaschin have died and been reborn? Even those who do not claim a dragon must be changed forever by this Winnowing.

What do you mean?

Feeling such pain, your life slipping away . . . you cannot be the same afterwards. I know this.

I don't want to learn this lesson, Bren thought, picking up her pace as she jogged deeper into the vast space.

Pray you never do, Ashika replied. *But here is where that will be decided.*

Something huge was resolving in the gloom, so large it nearly brushed the soaring roof. It was a tiered pyramid like she remembered from the caliphant's palace, but several times larger and much, much more ancient, its stone steps cracked and crumbling. And like back in Yestra, at its apex was the egg, resting in a curving piece of black metal atop a silver tripod. It shimmered with a metallic sheen from the daylight pouring down from the rents in the ceiling, and within its depths a shadow curled.

But that was not what brought her to an abrupt halt as she passed beyond the last of the great pillars. A massive winged snake lay at the base of the ziggurat, its black eyes staring at nothing and blood leaking from jaws that looked easily large enough to swallow a man whole. Cuts marred its iridescent feather-scales, and one of its wings had nearly been hacked from its massive body, dangling only by a thin, glistening tendon. Bren was sure this thing had grown too large to fly . . . though, admittedly, she also would have thought the same about dragons.

The monster's slayer slumped against one of the pyramid's lowest tiers, and for a moment Bren thought Zair Karth was also dead, but then he stirred, his dark eyes opening. His obsidian sword rasped as he dragged it from the step where it had lain, and then he set its curving tip onto the stone and used it to help him stand. He was clearly exhausted, his black hair damp with sweat, and his arms trembled as he pushed himself upright.

"I suppose this is fitting," he said.

Bren drew her own sword, taking a quick step back to stay beyond the reach of Zair's longer blade. "Where are your friends? I thought the girl and her nasty brother would be here."

Zair sighed dramatically and indicated the dead serpent with his blade. "I'm afraid this final guardian ended the Winnowing for them. Perhaps for the best, if I'm being honest, because I am fairly certain Alyia was going to try to claim the hatchling for herself. And as interesting as it would have been to see where Malisk's true loyalties reside, it would also have made future family gatherings rather awkward."

He is stalling to recover his strength, Ashika warned. *Do not let him. Bring the fight to him now!*

Zair must have noticed her sudden tensing because he quickly continued speaking.

"I know who your parents are," he said, and the shock of those words was like a blow to Bren's chest. She blinked, her sword dipping. "Or I think I do. I'm fairly sure. I wasn't supposed to hear the rumors, of course, but gossip so salacious is hard to suppress."

"Tell me," commanded Bren, raising her sword again.

Zair crooked a smile as he began to circle her. "No, I don't think I will. I think it better you go to your death never knowing." He chuckled. "Oh yes, your true death is coming. I am going to carve your heart out and chop it into tiny little pieces. And when I tell my father,

I think this will please him almost as much as knowing that his beloved son had done what he never could and become a rider."

"Who was my mother?" Bren whispered, but Zair just shook his head and settled into a guard position, knees bent and dark blade upraised.

And then he attacked.

He came at her in a flowing rush, his sword a flickering shadow. Bren had been expecting this, but still his speed and violence surprised her, and the fight was almost finished before it had even begun. Ashika's instincts seized her, and Bren just managed to turn aside the first slash and the following thrust. The clash of steel on dragon-fired obsidian was strangely discordant, though she had heard something similar when the paladin had drawn his moonblade outside her farmhouse in his final, desperate stand.

Stay close to him, Ashika said, a strained edge to her thoughts, as if it were really her who was parrying Zair's sword. *You must keep him from using his greater reach.*

But he's also so much stronger than me, Bren replied as a brutal shock traveled up her sword arm, numbing it. *And faster.*

Zair's lips were twisted into a frenzied grin as he pressed her, but despite the wildness in his face he managed to move with grace and precision, each strike carrying seamlessly into the next. Bren was driven backwards, until she could sense the vast bulk of the dead serpent behind her, and if the back of her legs bumped against those gleaming feather-scales she knew the fight would be finished, so she tried desperately to hold her ground against Zair's onslaught.

"How can you fight like this?" he spat, drawing back a step to catch his breath.

"My uncle taught me."

He shook his head vehemently, then lunged at her again. Bren blocked that thrust, skipping away to the side so that she wouldn't trip on any stray coils or scattered feather-scales.

"No," he sneered. "You fight like a sword dancer."

Nay, boy, answered Ashika, though of course Zair could not hear her. *It is you who fight like a blademaiden. Your people have preserved my art.*

After another rapid exchange, Zair's eyes narrowed and he paused again, panting heavily. Her first impression had been right – he *was* exhausted. "You are no simple orphan. Someone trained you and put you in this Winnowing. Why? To stop me?"

Bren attempted what she hoped was an infuriating smile. She was not the only one who could pretend to secrets. He was so much stronger and bigger and faster, but if his control slipped, she might gain the advantage.

"Was it that wench, Merith? Are you an Ahzan ploy?" Something occurred to him, concern entering his face. "Or is it the umbrari? What game is being played here?"

Bren could hear the frustration in his voice . . . the panic. He did not understand what was happening. She said nothing, merely holding the same sly smile that had driven him into this unbalanced state as she stalked forward. The uncertainty in his face deepened to something else.

Fear.

She slashed, for the first time going on the offensive. Zair caught her blade with his own, but that unearthly chime of steel on obsidian sounded different. Now it was he who was moving backwards as she pressed him, her sword a blur. With a snarl, he stopped himself from retreating and attempted to regain the initiative. This surprised Bren, for she had thought him faltering, and the edge of his black sword left a line of fire across her shoulder. She grimaced as a trickle of warmth began to run down her off-arm. This seemed to galvanize Zair, and he thrust forward again, but Bren twisted out of the way and opened up a gash on his thigh. He cried out, his leg nearly collapsing beneath him, and he just managed to hop backwards a step before she could bury her blade in his gut.

"I am the trueborn son of Bessam Karth!" he spat, his eyes wide and wild. "The dragon is *mine*!"

He lunged forward again, but this time his leg did betray him, and the strike was so clumsy Bren easily avoided it. She stepped fully inside his guard and thrust her sword into his midsection, and she felt Ashika guiding her hand, angling the blade upwards, seeking the boy's heart...

"No!" Bren cried, violently pulling her sword back. Zair watched the blade slide from his innards in mute astonishment, the hilt of his own sword slipping from his fingers. A harsh clang sounded as obsidian clattered on stone. He pressed both his hands to the wound, staring at the blood pouring from between his fingers as he stumbled backwards. With a grunt he collapsed onto the lowest step of the ziggurat, his face stricken.

You are still weak, Ashika told her reproachfully. *He said he was going to give you the true death. You must do that to him, or he will come for you again.*

For the first time since the ritual in the woods, Bren felt Ashika's will warring with her own, fighting for control. She stepped closer to where Zair was sprawled, raising her sword jerkily as she contested with the ghost; his breath was coming in ragged, rasping gasps, but still he realized what was happening, and he lifted a red-stained hand to ward her away.

"No . . ." he whispered, blood bubbling from his lips.

Pierce his heart! commanded the voice in her head. *Avenge your family!*

Bren's arm shook as she laid the tip of her sword against his chest. Zair stared at the steel in dazed horror, feebly twisting his body to try to escape.

She could feel Ashika straining with all her strength to force Bren to thrust down, to end the boy's life both in this world and in the other. She heaved a shuddering breath, so tempted to give in to what the spirit wanted.

And yet she did not.

"He has done nothing to me," Bren said hoarsely, drawing back the sword. Zair watched the blade retreat in astonished relief, and then a heaving spasm traveled up from deep within him and he sagged back into the steps, his limbs going slack. He looked almost peaceful as the pain and fear and anger drained away, smoothing the lines on his face.

He looked like a boy.

Bren cast her sword aside, a swell of nausea rising inside her. She had almost murdered him, and why? Because he had said unkind things to her? Threatened her? Dared to try to claim the hatchling she wanted?

He was your enemy, said Ashika. *And now he will stay your enemy.*

So be it! she thought savagely in reply. *I will not kill him!*

And then Zair's body was gone. Even his obsidian sword vanished, unlike the other weapons of this place, more evidence that it had been brought into the labyrinth from their world.

Bren felt Ashika's presence retreat, but she ignored the sulking ghost and turned her attention to the egg and the shadow within.

Letting out a steadying breath, Bren began to climb the steep steps. Her life had been building towards this moment ever since the Old Drake had told her of the Winnowing . . . no, it had begun even before that, when she'd peeked around the edge of the shutters and glimpsed those impossible monsters outside her farmhouse. They had destroyed her family, burned her heart to ashes, but now a dragon offered her a path to the strength she needed . . . She would turn the greatest weapon of the Velaschin against them, save the Silver Mother before they could tear her from the sky, stop this reign of fire from consuming the Flowering Coast and the Seven Valleys . . .

The shadow inside the egg shifted, as if to better watch her approach.

What would happen when she touched the shell? Would it break apart as the hatchling burst forth? Or would—

Something slammed into Bren's back, spinning her around and sending her sprawling onto the steps. She gasped in shock and pain as whatever had struck her was shoved deeper into her flesh by the stone she lay upon, so hard and sharp and terrible. With shaking hands, she touched the front of her tunic, expecting to feel this thing emerging from her chest, but it remained lodged deep inside her, filling her with searing agony. Her sight dimmed as she fought to keep from slipping into the black.

"What?" Bren murmured through lips wet with coppery blood, struggling to focus on the movement below her.

Her vision suddenly sharpened, and she could clearly see the sun-splashed, crumbling steps and the figure climbing them.

Seris loomed over her, still holding her bow. She paused, looking down at Bren with pursed lips, then she brushed a stray red curl from her face as she turned to what waited higher up the pyramid.

The egg.

Bren struggled to speak through the blood in her mouth. She raised a trembling hand, but Seris ignored her as she continued on. passing out of Bren's eyesight.

Why? she wanted to say, wanted to *scream*, but she could only shape this question inside herself and hurl it at the presence sharing her mind.

Ashika did not answer, stunned into silence.

Coldness welled up from below her, a numbing darkness. She felt like she was sinking into a frozen sea, her senses evaporating, growing more frayed until she was perceiving the world through a rapidly dwindling keyhole.

She was dying.

But that couldn't be . . . She would fall asleep here and wake back in her tent in Yestra.

Unless . . . unless . . .

The arrow Seris had shot into her back had nicked her heart.

Bren wanted to reach around her body and take hold of the shaft embedded in her flesh and rip it out, but her arms refused to move. She sank deeper and deeper into the abyssal depths . . . until suddenly she felt strong hands grasp her waist, lifting her upwards. Her head broke the surface, and she drew in a shuddering, life-sustaining breath. Someone was beneath her, holding her so she wouldn't slip fully into the dark.

Ashika.

The spirit was keeping oblivion away, but she could feel the strength fading in the spirit as Ashika strained to keep Bren's soul tethered to her dying body . . .

And then something changed.

The force dragging her down lessened and was gone. Instead, something new was drawing her upwards, out of the clinging dark and towards a great shining circle hovering high above . . . The Silver Mother beckoned her home, and sobbing with joy Bren spread her arms wide to embrace Her.

30

B ren coughed blood, spattering Jaleska. Shocked, the sister of the Temple Draconium reeled back from the bed, her face aghast. Beside her the young warlock who had ushered Bren into the Winnowing looked on in shock. Lamps had been lit, their light hazy with the residue of the smoke. Bren registered vaguely that night must have fallen in the City of Lotuses, but her immediate concern was the pain in her chest, like someone had jammed a knife between her ribs. She made a mewling sound, clawing at the front of her aspirant robes.

"What's wrong?" cried Jaleska, the whites of her eyes stark against the redness painting her face.

"It's her heart!" the warlock babbled. "It's been pierced in the other realm!"

"Save her!" Jaleska screamed, rushing to Bren's side as she gasped for breath.

"I can't!" the warlock yelled back, looking scared and helpless. "She's dying!"

"She can't die!" Jaleska seized hold of Bren's arm and shook it fiercely. "You can't die! Hold on!"

It's all right, Bren wanted to say to the terrified girl as she subsided back into the mound of pillows. A warmth was stealing over her as the pain faded. *My family is waiting for me . . .*

The roof of the tent vanished.

Crisp night air flooded what had a moment ago been enclosed by the tent, extinguishing the braziers and plunging everything into darkness. But the black was not seamless – stars gleamed in the great arc of the sky that had now been revealed, and the Silver Mother hung heavy and pendulous, pregnant with the next month's sun. The scars left by the demon Maliskaith were etched so clearly in her shining face that Bren imagined she could see them glistening wetly, as if fresh-carved. She concentrated on the Mother, and around her the screams of the others and the roaring of the wind grew fainter and fainter until Bren's entire world was bounded by the goddess's gentle curves and pitted surface.

Take me, she mouthed, reaching with a trembling hand.

The moon and the stars disappeared, blotted out by a great shadow.

"No," Bren moaned, but then she felt something enclose her, and she was lifted from the cushions, her blanket sliding away. A cool breeze licked her skin, but it was the thing that had slid beneath her and borne her upwards that made her shiver. Cold and smooth and hard, like iron on a winter night.

The Silver Mother had answered Bren's prayer. She would see her mother again – her true mother – and her father, and dear little Helat. Tears wet Bren's cheeks as she was devoured by the rushing dark.

WHEN BREN RETURNED to herself she didn't know where she was. A gray dawn had replaced the night, though faded stars and the faint outline of the Mother were still visible above. She lay on the same hard, pebbled surface she remembered carrying her into the sky, but it was no longer moving. Bren breathed in deeply, expecting to feel a stabbing in her chest, but there was nothing. The pain that had flared so bright and hot inside her was gone, as if it had never been. The sensation of Ashika's ghost in her head was also missing, a cold absence that to Bren's surprise made her feel empty. Where had she gone? She'd saved Bren after Seris had put an arrow in her, holding her up as the darkness rose.

And what was this place? Thick, crooked pillars rose around her like the bars in a cage, though the space between each was so wide she could have easily slipped between them. The uneven platform was just barely large enough for her curled body, and as Bren climbed slowly to her feet she steadied herself against one of the curving pillars. It felt odd, like it was covered with many overlapping pieces of metal. Bren frowned, then after bracing herself leaned out into the gap between two of the columns and looked down.

She jerked herself back, hissing in surprise. Impossible. Slowly and much more carefully, she brought herself to the edge again.

Below her a vertical wall of stone plunged down to where the sea dashed against jagged black rocks. She must be atop a tower, as no cliff so smooth could have come about naturally. Light was spilling from somewhere near the top of the structure, not very far beneath where she now stood, and the way it moved as it illuminated the wall below suggested there was a large fire burning in the uppermost floor.

Bren had heard of such buildings, though she had never seen one. This must be a lighthouse, where great fires were lit to guide ships away from rocks or into port. But how and why had she been brought to its roof just as dawn was breaking?

The pillar she was leaning against suddenly moved. Bren gasped, reeling backwards as a vision of this strange platform collapsing and toppling into the distant sea came to her. She staggered into the center of the space as it shifted beneath her, and she would have screamed if she hadn't suddenly felt something inside her.

"Ashika! What's going on?" Bren cried.

The ghost did not answer. It was not the blademaiden, she realized. This presence from outside pushing into her mind was so much greater and stranger than anything she had felt before. Bren fell to her knees holding her head, but after a moment something compelled her to look up again into the lightening sky.

Except that the sky had vanished. And in its place, gilded by the breaking dawn, was a dragon.

Bren whimpered when she realized it was staring down at her. That she was being held in its massive hand, the columns rising around her its talon-tipped fingers. With a gesture it could crush her or send her tumbling down to where the rocks waited.

Sensations trickled into her, which could only be from the dragon. Bren was safe; nothing would hurt her. It wanted her to know that.

"You saved me?" Bren whispered, far too softly to be heard over the gusting wind . . . yet in answer an image seeped into her consciousness. A memory.

The wind, rushing over scales. Stars blazing above. Tents scattered on tiny islands below, terrible emanations. Screams of pain.

The girl's screams.

The girl is dying. She knows her from before. She recognizes her . . . She senses what they share.

No time to waste. Claws hook the fabric of the tent, rip it open. And Bren sees herself writhing on a mound of cushions, Jaleska and the warlock staring up at her – no, not her, at the dragon – staring up in shock and terror as she seizes the girl and carries her into the sky. But still the life is trickling away. And so she does what she thought she would never do again and opens herself to the dying girl. She offers, and the girl accepts.

"We are bonded?" Bren murmured numbly, unable to fully understand what the dragon was trying to tell her. Another memory rose up unbidden – a man gesturing towards where she hid behind the shutters of her farmhouse and the great monsters crouching behind him stir, jaws opening wide.

"You are the storm dragon. The hatchling's mother," Bren said, groping for the name Jaleska had once told her.

Something flowed across the bridge that now spanned their minds, and Bren saw a thick fog lit by distant flickers of lightning. "Mist," she suddenly remembered. "Your name is Mist."

A warm pulse entered Bren. Was this its affirmation? No, not it, Bren corrected herself – this dragon was a mother. And she recalled what else Jaleska had told her about the storm dragon – she was in mourning for her rider. Her sadness – that terrible grief – had overwhelmed Bren on her first day in Yestra. She remembered this massive head that was now looking down at her lifting from within that great arena, the sorrow flowing from the dragon touching something similar within Bren.

Was that why the dragon had saved her?

Mist lowered her great head to peer more closely at Bren. She felt the hairs on her arm rise, but she wasn't sure if that was happening because of the crackling power wreathing the storm dragon or because she was now so close to those massive jaws that Mist could toss Bren into her mouth like a fresh-picked berry.

But Bren knew she would not do this . . . she felt it. Before when she'd stood in the presence of dragons, she'd sensed their emotions as a vague penumbra difficult to parse and comprehend. This was very different. Sharper. More layered. She felt the dragon's curiosity, her wariness, her affection . . . her excitement. The darkness clouding the dragon's mind had lifted, letting in a ray of light.

Bren swayed and nearly fell, overwhelmed by everything. She had been told to claim a hatchling, and yet somehow she had ended up with this ancient, terrifying creature.

Mist must have sensed her discomfort because the dragon's mind drew back, giving her the space to order her thoughts.

She had failed in the trials but won far more than Tharos and Desian could have ever dreamed. A storm dragon – a greater dragon, as Jaleska had explained to her what felt like ages ago – had chosen her as its new rider. Bonded with her. But what did that mean?

And what about Ashika? Bren turned inward, searching for the spirit, but there was nothing. The ghost of the blademaiden was gone. Bren hoped Ashika had been pushed down deep inside Bren, like what Desian had accomplished with his ritual, but she had a sinking suspicion that this time was different. She remembered Ashika holding her up as the dark waters rose, how the spirit had refused to let her slip into the black. Had she sacrificed herself to save Bren? Could a ghost die?

Thank you, Bren thought, even though she knew Ashika could not hear her.

The dragon tilted her head to one side as she regarded Bren, as if puzzled. It was a strangely human movement. Could she sense that Bren was trying to communicate with something else? Or was she reacting to the gratitude Bren felt towards Ashika? This was all so new and strange. She wondered if Seris was having the same experience with Mist's hatchling.

Seris.

Bren had avoided thinking about what had happened in the labyrinth, but now emotions rose within her, sharp and raw. Anger at the betrayal. Confusion. And sadness. Why had she done that? Why had Seris nearly *killed* her?

The dragon seemed to sense her agitation. A rumbling began deep inside Mist, making the scales Bren stood upon tremble. Wisps of crackling energy escaped from the corners of the dragon's mouth before quickly dissipating.

Another image slipped into Bren's thoughts: a silver-blue dragon, wings outspread, drifted over a sea of clouds burnished gold by the morning sun. Peace flooded her, and the distress Bren felt about Seris's actions lessened dramatically.

The dragon was trying to comfort her.

"I'm all right," she said, forcing a smile. She wasn't sure if dragons could even read human expressions, but she suspected Mist understood quite a lot, perhaps even speech. She certainly seemed to be offering responses when Bren spoke to her.

"I just need to—oh!"

Bren staggered as the hand she was standing on moved, the fingers rising around her curling in slightly so that the gaps were no longer large enough to fit through. She was lifted, passing over the dragon's massive, sharp-bladed shoulder and then deposited directly beside one of her wings. Mist relaxed her taloned hand, providing

Bren with an opportunity to clamber out onto this great expanse of scales.

But this wasn't where she wanted Bren to go. Beyond where this wing joined with Mist's body a line of low, blunted spines ran down the center of the great dragon's back. And wedged between two of these protrusions, held in place by straps that curved downwards and out of sight, was a saddle.

"Oh," Bren murmured, awed by the implications. "I don't know if—"

Once again, the dragon did not wait for Bren. Gently she tipped her wing, and with a surprised yelp Bren staggered forwards. The wing was very slightly canted, but Mist apparently had quite a bit of experience helping her rider to mount this way because the slope was easy enough to keep her balance. Swallowing hard and trying not to imagine the thousand-span fall that yawned below the membrane she stood upon, Bren gingerly walked the length of the wing until she reached Mist's body. Then by using a series of natural handholds – gnarled barbs and bristles emerging from among the scales – she pulled herself over to where the saddle was situated. It was taller than what would be used on a horse, so that the rider's legs could dangle down rather than have to splay out wide across the dragon's broad back.

Staring down at the beautifully tooled saddle, the uncracked leather clearly well-cared for given the lacquer that had built up after countless applications of animal fat, Bren couldn't help but think about who had last been in this seat. A warrior of Velasch. Had she swooped over battlefields and cities, directing Mist to kill? Was Bren joining herself to a creature that had laid waste to her lands and people?

The image came again of the storm dragon soaring through the morning sky. Bren felt Mist's yearning to show her the beauty that could be found above the clouds. Perhaps the dragon was just like a soldier pressed into service by her lord. Maybe she was like Bren, merely a piece in a game played by queens and emperors and sorcerers.

As Bren settled into the saddle, she felt something like a shiver or a sigh pass through the dragon. She fumbled with the saddle's straps as the wings to either side of her lifted and stretched, and then with a roar that shook the heavens Mist launched herself from the top of the lighthouse and ascended into the sky.

Bren shrieked in terror and joy.

31

Bren rolled Tal's pebble around in her pocket, more nervous than when she had been plummeting through the clouds astride Mist. She stood in an uncomfortably tight uniform of red and black riding leathers – or flying leathers, she supposed – on the highest dais in the caliphant's palace, looking out over a sea of Velaschin. The last time she had been in this hall, the hatchling's egg had been placed just about where she was now, and she had fainted after brushing her fingers against the shell. Staring down at the steepness of the steps cascading to the floor below, Bren was grateful she hadn't dashed her skull open back then.

She had never met the man who stood beside her, but as soon as he'd entered the hall she'd known who he must be. The resemblance to Zair was uncanny, right down to the sardonic tilt of his mouth and the sharpness of his dark eyes, though he walked with a limp, his left foot dragging slightly on the pink marble tiles. When he'd introduced himself as Bessam Karth, governor of Yestra, she had not been surprised. What *had* surprised her was the tenor of his greeting – she had stabbed his son in another world, ending his dream of claiming a dragon, yet she had felt no ill will emanating from the Velaschin lord. Zair was another matter. She had glimpsed him slinking into the hall from where she stood up on the dais, and this had reminded her of his claim that he knew who her true parents were. A ploy to unbalance her before their fight, surely, and it had very nearly worked. If Ashika had not been there to steady her, she likely would have lost her focus and her life.

Before Zair had disappeared into the milling Velaschin their eyes had met, and the sullen hate in his face – deathly pale just like her own, a result of dying during the Winnowing – had sent a little thrill through her, and she'd stuck out her tongue to infuriate him further.

At least he wasn't dead – he should be grateful to her for that.

She felt no such thanks towards the other person who shared the top of the dais with her and Bessam. Seris stood on the far side of the governor of Yestra, tall and straight-backed as she watched the shifting crowd. The kalishwoman had not so much as glanced over at Bren since she'd ascended the steps to join her, though from her stiffness she couldn't entirely hide the tension she must be feeling.

And she was right to feel uncomfortable, since she was being forced to share this moment with someone she had fought beside and then betrayed. Not only betrayed, but very nearly killed. The desire to know *why* Seris had done what she did burned inside Bren, and when the formal ceremony concluded, she wouldn't let the kalish girl escape without confronting her. She owed Bren an explanation. At least she hadn't done anything terrible to Jerym – Bren hadn't seen the boy since the Winnowing concluded, but she'd asked around and learned he'd also returned to Yestra unscathed.

Beside her, Governor Bessam raised his hands for quiet and the hum of conversation filling the palace almost instantly subsided. For a moment his gaze swept those gathered, and then he lowered his arms and cleared his throat.

"Lords and ladies of the four families! Esteemed merchants and scholars of the empire! We come here today to celebrate the conclusion of the first Winnowing ever held on this side of the Cull and to honor the champion who has defeated her rivals." He grasped Seris's wrist, lifting her arm high as if to ensure all knew which of them had actually triumphed in the trials. "Seris of clan r'Haeth of the Kalish

Marches, today reborn as Seris ben-r'Haeth, new rider of a male sun dragon. All the empire rejoices!"

A cheer went up from the Velaschin, but given the fullness of the hall Bren thought it was more than a little muted. Were they disappointed that an aspirant not from their family had won the Winnowing? Or were they upset that a common-born kalishwoman could now call herself a dragon rider? Bren suspected it was the latter, and from the look on Seris's face she must have thought the same – the slight sneer had broadened into a grin, as if she was reveling in the displeasure her triumph had caused.

Bessam seemed to notice this as well, though he looked more amused than irritated. He let Seris's hand fall, and then Bren felt his fingers go around her wrist. She winced at the tightness of his grip, but his expression remained friendly as he raised her arm high.

"And this Winnowing is momentous for another reason. At its conclusion, the great storm dragon Mist – who had been deep in mourning since the tragic passing of her rider Vera ben-Ahzan – unexpectedly emerged from the depths of her sorrow to choose a new rider, the aspirant Brenna Gelindotter, now Brenna ben-Gelindotter, a daughter of Velasch raised in these lands who now returns to the empire. She was lost and now has been found, and this, too, we must celebrate."

The cheers this time were even less enthusiastic. The crowd seemed confused about how this could happen – an outsider was now the rider of a greater dragon . . . one of the *greatest* dragons, if what Jaleska had told Bren was true – and to be fair, this response was entirely reasonable. Bren could scarcely believe it herself. She had dreamed of bonding with a newborn dragon barely larger than a dog. It would have been years – decades? – until the hatchling had grown large enough that she could call herself a true rider. Yet here she was, bonded to a fully mature dragon. If she turned inward even now, concentrating on the thread connecting her to Mist, she could see the white-capped waves flashing below as the storm dragon skimmed low over the ocean's swells hunting for breaching whales or pods of dolphins. It was all so incredibly surreal.

The swell of applause jolted her away from what Mist was doing and returned her to the caliphant's hall. Bessam had released his hold on her and taken a step back to better focus the attention on the new riders.

"The families may contest with each other," Bessam cried, shouting to be heard. "But in the end, it is Velasch that we are loyal to above all else. And the empire is strengthened with this new blood! Let us welcome these riders with glad hearts and open arms!"

Bren looked over at Seris, but the kalishwoman still refused to meet her gaze. Indignation flared in her, and she prepared herself to go confront the kalishwoman. The governor's final words must have concluded the ceremony, as the periphery of the crowd had already begun to disperse. Those at the base of the steps below Bren were turning to each other to engage in animated conversation, probably about what they had all just witnessed.

"Brenna!"

The voice was familiar, and Bren stopped in surprise just as she was turning towards Seris. She glanced down to find Agiz ben-Ahzan ascending the tiers, his smile broad behind his silver mustache. The old dragon rider was dressed in the same crisp uniform from that day at the Briar, a green doublet slashed with gold. He looked the part of an indolent noble . . . but she remembered him in his intricate black armor, the point of his obsidian sword planted in the earth outside her house. That was his true self, she suspected, not the costume he donned for occasions like this.

"Lord ben-Ahzan," Bren said, inclining her head slightly as the Old Drake reached the top of the dais.

His smile persisted even as he waved away her greeting. "Call me Agiz. If we riders were always so formal, we'd never know who was being addressed – after all, almost all of us share the same family names. Though you two are now the very notable exceptions." Agiz chuckled at this, and Bren had to stop herself from clenching her jaw. Like before when they'd met, he was acting like a proud grandfather . . . but she knew what he really was. A soldier. A *killer*.

He continued, blithely unaware of her souring mood. "Of course, once we discover who your parents are, you may adopt their family name. You look like a Karth, but we can't simply assume that is truly your family. After all, I never would have thought Mist would choose a Karth to bond with given how much Vera disliked them." He glanced over at where Bessam Karth was descending the steps gingerly, careful not to put too much weight on his twisted leg. "Though you're not really a Karth, even if you share their blood."

"No, I'm not," Bren replied, more harshly than she'd intended. "I'm not from any of your families. My father was Gelin Kaelingsun of the Seven Valleys."

The Old Drake's face creased with sympathy. "And he died – I remember you told me that. My apologies, I did not mean to dismiss the ones who raised you. They must have been good people to bring up such a daughter." He touched his forehead with two fingers, which Bren assumed must be a gesture asking for forgiveness.

She was not in the mood to give it to him, but she had to admit his talk of Mist's former rider had piqued her interest. "Vera . . . she was from your family? An Ahzan? What was she like?"

Something sparked in the old warrior's eyes. "She was the best of us. We riders try to hold ourselves to a strict code of honor, and for the most part we succeed, but she never wavered from the straightest path."

A strict code of honor . . . The anger that had been bubbling inside Bren threatened to boil over. She knew how well these riders adhered to whatever 'code' Agiz was talking about.

"I heard a tale," she said, finally unable to contain herself, "when I was traveling to Yestra. From a boy who had fled the lands near Leris. He said . . ." She swallowed back the sudden tightness in the throat. "He said his farm had been destroyed by three dragon riders. He watched in hiding as one of them killed a paladin of the Silver Mother, and then their dragons burned his house to ashes with his family still inside." Her nails were digging so deep into her palms that she was surprised she hadn't drawn blood. "Is that the kind of *code* the riders follow?"

Agiz seemed to finally realize the emotions roiling her, but rather than look outraged that maddening sympathy crinkled the corners of his eyes again. "Oh, my child. I know of what you speak. That was . . . a mistake."

"A mistake?" she hissed.

"Aye," Agiz said with a deep sigh. "I was there, Bren. The boy spoke true. Our dragons burned the poor lad's house . . . but it was because we were tricked."

Bren blinked, knocked off-balance.

The old warrior grimaced. "It was not a paladin we chased to that farm, but the ones he was protecting. We had been hunting a pair of sorcerers, powerful servants of the demon goddess worshipped in these lands. I swear with my own eyes I saw them take refuge in that house! And we dared not risk a direct confrontation – those creatures wield terrible powers that can threaten even dragons. So Vanoc commanded our dragons to destroy them . . . but we discovered that we had been deceived. It must have been some sort of illusion, because some time later Thalia found these same sorcerers performing a dark ritual in the undercity of Leris. One she slew, but the other disappeared into the depths."

Coldness flooded Bren. Surely he couldn't be telling the truth. Surely what he was saying was impossible.

Agiz shook his head sadly. "I grieve for that boy's family, I truly do, and I can see now why you hold some resentment in your heart. In war, I'm afraid mistakes are often made."

"Mistakes . . ." Bren repeated numbly.

"Aye," Agiz continued. "Although for Thalia, such a mistake is a very rare thing. She is among the best of the keth-chathan, those trackers who serve the masters of the Red Tower by hunting down renegade warlocks." He turned, squinting into the crowd of Velaschin. "She is here, you know, and can confirm what I have told you. Where . . . ah, there," he said, indicating one of the great pink pillars holding up the dome. "That is her, Thalia ben-Karth. Speak to her later, if you wish."

Bren followed where he was pointing and saw the third dragon rider from that terrible, tragic night . . . the one who had ambushed them in the ancient temple under Leris. It was like looking into a mirror. But what made Bren's skin crawl was the intensity with which Thalia – the one Tharos had called the Huntress – was already staring up at Bren, as if trying to glimpse what might be hidden beneath her flesh.

Why was she looking at Bren like that? Was it possible Thalia *recognized* her? Surely not, or the guards in their crimson armor would have already dragged her away for questioning.

Bren's head was spinning from having her entire world upended. Bren had once explained to Desian what had happened to her family, and now she remembered that sharp look he had cast her way when she'd mentioned the paladin who had taken refuge in her house. He must have known that it had been his fault that the riders had burned her farmhouse, and yet he had said nothing. Had he known at the time that there were people inside? Would he have cared at all if he had?

"Careful, lass," Agiz murmured, reaching out to steady her, concern deepening the lines around his eyes. "I can tell you're still suffering from what happened in the Winnowing. Even bonding with a dragon can't compensate for dying in that place. It's a terrible feeling." He paused, looking faintly embarrassed. "Not that I would know, of course. I won my Winnowing. But I've seen the effects in countless young folk since then."

"I . . . uh, thank you," Bren murmured. She glanced into the crowd, trying to find the Huntress again, but the dragon rider had vanished. Hopefully she hadn't slipped away to tell the warlocks of Velasch that Bren consorted with the sorcerers of the Jade House.

"Let me help you down the stairs," Agiz offered, and she could hear the care in his voice. Somehow this both gladdened and infuriated her. A part of her still hated him for what had happened . . . but if what he'd said was true, there was much she did not understand.

The old rider linked his arm with hers and began to guide her gently down the tiered steps. Her thoughts were scattered, but she suddenly remembered she had wanted to confront Seris. She glanced back to find that the kalishwoman had already left the top of the dais.

Another time, Bren promised herself. She was sure they'd cross paths again.

When they reached the bottom of the steps the crowd drew back a little, as if she was sick with something contagious. Bren swallowed as her gaze traveled over the nearby faces. She saw curiosity, wariness, skepticism . . . but little friendliness. She was a mystery to them. A stranger. Their scions had failed, and she had emerged from the Winnowing a dragon rider.

One face, however, wore an expression of absolute jubilation.

"Bren!" Jaleska cried, then lowered her eyes sheepishly, as if afraid what the Velaschin lords and ladies around her would think of her outburst.

Bren pulled away from Agiz, going over to the girl. "Jaleska," she said, and the warmth in her voice was not feigned. It felt good to see her again. Bren turned her body so that they were shielded from the crowd, and she must have made her point understood because she heard the hum of conversation swelling again behind her.

"I was so worried for you," Jaleska said, keeping her voice low. "When Mist grabbed you up, I thought for sure she was going to eat you." She frowned, looking guilty. "Sorry, that's not a nice image."

Despite the disturbing revelations concerning what had really happened to her family, Bren still couldn't hold back a smile. "It's fine. I'm glad I didn't end up a dragon's dinner."

"Aha," Agiz said, coming to stand beside Bren and looking Jaleska up and down. "Greetings, Sister. You must be Bren's handmaiden. I'm sure you're excited about all that's happened."

"This is Jaleska, Agiz," Bren told the old dragon rider, and she saw the girl's eyes go round as dinner plates.

"Oh! Lord ben-Ahzan!" squeaked Jaleska, clumsily attempting a curtsy. "It is an honor, Ser!"

"And an honor to meet you as well, Sister," he replied, offering a much more graceful bow in return. Jaleska visibly swooned at this, and Bren debated whether she should move closer so to catch her if she fainted.

"You will find that the bond between handmaiden and rider is nearly as strong as the one between dragon and rider. Your loyalties to each other will run deeper than to anything else, even blood and empire and temple, and that is the way it should be. You must trust and defend your rider always. Do you promise to do that, Sister?" Agiz's tone was grave, like he was formally investing her with a great responsibility.

Jaleska's mouth worked silently for a moment, as if she'd forgotten how to form words. Then she nodded jerkily. "Yes, of course, my lord. I promise!"

"Good," Agiz said, stroking the ends of his drooping mustache. "Then I will leave you two so you can discuss all that has happened. Sister, I would suggest you take your rider to her quarters so she can recover. The last few days have been very taxing, and she should be well-rested before she has to spar with these sorts of folks again." He made a gesture encompassing the Velaschin, then winked at Bren before vanishing into the crowd.

Jaleska watched him go with such awe that Bren had to stop herself from rolling her eyes.

"Come on," she said, touching Jaleska on the shoulder to wake her from her daze, "there's nothing I want more right now than a hot cup of kefa."

32

Bren slouched against a wall under a portico of gray-green stone, watching the entrance of *The Windblown Inn* through a hissing curtain of rain. She had wrapped herself in her father's cloak and drawn up the hood, though the fierceness of the sudden storm had chased the Yestrians inside, and she also doubted she would be anything other than a hazy smudge unless someone was standing right beside her.

Unless they were like her, she supposed. A dragon rider. Because Bren had changed in the days since Mist had rescued her. Her eyesight – which had always been excellent – had noticeably sharpened. Now, she could easily pick out a frog hiding in a spray of reeds and the pattern on the feathers of a hawk floating on the wind. And this wasn't the only way she was different. Before bonding with the dragon a rain like this would have chilled her to the bone – she remembered how clammy Yestra had felt even on clear days. Yet she was wearing damp wool and sodden boots and she was not cold at all. Jaleska had told her this happened to all riders, that some dragon traits would seep across the bond, making her less susceptible to the elements and heightening her senses. Even her body would gradually change until she was more powerful than others, faster and stronger.

Which explained how Vanoc ben-Karth had defeated a paladin of the Silver Mother in single combat, for such a feat should have been impossible for any mere man.

Movement further down the street drew her attention. A cloaked figure dashed from stoop to portico to overhang, drawing closer to where she waited. Bren frowned, trying to make sure it was really who she thought and hoped it was. In the end, she simply threw caution to the wind and called out before the figure could scurry inside the inn's doors.

"Shadows!" she cried, and her heart leaped in her chest as the figure stiffened and turned towards her. Slim hands drew back the cloak's hood, revealing messy black curls and wide dark eyes, and then Tal was dashing through the rain to wrap her in an embrace.

"Bren!" he said when he finally drew back, looking her up and down. "Oh, saints and sages, it's good to see you!"

Her smile felt like it was about to split her face. "And you. I asked the innkeeper where you were, and he said you were out, but that you'd likely return soon despite the weather."

Tal brushed back his long wet hair. "Well, you should have waited in the common room. They have good spiced wine here – come, let's get you a glass and you can tell me everything that's happened. I've heard stories, of course, about a girl from the Flowering Coast who bonded with a fully grown dragon. There are so many rumors flying about I didn't know what to believe."

He made to turn away, but Bren caught his arm. "Wait, Tal, I don't want to go in there with you."

Tal frowned, glancing up and down the rain-shrouded street. "Were you followed?"

"No, no." She bit her lip, unsure where to begin. "I've learned things, Tal. I don't trust Desian anymore. He kept things from me . . . important things. The innkeeper said he hasn't emerged from his room for days, but I'm still worried he might come downstairs . . . or that he could sense me if I get too close."

Tal blew out his cheeks and shook his head in something like resigned exasperation. "You know I never trusted him! Though I'm glad you've finally seen some sense. But you shouldn't be worried. This morning I got tired of knocking on his door and getting no response, so I crept around the outside of the inn and looked in his window. Everything was gone. He's not here."

A shiver went through Bren. Desian had told her he would be waiting for her after the Winnowing had concluded. Instead, he'd left before she could return with exactly what he'd always wanted – a dragon. Or perhaps Mist being grown was a stick shoved into the spokes of the Jade House's plan. A hatchling could be molded, but how would Mist ever be convinced to betray Velasch? Perhaps he had abandoned all hope and fled the city.

But she didn't think so.

"We'll see him again, I suspect," Bren said. "Or at least you will."

Tal's face crinkled in confusion. "What do you mean?"

Bren took a deep breath, dreading what would follow. "I'm leaving, Tal. There are three ships sailing to Velasch tomorrow, and I'll be on one of them. Riding a dragon is not simply sitting on its back . . . There's so much to learn, and that is done across the Cull in the aeries."

"Tomorrow?" he murmured, and she could hear the dismay in his voice. "That's so soon."

"It has to be," she said softly. "Apparently, without training there's a chance the bond, uh, goes bad. Especially when one of the pair is so much older and stronger. It's a delicate situation that needs the guidance of the Temple Draconium."

"What's it like?" Tal muttered, looking dejected. "Being bonded, I mean."

"It's strange," she replied. "I can feel her out there at all times and even see what she's seeing if I concentrate hard enough. Her thoughts, her emotions . . . they're so different. So alien. She doesn't communicate with language, but I can usually understand." Bren quirked a half-smile. "I suppose I have a better background for this than most. After all, I'm no stranger to feeling something else in my head. Mist is far less intrusive, to be honest."

Tal scratched his cheek, looking thoughtful. "That never occurred to me. With the ghost of the sword inside you as well, it must be getting pretty crowded."

"Ashika's gone," Bren told him, and she was surprised at the sadness that accompanied this admission. "She saved me, though. I was dying, and I felt her straining to keep my spirit tethered to my body. She held me together long enough for Mist to forge the bond that healed me. It was a sacrifice – I haven't felt her inside me since."

"She's dead?"

"Well, she was already dead. I guess I can just hope she returned to whatever afterlife she was pulled from. She deserves to be with her people."

"Then your sword skills . . ."

"Gone," Bren admitted. "I'm no more than a shepherdess with silly dreams again."

"Not silly," Tal told her, putting a hand on her shoulder. "And you're a dragon rider. I'm sure across the Cull they'll teach you how to wield one of those black swords."

"Banevak is my blade. It's special, with or without Ashika inside it."

Bren realized he was looking at her strangely.

"You've changed," he said with a sigh. "The girl I first met, the one who saved me from those soldiers . . . she's gone. You're so confident now. So strong."

"A lot has happened," Bren admitted, then tapped her chest with two fingers. "But deep inside I'm still the same, I promise you."

She reached into her pocket and pulled out Tal's pebble. "Since I'm leaving, I wanted to return this. I don't know when I'll be back. But it meant so much to me that you let me borrow your mother's gift. I wish I could have brought it into the Winnowing – it would have been very useful."

Tal smiled sadly, folding her fingers around the smooth stone. "I want you to keep it," he told her. "But you have to give it back some day. Which means you have to return to the Flowering Coast after your training is finished."

"Of course I will," Bren said, a tightness in her throat. "I promise I will end this war, Tal. I don't know how I'm going to do it, but I will." She smiled, blinking back tears. "And I have to come back for Moon. You better take good care of that horse."

"Be careful, you'll make your dragon jealous," Tal said, covering her hand with his own. "We'll be waiting for you."

33

I promise I will end this war.

Bren gripped the lacquered wooden railing fiercely as the Velaschin carrack slid between the rocks guarding Yestra's lagoon. The size of the ship was staggering, but it paled in comparison to the endless dark waters of the Cull that now unraveled before them. Her breath quickened at the thought of the distance they had to traverse – the captain had informed her it would be over a month before they'd stand on land again. How they were ever going to survive such a crossing she had no idea, but the Velaschin had done it before, and she supposed they would be able to do it again.

I promise I will end this war.

Bren had been turning over what she said to Tal ever since she'd left him. The words had slipped out unbidden, surprising her, and it was only later that she'd realized what they truly meant. Once she had wanted nothing more than to bring ruin to the Velaschin. She had begged the Silver Mother to give her the strength to find bloody vengeance on the riders who had ordered the death of her family. She had even dreamed of slaying *all* the Velaschin who had brought death and fire to her land. But everything had changed. She did not want Jaleska dead. Or Jerym. Or even Agiz ben-Azhan, despite his presence on that terrible night.

Now she was traveling to their city, to the beating heart of their empire. She had been chosen by the greatest of their dragons, and she would find a way to end this war.

This she promised to the Silver Mother and to Her daughters and to the memory of her family. This she promised herself.

"It is a daunting view the first time one beholds it."

The voice startled Bren, as she hadn't heard anyone come up beside her on the deck. She turned and found a tall, severe-looking woman staring out to sea, her hands clasped behind her back. She was wearing a simple blue dress that was nevertheless clearly of very fine make, and though Bren could not see the glitter of gold or jewels, she knew from her bearing that this was a woman of rank.

"A vast, gnawing waste, inimical to man. The mouth of the world, as the poet Ajantis called it during the first crossing." The woman shifted slightly to face her, studying Bren with sharp eyes. "Do you know what 'cull' means, Brenna?"

Bren shook her head, intimidated into silence.

"It means a selective slaughter to reduce an animal's population. Not a very fitting name, given how indiscriminate the ocean truly is."

Behind this woman, the mainsail of the carrack was being unfurled, sailors scurrying along the rigging. And far beyond them she glimpsed a dark silhouette in the pale blue sky, Mist drifting on the high winds. Bren could sense the dragon's joy at the thought of the long days of flying before her and the excellent hunting she would find in the deeper waters. She was less excited about curling up at night on the massive barge this ship was towing, but nothing could be helped about that. The Cull was far too vast to be traversed without rest, even for a dragon as large and strong as Mist.

The woman lifted an eyebrow and turned to see what had drawn Bren's attention. "Ah. The dragon pulls you away. It was the same with my cousin when she was given Reed. Before she had been perfectly happy to while the afternoons away reading in father's library with me. After she did nothing except spend her days lazing on the riverbank communing with her dragon. A waste of a perfectly good mind. That was one reason why I never wanted Jerym to have his own."

That jolted Bren's gaze back to the woman. "Are you his mother?"

Thin lips quirked at the tone of her voice. "I am." She extended her arm, and after staring at it stupidly for a moment Bren reached out with her own. The woman squeezed her hand briefly and then let go. "I am Seliana Regast. Jerym has spoken fondly of you, and he claims to owe you quite the debt."

Bren felt the color rising in her cheeks. "I . . . it was nothing. He was very helpful in the labyrinth." She craned her neck, searching the deck for the golden-haired boy. "Is he here? May I see him?"

Seliana made a sharp motion with her hand, as if to dismiss the very idea as absurd. "No. My son is recovering from his ordeal and is resting below. You might not know what happened at the end of the Winnowing, but he was stabbed by one of the Karths. It is a harrowing experience to die in that place, or so I am told."

"I know," Bren said softly. "I died there as well."

"You failed and yet triumphed," Seliana murmured, placing her long-fingered hands on the railing and returning her gaze to the Cull. Most of her fair hair was bound up in a silver net, but a few loose strands twisted in the salty sea breeze. "Such a fascinating outcome. I admit I am not a historian of the Winnowing, but I believe something like this has never happened before."

"My understanding is that dragons don't often lose their riders. Even in war."

Seliana's lip curled. She stayed watching out at the white-capped swells for a time before speaking again. "I want you to know something, Bren. Not all Velaschin are as wedded to violence as most of those who have come to these shores. The Winnowing is a barbaric relic from an earlier time. And this . . . conflict is not how I would want my people to be judged."

Bren said nothing, surprised by the frustration she heard in the woman's voice.

"I am a scholar," Seliana continued. "A naturalist. I want to learn about your lands, not subjugate them. And because of that, I have a favor to ask of you." She began to turn the one ring she wore on her finger, an iron band of interlocking wings joined beneath a bird's head. "You see, I am a senior member of a group that is dedicated to exploring and cataloging. You, Bren, would be one of the first from the old world to come to Velasch, and so I wish to invite you to come meet my colleagues in the Peregrine Society. I am certain they have many questions they would like to ask you. What do you think? Will you be able to pull yourself away from your dragon for a while?"

"Yes, my lady," Bren replied, feeling more than a little overwhelmed by the force of this woman's personality. She doubted she could have refused even if she'd wanted to.

"Call me Seliana. I am not one to stand on ceremony, I assure you. And I'm pleased, Bren. I believe we have much to learn from each other." Seliana lapsed into silence, as if imagining this future meeting and just what knowledge might be shared.

Bren could understand now the awe she had heard in Jerym's voice when he'd spoken about his mother. This was a formidable woman.

She turned away from Seliana as one of the two sister-ships accompanying them across the Cull began to pass. This carrack was not hauling a dragon barge, and it slid through the water faster than their ship. Bren watched the frantic activity on that other deck, wondering if Seris was somewhere on board. The desire to know why the kalishwoman had betrayed her was still burning hot, but it would have to wait until they arrived in Velasch.

Her attention was drawn to a group of sailors clustered on the closest side of the passing ship. They were dressed differently from the others, with strikingly bright shirts instead of the drab gray or brown worn by the Velaschin sailors, and their skin was several shades darker. One of them was wearing a familiar cap topped with an iridescent feather, and he doffed it before waving enthusiastically in greeting when he saw her. Bren couldn't restrain a smile. So the Azakani she'd met on the Isle of Broken Swords had gotten their wish and would be the first of their people to cross the Cull. That made her happy. They'd realized their dreams, and she also suspected they would prove to be excellent ambassadors. The war could only end when the people on each side of the Cull saw each other as something other than enemies.

Though it was also true that one of the Umber Isle folk looked to be far less friendly than his fellows. He was standing a little way off, watching with his arms folded as the others worked on securing some rigging. He must have felt Bren's gaze on him, because he suddenly looked directly at her.

Bren gasped, her hands tightening on the railing.

The Azakani had already turned away, but Bren was certain about what she'd seen.

His eyes. His eyes had been silver.

"Do you know them?" asked Seliana, her tone suggesting that she was mildly affronted by the behavior of the Azakani.

"Yes," Bren replied softly, gripping the railing so hard she felt splinters digging into her palms. "I know them."

ABOUT THE AUTHOR

Alec Hutson grew up in a geodesic dome and a bookstore and currently lives in Shanghai, China. If you would like to keep current with his writing, please sign up for his newsletter at authoralechut son.com.

ALSO BY ALEC HUTSON

The Raveling

The Crimson Queen

The Silver Sorceress

The Shadow King

Swords & Saints

The Cleansing Flame

The Twilight Empire

The Hollow God

The Sharded Few

The Umbral Storm

Standalones

The Shadows of Dust (space fantasy)

The Book of Zog (eldritch cozy fantasy)

The Manticore's Soiree (short stories)

Printed in Great Britain
by Amazon

38563141R00260